ACCLAIM FOR THE BOURNE THRILLERS

ROBERT LUDLUM'S™
THE BOURNE IMPERATIVE

"Bourne lovers should be delirious."

—*New Haven Register*

"Plenty of intrigue and excitement...Lustbader keeps the action and plot moving forward, and the tension never lets up...Readers most assuredly will be gasping for breath as each eye-opening chapter unfolds."

—**BookReporter.com**

"Another terrific thriller...an action fest...Fans will discover this to be the best Lustbader Bourne novel yet."

—*Library Journal*

"This offers more Bourne action with traitors, counterspies, subplots, and daring escapes."

—*Oklahoman*

"In true Bourne fashion, THE BOURNE IMPERATIVE is fast-paced and full of action. There are twists and turns that even the grandest of plot detectives could not foresee."

—*Spencer Daily Reporter* (IA)

"Chocked-full of clandestine operations and international espionage, this thrill-a-minute novel is a winner."

—**FreshFiction.com**

"Action-packed thriller...The unrelenting action in the novel clearly shows how this series has become so popular both in print and on the screen."

—*Suspense Magazine*

"Lustbader offers plenty of thrills...showing why this remains one of the best high-octane series for readers."

—**Suite101.com**

"Fans will find all the usual cliffhangers, hairbreadth escapes, and multiple betrayals they expect from this series."

—**Publishers Weekly**

THE BOURNE DOMINION

"Fans of the book and movie franchise will love this new plot-driven international thriller...This is classic Bourne."

—**USA Today**

"The twists, the nonstop action, and the multilayered plot that Ludlum fans expect are here in abundance. Fans of the Bourne films will eat this one up."

—**Booklist**

"A wealth of information flows as smoothly as a swallow of single-malt scotch. With more twists and turns than a Napa Valley of grapevines, the nonstop action and resourceful Bourne plucked a fourth from my Star Jar."

—**BookReporter.com**

"Action-packed...It's a testament to Lustbader's skills that he can keep everyone in place and blazing away without losing track of the ongoing plot."

—**Publishers Weekly**

"Fans of the book and movie franchise will love this new plot-driven international thriller...This is classic Bourne."

—**Des Moines Sunday Register (IA)**

THE BOURNE OBJECTIVE

"Thriller addicts who love intricate webs of conspiracy mixed with an adrenaline rush of action and global adventure will snap this one up."

—Library Journal

"The rogue spy is one of the best characters in the genre."

—US Metro Newspapers

"This novel rocks—it's filled with action, adventure, and has plenty of plot twists and turns...an entertaining, thrilling roller-coaster ride you won't want to end."

—BestsellersWorld.com

THE BOURNE DECEPTION

"Powerful and poignant development of characters old and new, as well as a hard-hitting plot, reinvent the series and ensure its place in contemporary political fiction...Once again, Van Lustbader has written a gripping novel that the reader can easily imagine being developed into another blockbuster film."

—Fredericksburg Free Lance-Star

"I plowed through [this book], my heart racing at every turn of the page."

—Wichita Falls Times Record News **(TX)**

THE BOURNE SANCTION

"Twisted, dark, and exciting."

—Oklahoman

"A thrill-a-minute work...This is one novel that will keep you reading long into the night."

—BookReporter.com

THE BOURNE BETRAYAL

"Breathless writing that makes the pages fly."

—*Kirkus Reviews*

"A cleverly plotted, incisive thriller with a hero I'm glad is on the good guys' side. In an amazing work of fiction, Lustbader takes us into the minds of terrorists."

—NightsandWeekends.com

"Lustbader is an excellent storyteller and is not afraid to keep the twists and turns coming in this sequel ... This is an explosive addition to a series with an unrivaled heritage and storied pedigree."

—BookReporter.com

THE
BOURNE
IMPERATIVE

Also by Eric Van Lustbader

ROBERT LUDLUM'S™

THE
BOURNE
IMPERATIVE

A NEW JASON BOURNE NOVEL BY
ERIC VAN LUSTBADER

GRAND CENTRAL
PUBLISHING

NEW YORK   BOSTON

Grand Central Publishing
Hachette Book Group
237 Park Avenue
New York, NY 10017
www.HachetteBookGroup.com

Grand Central Publishing is a division of Hachette Book Group, Inc. The Grand Central Publishing name and logo is a trademark of Hachette Book Group, Inc.

The Hachette Speakers Bureau provides a wide range of authors for speaking events. To find out more, go to www.hachettespeakersbureau.com or call (866) 376-6591.

The publisher is not responsible for websites (or their content) that are not owned by the publisher.

Printed in the United States of America

Originally published in hardcover by Hachette Book Group
First international mass market edition: January 2013
First U.S. mass market edition: January 2013

10 9 8 7 6 5 4 3 2 1
OPM

Acknowledgments

Thanks are due to my cousin, David Schiffer, for keeping me up to date on the latest methods of finding terrorists, international arms dealers, and drug dealers; to my friend, Ken Dorph, for his unique perspective on the Middle East and for his insightful stories of foreign lands; and to my wife, Victoria, for her editorial suggestions and proofing skills.

Special mention must be made of Carlos Fuentes. His marvelous novel, *Destiny and Desire*, served as a major inspiration for Bourne's trip to Mexico City, meshing with and enlarging upon my own personal experiences, along with other firsthand sources.

Prologue

S**HE CAME OUT** of the mist, and he was running, just as he had been for hours, days. It felt like he had been alone for weeks, his heart continually thundering inside his chest, his mind befogged with bitter betrayal. Sleep was unthinkable, rest a thing of the past.

Nothing was clear now except that she had come out of the mist after he had been certain—for the thirteenth, or was it the fifteenth, time?—that he had eluded her. But here she was, coming for him like a mythical exterminating angel, indestructible and implacable.

His life had been reduced to the two of them. Nothing else existed outside the wall of white—snow and ice and the wispy brushstrokes of fishing cottages, deep red with white trim, small, compact, containing only what was necessary. He admired such judiciousness.

The mist burned like fire—a cold fire that ran up his spine and gripped the back of his neck, just as she had gripped the back of his neck—when? Days? A week ago? When they had been in bed together, when she had been another person, his lover, a woman who quickly discovered how to make him shiver and melt with pleasure.

Half-skating across a large frozen lake, he slipped, lost his gun, which went skittering over the ice. He was about to make a lunge for it when he heard the snap of a twig, as clear and sharp as a knife thrust.

Instead, he continued on, made for a stand of shivering pines. Powdery snow sprayed his face, coating his eyebrows and the stubble of a long flight across continents. He did not dare waste another moment looking back over his shoulder to check the progress of his pursuer.

She had dogged his tracks all the way from Lebanon. He had met her in a packed, smoke-blurred bar in Dahr El Ahmar—or maybe now he would admit to himself that she had met him, that every gesture, every word out of her mouth, had been by design. Events seemed so clear now that he was on the precipice of either escape or death. She had played him instead of the other way around—he, the consummate professional. How had she so easily slipped inside his defenses? But he knew, he knew: the exterminating angel was irresistible.

Inside the pines he paused, his breath clouding the air in front of his face. It was bitterly cold, but inside his winter camo coat, he felt as if he were burning alive. Clinging to one of a maze of black tree trunks, his mind returned to the hotel room, stinking of bodies and sex, recalling the moment when she had bitten his lip, her teeth clamped down on his flesh while she somehow said, "I know. I know what you are."

Not *who*, but *what*.

She knew. He looked around now at the city of interlocking branches, at the labyrinth of needles in which he hid. It was impossible. How *could* she know? And yet...

Hearing again the snap of a twig, he started, turned slowly in a circle, all his senses questing toward the direction of the sound. Where was she? Death could come at any minute, but he knew it wouldn't be quick. There were too many secrets she needed to know, otherwise she would have killed him during one of their animalistic trysts. Nights that still gave him shivers of arousal, even though he now knew how close he had been to death. She had been playing with him—perhaps because she came to enjoy their lovemaking as much as he did. He gave a silent laugh, his lips pulled back from his teeth, more a snarl than a smile. What a fool! He kept deluding himself that there had been something between them, even in the face of the most explicit evidence to the contrary. What a spell she had woven over him! He shuddered, crouching down, contracting into himself as he pressed his spine against the rough pine bark.

Suddenly he was tired of running. It was here, in the frozen back of beyond, that he'd make his stand, even though he had no clear idea of how to emerge alive from this killing field. Behind him, he heard the insistent burble of water. In Sadelöga, you were never far from inlets of the Baltic Sea, the air mineral-thick with salt and seaweed and phosphorus.

A blur caught like a fish on a line at the corner of his eye. There she was! Had she seen him? He wanted to move, but his limbs felt as if they were filled with lead. He could not feel his feet. Turning his head slowly brought a sliver of her advancing into the tree line.

She paused, her head cocked to one side, listening, as if she could hear him breathe.

Unbidden, his tongue ran across his severely swollen lower lip. His mind raced backward, to an exhibit of Japanese wood-block prints—stately, serene, calming. All except one piece of erotica that was so famous everyone had heard of it even if they hadn't actually seen it in person. It hung before him, a depiction of a woman in the throes of unimaginable ecstasy, administered by her octopus-lover's dextrous eight arms. That was how he thought of his lover, his stalker. In the overheated Dahr El Ahmar hotel room he had known the depths—or heights—of the ecstasy experienced by the woman depicted in the wood-block print. In that respect, he wasn't sorry. He had never imagined, let alone expected, that anyone could give him so much pleasure, but she had, and he was perversely grateful, even though she might very well be the death of him.

He started. She was coming now. Even though he didn't hear her, had lost her in the maze of trees, he could feel her moving closer, drawn to him in some inexplicable manner. So he sat and waited for her to appear, considering what he would do when that happened.

He did not have long to wait. Seconds passed slowly, seeming to float away in the water somewhere behind him, at the far edge of the stand of pines. He heard her call his name, softly, gently as she had when they were lovers, entwined, locked in their own ecstasies. A shiver ran down his spine, lodged between his legs, and would not dissipate.

Still...He had resources left, surprises, chances to walk out of this killing ground alive.

Putting his head down, he slowly drew his knees up to his chest. It must have started snowing fairly hard because more and more flakes were pushing their way through the tangle of needles. Green shadows morphed to charcoal-gray, obscuring him further. Snow began to cover him, light as the flutter of angel wings. His heart thudded within his rib cage and he could feel his pulse in the side of his neck.

Still alive, he thought.

He sensed her as she slipped between the trunks of two pines. His nostrils flared, one animal scenting another. One way or another, the hunt was at an end. He felt a certain relief. Soon it would be over.

She was so close now that he heard the crunch as her boots cracked the gossamer-thin crust, plunged into the snow with each careful step. She stopped six feet away. Her shadow fell over him; he had felt it for weeks now as he traveled north by northwest in his vain attempt to dislodge her.

I know what you are, she had said, so she must know that he was on his own. There was no contact to call in case of emergency, in case of *her*. He had been cut out of the herd, so there would be absolutely no chance of the herd being disturbed or, worse, probed, should he be caught and put under articulated interrogation. Nevertheless, she also knew that he held secrets in the darkest corners of his mind, secrets she had been sent to extract from him in the same way a diner extracts the meat from the very top of a lobster's claw.

Octopus and lobster. Those terms more accurately characterized the two of them than any more traditional definition.

She spoke his name again, more definitively this time, and he raised his chin off his chest to look her in the eye. She held a 10 mm EAA Witness Pistol aimed at his right knee.

"No more running," she said.

He nodded. "No more running."

She looked at him with a curious kindness. "Pity about your lip."

His laugh was short and savage. "It seems I required a violent wake-up call."

Her eyes were the color and shape of ripe olives, vivid against her Mediterranean skin and black hair pulled back tight, tucked, except for a couple of wisps, inside her hood. "Why do you do what you do?"

"Why do you?"

She laughed softly. "That's easy." She had a Roman nose, delicate cheekbones, and a generous mouth. "I keep my country safe."

"At the expense of all other countries."

"Isn't that the definition of a patriot?" She shook her head. "But then you wouldn't know."

"You're very sure of yourself."

She shrugged. "I was born that way."

He stirred infinitesimally. "Tell me one thing. What did you think of when we were in bed together?"

Her smile changed character subtly, but that was the extent of her answer.

"You'll give me what I want to know," she said. "Tell me about *Jihad bis saif.*"

"Not even," he said, "on the point of death."

Her smile changed yet again, into the one he remembered from the hotel room in Dahr El Ahmar, a secret smile, he had thought, just between the two of them, and he hadn't been wrong. It was only the context he'd missed.

"You have no country, no innate allegiance. Your masters have seen to that."

"We all have masters," he said. "It's only that we tell ourselves we don't."

When she took a step toward him, he flicked the knife he had been holding close to his side. The short distance between them made it impossible for her to duck out of the way. She had just begun to react when the blade penetrated her Thinsulate parka and buried itself in the flesh of her right shoulder. The EAA swung away as she was spun 45 degrees. As her arm came down, he leaped at her, taking her down flat on her back. He bore down, using his superior weight to half-bury her in the snow, sinking her into the frozen, needle-packed earth beneath.

He struck a hard blow to her jaw. The EAA lay in the snow, some distance away. Shaking off the effects of the blow, she heaved him off her. He rolled back, and before she had a chance to move, grabbed the hilt of the knife, and ground the blade deeper into the muscle of her shoulder. She gritted her teeth, but she didn't scream. Instead, she jabbed the tips of her fingers into the cricoid cartilage of his throat. He coughed, gagging, and his hand came off the knife. Grabbing hold of it, she drew it out. Her blood glimmered darkly as it ran down the narrow blade.

Rearing back away from her, he lunged for the EAA, snatched it up and aimed it at her. When she laughed at him, he pulled the trigger, pulled it again and again. It was empty. What had she meant to do? This thought was racing through his mind when she pulled a Glock 20 out of her parka. Throwing the useless EAA at her, he lurched up, turned, and ran a patternless path through the pines, toward the water. It was his only chance now to escape her.

As he ran, he unzipped his coat, shrugged it off. In the water, it would only help to carry him down. The water would be frigid—so cold that he would have only five or six minutes to swim away to safety before the temperature penetrated to his bones, anesthetizing him. Paralysis would not be far behind, followed by death.

A shot from behind him whistled past his right knee, and he stumbled, crashed into a tree, bounced off and kept running, deeper and deeper into the woods, closer and closer to the water, whose sound rushed at him like a conquering army. He pushed himself on, panted breath streaming from him.

When he saw the first glint of the water, his heart lifted and the breath came easier in his chest. Breaking free of the pines, he lurched along snowy scrub grass sprouting between bald rocks that sloped steeply down to the sea.

He was almost there when he skidded on a slick of muck, and the second shot, meant for his shoulder, grazed the side of his head. He spun around, arms flung wide, continued blindly, legs churning as he reached the lip of land, and, blinded by his own blood, plunged down into the icy depths.

Gazing at the spattering of tiny islets around him, rimed in ice, Jason Bourne sat in the center of the small fishing skiff, rod in one hand, flicking it back and forth as he trolled for sea trout, pike, or perch.

"You don't like fishing much, do you?" Christien Norén said.

Bourne grunted, brushing himself off. The brief eruption of intense snow had vanished almost as quickly as it had appeared. The sky was an oppressive icy gray.

"Keep still," Christien admonished. He held his rod at a careless angle. "You're scaring the fish away."

"It's not me." Bourne frowned, peering down into the water, which was streaked brown and green. Shadows swayed as if to an unheard melody. "Something else is scaring them away."

"Oh, ho." Christien laughed. "There's an underwater conspiracy coming to light."

Bourne looked up. "Why did you take me out here? It doesn't appear that you like fishing much, either."

Christien regarded him steadily for some time. At length he said, "When discussing conspiracies, it's best to do so in a space without walls."

"A remote location. Hence this trip outside of Stockholm."

Christien nodded. "Except that Sadelöga isn't quite remote enough."

"But out on the water, this boat finally meets your requirements."

"It does."

"The explanation for what you and Don Fernando have been up to had better be good. What I learned from Peter Marks in DC—"

"It's not good," Christien said. "In fact, it's very, very bad. Which is why—"

Bourne's silent signal—the flat of his free hand cutting through the chill air—silenced Christien immediately. Bourne pointed at the disturbance near them, the sudden rushing curl of water arched like a dorsal fin. Something was surfacing, something large.

"Good God," Christien exclaimed.

Abandoning his rod, Bourne leaned forward and grabbed the rising body.

Book One

Book One

1

Rumor, innuendo, intimation, supposition." The president of the United States skimmed the buff-jacketed daily intel report across the table, where it was fielded by Christopher Hendricks.

"With all due respect, sir," the secretary of defense said, "I think it's a bit more than that."

The president leveled his clear, hard gaze at his most trusted ally. "You think it's the truth, Chris."

"I do, sir, yes."

The president pointed at the folder. "If there's one thing I've learned in my long and storied political career, it's that a truth without facts is more dangerous than a lie."

Hendricks drummed his fingers on the file. "And why would that be, sir?" He said this without rancor; he sincerely wanted to know.

The president heaved a sigh. "Because without facts, rumor, innuendo, intimation, and supposition have a way of conflating into myth. Myths have a way of worming their way into people's psyches, becoming something more, something larger than life. Something indelible. Thus is born what Nietzsche called his 'superman.'"

"And you believe that's the case here."

"I do."

"That this man does not exist."

"I didn't say that." The president swiveled his chair around, put his forearms on his gleaming desk, steepled his fingers judicially. "What I don't believe are these rumors of what he has done—what he's capable of doing. No, as of this moment I don't believe those things."

A small silence descended over them. Outside the Oval Office, the sound of a leaf blower was briefly heard, just inside the wall of reinforced concrete barriers at the perimeter of the sacred grounds. Looking out, Hendricks could see no leaves. But then, all work in and around the White House was inherently secretive.

Hendricks cleared his throat. "Nevertheless, sir, it's my unwavering belief that he is a significant threat to this country."

The American flag stood curled by the right side of the window, stars rippled. The president's eyes were half-closed, his breathing deep and even. If Hendricks didn't know better, he'd think the president had fallen asleep.

The president gestured for the file and Hendricks slid it back to him. The president opened it, leafing through the dense paragraphs of typescript. "Tell me about your shop."

"Treadstone is running quite well."

"Both your directors are up to speed?"

"Yes."

"You say that too quickly, Chris. Four months ago, Peter Marks was struck at the periphery of a car bomb. At almost the same time, Soraya Moore was hurt, involved as she was in tragic circumstances in Paris."

"She got the job done."

"No need to be defensive," the president said. "I'm simply voicing my concern."

"They've both been cleared medically and psychologically."

"I'm sincerely glad to hear it. But these are unique directors, Chris."

"How so?"

"Oh, come on, I don't know any other intelligence directors who routinely deploy themselves in the field."

"That's the way it's done in Treadstone. It's a very small shop."

"By design, I know." The president paused. "And how is Dick Richards working out?"

"Integrating into the team."

The president nodded. He tapped his forefinger ruminatively against his lower lip. "All right," he said at length. "Put Treadstone on this business, if you must—Marks, Moore, Richards, whichever. But—" he raised a warning forefinger "—you'll provide me with daily briefings on their progress. Above all, Chris, I want facts. Give me proof that this businessman—"

"The next great enemy to our security."

"Whatever he is, give me proof that he warrants our attention, or you'll deploy your valuable personnel on other pressing matters. Understood?"

"Yes, sir." Hendricks rose and left the Oval Office, even more troubled than when he had entered.

When Soraya Moore had returned from Paris three months ago, she had found Treadstone a changed place. For one thing, because security had been breached when the car bomb that had injured Peter went off in the underground garage of the old offices, Treadstone had been moved out of Washington to Langley, Virginia. For another, the presence of a tall, reedy man with thinning hair and a winning smile.

"Who moved my cheese?" she had said to her codirector and close friend Peter Marks in a parody of a stage whisper.

Peter had barked a laugh as he embraced her. She knew he was about to ask her about Amun Chalthoum, the head of al Mokhabarat, the Egyptian secret service, who had been killed during her mission in Paris. She gave him a warning look and he bit his tongue.

The tall, reedy man, having emerged from his cubicle, was wandering over to them. He stuck out his hand, introducing himself as Dick Richards. An absurd name, Soraya thought.

"It's good to have you back," he said affably.

She shot him a quizzical look. "Why would you say that?"

"I've heard lots about you since my first day on

the job, mostly from Director Marks." He smiled. "I'd be pleased to get you up to date on the intel files I've been working, if you like."

She plastered a smile on her face until he nodded to them both. When he was gone, she turned to Peter. "Dick Richards? Really?"

"Richard Richards. Like something out of *Catch-22*."

"What was Hendricks thinking?"

"Richards isn't our boss's doing. He's a presidential appointee."

Soraya had glanced at Richards, who was back toiling away at his computer. "A spy in the house of Treadstone?"

"Possibly," Peter had said. "On the plus side, he's got a crackerjack rep at IDing and foiling cyber spying software."

She had meant it as a joke, but Peter had answered her in all seriousness. "What, all of a sudden the president doesn't trust Hendricks?"

"I think," Peter had said in her ear, "that after what has happened to both of us, the president has his doubts about us."

Eventually, Soraya and Peter tackled the twin traumas the two of them had suffered four months ago. It took a long time for her to get around to saying anything about Amun. Not surprisingly, Peter showed infinite patience with her; he had faith that she would tell him when she was ready.

They had just gotten a call from Hendricks, calling for a crash briefing an hour from now, so, while they had the time, the two of them by silent mutual consent grabbed their coats.

"Field assessment meeting in forty minutes," the chubby blonde named Tricia said to Peter as they pushed out the door. Peter grunted, his mind elsewhere.

They left the offices, went out of the building and across the street where, at the edge of a park, they bought coffees and cinnamon buns from their favorite cart and, with hunched shoulders, strolled beneath the inconstant shelter of the bare-branched trees. They kept their backs to the Treadstone building.

"The really cruel thing," she said, "is that Richards is a sharp cookie. We could use his expertise."

"If only we could trust him."

Soraya took a sip of her coffee, warming her insides. "We could try to turn him."

"We'd be going up against the president."

She shrugged. "So what else is new?"

He laughed and hugged her. "I missed you."

She frowned as she ripped off a hunk of cinnamon bun and chewed it reflectively. "I stayed in Paris a long time."

"Hardly surprising. It's a city that's hard to get out of your system."

"It was a shock losing Amun."

Peter had the grace to keep his own counsel. They walked for a while in silence. A child stood with his father, paying out the string on a kite in the shape of the Bat-Signal. They laughed together. The father put his arm around the boy's shoulder. The kite rose higher.

Soraya stared at them, her gaze rising to watch

the kite's flight. At length, she said, "While I was recovering, I thought, *What am I doing? Is this how I want to spend the rest of my life, losing friends and—?*" For a moment, she couldn't go on. She had had strong, though conflicting, feelings for Amun. For a time, she had even thought she loved him but, in the end, she had been wrong. That revelation had only exacerbated her guilt. If she hadn't asked him, if he hadn't loved her, Amun would never have come to Paris. He'd be alive now.

Having lost her taste for food, she handed her coffee and the rest of her bun to a homeless man on a bench, who looked up, slightly stunned, and thanked her with a nod. When they were out of his earshot, she said softly, "Peter, I can't stand myself."

"You're only human."

"Oh, please."

"You've never made a mistake before?"

"Only human, yes," she echoed him, her head down. "But this was a grievous error in judgment that I am determined never to make again."

The silence went on so long that Peter became alarmed. "You're not thinking of quitting."

"I'm considering returning to Paris."

"Seriously?"

She nodded.

A sudden change came over Peter's face. "You've met someone."

"Possibly."

"Not a Frenchman. Please don't tell me it's a Frenchman."

Silent, she stared at the kite, rising higher and higher.

He laughed. "Go," he said. "Don't go. Please."

"It's not only that," she said. "Over there, in Paris, I realized there's more to life than clinging to the shadows like a spider to its web."

Peter shook his head. "I wish I knew what to—"

All at once one leg buckled under her. She staggered and would have fallen had Peter not dropped his food, the coffee spilling like oil at their feet, and grabbed her under the arm to steady her. Concerned, he led her over to a bench, where she sat, bent over, her head in her hands.

"Breathe," he said with one hand on her back. "Breathe."

She nodded, did as he said.

"Soraya, what's going on?"

"Nothing."

"Don't bullshit a bullshitter."

She took a deep breath and let it out slowly. "I don't know. Ever since I got out of the hospital I've been getting these dizzy spells."

"Have you seen a doctor?"

"There was no need. They were getting less and less frequent. I haven't had one for over two weeks."

"And now this." He moved his hand in a circular motion on her back in an attempt to soothe her. "I want you to make an appointment—"

"Stop treating me like a child."

"Then stop acting like one." His voice softened. "I'm concerned about you and I wonder why you aren't."

"All right," she said. "All right."

"Now you can't go," he said, only half in jest. "Not until—"

She laughed, and at last her head lifted. Tears glimmered in the corners of her eyes. "That's my dilemma precisely." Then she shook her head. "I'll never find peace, Peter."

"What you mean is you don't deserve to find peace."

She looked at him and he shrugged, a wan smile on his face. "Maybe what we need to concentrate on is explaining to each other why we both deserve a bit of happiness."

She rose, shaking off his help, and they turned back. The homeless man had finished the breakfast Soraya had provided and was curled on his side on a bench beneath sheets of *The Washington Post*.

As they passed him they could hear him snoring deeply, as if he hadn't a care in the world. And maybe, she thought, he didn't.

She shot Peter a sideways glance. "What *would* I do without you?"

His smile cleared, widening as he walked beside her. "You know, I ask myself that all the time."

Gone?" the Director said. "In what way gone?"

Above his head was engraved the current Mossad motto, excerpted from Proverbs 11:14: *Where no counsel is, the people fall, but in the multitude of counselors there is safety*.

"She's vanished off the grid," Dani Amit, head of Collections, said. "Despite our most diligent efforts, we cannot locate her."

"But we *must* locate her." The Director shook his shaggy head, his livery lips pursed, a clear sign of his agitation. "Rebeka is the key to the mission. Without her, we're dead in the water."

"I understand that, sir. We all do."

"Then—"

Dani Amit's pale blue eyes seemed infinitely sad. "We are simply at a loss."

"How can that be? She is one of us."

"That is precisely the problem. We have trained her too well."

"If that were the case, our people, trained as she was trained, could find her. The fact that up till now they haven't would argue for the fact that she is something more, something better than they are." The rebuke was as clear as it was sharp.

"I'm afraid—"

"I cannot abide that phrase," the Director said shortly. "Her job at the airline?"

"Dead end. Her supervisor has had no contact with her since the incident in Damascus six weeks ago. I am convinced he does not know where she is."

"What about her phone?"

"She's either thrown it away or disabled its GPS."

"Friends, relatives."

"Have been interviewed. One thing I know for certain is that Rebeka told no one about us."

"To break protocol like this—"

There was no need to finish that sentence. Mossad rules were strictly enforced. Rebeka had violated the prime rule.

The Director turned, stared broodingly out the window of his satellite office on the top floor of a curving glass-faced structure in Herzliya. On the other side of the city were the Mossad training center and the summer residence of the prime minister. The Director often came here when he grew melancholy and found the Mossad's ant-colony central HQ in downtown Tel Aviv oppressive and enervating. Here, there was a fountain in the middle of the circular driveway and fragrant flower beds all year round, not to mention the nearby harbor with its fleet of sailboats rocking gently in their slips. There was something reassuring about that forest of masts, even to Amit, as if their presence spoke of a certain permanence in a world where everything could change in the space of a heartbeat.

The Director loved sailing. Whenever he lost a man, which was, thankfully, not all that often, he went out on his boat, alone with the sea and the wind and the plaintive cry of the gulls. Without turning back, he said rather harshly, "Find her, Dani. Find out why she has disobeyed us. Find out what she knows."

"I don't—"

"She has betrayed us." The Director swung back, leaned forward, his bulk making his chair squeal in protest. The full force of his authority was explicit behind each word he spoke. "She is a traitor. We will treat her as such."

"*Memune*, I wonder at the wisdom of rushing to judgment." Amit had used the Director's internal title, *first among equals*.

The bullet- and bombproof windows were coated with a film that reflected light as well as the possibility of long-range surveillance, lending the room a distinctly aqueous quality. The Director's eyes seemed to glimmer in the office's low lamplight like a deep-sea fish rising into the beacon of a diver's headlamp. "It isn't lost on me that she has been your pet project, but it is time now to admit your mistake. Even if I were inclined to give Rebeka the benefit of the doubt, we are out of time. Events threaten to overrun us. We are old friends as well as comrades in arms. Don't force me to call in the Duvdevan."

Invoking the specter of the Israeli Defense Forces' elite strike unit caused a blade of anxiety to knife through Amit. It was a measure of Rebeka's extreme importance to Israeli security that the Director would even use the threat of the Duvdevan to induce Amit to do what the Director knew full well he was reluctant to do.

"Who will you use?" The Director said this conversationally, as if he were asking after Amit's wife and children.

"What about her unique skills, her usefulness—"

"Her betrayal has trumped everything, Amit, even those extraordinary skills. We must assume that what she discovered has sent her to ground. What if her intent is to sell that knowledge to the highest—"

"Impossible," Amit flared.

The Director contemplated him for a moment from beneath half-closed eyelids. "And I daresay up until today you would have said her disappearing off the grid was impossible." He waited. "Am I wrong?"

Amit hung his head. "You're not."

"So." The Director knit his fingers together. "Who will it be?"

"Ilan Halevy," Amit said with a heavy heart.

"The Babylonian." The Director nodded, seemingly impressed. Ilan had garnered his operations name by almost single-handedly shutting down the Iraqi Babylon Advanced Weapons Project. He had killed more than a dozen enemy operatives in that pursuit. "Well, now we're getting to the heart of the matter."

The Director loved nothing better; it was one of his many admirable traits. His inflexibility was not. However, it was his iron hand on the tiller that for the past five years had guided them successfully through the rough seas of international espionage, clandestine forays into the territories of their enemies, and state-sanctioned executions while keeping their casualties to a minimum. He felt the deaths of his people like body blows, which was why, when they occurred, he needed to take to the sea. Out there, he buried his sorrow and cleared his head.

"You'll start him—"

"Immediately," Amit said. "He knows Rebeka well, better than most."

"Except you."

Amit knew what the Director was implying but as yet he was unwilling to engage the notion. "I will brief the Babylonian myself. He will know everything I know."

That was a lie, and Amit suspected his old friend knew it, but mercifully the Director remained silent. How could he tell the Babylonian everything he knew about Rebeka? That was a betrayal he was not about to commit, even to curry favor with the Director. He had lied to forestall the possibility of being given a direct order to divulge all he knew to the Babylonian. Such a moral choice might possibly spell the end of him or, at the very least, his effectiveness within Mossad.

The chair squealed again as the Director returned to his survey of the port city. Who knew what he was thinking? "Then it's settled." He said this as if he were speaking to himself. "It's done."

Amit rose and silently departed. There was no need for the two men to continue the conversation.

Out in the hall, the air-conditioning was fierce. For a moment, Amit stood immobile, as if lost. Occasionally, when it was appropriate, the Director requested that Amit go sailing with him, mourning side by side the man or woman they knew well who had delivered up their life to keep their country secure. Amit imagined this necessary ritual would come again after Rebeka was dead.

2

WHEN HE AWOKE, he was still swimming through frigid water, black as night. It had already infiltrated his nostrils, burning them, threatened to surge down his throat and inundate his lungs. Drowning, he was drowning. He kicked off his shoes, scrabbled in his pockets, divesting himself of keys, wallet, a thick roll of krona, anything that might have been weighing him down. Still he spiraled downward.

He would have screamed, but he was terrified that opening his mouth would let the water gush in, filling him up. Instead, he rose off the bed and, his torso shaking, his limbs spasming, shook himself violently as he tried to claw his way up through the icy water to the surface.

Something grabbed his arms, trying to restrain him, and he opened his eyes into aqueous semi-darkness. His dread bloomed anew. He was at the bottom of the sea, hallucinating as he drowned.

"It's okay," someone said. "You're safe. Everything's all right now."

It took moments—moments that felt like an eternity. Intense anxiety clamped him in its tenacious grip. He heard the words spoken again, but they still made no sense: the brightness, the fact that he could breathe, the sight of two faces in front of him, breathing quite normally, which was inexplicable because they were all under water.

"The light," a second voice said. "He thinks... Turn up the lights."

A sudden blaze made him squint. Could there be such a dazzle on the sea floor? The third time he heard the words repeated, they began to seep through cracks in the armor of his anxiety, and he realized that he was breathing as normally as they were, which must mean that he was no longer in danger of drowning.

With that dawning came the realization of the pain in his head, and at the next pulse, he winced. But at least his body relaxed; he ceased fighting against the hands that held him. He let them lay him back down. He felt something soft beneath him, dry and solid—a mattress—and knew he wasn't on the floor of the sea, there to die while he stared up helplessly into swaying nothingness.

He sighed deeply, and his legs relaxed, his arms came down to his sides and were released. He stared up into the face swimming above him, shuddering at the recurring thought of the water closing over him. He'd never go out on a boat again or even plunge through breakers as he used to do when he was a child. He frowned. Had he really done that? With an enormous effort to focus himself, he realized that he couldn't remember his childhood. His frown deepened. How was that possible?

He was distracted by the face above him speaking to him. "My name is Christien. What is yours?" Christien repeated the question in a number of languages, all of which he understood, though he had no idea how he understood them. He had no memory of learning any language.

After Christien had finished, he said automatically, "My name is—" and then stopped.

"What is it?" Christien said. "What's happened?"

"I don't know." He looked around the room, almost in panic. "I can't remember my name."

Christien, who had been leaning over, now stood up and, turning, said something he couldn't make out to a shadowy figure behind and just to the right of him. He strained to make out the face, but then the figure stepped into the light.

"You can't remember your name?" the second man said.

He shook his head, but that caused a fierce throbbing.

"What do you remember?"

He took a moment, but this only made him break out into a cold sweat as, his brow deeply furrowed, he strained to recall anything—even a single memory.

"Relax," the second man said. He seemed to have taken over from Christien.

"Who are you?" he said.

"My name is Jason. You're in a private clinic in

Stockholm. Christien and I were out fishing when you surfaced. We pulled you into our boat and flew you here. You were suffering from hypoxia and hypothermia."

He thought, *I should ask Jason what those words mean*, but to his shock, he already knew. He licked his lips and Christien, leaning over, poured water from a carafe into a plastic cup and stuck a bendy straw in it. Christien stepped on a pedal, and his head and torso were raised to a modified sitting position. He took the cup gratefully and sipped the water. He felt parched, as if his thirst would never be slaked.

"What . . . what happened to me?"

"You were shot," Jason said. "A bullet grazed the left side of your head."

Automatically his left hand went to the side of his head, felt the thick layers of bandages. He had identified the source of his headache.

"Do you know who shot you? Why you were shot?"

"No," he said. He drained the cup, held it out for more.

While Christien refilled it, Jason said, "Do you know *where* you were shot, where you went into the water?"

At the mention of going into the water he shuddered. "No."

Christien handed him the cup. "It was Sadelöga."

"Do you remember Sadelöga?" Jason said. "Does the name sound familiar?"

"Not in the least." He was about to shake his head again, but stopped himself in time. "I'm sorry, there's nothing I remember."

This seemed to interest Jason. "Nothing at all?" he said.

He stopped sipping his water. "Not where I was born, who my parents are, who I am, what I was doing in—where did you say?"

"Sadelöga," Christien said.

"Maybe I was fishing there," he said hopefully, "like you."

"I very much doubt that fishing involves being shot, and there's no hunting to speak of there," Jason said. "No, you were in Sadelöga for another reason entirely."

"I wish I knew what it was," he said sincerely.

"There's another thing," Jason said. "You had no identification on you—no wallet, passport, keys, money."

He thought a moment. "I threw them all away, along with my shoes, to lighten myself. I was desperate to get back to the surface. They must all be at the bottom of the sea now."

"You remember getting rid of these things," Jason said.

"I ... Yes, I do."

"You said that you remembered nothing."

"*That* I remember. Nothing else." He looked at Jason. "I don't recall you pulling me out of the water, or the trip here. Only those first panic-stricken moments after I went under, not going under itself. Nothing of that."

Jason seemed lost in thought. "Maybe when you're sufficiently recovered we should take you back to Sadelöga."

"Would you agree to that?" Christien asked.

He thought about that for a moment. On the one hand, the idea of returning to the spot where he went into the water terrified him; on the other, he felt an overwhelming, desperate desire to know who he was.

"When can we leave?" he said at last.

What do you think?"

Bourne looked at Christien. They were downstairs in the lounge of the private clinic owned by Christien's company. Outside, the traffic along Staligatan was fierce, but the clinic's thick windows muffled all noise. Clouds were gathering as if for a battle. Once again, it looked like snow. They sat on low Swedish-modern furniture, stylish as well as practical: a sofa in a sturdy print, its colors suitably muted, that was the focal point of one of several conversation areas.

"He reminds me of me," Bourne said.

Christien nodded. "I had the same thought, though this man's amnesia appears virtually complete."

"If he's telling us the truth."

"Jason, he was quite clearly in serious distress. Is there any reason to doubt him?"

"The bullet that grazed the side of his head," Bourne said. "He isn't a tourist. Also, he quite clearly, as you would say, understood all five languages you spoke to him in."

"So he's a linguist. So what?"

"So am I."

"You're also a professor of comparative linguistics."

"Used to be."

"He could be one, too."

"What's he doing out here with a bullet crease in the side of his head?"

"Noted."

"I want to find out whether he's in our business."

Christien gave him a skeptical look. "Just because he's a linguist?"

Bourne gestured. "Look, if he's not a spy we have nothing to worry about. But given what you've told me..."

Christien spread his hands. "All right, what do you suggest?"

"We have some time before we can take him back to Sadelöga."

"What does it matter? We won't get anything out of him in his current state."

"Untrue. We can subject him to a series of tests."

Christien shook his head. "Tests? What do you mean?"

Bourne sat forward, perched on the edge of the sofa. "You discovered that this man speaks at least five languages when he himself didn't know that. Let's find out what else he doesn't know he knows."

Soraya and Peter left the briefing with Hendricks filled with mixed feelings.

"This so-called Nicodemo sounds like a ghost," Soraya said. "I don't like chasing ghosts."

"For some reason, Hendricks is obsessed with finding and eliminating Nicodemo," Peter said. "He gave it his highest priority. And yet, he had no specific intel, no chatter as to a clear and present attack that Nicodemo might be planning against American personnel or citizens abroad or here at home. I smell a political hot potato."

"I never thought of that."

Peter laughed. "That's because you still have one foot in Paris."

She turned to him. "Is that what you think?"

He shrugged. "Can you blame me?"

The hallway was quiet, save for the hum of the HVAC vents high up in the walls. Far away at one end, she thought she saw Dick Richards coming toward them, and she groaned inwardly. The guy was like a leech.

She gestured with her head toward Richards. "If we can't trust each other, we're fucked."

"My thought exactly."

"About your leaving..."

"Let's not talk about that now, Peter." She sighed. It was definitely Richards coming toward them. "So how important to us is finding Nicodemo?"

"If, as you surmise, the issue is political, not very. I didn't take this job to carry Hendricks's water."

"I think I know just what to tell Mary's little lamb."

She smiled broadly as they met Dick Richards halfway along the hall.

Richards handed a dossier to Peter. "I have some intel briefs I thought you'd want to see," he said helpfully.

"Thanks." Peter, opening the file, glanced through the pages with no real interest.

Soraya shoved the fuzzy intel on Nicodemo that

Hendricks had given them in the briefing at Richards.

"Peter and I would like you to run this person of interest down," she said, "see if there's anything substantive to him, see what level of danger he represents to US interests abroad."

Peter looked up as Richards nodded. He gave her a sharp glance to which she responded with her sweetest smile.

"We'd appreciate your dropping whatever it is you're working on now," she continued, "and concentrating on this until you can give us a yea or a nay. If you need any help, ask Tricia." She pointed in the general direction of the chubby blonde.

"Great." Richards, having no interest in assistance of any kind, slapped the back of his hand against the thin file Soraya had given him. "I'll get on it ASAP."

"Atta boy," she said. "Make it so, Number One."

"*Star Trek TNG*, right?" He gave her a lopsided grin. "I won't let you down, Captain." Turning on his heel, he retreated down the hallway to his cubicle to begin his data search.

Peter frowned. "That was wicked cold."

She shrugged. "It saves us some busywork and it keeps him off our streets. Where's the harm?"

When Dick Richards heard their muffled laughter behind him, he began to change his mind about at last feeling included. Or perhaps he only imagined their laughter. What he knew was real, however, was their contempt. Director Marks had been okay—

cool, but helpful—when he had arrived at the president's beckoning. The atmosphere started to deteriorate, however, the moment Director Moore returned from her medical leave in Paris. Regarding the co-directors of Treadstone, Richards had no more to go on than hearsay, office scuttlebutt, and, least reliable of all, the inter-agency mythos that always arose like smoke obscuring the true contours of the land.

The president's orders had been most specific. He had come to the great man's attention through his job at the NSA, cracking the core code to the horrific Stuxnet worm, the most advanced malicious software worm to date, the first to be called a cyberweapon, that had baffled the best cyber security analysts for months. Variations on the Stuxnet worm had sucked up information on US advanced weapons systems, clandestine asset locations, forward initiatives by the military in both Iraq and Afghanistan, and drone strike targets in western Pakistan. He had also been the one to realize that the SecurID tokens the federal clandestine operatives used had been hacked. He identified the security flaw that had allowed the breach and sealed it.

He was like Einstein formulating the equation for the speed of light. At least that was how he had been described to the president by Mike Holmes, his former boss at NSA. Now he worked strictly for the president, reported to him directly. Their relationship was unprecedented, and quite naturally caused no end of jealousy among the members of the president's cabinet, who resented his presence, let alone his cyber triumphs. What it boiled down to, Richards thought now, as he climbed into his chair and faced his computer screen, was that they didn't understand him. Human beings, he had discovered, hated and feared anyone or anything they couldn't understand.

Now his new directors were firmly in that restive camp. Pity. He had begun to like Director Marks, and he might have felt the same way about Director Moore had either of them given him a chance. Someone else might have been angry at them for this gross disservice, but Richards's mind didn't work that way. He knew, also from experience, that the best way for him to not only survive at Treadstone, but to flourish, serving the president as he was expected to do, was to change the co-directors' opinion of him.

Opening the slim file Director Moore had handed him, he read through the close-set typescript, which, he saw immediately, was little more than unreliable bits and pieces—ephemera from the field. Still, there remained the possibility, slim though it might be, that at the heart of this smoke-and-mirrors show there lay an actual piece of uncharted topography. And he knew without a shadow of a doubt that if he could reveal this topography for the directors, they would begin to see him in a new light. This, more than anything else, was what he desired. It was what needed to happen. His master's command.

He opened his Iron Key browser to the Internet and, fingers flying over the keyboard, began his search for a myth.

Rebeka stared out at the beautiful, bleak expanse

of Hemviken Bay. Sitting at a waterside table at
Utö Wärdshus, the only restaurant in this area of the
southern Swedish archipelago, she nursed a coffee
and her sore right shoulder. She'd received no more
than a flesh wound from her quarry's sudden attack.
Anyone else would have berated herself for failing
to deflect the attack, but not Rebeka. She had trained
herself to let go, not to feel remorse or, worse, to
castigate herself. She lived in the present, thinking
only of the perilous future, and how to get there successfully while absorbing the minimum of damage.

Upon entering the restaurant, her practiced eye
had noted all sixteen tables, only three of which
were inhabited, one by a pair of old men, one of
them in a wheelchair, slowly and deliberately playing chess, another by an ancient mariner with rough
hands the color of a boiled lobster claw, reading a
local paper while smoking a small-bowled pipe, and
the third by a pregnant woman and her daughter,
who Rebeka judged to be five or six. Her professional assessment was that none of them posed a
threat, and she promptly forgot about them.

After her target had gone into the water, Rebeka,
completely ignoring her knife wound, had spent the
better part of an hour wading in looking for him. For
all her efforts, standing firm against being pulled out
with the tide, for the almost-frostbite in her toes, she
had failed to find him. This was both unfortunate
and frightening. She was fairly certain her shot had
done nothing more than crease her target's head. If
she hadn't killed him, she wanted to make certain
the frigid water didn't. She needed what was in his
brain, and she cursed herself for shooting at him at

all. She should have simply jumped in after him. Overpowering him in the water, she felt certain, would have been no difficult matter. Instead he was gone and, with him, the intel he carried that would save her.

Absentmindedly, she stirred more sugar into her coffee, then took a sip. Her own people were now after her. No one knew better than she how ruthless and relentless the Mossad could be when they believed one of their own had betrayed them. She fervently wished there had been another way to tackle the problem, but she knew Colonel Ari Ben David better than to think he would believe her wild tale, and there was simply no one else to go to. Well, there was one person, but her training made her reluctant to involve anyone outside Mossad.

She heard the waitress's voice, and turning, winced. The knife wound she had received in Damascus was not yet fully healed, and certain sharp movements of her upper torso reminded her it was still there.

"Would you care for more coffee?"

The waitress smiled at her. She looked like a Valkyrie. Rebeka could imagine her, armored, riding to Ragnarök, or, more realistically, out on a fishing boat, hauling in the morning's catch. She nodded, returning the smile.

Turning back to the bay, she saw that a storm was coming in. Fine. The increasing bleakness matched her mood. She drank her coffee, added more sugar, and reflected on her life since she had met Jason Bourne on her regularly scheduled flight to Damascus. Though it was only six weeks ago, her former cover as a flight attendant seemed like a hundred years ago. How her life had changed since then! She and Bourne had both been after the same terrorist target, Semid Abdul-Qahhar. During their showdown with him, they had both been wounded. Though he had been shot in the shoulder, Bourne had flown her in a stolen helicopter across the southern border into Lebanon and, at her whispered instructions, had set down inside the Mossad encampment in Dahr El Ahmar.

Now she had no idea where he was or whether he would even talk to her. After all, it was she who had directed him to the encampment commanded by Ben David. For all she knew, he blamed her for what had happened.

No, even if she had been able to find him, she couldn't go to Bourne with her suspicions, in spite of the fact that they had arisen during her convalescence in Dahr El Ahmar. As far as he was concerned, she was the enemy. She had betrayed him. After what had happened, how could he think otherwise?

And, of course, she herself had come under suspicion from having brought Bourne into the encampment. Colonel Ben David was not a forgiving man—in truth, he could not afford to be—but the change in how he viewed her shocked, then saddened, her. She was inured to the byzantine ways of her world, but nothing she had experienced before could have prepared her for how quickly and thoroughly he had turned on her. In fact, he had acted more like a jilted lover than her commanding officer. It was only later, after she had left, after she had decided to act on the intel she had overheard while convalescing, after she had been in full pursuit of her target, that the nature of Ben David's true feelings had dawned on her. In hindsight, she realized that she had never been just an agent to him. Now, of course, it was too late to do anything about that, even had she wished to.

The stormfront hurled the first fistfuls of snow against the window with a force that startled her. The glass shivered and creaked in the wind. It was then that she turned around and saw the man, thin as a blade, sitting at a table near the door farthest from her, and knew that all was lost.

One man. A single man." Christien looked at Bourne. "His name is Nicodemo, but he is more commonly known at the Djinn Who Lights The Way."

"Meaning?"

"He is the advance guard, the outrider."

"In other words, he gets things done."

Christien nodded.

Bourne stared out the window. It was late morning. Clouds kept rolling in from the north like waves on a seashore. Off and on, snow gusted in the wind eddies. The nameless man, who Bourne had come to think of as Alef, had passed into an exhausted sleep. Bourne and Christien had decided to take a break from interrogating him, though neither of them had wanted to.

"Tell me about Nicodemo," Bourne said. "Why are you and Don Fernando so concerned about him?"

The restaurant occupied the top floor of a chrome-and-green-glass ultramodern building on Kommendörsgatan in the posh Östermalm section of Stockholm, close to where Christien lived.

Christien shrugged. "I'll tell you as much as I know, which, quite honestly, isn't much; his origins are obscure. Some say he's Portuguese, others maintain he's Bolivian, still others swear he's Czech. Whatever the truth, he came out of nowhere, quite literally. For some time, a decade ago, he seemed to be an investment conduit for Core Energy. During that time, the company mushroomed into a multinational powerhouse that buys and sells all forms of energy. No one seems to know whether he is still involved, or in what way. By comparison, the CEO of Core Energy, Tom Brick, is an open book. He was born in London's World's End, graduated from London Business School. Don't let his lack of degrees fool you, he's a very savvy guy."

"Let's get back to Nicodemo."

"That's the problem. Nicodemo seems inextricably linked with Core Energy."

"Nicodemo is a terrorist," Bourne said, "and Core Energy is a legitimate company, a leader in the burgeoning energy markets, green and otherwise."

"That's the most troubling part, Jason, the one Don Fernando and I have been investigating for months now. We believe that Core Energy is on the verge of making a deal that will be a game-changer, that will give it such an advantage in the new energy markets as to cause its profits to explode tenfold."

Bourne shrugged. "Business is business, Christien."

"Not when it leaves death and destruction in its wake."

"Which is where, I assume, Nicodemo comes in."

Christien nodded. "This is what we believe, yes."

"Are you certain this man actually exists?"

"What d'you mean?"

"Have you ever heard of Domenico Scarfo?"

Christien shook his head.

"He was a notorious boss of the Philadelphia mob in the forties and fifties. Behind his back, people called him 'Little Nicky' because he was five-six, but his full name was Nicodemo Domenico Scarfo."

"What are you saying?"

Bourne set aside his menu. "I've come across this kind of thing several times before. A name is created, a legend is built, fed first by myth, then by rumors and innuendo, sometimes even by murders committed by a cadre of people who work for the people who created the name in the first place."

Christien plucked a warm roll from a basket in the center of the table and began to butter it. "Your own origin, if my sources are correct."

"The Jason Bourne identity was created this way, yes." Bourne took a sip of fresh orange juice.

Christien spooned up some lingonberry jam. "And now you *are* Jason Bourne."

Bourne nodded. "I am. Identities are powerful images that often take on a life of their own and have unintended consequences. But if I hadn't lost my memory..."

Christien nodded thoughtfully. "We're back to Alef. I take your point." He bit into his roll and looked up at the waiter, who had appeared by their side. He raised his eyebrows at Bourne, who ordered scrambled eggs and gravlax, toast, and more coffee. "I'll have the same," he said.

When the waiter left, Bourne said, "Have you or Don Fernando entertained the notion that Nicodemo is an identity Tom Brick created so that he could circumvent the law without any blowback for either him or Core Energy?"

Christien said, "Nicodemo exists, believe me."

Bourne looked up. "You've met him?"

"Don Fernando believes he has." He was speaking of Don Fernando Hererra, his sometime partner, an industrialist, banker, and friend with whom Bourne had had dealings previously.

"Even if I accept what you tell me, all we know for certain is that he's met someone purporting to be Nicodemo. It doesn't mean that Nicodemo actually exists."

"I should take lessons from you on cynicism."

"One man's cynicism is another man's prudence," Bourne said. "Speaking of Don Fernando, where is he? It would be helpful to speak with him."

"He's away."

"You'll have to do better than that," Bourne said shortly.

The food came then. They were both silent until the waiter left and they began to eat.

"The truth is," Christien said, "he has asked me to keep his whereabouts secret."

Bourne put down his fork and sat back. "Look, make a decision. Do you and Don Fernando want my help or not?"

"Either way, you'll have to deal with this growing

menace. Core Energy forced us to use subterfuge to buy into the Indigo Ridge Rare Earths mine in California. If we hadn't, it would have bought it out from under America. We couldn't allow that to happen. But Core has been busy elsewhere, buying up rare earth, uranium, gold, silver, copper, and base metals mines in Canada, Africa, and Australia. In the decades to come, these resources will increase in value exponentially as one nation after another is forced to phase out machines that run on oil, coal, and even natural gas. The world is running out of oil. As for coal, we'll all be choking on the carcinogenic fumes that plague every city in China, India, and Thailand unless we abandon it as an energy source. Solar panels aren't energy efficient and as for those much-hyped wind turbines, each one requires four hundred pounds of rare earths. Besides, you can't put a windmill on a car or an airplane. Hybrid cars are dependent on rare earth components as well, and as for electric cars, where d'you think the electricity comes from?"

Christien shook his head. "Nicodemo has seen the future and it's energy."

"But Core Energy is run by Tom Brick."

"Right. Brick is the company's public face. But it's altogether possible that he is getting his orders from Nicodemo. This is what Don Fernando intends to find out. If it's true, it would allow Nicodemo the freedom to work on the nether side of the law. Don Fernando believes that he is the first of the coming generation of terrorists. He can make deals in the shadows, the gray areas—by outright bribery, extortion, or other methods of coercion—that Brick and Core Energy itself can't. He's motivated by neither religion nor ideology. Corner the market on the next century's major fuel sources and you have the entire world at your feet. In one fell swoop you've choked off free trade, you've compromised nations' economies and security. These days, no one can build a competent army without weapons that rely heavily on rare earths."

"Where has Don Fernando gone?"

Christien, too, put down his utensils and wiped his mouth. "Jason, there is a very good reason why Don Fernando asked me to keep his whereabouts secret. He was afraid that you'd try to follow him."

"Why?" Bourne leaned forward. "Where has he gone? Tell me."

Christien sighed. "Jason, we have our own mystery to solve here."

"There's no going back. You'll tell me now."

The two men's gazes locked in a contest of wills. At length, Christien looked down at his plate. He picked up his knife and fork and returned to eating. He did not look up from his food. Between bites he said, "Don Fernando has gone to find the Djinn Who Lights The Way."

Rebeka paid her check, rose, and walked to the door. At the last minute, she turned and sat down at the table where the blade-thin man had installed himself some time before.

"Edge of the world," he said dryly.

She eyed him. "Not nearly."

"For us, at least."

"You mean Jews?"

"That, too."

He had curiously dainty hands, milky white, the knuckles prominent, as if the bones were about to burst through the skin. His eyes were black, his thinning hair of a nondescript color. His features were sharp: a slash of mouth, a knife-like nose. She had seen him only once before, years ago, when she had finished her training and had been summoned to Mossad's Tel Aviv headquarters. He had watched, silent as death, as Dani Amit, head of Collections, had given her her first commission. She remembered him, though, his face indelible on the screen of her mind. His name was Ze'ev—*wolf*, in Hebrew—though she seriously doubted it was the one he had been born with.

"You're lucky I found you," Ze'ev said.

"How does that work?" She cocked her head.

He took an almost dainty sip of coffee. "They've activated the Babylonian."

Beneath her cool exterior, Rebeka felt the first ripples of apprehension. She tamped down on this emotion before it could turn into outright fear. "Why would they do that?"

"What the devil are you up to?" Ze'ev said.

At first, she thought he had deliberately ignored her question, but she quickly realized that his counter-question *was* his answer. The depth to which she had shaken her bosses was signified by their extreme response.

She shook her head.

"I don't understand you, Rebeka. You've had a

stellar career so far. Then you go and bring Jason Bourne into Dahr El Ahmar, into the heart of—"

"He saved my life. I was bleeding out. There was nowhere else to go."

Ze'ev sat back, his black eyes contemplating her. She wondered what he was thinking.

"You had clearance. You knew the secret nature of Dahr El Ahmar."

She met his gaze, said nothing.

"And yet—"

"As I said."

He shook his head. "Colonel Ben David is out for your blood—and, of course, Bourne's."

"I had no idea of the Colonel's intense antipathy toward Bourne."

"Are you saying he's not justified?"

She thought about this for a moment. "I suppose not. But at the time of the crisis I had no knowledge—"

"But you did have the one piece of crucial knowledge: the absolute secrecy in which Dahr El Ahmar operates. Bourne escaped. He knows—"

"You have no idea what he knows," she snapped. "He was in the encampment for less than fifteen minutes. He was wounded and fighting for his life. I hardly think he had time to—"

"One, Bourne is a trained agent; he sees and hears everything. Two, he knows, at the very least, that Dahr El Ahmar exists. Three, he escaped via helicopter, which means he overflew the compound."

"That doesn't mean he made sense of what he saw. He was too busy trying to evade the ground-to-air missile Ben David sent up after him."

"So far as Colonel Ben David—and, I have it on good authority, Dani Amit—are concerned, Bourne's presence at Dahr El Ahmar is more than enough to condemn him. The security breach is of the most serious level. Following this, you vanish off the grid. Rebeka, you must see where their thinking has taken them."

"The two incidents are wholly unrelated."

"Of course you'd say that."

"It's the truth."

He shook his head. "They don't buy it and, frankly, neither do I."

"Look—"

"The Babylonian has been loosed, Rebeka. He's coming for you." He sighed. "There's only one way to stop him."

"Forget it," she said. "Don't even ask me."

He shrugged. "Then I'm talking to a dead woman. Pity." He threw down some money, then rose.

"Wait."

He stood, staring down at her with an expression that made something inside her wither.

Rebeka's mind was working furiously. "Sit."

He hesitated, then did as she requested.

"There's something—" She stopped herself, abruptly frightened. She had promised herself to tell no one what had happened at Dahr El Ahmar. She looked away, chewing her lower lip in uncertainty.

"What is it?" Ze'ev said, leaning forward.

Some tone in his voice—conciliatory, as if he harbored a real concern for her—caused her to turn back. *This is the moment*, she thought. *To trust or not to trust. It's now or never.* Of course, there was an entirely different route she could take.

She took a deep breath, trying to settle herself, but nothing could stop the almost painful hammering of her heart. The not-quite-healed wound in her side began to throb.

"Rebeka, look, there are two reasons someone in your position bolts. These days, we can forget ideology. So what are we left with? Money and sex." He regarded her with great sympathy, even during her continued silence. "I'm going to hazard a guess. There's been only one change in your recent life—Jason Bourne. Am I right?"

Oh, my God, she thought. *He believes I betrayed Mossad at Bourne's request.* But perhaps she could use that misconception.

She rose abruptly and pushed out the door, only to be slapped in the face by the storm. She stood under the eaves of the restaurant, which sheltered her partially from the stinging snow but not at all from the ferocious wind.

It wasn't long before she sensed that Ze'ev had pushed through the door to stand close beside her.

"You see," he said, his voice raised over the unearthly howling, "there's nowhere to go from here."

She allowed a long silence to build before she let out a breath and said, "You're right." She made herself look slightly ashamed. "It is Bourne."

Ze'ev's eyebrows knitted together. "What did he say to convince you? What did he do?"

"I was with him for two nights in Damascus." Her eyes engaged fully with his. "What d'you think?"

* * *

Life at Treadstone was difficult for Dick Richards. Going from NSA, where he was revered, even by the president, to being a virtual pariah was not easy on the nerves. That, on top of his duplicitous role, was getting to him. He was not someone cut out for the field; he did not have that nerveless sort of personality those agents did. You had to be born with it; no amount of training would give it to you. The fact was, he was a physical coward. He had lived with this humiliating knowledge since he was thirteen, in summer camp, in a house commanded by a bully who, sensing Richards's weakness, preyed on him mercilessly. Instead of fighting back, he had endured the humiliations until, at the end of the dreadful summer, he had held out his hand to the bully and said, "*No hard feelings, yeah?*" All he had gotten in return was a knowing smirk. That memory haunted him into adult life, where it had been repeated in other forms. His intellectual achievements sometimes masked this core failing in him, but not always, and certainly not, as now, in the dead of night, when even the city's golden glow failed to exorcise the feeling of helplessness from his heart.

He had been at his computer all afternoon, evening, and into the night, stopping only to relieve his bladder and to get himself a hurried bite of fast food that now sat like a congealed lump in his roiling stomach. Opening a drawer without taking his eyes off the screen, he twisted open a bottle of antacids and popped a handful into his mouth, then chewed desultorily as he continued to pretend to track down the ghost in the sketchy intel his directors had given him, half, he suspected, in jest. Another humiliation piled onto all the others. On the other hand, it was heartening to know they weren't much interested in Nicodemo themselves. The order must have come down from above, which meant that it was Secretary Hendricks who was trying to find Nicodemo. Richards had no idea who Nicodemo was; nevertheless, he knew far more about him than did anyone else at Treadstone.

His interest lay in the spate of Chinese cyber-attacks on government, military, and contractor servers worldwide, trying to glean classified knowledge. It was this investigation he had been working on all day and evening. There had been several moments when he had been certain he'd been onto something, following threads through firewalls, breaking into encrypted files, accessing site after vault-like site, his platoon of software Trojans and worms that he himself had tweaked to his own exacting specifications allowing him access to sites in Russia, Romania, Serbia, and, finally, China. Always China. Each path he took, however, proved to be either a dead end or a false lead, leaving him, after eight hours, back where he had started. But not quite. Knowing where *not* to look was an excellent tool for first changing his search parameters, then narrowing them down.

He stood up, stretched, and walked over to the bulletproof window. Small sensors were embedded in the glass that sent out electronic signals proven to jam any audio surveillance system. He stared down at the deserted streets below. Occasionally a car or truck rumbled by. Unbidden, thoughts of his father and his stepfather bloomed in his mind like poisoned flowers. His father, who had left when Richards's mother had gone blind. Richards had been four. Years later, he had used his computer skills to track his father down only to find that the man denied ever having sired him. As for Richards's stepfather, he had entered the damaged family in order to live off Richards's mother's money. He had made fun of her, had repeatedly betrayed her with a virtual harem of women. When Richards had tried to tell his mother, she had not only refused to believe him but had grown visibly angry, castigating him for refusing to accept her new husband. It was only then he realized that she knew everything, but was so terrified of being on her own that she had sunk deeper and deeper into her own manufactured reality.

Abruptly, he returned to his desk. Standing at the window made him feel like an animal in a cage, imprisoned within the stronghold of the modern Treadstone castle. He was only dimly aware that it was his life in which he felt imprisoned. Unconsciously, he had chosen his mother's solution. He had made the Internet, endlessly morphing, always fascinating, more real to him than anything else in his life.

Flexing his fingers, he cracked his knuckles, then placed his fingertips on the keys. What he needed to do was something more constructive. He decided to fabricate intel on Nicodemo that he could present to his directors, maybe get into their good graces. He felt that old familiar desperation to have superiors like him, and his cheeks flamed with shame.

He took a deep breath. *Concentrate*, he thought. *Do what you do best; you'll feel better for this small success.* Looking for one man in the complex ISP stew of the Internet was always difficult, he knew. He also knew that no man—not even a ghost—could exist as an island. He had to have associates, friends, family—in other words, an infrastructure, just like everyone else. Even if he didn't so far exist on the Net, they certainly would. And then there was the fact that he made money, lots of it, according to the scraps Richards had been given. Money did not exist in a vacuum; it came from somewhere and went somewhere else. Those places might be well hidden, but they existed; their routes existed online as well as in the real world. None of this, however, applied to Nicodemo; Richards knew this much about him.

Not to worry, he decided, his pulse rate climbing; he'd manufacture an oblique approach to finding the Djinn Who Lights The Way. So thinking, he returned to the pathetically few crumbs in the file, reading them over in this new light, for a way to begin writing his bogus trip through the cyberworld of the Net.

As if of their own volition, his fingers began their familiar tattoo on the keyboard. Moments later, he was once again immersed in his beloved virtual universe.

3

THE TROUBLE IS you flew."

"What do you mean?" Soraya shook her head. "I don't understand."

Dr. Steen glanced up from the folder that contained the results of her EEG and MRI tests. "You were injured in Paris, is that right?"

"Yes."

"And you were treated there as well."

She nodded. "That's right."

"Were you not cautioned about the risks associated with flying?"

Soraya felt the beating of her heart. It was far too rapid, as if it had broken free of its cage and had risen into her throat. "I thought I was fine."

"Well, you're not." Dr. Steen swiveled in his chair, switching on an LED monitor. He brought up the MRI of her brain. Nodding toward the screen, he said, "You have a subdural hematoma. Your brain is bleeding, Ms. Moore."

Soraya felt chilled to the bone. "I saw my previous MRI. It revealed no such thing."

"Again," Dr. Steen said, "the flying."

He swiveled back, but the MRI of her brain remained on the screen, a horrible reminder of her un-wellness.

Dr. Steen clasped his hands on his desktop. He was a middle-aged man who shaved his head rather than deal with his balding pate. "I suspect that this— tear, let's call it—was microscopic. The previous MRI didn't pick it up. Then you flew and…" His hands opened.

She leaned forward, anger supplanting her fear. "Why do you keep intimating that it's somehow my fault?"

"You shouldn't have—"

"Shut the fuck up." She didn't say it loudly, but the intensity of her words rocked him backward and rendered him mute. "Is this how you talk to all your patients? What kind of a human being are you?"

"I'm a doctor. I—"

"Right," she interrupted. "Not a human being. My mistake."

He watched her steadily, waiting for her to calm down. "Ms. Moore, my extensive experience in neurosurgery has taught me that it does not pay to sugarcoat my diagnoses. The quicker a patient understands their condition, the quicker we can work together to make them well again."

She paused for a moment to control herself, but

her heart still felt like a runaway train. Then she winced at the sudden spike of pain in her head. At once, Dr. Steen came around his desk and was at her side.

"Ms. Moore?"

She rubbed the side of her head.

"That cuts it." He reached for his phone. "You're going to the hospital this minute."

"No." She grasped his arm. "No, please."

"I don't think you understand the gravity of—"

"My job is my life," she said.

"Ms. Moore, pressure is building in your brain. You won't have a life unless we relieve that pressure. I cannot allow—"

"I'm okay now. The pain is gone." She gave him a smile that almost faltered. "Absolutely, I'm fine."

Dr. Steen looked around, pulled a chair over to sit beside her. "Okay," he said, "what's really going on?"

"What happened to the doctor with the attitude?"

"I put him on the shelf for the moment." He allowed himself a thin smile. "Patient needs me."

"I needed you, it seems, the moment I stepped into your office."

She was silent for some time. She could hear the phone ring in the outer office, a voice raised suddenly, then stillness returned.

Dr. Steen tapped her wrist lightly to make certain she was still with him. "We have to resolve your physical problem. Clearly, we can't do that until your other problem is resolved."

Slowly, almost infinitesimally, she raised her eyes to his. "I'm frightened," she said.

He seemed in a way relieved. "That's perfectly normal, only to be expected, in fact. I can help—"

"Not for me."

He looked at her, momentarily confused.

"For my baby," Soraya said. "I'm pregnant."

How are you feeling?" Bourne said when he appeared in the room where Alef was recovering.

"Better, physically."

The man was sitting up. He was trying to read a copy of the *International Herald Tribune* someone had given him, but he appeared to be having difficulty.

Bourne set down a black leather briefcase and peered at the page, which was filled with stock market quotes, company mergers, quarterly results, and the like. "Eyes not focusing right?"

Alef shrugged. "In and out. The doctors said it's to be expected."

"See any companies you own?"

"What?" Alef laughed uneasily. "No, no, I was just trying to adjust my eyes to the smaller print."

Bourne took the paper away, opened the attaché case, and laid a handgun on Alef's lap. Before he could open his mouth, Bourne said, "What is that?"

Alef picked it up. "It's a Glock 19 9 mm." He checked the magazine, saw that it was unloaded. Sighted down it. A professional.

Bourne took it from him and, in the same motion, handed him another. "And this?"

"A CZ-USA 75B Compact Pistol."

"How many rounds does it take?"

"Ten."

Bourne took the CZ and replaced it with a far smaller handgun. "Know what that is?"

Alef handled it. "This is a Para-Ordnance Warthog Pistol, WHX1045R, Alloy Regal Finish, 45 ACP Caliber, 10 round capacity, single action." He looked up at Bourne with an astonished expression. "How do I know all that?"

By way of an answer, Bourne plucked up the Warthog and, throwing down a magazine open to a detailed photo, said in Russian, "*Pozhaluysta, skazhite mne, chto izobrazheno tam.*" *Please tell me what is pictured there.*

"A Dragunov SVD-S rifle with folding butt and polymer furniture." His forefinger traced a pattern across the photo. "It's a sniper's rifle."

"Good, bad, what?" Bourne demanded.

"Very good," Alef said. "One of the best."

"What else can you tell me?" Bourne said, switching to English. "Have you ever used one?"

"Used one?" Alef appeared confused. "I...I don't know."

"What about the Glock or the Warthog?"

Alef shook his head. "I'm drawing a blank."

"You knew them immediately."

"Yes, I know, but...how is that possible?" He rubbed his temples as Bourne packed away all the weapons. "What the hell does this mean?"

"It means," Bourne said, "that it's time to see whether a return to Sadelöga will jog your memory."

Here's a flash for you," Peter Marks said when Soraya came through Treadstone's security door, "our new boy Richards claims the Djinn Who Lights The Way isn't a ghost after all. He's real."

"Is that so?" Soraya shrugged off her coat and started toward her office.

"Yeah." Peter strode at her side. "And what's more, he came up with a name—it's tentative, mind you, but still...his name's Nicodemo."

"Huh." She threw her coat over the heating sill and sat down at her desk. "Maybe we should go have a talk with Richard Richards."

"Not right now. I don't want to break his concentration. He's hip-deep in it." He glanced over at Richards's cubicle. "I think he's been at it all night."

She shrugged and pulled the stack of files out of her in-box. In them were transcripts of the night's oral reports filed by her agents-in-place in the Middle East: Syria, Lebanon, Somalia, and so forth. She flipped open the first file and began to read.

Peter cleared his throat. "So how did things go at the doctor's?"

She looked up. Putting a smile on her face, she said, "All the tests were negative. It's just fatigue." She shrugged. "He thinks I came back to work sooner than I should have."

"I tend to agree," Peter said. "You don't look yourself."

"No, who do I look like?"

He didn't laugh at her weak joke. "Go home, Soraya. Get some rest."

"I don't want to go home. After what happened, and my forced bed rest, the best thing for me is to keep working."

"I disagree, and so does your doctor. Take a couple of days off. In fact, don't even get out of bed."

"Peter, I'll go out of my mind."

He put a hand over hers. "Don't make me bring Hendricks into this."

She looked at him for a moment, then nodded. "Okay, but I want this just between the two of us."

He smiled. "So do I."

"Anything important comes up you'll call me."

"Of course I will."

"Use my mobile, the landline at my apartment is out again."

He nodded, clearly relieved that she had acquiesced. "You got it."

"Okay." She took a breath. "Just give me a minute to finish this report, then I'll hand them all over to you." As he rose, she said softly, "Keep an eye on Richards, will you?"

Peter bent over. "Sure thing." He went to her door, turning back for just a moment. "Do as you're told, okay?"

"Okay."

Soraya watched Peter return to his office across the corridor, then she finished reading the report, scribbled some notes on the margin for Peter, and gathered the files up, stacking them to bring over to him. As she did so, she saw the file containing the reports from her agents in Egypt. An image of Amun bloomed in her mind, and immediately she felt her eyes burning. Angry and heartsick in equal measure, she wiped the tears away with the back of her hand.

Taking several deep breaths, she rose and brought the files over to Peter. On the way down to the ground floor, she checked her watch. It was just before noon. Punching a speed dial number on her mobile, she called Delia Trane, who was an explosives specialist at the Bureau of Alcohol, Firearms, Tobacco, and Explosives. She and Delia had worked closely together on several cases when Soraya had been at Central Intelligence, and beyond that the two were close friends.

"Raya, how are you?"

"Needing to see you," Soraya said. "Can you do lunch?"

"Today? I have something, but I'll reschedule it. Are you okay?"

Soraya told her where and when to meet, then rang off. She had no desire to talk any longer over the phone. Forty minutes later, she entered Jaleo, a tapas restaurant on Seventh Street NW, and saw Delia already seated at a table by the windows. She smiled broadly when she spotted Soraya and waved her over.

Delia's mother was an aristocratic Colombian from Bogotá, and the daughter carried much of her maternal ancestors' fiery blood. Though her eyes were light, her skin was as deep-toned as her friend's, but there the similarity ended. She had a plain face and a boyish figure, short-cropped hair, and strong hands. At work, her blunt, no-nonsense manner was legendary, but with Soraya, she was completely different.

Delia rose and the two women embraced.

"Tell me everything, Raya."

Soraya's smile faltered. "That's why I called you."

They sat facing each other. Soraya ordered a Virgin Mary. Delia was nursing a caipirinha, a drink prepared with *cachaça*, Brazilian sugar cane liquor.

Soraya glanced around the room, grateful that it was filling up, the hubbub rising around them like walls. "The doctor was surprised I wasn't showing, given that I'm at the beginning of my second trimester. He said he can usually tell."

Delia grunted. "Men are so full of shit about their pregnancy radar."

"In my case, just like my mother, I may not begin to show until I'm about five or six months."

A small silence rose between them amid the increasing clamor of the restaurant as more and more diners were seated and those already there became boisterous. The laughter, in particular, seemed shrill and ugly.

Delia, sensing her friend's mounting distress, reached out and took Soraya's hand in hers. "Raya, listen to me, I won't let anything happen to the baby, or to you."

Soraya's grateful smile flickered on and off. "The tests came back. I have a subdural hematoma."

Delia caught her breath. "How bad is it?"

"Like a slow leak in a tire. But the pressure…" Soraya's gaze flicked away a moment. "Dr. Steen thinks I should have a procedure. He wants to drill a hole in my head."

Delia squeezed her hand tighter. "Of course he thinks that. Surgeons always want to cut and paste."

"In this instance, he may be right."

"We'll get a second opinion. A third, if necessary."

"The MRI is clear," Soraya said. "Even I could see the problem."

"Hematomas can be self-healing."

"I suppose this one could have been. Unfortunately, I flew. The trip from Paris exacerbated it, and now ..."

Delia saw the fear in Soraya's eyes. "Now what?"

Soraya took a deep breath and let it out. "Surgical procedures are done on pregnant women only in emergencies because there's a double risk for the fetus—the anaesthesia and the procedure itself." Tears glittered in her eyes. "Delia, if something goes wrong—"

"Nothing's going to go wrong."

"If something goes wrong," Soraya persisted, "the mother's well-being comes first. If there are complications, they'll abort the baby."

"Ah, Raya." It was a kind of helpless cry, half submerged in the restaurant clamor.

Then Delia's face cleared. "But why think like that?"

"I *have* to think like that. You know why."

Delia bent in closer. "Are you absolutely certain?"

"I did the math. Days and menstrual cycles don't lie, at least mine don't. There's no doubt about the father's identity."

"Well, then ..."

"Right."

Both women looked up as the waiter appeared tableside. "Have you made your choices, ladies?"

After receiving his latest commission from Dani Amit, Ilan Halevy, known as the Babylonian, flew from Tel Aviv to Beirut on an Argentinian passport, part of a Mossad-created legend. From Beirut he traveled via private aircraft to Sidon, from Sidon to the Dahr El Ahmar encampment by Jeep.

Colonel Ben David was shaving when the Babylonian was shown into his tent. Ben David did not turn, but glanced at the assassin in the mirror before returning to the scrutiny of his bluish jawline. A livid scar of fire-red flesh, barely healed, ran down from the outside corner of Ben David's left eye to the lobe of his ear. He could have opted for cosmetic surgery but hadn't.

"Who knows you're here?" he asked without preamble.

"No one," the Babylonian said.

"Not even Dani Amit?"

The Babylonian looked at him steadily; he'd already answered this.

Ben David took the straight razor from his skin and nodded as he washed it free of cream and stubble. "All right then. We can talk."

He carefully dried the razor before he closed it and put it away. Then he took up a towel and wiped his face clean. Only then did he turn to face the Babylonian.

"Killing becomes you."

A slow smile spread across the Babylonian's face. "It's good to see you, too."

The two men embraced briefly but intensely, then they stepped back and it was as if the intimacy had never happened. They were all business, and their business was deadly serious.

"They've sent me after Rebeka."

Something dark flitted across Ben David's eyes and was immediately gone.

"I know what that means to you," the Babylonian said.

"Then you're the only one."

"It's why I'm here." The Babylonian regarded Ben David with no little curiosity. "What do you want me to do?"

"I want you to follow through on your commission."

The Babylonian cocked his head. "Really?"

"Yes," Ben David said. "Really."

"I know how you feel about the girl."

"Do you know how I feel about this project?"

"I do," the Babylonian said. "Of course I do."

"Then you know my priorities."

The Babylonian eyed him for a moment. "She must have pissed you off royally."

Ben David turned away, busying himself with aligning his shaving equipment in regimental order.

After a moment of observing him, the Babylonian said, "You only go OCD when you're extremely agitated."

The Colonel froze, pulling his fingers away from the implements.

"Don't deny it," the Babylonian said. "I know you too well."

"And I know you," Ben David said, turning back to face him. "You've never failed at a commission."

"That's not, strictly speaking, true."

"But only you and I know that."

The Babylonian nodded. "True enough."

Ben David took a step toward the other. "The

thing is, Rebeka has become tangled up with Jason Bourne."

"Ah," the Babylonian said. "Dani Amit didn't inform me of that complication."

"He doesn't know."

The Babylonian eyed Ben David for a moment. "Why didn't you tell him?"

"Bourne is none of his fucking business."

"In other words," the Babylonian said, "Bourne is *your* business."

Ben David took another step toward the assassin. "And now he's yours, as well."

"Which is why you brought me here."

"As soon as I learned about the commission."

"Yes," the Babylonian said. "How exactly did you find out about it? So far as I know, only Dani Amit and the Director know."

A slow smile spread across Colonel Ben David's face. "It's better this way," he said, "for all of us."

The Babylonian seemed to accept this. "So it's Bourne you want."

"Yes."

"And Rebeka?"

"What about her?" Colonel Ben David said sharply.

"I know how you feel—"

"Keep your eye on what's important. You cannot give Dani Amit the slightest reason to suspect you. You must fulfill your commission."

The Babylonian looked on with some sympathy. "This can't be easy for you."

"Don't worry about me," Ben David snapped. "I'm perfectly fine."

"And we're on schedule."

"To the dot."

The Babylonian nodded. "I'll be off then."

"That would be wise."

After the assassin was gone, Colonel Ben David stood staring at himself in the mirror. Then he strode over, picked up his straight razor, and threw it. The mirror shattered and, with it, Ben David's reflection.

4

THE MAN, BIG, BURLY, and round-shouldered, resembled a bear. Clad in a bespoke sharkskin suit that cost more than the yearly salaries of many of his minions, he stood in the sun-splashed Place de la Concorde. The ceaseless clamor of tourists sounded to him like the hammering of a flock of woodpeckers. The endless spiral of traffic surrounding the cement island on which he stood was like death, speeding by always a little out of reach, until the moment when it ran over you, pounding you into the cobbles before speeding onward. He thought of the wasted days of his youth, before he had found himself, before he had discovered how to work his inner strength; time wasted, and now gone forever.

The Place de la Concorde was a favorite meeting place of his when he was in Paris because of its proximity to death, both present and past. It was the place where the guillotine had sliced off the head of Marie Antoinette, among many others, guilty and innocent alike, during France's notorious Reign of Terror. He liked the sound of that phrase, *Règne de la Terreur*, in any language.

His head turned and he saw her striding across the wide street on impossibly long legs as the light turned, favoring her. She came hidden within a cloud of tourists, seeing him, but totally ignoring him until she was on the far side of the 3,300-year-old Egyptian obelisk glorifying the reign of Rameses II. Given to France by Mehmet Ali, the Ottoman viceroy in 1829, it had originally marked the entrance to the Temple of Luxor. As such, it was a remarkable historical treasure. The man thought about this as the crowds of tourists ebbed and flowed around it without giving it more than a cursory glance. Every day now the history of the world was being lost, plowed under by the mountains of digital effluvia venting off the Internet, scanned by growing millions on their smartphones or iPads. The lives of Britney Spears, Angelina Jolie, and Jennifer Aniston were of more interest to the new masses than were those of Marcel Proust, Richard Wagner, or Victor Hugo, if they even knew who these august personages were.

The man resisted the urge to spit, instead smiling as he slipped through the throngs to the west side of the obelisk where Martha Christiana stood, hands in the pockets of her avant black-and-red L'Wren Scott swing coat, beneath which a deep plum suede pencil skirt from the same designer showed off the shapely lower half of her body. She did not turn when she felt his presence at her left shoulder, but tilted her head in his direction.

"It's good to see you, my friend," she said. "It's been a long time."

"Too long, *chérie*."

Her full lips curved slightly in her Mona Lisa smile. "Now you flatter me."

He barked a laugh. "There's no need."

He was right: she was a strikingly beautiful woman, dark-haired, dark-eyed, Latin in both features and temperament. She could be fiery as well as feisty. In any case, she knew who she was. She was her own woman, which he admired, all the while attempting to tame her. So far, he had not succeeded, for which a part of him was grateful. Martha would not have been half as useful to him if he had managed to break her spirit. Often, in his infrequent idle moments, he found himself wondering why she kept coming back to him. He had nothing on her; besides, she was no one to be coerced—he had found that out on their second meeting. He turned his mind away from that dark time to the pressing matter that necessitated today's meeting.

Martha was leaning back against the massive obelisk, legs crossed at her tiny ankles. Her Louboutins glittered richly.

"When I was young," he said, "I used to believe in the concept of reward, as if life were fair and predetermined, as if life couldn't put undreamed-of and unacceptable obstacles in my path. So what happened? I failed, again and again. I failed until my head hurt and I realized that I had been fooling myself. I knew nothing about life."

He shook out a cigarette, offered her one, then took one himself. He lit them both, first hers, then his. When he leaned in, he smelled her perfume, which held notes of citrus and cinnamon. Something deep inside him quivered. Cinnamon, especially, presented a special erotic note for him. Many intimate associations flooded his mind before he clamped down on them. Standing up straight, he filled his lungs with nicotine as a way of distancing himself from the past while he spoke.

"I realized that life was trying to guide me," he continued, "to teach me the lessons I would need in order not only to survive, but to prosper. I realized that I would have to shed my pride, I would have to embrace the unacceptable obstacles, to find the way through them, rather than turning away from them. Because the path to success—anyone's success, not only mine—lies through them."

Martha Christiana listened to him silently, solemnly, following every word. He liked that about her. She was not so self-involved that she failed to hear what was important. This quality alone separated her from the masses. She was like him.

"Every time the unacceptable is accepted, there is a change," she said finally. "Change or die, that is the central thesis we both absorbed, isn't it? And as the changes add up, a certain metamorphosis occurs. And, suddenly, we are different."

"More different than we ever thought we'd be."

She nodded, her gaze fixed on the rows of horse chestnuts flanking the wide, perfectly straight Champs. "And now here we are, once again waiting for the shadows to fall."

"On the contrary," he said, "we are the shadows."

Martha Christiana chuckled, nodding. "Indeed."

They smoked silently, companionably, for several minutes while the crush of people and traffic ebbed and flowed around them. In the distance, down the Champs, he could see the Arc de Triomph, shimmering like Martha's Louboutins.

At length, he dropped his cigarette butt and ground it under his heel. "You have a car?"

"Standing by, as usual."

"Good." He nodded, then licked his lips. "I've got a problem."

He always began the business end of their conversations in the same way. The ritualistic opening calming him. He always had problems, but he rarely called on Martha Christiana to solve them. He hoarded her special talents for the problems he felt certain no one else could handle.

"Male or female?" asked Martha Christiana.

He slipped a photo out of an inner pocket and handed it over.

"Ah, what a handsome devil!" Her lips curled up. "I could go for this one."

"Right." He laughed as he handed over a USB thumb drive. "All the relevant information on the target is on here, though I know you like to do your own digging."

"On occasion. I like to hit all the notes, even the trivial ones." She looked over at him. "And where is this Don Fernando Hererra currently residing?"

"He's on the move." He showed bits of his teeth, the color of ivory mah-jongg tiles. "He's searching for me."

Martha Christiana raised her eyebrows. "He doesn't look like a killer."

"He isn't."

"Then what does he want? And why do you want him terminated?"

He sighed. "He wants everything. Don Fernando wants to extract something from me far more precious than my life."

Now Martha Christiana turned to him fully, her face full of concern. "What would that be, *guapo*?"

"My legacy." He puffed air out of his mouth. "He wants to take everything I have, everything I ever will have, away from me."

"I will not let him."

He smiled like beaten brass and touched the back of her hand as lightly as the brush of a butterfly's wing. "Martha, when you are finished, I will have someone come fetch you. There is a very special commission I need you for."

Martha Christiana returned his smile as she pushed herself off the obelisk. "Don Fernando Hererra will be taken care of."

He smiled. "I know he will."

This thing with Bourne, this liaison," Ze'ev said, "is fucking foolish, it isn't worth it. It will be the death of you, Ben David will see to that."

Rebeka clucked her tongue. "This is what you traveled all the way from Tel Aviv to tell me?"

"I'm trying to help you. Why can't you see that?"

She narrowed her eyes against the glare of sunlight peeking through shredding clouds in the wake of the swiftly moving storm. They were tramping through the freshly fallen hillocks of white. Ahead of them, the water was a pearlescent gray, as if it were an extension of the steeply sloping shingle. They were walking, maybe in circles. It seemed like it, anyway. Small blue-roofed cottages dotted the landscape. Here and there, men could be seen uncovering walkways to their front doors. She wanted to get back to Sadelöga, but Ze'ev was making things difficult. She knew she had to find a way to turn his appearance to her advantage, and she had precious little time in which to do it.

"I'm trying to understand what you get out of it."

He cracked his large knuckles. He wasn't wearing gloves. His hands were as white as a corpse's. Though stationed in Tel Aviv, Ze'ev was one of Colonel Ben David's men. That, in and of itself, made him dangerous. But there were other reasons to be wary of him if what she had heard at Dahr El Ahmar could be trusted.

"Out of what?" he said.

"I'm willing to bet that your helping me won't sit well with either Amit or the Director."

He flexed his powder-white fingers. A show of strength or a warning? "Neither of them know, or will know."

She regarded him with a hard, skeptical glance, and he sighed.

"All right, here's the deal. Ilan Halevy has had it in for me ever since he's risen in the ranks." Ilan Halevy, the Babylonian.

"Why would that be?"

Ze'ev blew a breath out through his nose, a horse

snorting under a too-tight rein. "I tried to get him sectioned out of Mossad. It was at the beginning of his career; he was a loose cannon, learned his lessons, then did everything his way, not Mossad's way."

"Turns out you were wrong."

Ze'ev nodded. "He's never let me forget it, either. He won't be happy till he forces me out."

"Ilan Halevy doesn't know the meaning of the word *happy*."

"Still . . ."

She nodded. "So, all right, the two of you hate each other's guts. What does that have to do with me?"

"I want him to fail."

"Not just fail."

"No. I want him to fail spectacularly, a failure he cannot crawl out from under."

Rebeka considered a moment. "You have a plan."

The ghost of a smile made a brief appearance, then was gone.

"There's no way to turn him back. You said so yourself."

"Yes, that would be a complete waste of time. Instead, we lure him to Sadelöga."

"And then what?"

"Then we'll be waiting."

The DC offices of *Politics As Usual* were on E Street NW. Soraya tried not to think as she rode up to the sixteenth floor along with a fistful of suits talking options, margin calls, and Forex strategies.

She forced herself off as soon as the doors opened, striding right to the curving front banc formed of sheets of burl maple and stainless steel.

"Is Charles in?" she said to Marsha, the receptionist.

"He is, Ms. Moore," Marsha said with a thoroughly professional smile. "Why don't you have a seat while I call him."

"I'm fine right here."

Marsha gave her a brief nod as she dialed Charles's extension. Even this close, Soraya could only hear an indistinct murmur. While she waited, she glanced around the reception area, even though she knew it well. Laminated plaques commemorating the online news agency's Peabody- and Pulitzer-Prize–winning stories were everywhere in evidence. Her eye fell inevitably on the brilliant piece Charles had written two years ago, centering on a powerful but little-known Arab terrorist cell in Syria. Hardly surprising, since that was how he had come to her attention. She had called on him in order to appropriate at least some of his sources, with little result.

She sensed him then, as she always did, and her head came up, a smile on her full lips. He was tall and slender, with a crop of unruly and prematurely gray hair. He was, as usual, impeccably dressed in a midnight-blue suit, dove-gray shirt, and water-print tie in muted colors.

He beckoned to her as soon as he saw her, but there was something troubling in his smile that she couldn't place and that sent a thread of disquiet through her. She began to question her decision. Part of her wanted to turn, enter the elevator, and never see him again.

Instead, she stepped forward and, with his hand lightly at the small of her back, walked with him down the hallway to his corner office. Just before she stepped inside, she saw the plaque affixed to the wall just to the right of the doorway: CHARLES THORNE, DEPUTY EDITOR IN CHIEF.

He closed the door behind him.

I need to get this over with as quickly as possible, she thought, *before I lose my nerve.* "Charles," she said as she sat down.

"It's fortuitous you came here just now." He raised a hand, forestalling her, and carefully and deliberately drew the blinds. "Soraya, before you say anything—"

Oh, no, she thought. *He's going to give me the "I love my wife" thing. Not now, please not now.*

"I have to tell you something in strictest confidence. Yes?"

Here we go. She swallowed hard. "Yes, of course."

He took a deep breath and let it out with a kind of thin whistling sound. "We're being investigated by the FBI."

Her heart lurched in her chest. "We?"

"*Politics As Usual.* Marchand." The publisher. "Davidoff." The editor in chief. "Me."

"I...don't understand." Her pulse was beating an unpleasant tattoo in her temples. "What for?"

Charles ran a hand across his face. "Wiretapping—specifically victims of crimes, prominent celebrities, NYC police, some pols." He hesitated, pain in his eyes. "Nine-eleven victims."

"Are you kidding?"

"Sadly, I'm not."

She felt hot, as if she had contracted a tropical fever. "But...is it true?"

"You and I have to..." He coughed, cleared his throat. "We have to go our separate ways."

"But you—" She shook her head, her ears ringing. "How could you possibly—?"

"Not me, Soraya. I swear it wasn't me."

He's not going to answer my question, she thought. *He's not going to tell me.* And then, looking into his eyes, she heard his voice again: "*We have to go our separate ways.*"

Stumbling, she struck the backs of her knees on a chair and she sat down, quickly and hard.

"Soraya?"

She did not know what to say, did not even know what to think. She was struggling simply to breathe normally again. In the space of a heartbeat, her world had been turned upside down. They couldn't separate, not now. It was unthinkable. All at once, she remembered a dinner she'd had with Delia the night after she had met Charles.

"Are you insane?" Delia had said, wide-eyed. "Charles Thorne? Seriously? Do you know who he's married to?"

"I do," Soraya had said. "Of course I do."

"And still you...?" Delia had broken off in disbelief.

"We couldn't help ourselves."

"Of course you could help yourselves." Delia was angry now. "You're adults."

"This is something that adults do, Dee. That's why they call it—"

"Don't," Delia had said, holding her palms up toward her friend. "Dear God, don't you dare say it."

"It isn't a one-night stand, if that makes a difference."

"Of course it makes a difference," Delia had said, a bit too loudly. Then she lowered her voice to a fierce whisper. "Dammit, Raya, the longer this goes on, the worse it becomes!"

Soraya remembered how she had reached out and taken her friend's hand. "Don't be angry, Dee." She hadn't been listening, not really. "Be happy for me."

"The longer this goes on, the worse it becomes."

"Soraya?" Thorne had repeated. When he saw her expression, he looked stricken.

And now, Soraya thought, returning to the dreadful present, the worst had happened. Now she had to tell him. It was the only way for them to stay together, to ensure their relationship continued uninterrupted.

She opened her mouth to do it but, instead, her mind rebelled. *Is this what I've reduced the baby to—a pawn?* An immediate wave of disgust overwhelmed her and, leaning forward, she grabbed his wastepaper basket and vomited into it.

"Soraya?" He hurried toward her. "Are you ill?"

"I don't feel well," she whispered thickly.

"I'll call a taxi."

She waved away his words. "I'll be all right soon enough." She had to tell him, she knew she had no choice, but another wave rose up into her throat, gagging her, clogging her throat, and she thought, *Not today. Just give me a day's respite.*

* * *

An hour before he was set to embark with Alef for Sadelöga, Bourne had a dream. In the dream, he had been shot, pitched into the storm-dark waters of the Mediterranean, but instead of losing consciousness, as he had when this had occurred many years ago, he remained alert to the electric bolts of pain transfiguring his head into a short-circuiting engine.

As he struggled in the darkness, he became aware that he was not alone. There was a presence eeling its way up from the depths of the sea, long and thin, a monstrous sea snake of some sort. It wrapped its long length around him while its fanged mouth darted in toward him. Again and again, he fought it off, but with each second that ticked by strength passed out of him, dissipating into the inky water. And as his strength waned, so the monster's strength waxed, until it reared back, opened its mouth, and said, *"You'll never know who I am. Why don't you stop trying?"*

It unwound itself from him, slipping away even as he grabbed for it, even as his desire to know it became unbearable...He woke up.

Sweating heavily, he threw the covers off his naked body and padded into the bathroom, stepping into the shower even before he turned on the taps. The icy water hit him like a fist, which is what he wanted, to get away from the last coiling tendrils of the dream as quickly and completely as he could. It wasn't the first time he'd had that dream. It always ended the same way. He knew the sea eel was his past, lurking in the deepest depths of his unconscious, coiling and uncoiling, but never revealing itself to him. If the sea eel was to be believed, it never would.

When he was shaved and dressed, he sat on the edge of his bed and called Soraya, using his new sat-phone. They had an arrangement to check in with each other periodically, which worked well for both of them. Often they were able to swap intel to their mutual advantage.

It was the middle of the night in DC, and it was clear that he had woken her up.

"Are you all right?" he asked.

"I'm perfectly fine. I just had a long, difficult day."

At once he knew she wasn't telling him the whole truth, even though she insisted nothing was wrong. He kept at her until she admitted that the concussion she had gotten in Paris had become worse. That was all she would say, other than that she was being closely monitored by her doctor. Then she mentioned Nicodemo, and Bourne told her about his conversation with Christien, that Nicodemo was somehow involved with Core Energy and, specifically, its CEO, Tom Brick.

"You mean Nicodemo is real?" she said when he had finished.

"Christien and Don Fernando certainly think so. Can you do some digging into Core Energy and Brick for me?"

"Of course."

"Take care of yourself, Soraya."

There was a slight hesitation before she said, "You, too."

Ninety minutes later, with the sky clearing in the east, the last clots of night gathered like refuse in the street gutters, he and Alef were in one of Christien's cars, heading out of Stockholm toward Sadelöga.

"You don't look too good," Alef said as they hit the highway and hurtled down it at breakneck speed.

Bourne said nothing. Every few minutes his eyes flicked to the rearview mirror, memorizing the makes, models, and positions of the vehicles behind them.

Alef's gaze automatically went to the side mirror. "Expecting company?"

"I'm always expecting company."

Alef laughed shortly. "Yeah, I know what you mean."

Bourne gave him a long, keen look. "You do?"

"What?"

"You said you knew what I meant when I said I'm always expecting company. *How* do you know?"

Alef returned his gaze and shook his head helplessly. "I have no idea."

"Think!"

Bourne said it so sharply that Alef jumped.

"I don't know. I just do." His eyes returned to the side mirror. "Nothing suspicious."

"Not yet, anyway."

Alef nodded, accepting this judgment. "I have a good feeling about Sadelöga. Going back, I mean."

"You think it will help you remember."

"I do, yes. If anything will..."

His voice dropped off and they rode the rest of the way in silence. Christien had a boat waiting—

the same one he and Bourne had been fishing in when they pulled Alef out of the water. Someone had cleaned it up. No trace of blood could be detected on its interior.

Bourne saw Alef into the boat, then untied the ropes and, pushing off with his boot, jumped in. They motored slowly over to Sadelöga. The air was wet and heavy. A low mist lay over parts of the water like a shroud. As they neared Sadelöga, Alef began to look around.

"Anything look familiar?" Bourne's breath made little clouds in the icy air.

Alef shook his head.

Several minutes later, Bourne slowed. "This is where we hauled you out of the water. You couldn't have been in too long, so we must be near where you were shot."

Slowing further, he nosed the boat in closer, paralleling the shore.

"Let me know," he said.

Alef nodded. He appeared increasingly agitated, like someone approaching his own death. Bourne knew the feeling. Beneath the tendrils of fog, chunks of ice could be seen milling against the shoreline. In just the few days since they had been here, the temperature had dropped at least ten degrees. The cold had silenced even the usually gregarious gulls. It was painful to pull air into the lungs.

"I don't know," Alef said miserably. "I don't know." And then, all at once, his head came up like a hunting dog on point. "There!" He was quivering. "Over there!"

Bourne turned the boat, heading in to shore.

* * *

You've been spying on her!" Delia looked at Peter incredulously. "She's your friend, for God's sake."

"I know, but—"

"You people are incredible." She shook her head. "Inhuman."

"Delia, it's *because* I'm Soraya's friend that I followed her."

Delia snorted skeptically. They were in her office, where Peter had come to see her. She had kicked the door closed as soon as he had asked his first question.

"What was she doing at the offices of *Politics As Usual*?"

"Gosh," Delia said, "aren't you going to ask me what she and I talked about at lunch?"

"I assumed it had something to do with her visit to Dr. Steen."

Delia, head shaking again, backed away from him until she was behind her desk. "I don't know what you think is going on—"

"I'm asking you to tell me."

"You need to ask Soraya these questions, not me."

"She won't talk to me about them."

"Then you have to understand that she has good reason."

"See, that's the thing," Peter said, taking a step toward her, "I don't think her reasoning is sound."

Delia spread her hands. "I don't know what—"

"I think she's in trouble," he said. "I'm asking you to help me help her."

"No, Peter. You're asking me to betray her trust."
She crossed her arms beneath her breasts. "I won't,
no matter what you say or do."

He stared at her for what seemed a long time. "I
care about her, Delia. Deeply and truly."

"Then go back to your work. Leave this alone."

"I want to help her."

"*Help* is a relative term. If you pursue this, I
promise you it will only end in tears."

He shook his head. "I'm not sure what you—"

"Whatever she's going through, she doesn't want
to share it with you." Delia smiled coldly at him. "It
will be the end of your friendship, Peter. That's what
I mean."

Alef scrambled ashore even before the boat had run
up onto the snow-covered shingle.

"Wait!" Bourne called as he cut the motor. Then,
cursing, he leaped onto the bank, sprinting after Alef.

"There's a copse of pines and a lake," Alef said,
as if to himself. "Somewhere, somewhere." His eyes
were wide and staring and his head jerked back and
forth on the stalk of his neck.

Bourne was almost upon him when he burst
through a small stand of pines and saw the lake. It
looked solidly frozen.

"I remember crossing this," he said as Bourne
caught up with him.

"Let's take it one step at a time," Bourne said.
"Why were you here?"

Alef shook his head. "I crossed the lake or—" He
took a step onto the ice. "I was trying to get away."

"Get away from who?" Bourne pressed him. "Who was chasing you?"

"That lake." Alef had begun to shake. "That damn lake."

A kind of electric storm bursts behind his eyes as shards of memories bubble up from the fog of his amnesia. He sees himself, hears the panting of his breath, sees the slim figure skating lithely after him as if on blades. An abrupt blank, the memory-lamp inside his head extinguished, then he feels himself stumbling. The next instant, he is down on his knees, the figure is rushing inexorably toward him, and he turns, aims his handgun, but he stumbles, and it goes flying. He wants to scramble after it, but there's no time. He's off and running again, running for his life.

These memories rush at him like an attacking army, flickering in and out of focus. In between is the darkness of the befogged abyss he has come to know as amnesia—his life ripped away from him, forever beyond his grasp. The grief that had held him fast quickly morphs into panic welling up inside him as shards of memory stab him so fast and furiously that he becomes overwhelmed, disoriented, briefly insane.

Alef blinked, back in the present.

"Okay." Shadowed by pines, at the edge of the flat, glittering expanse, Bourne began to guide him back toward the shoreline where he had moored the boat. "I think that's enough for today."

"No! My life is back there! I have to get it back!" Alef broke away, hit the ice, but before he could take another step Bourne grabbed him, jerking him back into the shelter of the trees.

"You can't go out there," Bourne said. "It's too exposed, too dangerous."

"Dangerous?"

Bourne shook him briefly, trying to get him to focus. "You were shot, remember? Someone is after you."

"I'm dead, Jason." He stared wide-eyed. "Don't you see? No one's after me now."

Bourne saw that this trip that he and Christien had decided on was a mistake. It was too soon. Alef was losing his grip on reality. "Let's go back to the boat and talk it through calmly and rationally."

Alef hesitated, staring out across the icy expanse of the lake, then nodded. "Okay."

But the instant Bourne let go, he broke away, began to skate onto the lake, his legs splayed, his arms straight out like airplane wings to keep himself from sprawling headfirst onto the ice.

Bourne lunged after him, one eye on Alef, the other on the trees, dense enough to hide a regiment, that ringed the lake. The wind whipped slivers of ice into his face. He raised one hand to shield his eyes, and heard the sharp report as if it were an afterimage, there and gone before it registered. Thick shards of ice fountained up as the sharpshooter squeezed off two more shots, creating a deep gouge in the ice just in front of where Alef stood.

Bourne slammed into Alef, covering him but, at the same time, sliding both of them forward into the gouge made by the sniper's bullets. The ice cracked in a spiderweb beneath them. Bourne tried to back up, hauling Alef with him, but bullets struck the ice behind him, pinning him down, and now, with a deep groan, the ice gave way, plunging both of them down, a surprisingly strong current sucking them out into icy darkness.

5

WATER RUSHED INTO Bourne's nose, stinging
his nostrils. It was no wonder the ice cracked—this
was a salt water lake. He was forced to let go of
the gun in order to reach for Alef, who was sinking
faster. Bourne had to turn, aim himself down, giving
powerful kicks to force himself to accelerate like an
arrow loosed from a bow, in an attempt to catch up
with Alef.

Within moments, the cold penetrated his jacket
and boots. He could feel his heart hammering faster
as his core temperature came under attack. By the
time it actually started to drop, it would be too late.
He wouldn't have strength enough to push himself
up through the gelid water, let alone drag Alef with
him.

Without light there was no direction. Bourne, an
expert diver, knew how easy it was for even professional divers to become disoriented on night dives,

or when adverse conditions like nitrogen narcosis began to affect them. Extreme cold was another serious danger that could slow the mind and cause wrong decisions to be made. This far down in the icy depths, wrong decisions would be fatal.

Bourne's lungs were bursting, he could no longer feel his toes, and his fingers felt thick and unwieldy. Head pounding, he made one more desperate kick downward, felt Alef's collar, and hauled upward. Reversing his body, he kicked rhythmically, trying to keep his mind occupied in the present, even while flickers of his own near-drowning, which had caused his amnesia, flashed through his mind.

He found it increasingly difficult to stay in the present, to keep his body working at peak level, never mind peak efficiency. There was nowhere for him to go in the Mediterranean, only he wasn't in the Mediterranean, he was far, far to the north. But a kind of peaceful warmth was stealing over him, a great lethargy even as his legs continued to pump, even as he continued his hold on Alef. But if he was warm, wasn't he in the Mediterranean? He must be. He had been shot, cast overboard out of Marseilles and now...Now he saw himself held fast in the dense shadows of jungle foliage. He was standing behind a man who knelt on the ground, wrists bound at the small of his back. He saw himself gripping a military-issue .45, saw himself pressing its muzzle against the base of the man's skull, saw himself pull the trigger. And saw Jason Bourne crash to the jungle floor, dead...

He wanted to cry out. An icy shiver slithered down his spine and he twisted back and forth, as if trying to rid himself of the nightmarish images. Then he looked up, saw a lighter patch in the endless darkness, a way out!

Glancing down, he saw Alef's pinched, white face, and the sight galvanized him, dissipating his lethargy, his slide into the nightmarish watery wastes. Kicking out with renewed energy, he saw the pale patch widening, growing brighter and brighter until he breached the surface, gulping air into his burning lungs. He renewed his grip on Alef as the unconscious man grew heavier the farther he hauled him out of the water.

But Bourne still wasn't thinking clearly, and time after time Alef's body kept slipping back into the darkness, until Bourne climbed slowly and painfully out of the water, then turned, using all his strength. Inch by inch, he drew Alef out of the water, hauling first on his collar, then under his arms, and finally, grasping his belt and sliding him the rest of the way, onto the ice.

He was finished then. The cold and the dread of memories long buried had sapped all his energy. Collapsing onto his back, he concentrated on breathing, even though a small voice in the back of his mind screamed at him to find shelter, to get out of his wet clothes before they froze onto his flesh.

It was then a shadow fell over him, and he looked up to see a man standing over him. He was holding a handgun at his side. The sniper? Then where was his rifle? Back in the woods? Bourne's clouded mind couldn't think straight.

"No need to introduce yourself, Bourne," the man said, sliding down to his knees, "I know who you are."

He grinned as he pressed the muzzle of the handgun against the side of Bourne's head. Bourne tried to lift his arm up, but his clothes were partially frozen, weighing him down like armor. His fingers felt frozen in place.

Clicking off the safety, the man said, "Pity there's no time to get to know each other."

The report of the pistol shot echoed across the lake, around and around like a frenzied shout. A clutch of gulls rose, screaming in fright, into the heavily striated sky.

I can't get a read on either of them."

"What the hell does that mean?" the president said. "You're my eyes and ears inside Treadstone."

Dick Richards crossed one leg over the other. "It seems to me that your problem lies not with Marks and Moore but with Secretary Hendricks."

The president glared at him over his desk. The Oval Office was quite still; even the occasional footfalls, phones, and various secretaries' and assistants' voices were muffled, as if coming from a great distance, rather than just outside the doors.

"I don't need you to tell me what my problem is, Richards."

"No, sir, of course not. Nevertheless, Treadstone is Hendricks's baby."

The president raised his eyebrows. "What's your point?"

"Marks and Moore take their orders from him."

The president swiveled around to stare out the window. "What *have* you found out about them?"

Richards took a moment to marshal his thoughts. "They're both smart—smart enough to keep me at arm's length. Their mistake, however, is in thinking the assignment they gave me is merely make-work."

The president swung back around, his hooded eyes fixed on his mole. "Meaning?"

"Did you know that the identity of Jason Bourne was created by Treadstone personnel?"

"Richards, you're sorely trying my patience today."

"Also, that Jason Bourne was a real human being. He was a soldier of fortune who was killed because he sold out his unit."

The president frowned deeply. "That knowledge is Archive Omega–level. How the devil did you get hold of it?"

For an instant Richards wondered whether, in trying so hard to make his point, he had overplayed his hand. "There's no leak, if that's what you're thinking. The Archivist asked me to vet a new priority-one algorithm for all Archival data, for security holes." He waved his hand as if to downplay the importance of his explanation, which was the truth only on the surface. He certainly didn't want anyone probing beneath. "The point is, I'm making headway finding out whether or not the Djinn Who Lights The Way is real or fictional. One thing I can tell you is that one man cannot be responsible for all the influence attributed to him."

The president sat forward. "Listen, Richards, you're not understanding."

"It's most likely that this Nicodemo is an agglomeration of many people."

"Fuck Nicodemo," the president said harshly. "I'm not interested in him; that's Hendricks's bogeyman. What interests me are Peter Marks and Soraya Moore."

Richards shook his head. "I don't understand."

"Soraya Moore was a rogue agent at CI; now both of them are rogue directors at Treadstone."

"Surely they're not security risks. I'm still not—"

"They're both close to Jason Bourne, you fool! It's his toxic influence that's made them unreliable." The president seemed as shocked as Richards by the ferocity of this statement. He drummed his fingers on his desk, then took a deep breath and let it out slowly. When he resumed speaking, it was in a more normal voice. "Moore and Marks are close to Bourne, therefore they must be in touch with him."

Richards took a moment to regroup. "You're after Bourne."

"Why d'you imagine I placed you inside Treadstone, Richards? Bourne's not subject to any rules or regulations. He does whatever he pleases. I can't have that."

"I've heard that he's helped us in the past."

The president's hand cut through the air. "Those rumors may or may not be true, Richards. What they don't address, however, is Bourne's own agenda, and believe me, he has one. I want to know what it is. Anyone that far out on the rim, beyond our control, is not only a security risk, but a potential danger to our foreign policy programs. And that's not even taking into account his unstable mental state. He's an amnesiac, for Christ's sake! Who the hell knows what he'll do next. No." He shook his head emphatically. "We've got to take care of him once and for all. The direct approach hasn't worked, we'll never find him that way. And tracking him is an exercise in futility. Besides, Hendricks doesn't share my concern, so he's out of this loop."

You and Secretary Hendricks are at odds, Richard thought. *Hendricks condones thinking outside the box; clearly, you don't.* All at once, he realized that he desperately wanted to be on the winning side. For once in his life.

The president stood abruptly, went to stand by the furled flag of the United States at one side of the curtained window. "Forget Nicodemo. He's a smokescreen at best, more likely disinformation, a mirage perpetrated by our enemies to keep us running in circles. Get me now?"

"Yessir, but I can't just drop my search for Nicodemo. The directors will become suspicious."

"Do just enough Internet snooping to keep their suspicions at bay. Concentrate on finding Bourne."

Now his plan for getting Peter and Soraya to trust him by successfully completing the assignment they had given him was blown out of the water. He was growing more and more angry with how the president was treating him. Wasn't he supposed to be the president's golden boy? Hadn't the president himself plucked him out of NSA for this special assignment? And now to find out that the president had lied to him about the real nature of the assignment made him mad as hell. *Fuck it*, he thought. *It's every man for himself now.*

But then, he thought with a silent, sardonic laugh, *it always has been.*

For the rest of the briefing, he pasted a smile on his face, nodded occasionally, and made all the appropriate noises. The truth was, he wasn't listening. He was already forming a new strategy, one that would benefit only him. He berated himself for not having thought along that line before.

When he returned to Treadstone, Richards went straight to Peter Marks's office, only to find Soraya Moore sitting behind his desk, working at his computer. This both surprised and alarmed Richards, and he heard again an echo of the president's assertion that these two directors had rogue personalities. Even in business, it was frowned on to use someone else's computer terminal; in the clandestine services it was unheard of. He could see why they maintained their connection with Bourne.

Soraya looked up as he stood hesitantly on the threshold. "Yes? What is it, Richards?"

"I was—I was looking for Director Marks."

"And instead you've found me." She gestured. "Take a pew. What's on your mind?"

Another hesitation, even though momentary, brought home to Richards just how intimidated he was by her. Truth to tell, he'd never met a woman anything like her, and this made him deeply uneasy.

Soraya sighed. "Sit. Now."

He lowered himself, perched on the edge of the chair. His physical discomfort echoed his emotional disquiet.

"Are you going to say anything or just sit there like a toad on a log?"

He watched her, wary still. It was only then that he remembered he was clutching a file that contained a hard copy of his progress so far in finding the truth about Nicodemo. He placed the file on Marks's desk and shoved it across to her side. He found it curious that she had made no mention of what she was doing in her co-director's office, using his computer. Did she have the key code to his terminal? Everyone in Treadstone had their own personal codes to log in and out of their office computers. A second code was needed for their laptops, and a third for those who had been given the newest model tablet computers.

He found Soraya staring at him with her large liquid eyes. That she was beautiful and highly desirable as well as powerful made him angry beyond words. She took up the file and, without taking her eyes from him, opened it.

"What is this?"

The unexpected question unnerved him. Why was she asking him when a simple glance down would give her the answer?

He sucked in a ragged breath. "I've made significant progress on the assignment you and Director Marks gave me."

"Go on."

Why didn't she look down? Richards shook off the nagging question and continued. "If you check the printouts—"

"Hard copy is entirely without context or affect," she said. "I'd like to hear your findings in your own words."

So that was it, he thought. Clearing his throat

again, he continued. "It's increasingly clear that the person Nicodemo doesn't exist, per se. It's more than likely he's a clever construct, like the Bourne Identity."

"'Increasingly clear,' 'more than likely'?" Soraya said, not rising to the bait. "These are not phrases I like. They're not factual; they have no meaning."

"I'm working on rectifying that now," Richards said, wondering how he was going to get her to talk about Bourne.

"No, you're sitting here talking to me." Soraya cocked her head. "Tell me, Richards, why were you coming to Peter with this and not to me?"

Land mines, Richards thought. *She's placing land mines all over the place. I have to tread very carefully without letting on I know what she's up to.* He could say that Marks had told him he'd given Director Moore a couple of days off, but that wasn't strictly speaking true. He'd overheard it. *Snooping* might be a better term. He couldn't afford to have her catch him in a lie, or even a half-truth. "My first contact here was with Director Marks. I worked with him for several weeks, more or less collegially, before you arrived, and then..." He allowed his voice to trail off as he shrugged. She knew very well how she had frozen him out, treated him like a worm in the apple.

"I see." Soraya put down the file unread, and, steepling her fingers, leaned back in Peter Marks's chair. "So you're lodging a complaint against me, is that it?"

He saw his mistake immediately and silently cursed himself. He could sense that any denial on his part would only make things worse. He could tell now that she despised any form of weakness, whether merely apparent or real. "Director, allow me a moment to take my foot out of my mouth." He allowed a brief sense of relief as the flicker of her smile impressed itself on him. "I have a thick skin. I didn't used to, but you know NSA."

"Do I?"

"M. Errol Danziger, the current CI director, is NSA-trained, so I would judge that you know better than most."

"During your time at NSA did you form an opinion of Director Danziger?"

"He's an asshole, in my humble opinion." This answer appeared to please her, and he willed himself to relax. "If my tenure at NSA taught me anything, it was that in order to survive, I had to toughen up. Which is all to say that how you treat me is entirely your business."

"Thank you."

Noting her sharply sardonic tone, he said, "My business is to carry out to the best of my ability whatever orders you give me."

"Not whatever orders the president has given you?"

"I understand that you don't trust me. Frankly, in your place I'd feel the same."

"Just why the hell *did* the president press you onto us?"

"In the past, there has been too much leeway taken inside black-ops organizations. He's asked me to monitor—"

"Spy on us."

"If I'm to be honest, I don't think he's being adversarial."

"Then what?"

"He's cautious, I guess would be the best term for it."

Soraya smirked. "And you agree with him, I imagine."

"I guess I did before I got here. But now, seeing what Treadstone does..." He left a small silence to punctuate that statement.

"I'm all ears."

"And I'm doing my best to earn your trust."

"Uh-huh."

"The deeper I get into the Nicodemo assignment, the more of a tangle it becomes. I finally came to the conclusion that this tangle, which proliferated at every turn of whatever form of search I performed, was deliberate."

"Nothing would arouse as much suspicion as your finding Nicodemo easily."

"Exactly! Of course, this was the first thought that came to me as I made my way through the first layers. But, as you'll see in the file, this is more than a hacker's tangle. It's a goddamned Gordian knot. The more I unraveled one strand, the tighter the knot became."

"Isn't that simply superior security?"

"No," Richards said. "It's a double-blind."

"Meaning?"

"This Gordian knot is meant to *seem* like superior security, the better to suck in expert hackers who, unlike me, are conspiracy theorists at heart. But, in fact, it's nothing but bullshit. The Gordian knot is the product of some evil genius—sound and fury signifying nothing."

"So you're saying—what?—Nicodemo doesn't exist?"

"Not as you and I were trained to think of him— and maybe not at all."

"Okay." Soraya spread her hands. "Say you're right."

"I *am* right."

"Then who the hell owns Core Energy?"

Richards blinked. "I beg your pardon?"

"I have it on good authority that Nicodemo is connected with Core Energy."

"Where did you hear that? Tom Brick is CEO of Core Energy."

Soraya had learned about Core Energy and Nicodemo from Jason Bourne, with whom, by long-standing arrangement, she was in periodic phone contact, but she wasn't about to tell Richards that. "According to this source, Core Energy has a shit-load of masked subsidiaries that are buying up energy mines and producers worldwide, making deals Tom Brick or any other legit CEO couldn't touch with a fifty-foot pole. If, as you claim, Nicodemo doesn't exist, then who the hell is making those corrupt deals?"

"I...I don't know."

"Neither do I, though I've tried my damnedest to find out." She closed the file and skimmed it back across the desk to him. "Back to the salt pits, Richards. You want to impress me, dig me out some useful intel."

* * *

A hot spray of blood coated Bourne's face as the gunshot reverberated through his mind. Helpless, he stared up into the gunman's stunned face. An instant later, the gunman's eyes turned glassy, and he keeled over onto his side.

A second shadow passed across Bourne's vision. He turned his head, saw another figure, gun in hand. Sunlight turned the figure inky, no more than a silhouette. Then the sun slipped behind a racing cloudbank and, as the figure knelt beside him, Bourne recognized the face.

"Rebeka," he said.

She smiled. "Welcome back to the living, Bourne."

Trying to move, he crackled like an iceberg cleaving. Reversing her Glock, she used the butt to chip off the layer of ice that had turned his coat and trousers to armor.

"We'd better peel this stuff off you before it adheres to your skin permanently." As she worked, she said: "It's good to see you. I never thanked you for saving my life."

"All in a day's work," Bourne said now. "Is Alef okay?"

She frowned. "Who?"

"The man next to me. I pulled him out of the water several days ago."

"Oh, you mean Manfred Weaving." She glanced to Bourne's left. "He's fine. Thanks to you. But I need to get him inside, too."

Bourne was beginning to regain movement in his

limbs, but he was still dreadfully chilled. To keep his teeth from chattering, he said, "How d'you know him? What are you doing here?"

"I've been pursuing him for weeks now, all the way from Lebanon." She laughed. "You remember Lebanon, Bourne, don't you?"

"How's Colonel Ben David?"

"Pissed as a bear up a tree."

"Good."

"He hates your guts."

"Even better."

With a wry smile, she helped him up to a sitting position. "I've got to get you both warmed up."

He turned, glanced at the man lying in his own blood. "Who the hell is this?"

"His name's Ze'ev Stahl. He worked for Ari Ben David."

Bourne looked at her. "You killed one of your own?"

"It's a long story." She nodded at Manfred Weaving. "We'd better get going." She gave him a wry smile. "You, I don't know about, but he's far too valuable to let freeze to death."

Peter Marks sat in his unmarked car, enjoying a Snickers bar. He hated stakeouts so much that the only way to get through them was to give himself a constant supply of treats. It being a particularly mild day, he had all the windows down, breathing in the air of a coming spring. While he waited, he listened again to the relevant snippet of recording from his office:

Soraya: *"I have it on good authority that
    Nicodemo is connected with Core En-
    ergy."*
Richards: *"Where did you hear that?"*

Peter nodded in satisfaction. He had to hand it to Soraya. She was a fucking expert. When she had first
outlined her plan, he had counted on confronting
Richards himself, but she had made a clear case
otherwise. *"First, he won't expect me to be in the office, let alone be sitting at your desk,"* she had said.
*"Second, I give him the heebie-jeebies, I can tell. He
doesn't know whether to spit at me or ask me out.
When he looks at me, I can see the heat in his eyes.
I can use all that to rattle him."* As it turned out,
she had been dead-on in her psych profile of Dick
Richards.

Taking a last luxurious bite of his Snickers, Peter
glanced at the dashboard clock. Fifteen minutes
since the impromptu meeting in his office had concluded. Movement at the entrance to the Treadstone
building caused him to look up. Bingo! Here came
Richards, hurrying down the steps, turning left into
the guarded and electronically surveilled parking
lot.

Peter watched as he climbed into his car, started
the engine, and drove out. Putting his own car in
gear, Peter nosed out into the traffic flow, taking up
a position a car length behind Richards.

He had expected Richards to head across the Key
Bridge into DC, but instead he went the other way,
heading out past the suburban sprawl of Arlington,
into the rolling Virginia hills, so lushly verdant in

spring and summer, aflame in autumn, brown now, sleeping in winter's chill.

Exiting the highway, they passed through sleepy villages and tony residential enclaves, separated by long swaths of parkland, stands of trees beside golf courses and tennis courts.

On the old Blackfriar Pike, they rose up, then swung down into a broad valley. The road ascended again, cresting a hill, and Peter thought, *Really? This is where he's gone?*

Beyond, on the left, he could make out the thick brick walls of the Blackfriar, the oldest and still the most exclusive country club in the area, tendentiously outmuscling the clutch of multi-million-dollar pretenders that had sprung up over the decades. Blackfriar accepted only the most powerful pols, lobbyists, newsmen and -women, influence peddlers, and attorneys, starting, of course, with the president and the vice president.

> Soraya: *"I have it on good authority that Nicodemo is connected with Core Energy."*
> Richards: *"Where did you hear that?"*

Peter was playing the taped conversation again, homing in on the question that must have so shaken Dick Richards. *"Where did you hear that?"* The question had given him away. He had already known about Core Energy, but he had withheld that information. Peter was following him to find out why. According to Soraya, Bourne strongly suspected a connection between Nicodemo and Core

Energy. From where Peter sat now, it looked as if he was right on the money. As usual.

Richards's car turned into the driveway, stopped at the guardhouse that sat as ominous as a military installation just outside the front gate, which remained closed to the uninitiated and the uninvited alike.

Peter was not a member of Blackfriar, which, in any event, would not have him. Nevertheless, he needed to gain entrance. Showing his credentials to the guards was out of the question; he might as well announce his presence via loudspeaker.

Driving farther along until he was out of sight of the guardhouse, he pulled over, off the road, and onto the mowed grass strip that separated the wall from the tarmac. The brick wall was thick, topped by a wide, decorative concrete band in which were set, at precise intervals, a series of black wrought-iron spikes whose tips were fashioned in the shape of a fleur-de-lys.

Peter got out, clambered onto his car's roof, and from there scrambled up onto the concrete top of the wall. Turning himself sideways so as to slip between the spikes, he leaped down onto the other side, landing in a crouch behind a spindly-limbed Eastern rosebud, harbinger of spring, the first to bloom at winter's end.

Being inside Blackfriar made him profoundly uneasy. It was a place to which he had no desire to belong, but whose deep-seated contempt for people like him made it hostile and alien territory.

These thoughts passed through his mind as he rose and began to head back toward the area where

Richards would drive in. Passing a number of tennis players exiting the winter indoor courts, he saw the car almost immediately, which was a relief; it seemed as if it had been held up at the guardhouse, presumably because Richards wasn't a member and hadn't been expected by the president.

He was close by the pro shop. Rows of golf carts crouched in neat rows, drowsing idly for the first taste of spring to bring out the duffers. Commandeering one, he jump-started the engine and paralleled Richards's car as it drove slowly down the winding two-lane road that split the country club in two. When he was certain Richards was heading for the two-story colonial clubhouse, he veered off, taking a shortcut that got him onto the gravel surrounding the building like a moat. Ditching the cart, he strode into the clubhouse, nodding occasionally at the few who glanced his way.

Inside, the clubhouse was more or less as expected: grand wood-beamed spaces with crystal chandeliers, deep masculine chairs and sofas in the great room that opened into a dining room to his left. Straight ahead, through a line of enormous French doors, the great room led out onto an enormous veranda filled with expensive wicker chairs, glass tables, and uniformed waiters ferrying highballs, gin and tonics, and mint juleps to lounging members who were chatting about their stock market calls, their Bentleys, their Citations. The overripe atmosphere made Peter want to gag.

He saw Richards hurry in and stood back in the shadow of a potted palm, as if this were a scene from a 1940s Sydney Greenstreet potboiler. Glancing around the great room, Peter did not see the president, nor could he spot any of the Secret Service agents who, if he were there, would be discreetly scattered about the area, talking into the cuffs of their starched white shirts.

He moved to keep Richards in sight and was rewarded to see his quarry head toward a small grouping of upholstered wing chairs. He seated himself in one of them, facing a man the crown of whose head was the only part visible. He had silver hair, but that was all Peter could tell from his position. He continued around the periphery of the great room in a counterclockwise direction, but just as the person Richards had come all this way to see was about to appear from behind a wing of the chair in which he was seated, someone tapped Peter on the shoulder. Turning, he found steel-gray eyes locked on his; the needle nose and thin lips below showed not a trace of bonhomie, let alone humor. As Peter tried to pull away, the man jabbed something sharp against Peter's side—the point of a switchblade.

"The atmosphere is toxic for you in here," the man said. He had dark hair, long at the collar, and slicked back. Hardly a fashionable DC style. His English held a slight accent that Peter couldn't place for the moment. "Let's step outside, shall we?"

"I'd rather not," Peter said, then winced as the knife point slid through his clothes to prick his skin.

The steel-gray eyes grew icy. "I'm afraid you have no choice in the matter."

6

"THERE ARE ALWAYS two sides to a story," Rebeka said.

"Except," Bourne said, "when there are three—or four."

She smiled. "Drink your hot toddy."

Bourne, in clean clothes, crouched by the fire and stared at Alef—or, according to Rebeka, Manfred Weaving. Weaving was lying on a mattress Rebeka had dragged in from a spare bedroom to lay by the fire. She had cut off his frozen clothes, as she had done, quickly and professionally, with Bourne. Then she had dressed him in shirt and trousers extracted from a large cedar chest at the foot of the bed she was using, then swaddled him in a woolly striped blanket. He was breathing normally, but he was unconscious, as he had been since Bourne had dragged him out of the water a second time. Before leaving the frozen lake, Rebeka had rolled Ze'ev off the ice, into the darkness of the frozen water. He sank as purposefully as if he were wearing a diver's lead-weighted belt.

"We should get him to a hospital."

Rebeka sat down cross-legged beside Bourne. "That wouldn't be wise."

"At least let me call a friend of mine in Stockholm. He can send a—"

"No." She said it firmly, without fear of rebuke. She was in charge here, and she knew it.

Bourne took a longer swig of the hot toddy. The Aquavit with which it was heavily laced burned a trail of fire down his throat and into his stomach. Instant warmth. He wished he could get some of it down Weaving's throat. "We might lose him."

"I've given him antibiotics." Leaning forward, she unwrapped the bottom half of him. "A couple of toes might have to come off."

"Who's going to do that?"

"I will." She rewrapped Weaving, then turned her attention to him. "I have an enormous stake in keeping him alive."

"I've been meaning to ask you about that."

They were in a fisherman's cottage a stone's throw from the water. Rebeka had rented it for a month, using an unholy cash sum that guaranteed the owner's silence, as well as his generosity. Every day, he restocked the refrigerator and the larder, made the bed, and swept the floors. Neither his wife nor his children knew a thing about her. That hadn't stopped Ze'ev from finding her, and it surely wouldn't stop the Babylonian from finding her, too.

"We can't stay here," she said, handing him a

plate of bread, cheese, and cold meat. "Only long enough for you to recover."

"And Weaving?"

"He will take longer." She looked at him almost longingly. "But if we wait until he regains consciousness, chances are all three of us will be dead."

Bourne stared at her while he ate. He was ravenous. "Who's coming?"

"Ben David has sent someone. According to Ze'ev, he's already on his way."

"I see how much you trusted Ze'ev," he said, nearly draining his mug.

She gave a hollow chuckle. "Right. Ze'ev was totally full of shit." She lifted a forefinger. "But it's only logical that Ben David sent someone after me—and you. And if, in fact, it is the Babylonian, well, he's the best Mossad has."

Bourne ate some more, taking several moments to absorb this. "What did Ze'ev want?"

"He said he wanted to help me, but from the first I suspected his real agenda was getting to Weaving. I thought he was dead, but..." She shook her head. "I made a mess of this, Jason. Weaving was getting away and I shot him. I aimed for his shoulder."

"You missed." Bourne wiped his mouth and glanced over at the unconscious man. "I pulled him out of the water. I brought him back here because I thought it might jog his memory."

Rebeka's head snapped up, her eyes alight. "What d'you mean?"

"The shot you fired grazed the side of his head. That and the shock of falling into the water, of almost freezing to death, caused amnesia."

"Amnesia?" Rebeka looked stunned. "My God, how...how bad?"

"He doesn't remember anything, not even his name." Bourne set the mug down. He shivered in the warmth. "He remembered the lake, running across it. I think he was beginning to remember you coming after him when Ze'ev began to fire."

He looked at her. "If Ze'ev wanted to find Weaving, why did he try to kill him?"

"That's a question I've been asking myself."

"Could that have been his aim all along?"

Her brows knit together as she nodded slowly. "It's possible, yes. But then, I've had all the pieces on the chessboard in the wrong places. People's allegiances have been compromised."

"But you must know that to be true. You must have seen what I saw in Dahr El Ahmar."

A flash of fear crossed her face. "So you did see...?"

"After I took off, after I evaded the missile and its explosion, I overflew the encampment."

"Have you told anyone?"

Bourne shook his head. "I have no master, Rebeka, you know that."

"A Ronin, a masterless samurai. But surely you have friends, people you trust."

He rose abruptly, stood over Manfred Weaving. "What is so valuable about him?"

"His mind." Rebeka stood up and went to stand beside him. "His mind is a treasure-trove of invaluable intel."

Bourne looked at her. "What kind of intel?"

She hesitated for just a moment, then said, "I

think Weaving is part of a terrorist network called *Jihad bis saif.*"

"Jihad by the sword," Bourne said. "I never heard of it."

"Neither have I, but—"

"What proof do you have?"

She touched the figure, swaddled like a newborn, lying unconscious by the fire. "I spoke to him."

"When?"

"After the lake, in the forest. I caught up with him, briefly. We spoke for a moment or two." She touched her shoulder. "Before he stabbed me."

Bourne rose and took his empty plate into the kitchen, which was an area adjacent to the living room, and placed it in the sink. "Rebeka, all this is conjecture on your part."

"Weaving found out what Mossad is doing in Dahr El Ahmar."

"An excellent reason, then, for Ben David to send Ze'ev to kill him."

"But there's far more in his head."

Bourne returned to her and to the fire. "None of this makes sense. Manfred Weaving may not even be his real name. It's more than likely a legend."

"Like Jason Bourne."

"No. I *am* Jason Bourne now."

"And before?"

Bourne thought of the monstrous sea snake, lying in the deepest recesses of his unconscious. "I was once David Webb, but I no longer know who he was."

As Peter was herded out of the Blackfriar clubhouse, he felt a trickle of blood snaking its way down his side, staining his shirt.

"Pick up the pace," the man with the steel-gray eyes said under his breath, "or more blood will be spilled."

Peter, who had in the past several months been almost blown up by a car bomb, kidnapped, and nearly killed, had had just about enough of being pushed around. Nevertheless, he went obediently with his captor, out the entrance of the clubhouse, down the wide stairs, past duffers in sweaters and caps, and around to the side of the building.

He was prodded through a thick stand of sculpted azaleas and, behind them, a maze of dense boxwood as high as his head. Even at this time of year, the boxwood, only drowsing, gave off its peculiar scent of cat piss.

When they were hidden from anyone who might somehow be in the vicinity, the man with the steel-gray eyes said in his peculiarly accented English, "What is it you want here?"

Peter drew his head back as if staring at a serpent rising off the forest floor. "Do you know who I am?"

"It is of no moment who you are." The man with the steel-gray eyes twisted the knife point into Peter's side. "Only what you are doing here."

"I'm looking for tennis lessons."

"I'll walk you over to the pro shop."

"I would so appreciate that."

The man bared his teeth. "Fuck you. You are following Richards."

"I don't know what—" Peter grimaced suddenly, as the knife point grazed a rib.

"Soon enough you won't need the pro shop," the man said, close to his ear. "You'll need a hospital."

"Don't get excited."

"And if I puncture a lung, even a hospital won't help you." The knife point ground against bone. "Understand?"

Peter grimaced and nodded.

"Now, why are you following this man you say you don't know?"

Peter breathed in and out, slowly, deeply, evenly. His heart was racing, and adrenaline was pumping into his system. "Richards works for me. He left the office prematurely."

"And this prompts you to follow him?"

"Richards's work is classified, highly sensitive. It's my job to—"

"Not today," the man said. "Not now, not with him."

"Whatever you say." Peter prepared himself mentally while willing his body to relax. He slowed his breathing, turned his mind away from the pain, the increasing loss of blood. Instead, he fixed his thoughts on what needed to be done. And then he did it.

Bringing his left arm down, he slammed his forearm into the man's wrist. At the same time, he twisted his upper torso, driving his right elbow into the bridge of the man's nose. Briefly, he felt the fire in his side as the knife point scraped along his rib, slashing open a horizontal wound. Then the full heat of battle rose up, and he forgot all about it.

The man, forced to let go of the knife, drove the ends of his fingers into Peter's solar plexus. Peter breathed out, then in, and stiff-armed his adversary. The man's shattered nose spouted blood like a fountain, and he took an involuntary step backward. Peter moved into the breach, drove his knee into the man's groin, then, as the man doubled over, smashed his fist into the back of his neck. The man went down and stayed down.

Retrieving the knife from where it had fallen, Peter knelt down, put the bloody point to the man's carotid as he rolled him over. He was unconscious. Quickly Peter rummaged through his pockets, found car keys, a thin metal-mesh wallet with almost $800 in cash, a driver's license, two credit cards, all in the name of Owen Lincoln. He also found a Romanian passport in the name of Florin Popa. Peter had a good laugh at that one. Popa, which meant *priest* in Romanian, was by far the most popular surname, the Romanian equivalent of *Smith*.

Staring down at the man with the steel-gray eyes, he knew only two things for certain: first, his name was neither Owen Lincoln nor Florin Popa. Second, whoever he was, he worked for the man Richards had come here to meet. Not enough, not nearly enough.

Soraya found Secretary Hendricks in a briefing with Mike Holmes, the national security advisor, and the head of Homeland Security. High-level stuff. The highest, in fact. Her credentials got her into the White House grounds, through several layers of security with exponentially increasing scrutiny, and into the West Wing, where she sat in a tiny, exquisite Queen Anne chair opposite one of Holmes's press officers—a speechwriter, actually— whom she knew on a casual, nod-at-each-other, basis. The officer kept his head down, his fingers plucking away at his computer terminal. She rose once to get herself a cup of coffee from a heavily laden sideboard, then sat back down. Not a word was spoken.

Forty minutes after she sat down, the door opened, and a clutch of suits marched out, glassy-eyed, still in the grip of the power of the Oval Office. Hendricks was talking in low tones to Holmes. Hendricks, who had himself ascended from the position Holmes now held and who had recommended Holmes to be his successor, was no doubt passing on a well-considered kernel of accumulated wisdom to his protégé. He saw Soraya when she stood up. He was almost abreast of her and appeared surprised to see her. He raised a forefinger, indicating that she should wait while he completed his conversation with Holmes.

Soraya bent and put her coffee cup down on the sideboard. When she straightened up, she winced at the pain that lanced through her head. Immediately she broke out into a cold sweat, and, turning away from the men, wiped her brow and upper lip with the back of her hand. Her heart was pounding, whether in fear for her own life or for that of her unborn baby, she could not say. Instinct drove her to place one hand on her belly, as if to protect the fetus from whatever was happening inside her skull. But there was no protection, she knew, not really. Every option available to her was fraught with dire peril.

"Soraya?"

She started at the sound of Hendricks's voice so close to her, and when she turned, she was afraid that her face was ashen, that her boss would see what was happening to her. But his smile seemed unclouded with doubt. He projected only mild surprise and a certain curiosity.

"What are you doing here?"

"Waiting for you."

"You could have called."

"No," she said. "I couldn't."

His brow furrowed. "I'm not following."

"I need to talk with you, someplace secure." She was appalled to hear how breathless she sounded.

"Ride with me to my next meeting." He took her elbow lightly and escorted her out of the West Wing, out of the White House, to his armored, custom Escalade. A Secret Service agent opened the rear door. He signed for Soraya to climb in, then followed her inside. When the door slammed shut behind them and they were settled, he pressed a hidden button. A privacy wall rose up, cutting them off from the driver and an eagle-eyed Special Forces bodyguard who was riding shotgun.

They began to move out through the gates. The world looked blurred and indistinct through the blacked-out bulletproof glass.

"We're perfectly secure here," Hendricks said. "Now, what's on your mind?"

Soraya took a deep breath, then let it out, trying to slow her pulse, which was galloping like a terrified horse. "Sir, with all due respect, I need to know what the fuck is going on."

Hendricks seemed to consider this for some time. They had left the White House grounds and were gliding through the traffic on the streets of DC. "Putting aside the oxymoronic usage of 'respect' and 'fuck' in the same sentence, Director, I think you're going to have to be more specific."

She had gotten his back up, but she'd also gotten his full attention, which was the point. "Okay, straight up, Mr. Secretary," she said, mimicking his brusque formal tone. "Ever since you briefed Peter and me on this Djinn Who Lights The Way, strange things have been happening."

"What kind of strange things, Director?" He snapped his fingers. "Details, please."

"For one thing, I've discovered that there seems to be a continuing connection between Nicodemo and Core Energy. Only I can't fathom what it is. Core Energy's president is Tom Brick."

Hendricks turned to look at the ashy city outside the window. "Brick. Never heard of him," he said. "Ditto for—what was it again?"

"Core Energy."

And there it was, Soraya thought. Hendricks lied. He had a steel-trap mind; there was no way he would need to ask her to repeat the company's name. He must be familiar with Core Energy. Did he know Brick as well? And if so, why was he lying to her about it?

They crossed over the Key Bridge, into Virginia, and the Escalade picked up speed. Soraya wondered where Hendricks was headed.

The secretary sighed. "Is that all?"

"Well, then there's Richard Richards."

"Forget Richards." The disdain in his voice was palpable. "He's a nobody."

"A nobody who reports to the president."

Hendricks turned back to her. "What sort of snooping has he been up to?"

"It's not that, so much as—"

"What?" He snapped his fingers again. "Details, Director."

Should I tell him? she wondered. And then, she thought, *It might help to see his reaction.* She was about to speak when the Escalade slowed and turned into the entrance of a cemetery. They passed through high iron gates, drifted slowly down a narrow paved road that bisected the graveyard. Near the back they turned right, went three-quarters of the way down, and rolled to a stop.

Grabbing Florin Popa by his ankles, Peter dragged him deeper into the undergrowth, depositing him behind a thick boxwood hedge. As he maneuvered the body into place, one of Popa's shoes came off and, as it bounced over the hard ground, something spilled out of it. Peter crouched down, peering at it, then picked it up and inspected it. A key, not to a hotel room or a car—smaller than either of those—but to a public locker.

Pocketing the key, Peter replaced the shoe, then condensed Popa's footprint by folding him into a fetal position. Rising, he backed away, checking everything. Then he turned, made his way out of the labyrinth of hedges, and crossed to the front of the pro shop. Inside, on his right, was a board listing the names of all the tennis pros, along with the days they were working. Back outside, Peter went around to the rear and made his way to the changing lockers. Each one had a nameplate affixed to it. The narrow windowless room was deserted. Peter bent over the locker of one of the pros the board had marked as not working today and picked the lock. Quickly, he changed his clothes, pinned on the pro's ID tag, and exited the pro shop via the employees' entrance.

A short walk brought him again to the clubhouse. Trotting with a confident air up the steps to the front porch, he entered the now-familiar great room. He looked immediately to the small grouping where he had seen Richards sit down with the mystery man, but the chairs were empty now. Picking up a club phone and calling the guardhouse, he learned that Richards had driven out while he had been changing in the pro shop. Peter set down the receiver. Surely the mystery man would be looking for Florin Popa—people like that felt naked without their bodyguards. In fact, if Peter was any judge of human psychology, the man would be getting antsy as to Popa's whereabouts. As Peter continued around the great room, he looked for a lone male who was peering around the space with increasing urgency. An older gentleman stood waiting near the rest rooms. He had silver hair like the man Richards had come to see. Perhaps...but no, an older woman emerged from the ladies' room and smiled at the man—his wife. Chatting amiably, they strolled off. There was no one else.

Wending his way past the club members, Peter made his way out onto the expansive terrace. Sun-

light bathed a third of the tables, all of them occupied. The rest, in shadow, were empty. Moving
forward, he saw a man with his back to him, his
upper torso leaning forward, his hands gripping the
wrought-iron railing. He, too, had silver hair.

Peter lifted his head like a bloodhound catching
a scent. He unpinned his ID, then snagged a uniformed waiter as he passed by, a tray of empty
glasses held high.

"This is my first day and I'm looking for clients.
See that guy over there? Know his name?"

The waiter looked at where Peter was pointing.
"How could I not? That's Tom Brick. He's a fucking
whale." When Peter looked at him in puzzlement,
he added, "Big fucking spender. There's bedlam
among the staff to serve him. Tips twenty-five percent. You get him to sign on with you, my man,
you're in clover, no lie."

Peter thanked him and let him go on about his business. He affixed his ID to his shirt. Taking a circular
route to the railing afforded him several moments to
observe Brick before he approached him. He was
younger than Peter had imagined, perhaps in his very
early thirties. He was neither handsome nor ugly, but
possessed a face full of features that failed to mesh, as
if it had been fashioned from spare parts. He had a tattoo of a knotted rope on the back of his left hand.

He must have sensed Peter's approach because he
turned just before Peter reached the railing. Brick
had a wandering eye, which, oddly, seemed to take
Peter in from all sides at once.

Peter nodded. "A perfect day for tennis, wouldn't
you say?"

Brick's good eye took in Peter's ID while the other one continued its disconcerting scrutiny. "You'd know better than me, I should think." Like the late, unlamented Florin Popa, he had an accent. This one was British, however. "Are you new to Blackfriar?"

"You don't play tennis, I take it."

Brick turned to gaze out over the deserted eighteenth hole. "Golf's my sport. Are you soliciting, Mr.—" another hard look at Peter's ID "—Bowden? Bad form, I should think."

Peter cursed himself for botching the approach so badly. Mentally, he retreated, kept his mouth shut, and began to formulate Plan B, which, admittedly, he should have come up with before saying one word to this man.

He was about to attempt reestablishing contact when Brick turned to him and said in a low voice, "Who the bloody hell are you?"

Taken aback, Peter pointed to his ID. "Dan Bowden."

"Fuck you are," Brick said. "I've met Bowden." He turned fully to Peter, his eyes abruptly hard as crystal. "Time to own up, mate. Tell me who you are or I call Security and have you arrested."

Wait here," Hendricks said gruffly, then got out and, accompanied by his bodyguard, walked slowly between the headstones until he stopped in front of one. He stood, head down, while his bodyguard, several paces back, looked around, as always, for trouble.

Soraya pushed open the SUV's door and slipped out. A mild breeze, holding the first heady scent of spring, snaked through the headstones. She came around the back of the Escalade, then stepped carefully over the mounded turf. The secretary's bodyguard saw her, shook his head, but she kept on, close enough for her to get a partial view of what was engraved on the headstone Hendricks stood in front of: AMANDA HENDRICKS, LOVING WIFE AND MOTHER.

The bodyguard took a step forward and murmured something to his charge. Hendricks turned, glanced at Soraya, and nodded. The bodyguard beckoned her on.

When she had come up beside him, Hendricks said, "There's something peaceful about a cemetery. As if there's all the time in the world to think, to reconsider, to come to conclusions."

Soraya said nothing, intuiting that she was not meant to answer. Contemplating a loved one's death was a private and mysterious moment. Inevitably, she thought of Amun. She wondered where he was buried—surely somewhere in Cairo. She wondered whether she would ever get the chance to visit his grave and, if so, what she would feel. If, in the end, she had loved him, it would have been different. Her profound guilt would have, to a mitigating extent, been assuaged. But that she had let go of him, had, in fact, despised him for his ugly prejudice against Jews, against Aaron in particular, shoved her guilt into outsized proportions.

As if divining her thoughts, Hendricks said, "You lost someone in Paris, didn't you?"

A wave of shame rose inside her. "It never should have happened."

"Which? His death, or your affair?"

"Both, sir."

"Yesterday's news, Soraya. They ended in Paris—leave them there."

"Do you leave her here?"

"Most of the time." He thought for a moment. "Then some days..."

His voice trailed off, but there was no need to finish the thought. His meaning was plain.

He cleared his throat. "The difficulty comes in not letting it rest. Otherwise, there will be no possibility of peace."

"Have you found peace, sir?"

"Only here, Director. Only here."

When, at last, he turned away from his wife's grave, she said, "Thank you, sir, for bringing me here."

He waved away her words. As they walked slowly back to the waiting Escalade, accompanied by the bodyguard, he said, "Are you done, Soraya?"

"No, sir." She gave him a sideways glance. "About Richards. He lied about Core Energy. He knows about it, knows that Nicodemo is involved in it."

Hendricks stopped dead in his tracks. "How on earth would he know that?"

Soraya shrugged. "Who knows? He's the 'It Boy' when it comes to the Internet." She made herself pause. "Then again, maybe there's another reason."

Hendricks stood still as a statue. Very carefully, spacing the words out, he said, "What other reason?"

Soraya was about to answer when an abrupt pain in her head blotted out all sight and sound. Leaning forward, she pressed the heel of her hand to her temple, as if to keep her brains from spilling all over someone's headstone.

"Director?" Hendricks grabbed her, saving her from falling over. "Soraya?"

But she could not hear him. Pain flared through her like forked lightning, blotting out everything else apart from the darkness, which overtook her in a kind of blessing.

7

"WE HAVE TO MOVE him now," Rebeka said as she peered out the window of the fisherman's cottage. Darkness was falling at a rapid rate. Blue shadows rose like specters. The world seemed unstable.

"Not until he's regained consciousness." Bourne crouched beside Weaving, whose face was pale and waxen. He took his pulse. "If we move him now, we risk losing him."

"If we don't move him now," she said, turning away from the window, "we risk the Babylonian finding us."

Bourne looked up. "Are you afraid of him?"

"I've seen his handiwork." She came over to him. "He's different from you and me, Bourne. He lives with death every day; it's his sole companion."

"He sounds like Gilgamesh."

"Close enough. Except that the Babylonian loves death—he revels in it."

"My concern is Weaving, not the Babylonian."

"I agree, Bourne. We have to take the chance that he'll survive the journey out of here. He certainly won't survive the Babylonian."

Bourne nodded, slapped Weaving hard on one cheek, then the other. Color bloomed as blood rushed back into Weaving's face. His arms spasmed as he coughed. Bourne, leaning over him, pried his jaws open, flattened his tongue before he had a chance to bite through it.

Weaving shivered, a tremor, then a rippling of his limbs. Then his eyes sprang open and, a moment later, focused.

"Jason?" His voice was thin and fluty.

Bourne nodded. At the same time, he waved Rebeka out of sight, afraid that if Weaving saw her he'd start to hyperventilate and perhaps even relapse into unconsciousness.

"You're safe. Perfectly safe."

"What happened?"

"You fell through the ice."

Weaving blinked several times and licked his chapped lips. "There were shots, I—"

"The man who shot at you is dead."

"Man?"

"His name was Ze'ev Stahl." Bourne scrutinized the other's face. "Ring a bell?"

For a long moment, Weaving stared up at Bourne, but his gaze was turned inward. Bourne not only sensed, but felt acutely, what must be going on in Weaving's mind: a plunge into the morass of amnesia, trying desperately to pluck out even a single memory, a place, a name. It was a heart-wrenching, soul-destroying experience that often left you weak and gasping because you were alone, utterly and completely alone, severed from the world as if with a surgeon's scalpel. Bourne shuddered.

"I do," Weaving said at last. "I think I do." He reached for Bourne's arm. "Help me up."

Bourne brought him to a sitting position. He licked his lips again as he stared into the fire.

"Where am I?"

"A fisherman's cottage a mile or so from the lake." Bourne signaled Rebeka to bring a glass of water.

"You've saved my life twice now, Jason. I have no way to thank you."

Bourne took the glass from Rebeka. "Tell me about Ze'ev Stahl."

Weaving looked around, but by that time Rebeka had stepped back into shadow. His curiosity seemed to have leached away with his strength. Accepting the water from Bourne with a trembling hand, he gulped half of it down.

"Take it easy," Bourne said. "You've come back from the dead twice. That's more than enough to plow anyone under."

Weaving nodded. He was still staring into the fire, as if it were a talisman that helped him remember. "I was in Dahr El Ahmar, I recall that much."

Out of the corner of his eye, Bourne saw Rebeka move. *Ask him why he was there*, she mouthed to him.

"Where were you, exactly?"

Weaving scrunched up his face. "A bar, I think it was. Yes, a bar. It was very crowded. Smoke-choked. Some kind of raucous rock music playing."

"Did he approach you? Did you talk to him?"

Weaving shook his head. "I don't think he was aware of me."

"Was he with someone?"

"Yes...no." Weaving frowned, concentrating. "He...he was watching someone. Not openly, watching without looking." He turned to look at Bourne. "You know."

Bourne nodded. "I do."

"So I felt...I don't know, a kind of kinship with him. After all, we were both living in the margins, hidden by shadows."

"Who was he looking at, do you remember?"

"Oh, yes. Vividly. A very beautiful woman. She seemed to exude sex." He drank the remainder of his water, more slowly this time. "She was...well, I was powerfully drawn to her, you might say." The ghost of a smile skittered across his lips. "Well, of course I was. Stahl was interested in her."

Rebeka leaned forward. "So you knew Stahl from before?"

"Not knew, no." Weaving frowned again. "I think I was at the bar to observe him. I know I went after the woman because of his scrutiny of her. I figured she might be my best way to learn about him. Then—I don't know—she seemed to cast a spell over me."

Bourne sat back, absorbing this information. He thought the time had come to broach the question that, for the moment, most interested him. "You haven't up to now, but do you remember your name?"

"Sure," he said. "Harry Rowland."

* * *

She's crashing!" the EMS tech yelled to the team that met them at Virginia Hospital Center's ER entrance in Arlington. Hendricks had phoned ahead, using his clout to get a crack group mobilized even before the ambulance came screaming down the driveway, the Escalade hard on its heels.

Hendricks leaped out, following the gurney's hurried journey through the sliding doors, down corridors smelling of medication and sickness, hope and fear. He watched as the team of doctors transferred Soraya to hospital equipment and began their critical initial assessment. There was a great deal of murmured crosstalk. He took a step closer to hear what they were saying but couldn't make head or tail of their jargon-filled conversation.

A decision made, they wheeled Soraya out and down another corridor. He hurried after them, but was stopped at the door marked SURGERY.

He pulled at one doctor's sleeve. "What's going on? What's the matter with her?"

"Swelling of the brain."

A chill went through him. "How serious?"

"We won't know until we get inside her skull."

Hendricks was aghast. "You're going to open her up? But what about an MRI?"

"No time," the doctor said. "We have to think about the fetus as well."

Hendricks felt as if the floor had just fallen away beneath him. "Fetus? You mean she's pregnant?"

"I'm sorry, Mr. Secretary, but I'm needed inside." He pushed a metal button that opened the door. "I'll inform you as soon as I know something. Your mobile?"

"I'll be right here," Hendricks said, stunned. "Right here until I know she's safe and secure."

The doctor nodded, then vanished into that mysterious land ruled by surgeons. After a long moment, Hendricks turned away, walking back to where Willis, his Special Forces bodyguard, waited with coffee and a sandwich.

"This way, sir," Willis said as he led Hendricks to the waiting room closest to Surgery. As usual, he had cleared it out so that he and his boss were the only ones in residence.

Hendricks tried to raise Peter Marks, but the call went directly to voicemail. Peter must be out in the field, the only time he kept his phone off. He considered a moment, then asked Willis to get him the number of the main DC office of the Bureau of Alcohol, Firearms, Tobacco, and Explosives. When Willis gave it to him, he punched it in on his mobile and asked for Delia Trane. He spoke to her briefly and urgently. She told him she was on her way. She sounded calm and collected, which is what Soraya needed at the moment. In all honesty, it was what he needed, as well. He made several other calls of a serious and secret nature, and for a time he was calmed.

He sat at a cheap wood-laminate table, and Willis set his food in front of him before retreating to the doorway, hypervigilant as ever. Hendricks found he wasn't hungry. He looked around the room, which had a hospital's pathetic attempt at making a space feel homey. Upholstered chairs and a sofa were interspersed with side tables on which sat lamps. But everything was so cheap and worn that the only emotion evoked was one of sadness. *It's like the waiting room to Purgatory*, he thought.

He took a sip of coffee and winced at its bitterness.

"Sorry, sir," Willis said, as attentive as ever. "I've asked one of the guys to get you some real coffee."

Hendricks nodded distractedly. He was consumed by the twin bombshells the doctor had dropped on him. Soraya with a serious concussion *and* a baby in her womb. How in the hell had this happened? How had he not known?

But, of course, he knew the reason. He'd been too preoccupied—obsessed, one might say—with the mythical Nicodemo. The president did not believe in Nicodemo's existence, was only contemptuous of Hendricks's allocating any time and money to what he called "the worst kind of disinformation." In fact, Hendricks was certain that the president's antipathy to the Nicodemo project was fueled by Holmesian rhetoric. There wasn't a day that went by when Hendricks did not regret having helped Holmes up the security ladder.

The truth of the matter: Holmes had discovered that Nicodemo might very well be Hendricks's Achilles heel, the lever by which he could, at last, wrest control of Treadstone away from his rival. Ever since the president had named Mike Holmes as his national security advisor, Holmes had proved himself to be a power junkie. *Increase* and *consolidate* were the watchwords by which he formulated his career. And he had, more or less, been successful. Now, the only major roadblock was Hendricks's control of Treadstone. Holmes coveted Treadstone with an almost religious fervor. In this, he and Hendricks were well matched; both were obsessives. They clashed obsessively over antithetical goals. Hendricks knew that if he could smoke Nicodemo out and capture or kill him, he'd be rid of Holmes's interference forever. He'd have won his hard-fought battle. Holmes could no longer whisper poisoned thoughts into the president's ear.

But if his instincts failed him, if Nicodemo was, in fact, a myth, or, worse, an elaborate piece of disinformation, then his career would spiral downward, Holmes would get what he so desired, and Treadstone would be used for other, much darker purposes.

The search for Nicodemo was, in fact, a struggle for the very soul of Treadstone.

Harry," Bourne said, "do you remember where you were born?"

Alef nodded. Bourne had returned to thinking of him as Alef. "Dorset, England. I'm thirty-four years old."

Bourne softened his voice considerably, as if they were two old friends meeting after a long separation. "Who do you work for, Harry?"

"I—" He looked at Bourne helplessly. "I don't know."

"But you do remember that you were in Lebanon—specifically Dahr El Ahmar—to gain information about Ze'ev Stahl."

"That's right. Maybe I was doing a bit of industrial espionage, eh?"

"Stahl is Mossad."

"What? Mossad? Why would I—?"

"Harry, tell me about Manfred Weaving."

Alef's eyes clouded over, then he shook his head. "Don't know him." He looked at Bourne. "Why? Should I know him?"

Bourne risked a glance at Rebeka, but Alef picked up on it. He had to turn almost 180 degrees in order to see her. When he did so, his eyes opened wide and he shivered.

"What the hell is *she* doing here?"

Bourne put a hand on his arm as Rebeka came toward them. "She's not going to hurt you. She was the one who shot Stahl out on the lake while we were both almost frozen to death and helpless."

"Hello, Manny," she said.

Even though she was looking directly at him, he looked around, as if searching for someone else in the room. "What's she talking about? Who's this Weaving?"

"You are," she said. "Manfred Weaving."

"I don't know what you're talking about." He appeared genuinely confused. "My name is Harry Rowland. It's the name I was born with, it's the name I've always had."

"Possibly not," Bourne said.

"What? How—?"

"Your network, *Jihad bis saif*." Rebeka had crouched down beside them. "Tell us its goal."

Rowland opened his mouth, about to answer when they all heard a sound from outside. It was half concealed by the suck-and-wash of the low surf, but it could have been the scrape of a leather boot sole.

In any case, it was very close to the house, and Rebeka mouthed: *He's found us.*

"Who's found us?" Rowland said.

At that moment, the front door crashed open.

8

MARTHA CHRISTIANA found Don Fernando Hererra with little difficulty. After receiving her commission, she had hunkered down in her Parisian hotel suite with her laptop and spent the next eight hours scouring the Internet for every iota of information on the banking mogul. The basics were at her fingertips within seconds. Hererra, born in Bogotá in 1946, the youngest child of four, was shipped off to England for university studies, where he took a First in economics at Oxford. Returning to Colombia, he had worked in the oil industry, rapidly working his way up the hierarchy until he went out on his own, successfully bidding for the company he had worked at. This was how he had amassed his first fortune. It was unclear how he segued into international banking, but from what Martha read, Aguardiente Bancorp was now one of the three largest banks outside of the United States.

Further exploration turned up more. Five years ago, Hererra had named Diego, his only son, to head up the prestigious London branch of Aguardiente. Diego had been killed several years ago under mysterious circumstances that, no matter how she tried, Martha could not clarify; it seemed clear enough that he had been murdered, possibly by Hererra's enemies, though that, too, remained murky. Currently, Hererra's main residence was in the Santa Cruz *barrio* of Seville, though he maintained homes in London, Cadiz—and Paris.

When she had absorbed all the information available on the Web, she pushed back her chair, rose, and padded across the parquet floor to the bathroom, where she turned on the taps and stepped into a steaming shower.

By the time she emerged, she had the framework of a plan formulated. By the time she had dried off, blown out her hair, put on makeup, and gotten dressed, the plan had been fleshed out and detailed. Gathering up her coat, she went out of the hotel. Her car was waiting for her, its powerful engine humming happily in the chilly air. Her driver opened the door for her, and she climbed in.

Hererra lived in an apartment on the Île Saint-Louis, in the middle of the Seine River. It was on the western tip, high up with breathtaking views that encompassed the Pantheon and the Eiffel Tower on the Left Bank, Notre Dame Cathedral on the adjoining Île de la Cité, and the major buildings in that section of the Right Bank.

Martha Christiana had discovered that Hererra was a creature of habit. He liked to haunt certain bars, cafés, bistros, and restaurants in whichever city he was currently inhabiting. In Paris, that meant Le Fleur en Ile for breakfast, lunch at Yam'tcha, and dinner at L'Agassin. As it was too late for lunch and too early for dinner, she had the car take her past the Aguardiente Bancorp offices. In the shower she had considered all of these places and, for one reason or another—too awkward or obvious—had rejected them all. She had read in the paper of a concert of chamber music by Bach that evening at Sainte-Chapelle on the Île de la Cité, one of an on-going series at the magnificent jewel-box chapel. The concert was early so as to catch the last sparks of winter sunlight through the chapel's radiant west-facing stained-glass windows.

Martha Christiana had decided on the concert for several reasons. First, Hererra loved Bach, as she did. From her study of him, she surmised that he loved the strict order of the mathematical music, which would appeal to his precise banker's mind. Second, Sainte-Chapelle was his favorite place in Paris to hear music. Third, the chapel was small, the audience packed together. This would give her ample opportunity to find him and figure out the most natural approach. It would also provide a number of topics—music, architecture, Bach, religion—in which to engage him in conversation that would be both innocent and stimulating.

Yes, she thought, as she left her car and walked the last several blocks to the concert entrance to Sainte-Chapelle, she had chosen wisely. Joining the line, she inched along the sidewalk. She spotted him as he turned into the doorway and came into view.

She was pleased: She was only six people behind him. She had chosen an Alexander McQueen outfit, one of her favorites: a belted, navy V-neck military pencil dress, which she had paired with black ankle-high boots with a wedge heel. She wanted to stand out, but not too much.

Inside, the rows of folding chairs were neat and precise, and people took their seats silently, almost reverently, as if they were coming to Mass, not to a concert played by a string quartet. Perhaps, Martha thought, because it was Bach the two might not be so different. She had read that those who loved Bach's music above all others often felt that when the music rose around them, they were as close to God as they would get in this life.

Her seat was three rows behind Hererra, which was good; she could keep him in sight. He sat between a man more elderly than he and a woman who Martha judged to be on the good side of forty. It was unclear if he knew either of these people, and shortly it didn't matter, at least not while the quartet was playing Bach. This almost mystical composer elicited many different reactions in his listeners. For Martha Christiana, the music brought up memories of her past: the fogbound lighthouse off the coast of Gibraltar in which she had been born, her father, gruff and weather-beaten, tinkering constantly with the ever-revolving light, her mother, pale and fragile, so agoraphobic that she never left the lighthouse. When her mother looked up at the stars at night, she was overcome with vertigo.

The musicians played, the music unfurled, precise and rigorous in its progression of notes, and

Martha Christiana saw herself escaping the lighthouse, leaving her dysfunctional parents behind, stealing aboard a freighter, steaming out of Gibraltar harbor for North Africa, where for nineteen months, she roamed the streets of Marrakech, selling herself to stupid tourists as a virgin, over and over, after the first time using fresh goat's blood she bought from a butcher, before she was taken in by an enormously wealthy Moroccan, who made her his unwilling concubine. He kept her prisoner inside his house, took her roughly, often brutally, whenever the spirit moved him, which was often.

He furthered her education in literature, mathematics, philosophy, and history. He also taught her how to look inward, to meditate, to empty herself of all thought, all desire, and while she was in that transcendental state, to see God. He gave her the world, many worlds, in fact. Eventually, inevitably, the knowledge with which he endowed her opened her eyes to the terrible price he was exacting from her. Three times she tried to escape from her perfumed prison and three times he caught her. Each time, her punishment was more grievous, more monstrous, but she steeled herself, she would not be cowed. Instead, one night, while they made love, she rose up, intending to slit his throat with a shard of glass she had hoarded in secret. His eyes turned opaque as if he could see his death reflected in her face. He emitted a sound like the ticking of a massive grandfather clock. She spread her arms wide, as if summoning God to do her bidding. His clawed fingers dug in, scratched down her upper arms as if he wished to take her with him as he died of a massive heart attack. Gathering up what money she could find, leaving untouched anything that could be traced back to him, she had fled Marrakech, never to return.

These were not altogether pleasant memories, but they were hers, and after years of trying to deny them, she now accepted them as part of her, albeit a part known only to herself. Every once in a while, when she was alone in the dark, she played Bach on her iPod, re-evoking these memories to remind herself of who she was and where she had come from. Then she meditated, emptying herself in order for God to fill her up. It had taken her a long time, absorbing pain of all kinds, to reach this state of being. Always, she emerged from these introspective sessions feeling renewed and ready for the task at hand.

The concert over, the audience applauded, then stood and applauded some more, calling for an encore. The quartet re-emerged from the wings, where they had been absorbing the well-deserved accolades, took up their instruments, and played a short, thrumming piece. More applause, as the concert ended, for good this time.

Martha observed the woman on Hererra's left turn to him, tilting her head while she spoke and he responded. She was more stately than pretty, very well dressed. A native Parisian, no doubt.

The audience was breaking up, shuffling along the rows, filing slowly up the aisles, talk of the concert persistent and ongoing. Martha Christiana moved along with the people in her row, then hung back a bit at the end so that when she entered the aisle she was alongside the woman with Hererra.

"Le concert vous a-t-il plu?" she said to the woman. *Did you enjoy the concert? "J'aime Bach, et vous?"* I love Bach, don't you?

"En fait, non," the woman replied. *In fact, no.* *"Je préfère Satie."*

Martha, thanking God for the opening, finally addressed Hererra. *"Et vous, monsieur, préférez-vous aussi Satie?"*

"Non," Hererra said, with an indulgent smile toward his companion, "I favor Bach above all other composers—apart, of course, from Stephen Sondheim."

Martha emitted a silvery laugh as she threw back her head, revealing her long neck and velvety throat.

"Yes," she said. *"Follies* is my favorite show."

For the first time, Hererra looked past his companion, sizing Martha up. By this time they had reached the echoing marble hallway that led to the street. That was the moment for her to nod in friendly fashion and move ahead of the couple.

Outside, a drizzle was making the streets shiny. Martha paused to turn up the collar of her coat, take out a cigarette, and fumble for her lighter. Before she could find it, a flame appeared before her, and she leaned in, drawing smoke deeply into her lungs. As she let it out, she looked up to see Hererra standing in front of her. He was alone.

"Where is your companion?"

"She had a previous engagement."

Martha raised her eyebrows. "Really?"

She liked his laugh. It was deep and rich and came from his lower belly.

"No. I dismissed her."

"An employee, then."

"Just an acquaintance, nothing more."

Martha liked the way he said "nothing more," not dismissively, just matter-of-factly, indicating that circumstances had changed, that he was quick to adapt to the changes.

Hererra took out a cigar, held it up for her to see. "Do you mind?"

"Not at all," Martha said. "I enjoy the smell of a good cigar."

They introduced themselves.

As Hererra went through the ritual of cutting and lighting the cigar, precise as a Bach toccata, she said, "Tell me, Don Fernando, have you ever been to Eisenach?" Eisenach was the birthplace of Johann Sebastian Bach.

"I confess I haven't." He had the cigar going now. "Have you?"

She nodded. "As a graduate student, I went to the Wartburg Castle, where Martin Luther translated the New Testament into German."

"Your thesis was on Luther?"

She laughed that silvery laugh again. "I never finished it. Too much of a rebel." He had been a rebel, too, in his youth. She thought a kindred spirit would appeal to him. She was right.

"Mademoiselle Christiana."

"Martha, please."

"All right, then. Martha. Would you be free for dinner?"

"Monsieur, I hardly know you."

He smiled. "Easiest thing in the world to remedy, don't you think?"

* * *

My name isn't important," Peter said. "Richards was followed here."

Brick's eyes were adamantine. "I don't know what you're talking about."

"Seriously?" Peter looked around at the table crowd. "Any idea where your man is?"

"My man?"

"Right. Owen." Peter snapped his fingers. "What's his last name?"

A flicker like a passing shadow in Brick's eyes. "What about Owen?"

"Best I show you." Peter took a step away.

Brick pulled himself reluctantly away from the railing. "What's this about then?"

Without another word, Peter led him out of the clubhouse and around the side of the pro shop, passing through the labyrinth of high boxwood to where Florin Popa lay.

Brick stopped dead in his tracks. "What the fuck?"

"Dead as a doornail," Peter observed pitilessly as Brick bent over Popa's corpse. "Mr. Brick, you're clearly under threat. I think it would be prudent for us to get out of here."

Brick, one hand on Popa's shoulder, looked up at him. "Bugger off, mate. I'm not going anywhere with you."

Peter nodded solemnly. "Okay, then. I'll leave you to muddle through on your own."

As he began to make his way back through the boxwood, Brick called out.

"Wait a sec. Who the bloody hell are you and who do you work for?"

Bourne reached into the fire, grabbed a burning log, and hurled it at the intruder. The firebrand hissed and flickered, one end of it bursting into sparking fury when it struck the intruder's shoulder. He half-spun, flung up one arm to bat the burning log away. Thus engaged, he was poorly prepared for Bourne's hurtled body. Behind him, Bourne could hear a mad scramble as Rebeka dragged Rowland out of harm's way.

The intruder chopped down on Bourne's back, arching him backward, hauled him off, and delivered a blow to his solar plexus. He grabbed Bourne by the collar and threw him against the wall. Bourne ripped a print off the wall, smashing it as the intruder bull-rushed him. The glass shattered. Bourne, grasping a long, slender piece, and ignoring the cut in his palm as he grasped it, struck downward.

He had aimed for the intruder's neck, but missed, the point of the glass shard burying itself, instead, in the intruder's back. The momentum of the bull rush took both men down to the floor. Seemingly ignoring the glass shard, the intruder flicked out a knife, stabbing down with it. Bourne rolled away, and the knife point buried itself in a narrow gap between the ancient floorboards. Instead of wasting time trying to pry it free, the intruder simply let it go, freeing another weapon.

*   *   *

Rebeka recognized Ilan Halevy immediately. The moment Bourne engaged the Babylonian, she busied herself dragging Weaving back around the corner into the shadows of the kitchen cupboards.

With a whispered, "For the love of God, stay put," she drew a pair of scaling knives out of their wooden holder, slipped one into her waistband and hefted the other as she reappeared around the corner, just in time to see the Babylonian, a shard of glass protruding from his bloodstained back, stab brutally down with a folding dagger.

She moved swiftly and silently, the scaling knife held in front of her. It had a wicked-looking gut-hook on its top edge. If she could bury it deep enough and then jerk back on the hilt, she could do the Babylonian some serious damage.

Both his strength and his stamina were legendary. She knew he hardly felt the glass shard in his back, wouldn't feel the scaling knife, either, unless she was lucky enough to hit a vital organ, or skillful enough to bury the gut-hook in his viscera and then pull backward. The resulting gush of blood would give even him pause.

But despite her stealth, he sensed her attack, and at the last instant, turned his body sideways to her, in the process absorbing two heavy blows from Bourne. His left hand whipped out, his fingers like tentacles as they clasped her, twisting viciously, grinding the bones in her wrist against one another. The breath went out of her as flashes of light exploded behind her eyes. In that instant, the Baby-

Ionian wrenched the scaling knife from her and slashed it at her. He'd meant to open her throat from side to side, but her reflexes saved her from the lethal blow. The blade slit open her sweater and shirt, opening a horizontal bright-red bloom across her chest, just above her breasts. She gasped and fell backward.

When Harry Rowland—for he was absolutely certain now that was his name—heard the grunts, thumps, and hard exhalations of hand-to-hand combat, something clicked inside his brain. Completely ignoring Rebeka's order, he slithered around the corner of the kitchen. In an instant, his measured, professional gaze took in the chaotic situation. Something peeled away. He felt as if, after having been cast adrift in a hazy dreamworld since awakening in the clinic in Stockholm, everything now had become sharp and clear.

Without further conscious thought, he scrambled to his feet, ran to the fireplace, and snatched up the fire tongs. Deftly avoiding Rebeka, he stepped to where Bourne and the intruder grappled in lethal hand-to-hand combat. He regarded the two of them, one after the other. Everything seemed to move in slow motion except his mind, which, having flickered to life, was now racing at a fever pitch. Memories were surfacing, flashing like schools of silvery fish lifted from the depths. They came in rapid succession, but now in their proper order. So many things unknown he now understood, like a thick curtain being pulled back, revealing, layer by layer, his life before being shot. Not everything was there—the tapestry still had holes, missing pieces, curious dead ends that puzzled him, fish slipping through his fingers, returning to the unfathomable deep. Some thoughts still didn't make sense, but certain imperatives did, and these drove him to decisive, galvanic action.

Lifting the fire tongs over his head, Harry Rowland brought them whistling down toward the top of Bourne's skull.

Book Two

9

W E LIVE IN A world where information is constantly flowing, through servers, networks, intranets, the Internet."

Charles Thorne, typing notes on his iPad 3 as an app recorded every word Maceo Encarnación uttered, nodded.

"We are fast becoming a cloud-culture," Encarnación continued. "Each hour of each day the amount of information grows exponentially, and all of this expanding tsunami of information—all of it—exists in some form or other that can be read and understood by outsiders—by overhearing, bugging, or hacking."

Thorne, sitting with Encarnación in the offices of *Politics As Usual*, felt his mobile buzz against his thigh as it lay in his pocket. He ignored it, nodding encouragingly at Encarnación. It had taken him months of complex negotiations with a succession of underlings to get Encarnación, the president and CEO of SteelTrap, to agree to be interviewed. Steel-Trap, the world's largest Internet security firm, was an anomaly in the world of business—so large, so influential, so successful, yet privately held, therefore beholden to no one. Its internal structure was entirely opaque.

In the end, Thorne had lucked out. Encarnación, on his way from Paris to Mexico City, where part of his vast staff maintained one of his palatial residences, had agreed to the interview while his private jet was being refueled. He had insisted that no photos be taken of him. This hardly surprised Thorne since, as part of his research for the interview, he had discovered a curious fact: there were no photos of Encarnación anywhere online. He was a bear of a man, curious-looking owing to the fact that he was entirely hairless. Thorne found himself wondering if this was a deliberate deforestation or the result of a congenital condition. Another curious thing that he typed into his iPad: Encarnación had not once looked directly at him. His eyes were restless things, like caroming marbles, in constant motion.

"These days," Encarnación said, "no scrap of information, no matter how small or well hidden, is safe. All of it can be, and is, hacked. This is an indisputable fact. Every hour of every day, encrypted sites behind so-called firewalls are hacked. The latest and most devastating form of terrorism. To counteract these cybercrimes is something of a divine calling. This is my business. This is what I do." He paused to absorb everything in the office with his colorless eyes. He held his sunglasses between his thumb and forefinger, as if ready to don them at a moment's notice. "In the Internet age, this is how fortunes are made."

Thorne's mobile buzzed again. Ignoring it, he said, "Tell me, Mr. Encarnación, how you first became interested in Internet security."

Encarnación produced a thin smile that Thorne found horribly disquieting. "I lost everything, all the money I had made trading in equities online. My account was hacked, my hard-earned money stolen." That mysterious smile again, signifying an apocalypse, as if Thorne were looking into the face of a large, hungry carnivore. "It vanished into the colossal void of Russia."

"Ah, I see."

"No," Encarnación said, "you don't." He rocked his sunglasses back and forth. "I fought my desire to go to the place that swallowed my money, to find the person or people who had stolen what was mine, because I knew that if I went to Russia it would eat me alive."

Thorne pursed his lips as his mobile vibrated insistently for the third time. "What precisely do you mean?"

"I mean that if I had gone to Russia then, ignorant as I was, I would never have returned."

Thorne could not help a small chuckle. "That sounds a tad, oh, I don't know, melodramatic."

"Yes," Encarnación replied. "Yes, it does." The smile returned, insistent as the buzzing of Thorne's mobile. "And yet, it is the absolute truth. Have you been to Moscow, Mr. Thorne?"

Thorne did not want this to turn into an interrogation. "I have."

"Done business there?"

"Uh, no. But I've heard—"

"You've heard." Encarnación threw his words back into his face. "If you haven't *been* to Moscow, haven't engaged in business there, you have no idea." He shook his completely bald head, which Thorne could not now help thinking of as a skull. "Money, corruption, rotten politics, coercion. This is Moscow."

"I suppose you could say that about almost any big city."

Encarnación's gaze made Thorne feel small and, worse, weak. "Moscow is different. Special. This is why. Having money is not nearly enough. These people with whom you are forced to do business want more from you. Do you know what that something is, Mr. Thorne? They want to be able to shine in the eyes of the president. They curry his favor so badly, so absolutely, that if negotiations do not go the way they want, they will not hesitate to have you shot in the back of the head, or, if their need to be amused is such, to have you poisoned with plutonium long after you have left the rat's nest of Moscow behind."

"Plutonium poisoning christ almighty!" Thorne wrote on his iPad.

Encarnación did not blink an eye. "I decided then and there to find a way to retrieve my money. The authorities were worse than useless; in those days, they had even less knowledge about hacking the Internet than they do now."

Thorne felt as if he were in the presence of a reincarnated Baron Munchausen, the legendary teller of tall tales, except that he had the distinct impression that everything Encarnación was telling was the truth. "Then this is how SteelTrap came into being."

"That's correct."

"And that was..."

"Seven years ago."

"Did you ever recover your money?"

Encarnación's expression turned infernal. "With interest."

Thorne was about to ask for details when his mobile went off for the fourth time. He frowned, but at this point his curiosity overrode his annoyance. Excusing himself, he stepped out of the office as he pulled out his mobile. Four text messages from Delia Trane. He had met her several times. He'd had dinner with her and Soraya twice, and he'd been grateful that she had agreed to be their cover for the evening.

Call me ASAP

His frown deepened. One text from her he could ignore, not four. Scrolling through his phonebook, he pressed in her number, put his mobile to his ear. She answered on the first ring.

"Where are you?"

"Where d'you think I am?" His annoyance flared into renewed life. "Dammit, Delia, I'm in the middle of—"

"Soraya's in trouble."

At the mention of her name, he looked around the corridor. People were striding by. Minions who knew nothing about the impending FBI investigation. He went into the empty conference room.

"Charles?"

She never called him Charlie, as Soraya did. He closed the door behind him. He was in darkness.

"What kind of trouble?" He had his own troubles to worry about. The last thing he needed was—

"She's in the hospital."

His heart skipped a beat. "Hospital?" he parroted stupidly. "Why? What's the matter?"

"She was hurt in Paris. A concussion. Apparently, flying home made it worse."

"What? Delia, for the love of God—!"

"She has a subdural hematoma. Her brain is bleeding."

Thorne felt the sudden need to sit down.

"Charles?"

"How..." His voicebox seemed to have shut down. He cleared his throat violently, swallowed convulsively. "How bad is it?"

"Bad enough that they needed to do an emergency procedure."

"Is she...?" He couldn't say it.

"I don't know. I'm at the Virginia Hospital Center in Arlington, but she isn't out of surgery yet."

He found his thoughts drifting back to Maceo Encarnación, who even now was cooling his heels in his office, while Delia was further complicating his already overcomplicated life. He wanted to forgive her, but could not.

"They have to relieve pressure in her brain, stop

the bleeding," Delia was saying now. "The procedure is normally fairly straightforward, but in Soraya's case there's a complication."

Christ, there's more? he thought. "What...complication?"

"She's pregnant, Charles."

Thorne started as if jolted by a surge of electricity. "What?"

"She's carrying your child."

As Harry Rowland brought the fire tongs down toward the top of his head, Bourne raised an arm. His hand, grasping the fire tongs, redirected them down onto the intruder's shoulder. Immediately, Bourne kicked out, connected with the intruder's knee, then rolled away. Rowland struggled, refused to loosen his death grip on the fire tongs. Bourne connected with the point of his chin, snapping Rowland's head back, his teeth clacking together. But Rowland continued his grip on the impromptu weapon, and Bourne couldn't turn away. The intruder's leg swept out, connecting with Bourne's ankle, and he went down, pulling Rowland with him.

Rebeka figured she must have blacked out for a moment because when she roused herself, wiping blood off her face, she saw Bourne and Rowland tangled up with the Babylonian. Staggering to her feet, she ripped the tongs from Rowland's hand, grabbed him by the collar, and jerked him backward, away from the other two men.

"Idiot!" she spat. "What d'you think you're doing?"

He turned on her then and struck her soundly across the face. "You have no fucking idea what you've stepped into," he said.

Recovering, she hit back, but he blocked her, and, at the same time, used the heel of his hand in three percussive blows that brought her to her knees.

"It all comes down to this," he said as he bent over her. "I remember everything now. Everything, do you understand?"

She tried to get to her feet, but he wouldn't let her. With his memory, he seemed to have regained all his strength and cunning. He was once again the man she had been with in that hot and sweaty hotel room in Lebanon, the man with whom she had been in a kind of competition, part cat-and-mouse, part shell game.

He twisted her wrist back painfully. "In Dahr El Ahmar, you won. But here we'll have a different outcome."

With Rowland's distracting weight lifted off him, Bourne returned his attention to the intruder, who, he had concluded, must be the Babylonian. And not a moment too soon. The Babylonian had wrapped a powerful arm around his neck, twisting viciously in an attempt to snap it. Bourne, turning his body in the direction of the twist, bought himself several seconds, enough time to drive his elbow sharply into the Babylonian's kidney.

The Babylonian grunted, and Bourne, repeating

the devastating blow, snaked free of the hold, brought a rough stone ashtray he snatched off a table down onto the back of the Babylonian's head. Blood gushed, and the Babylonian fell onto his back. The shard of glass half-buried there snapped off.

Bourne, thinking him finished, began to stand up. That was when the Babylonian arched up, slamming his forehead into Bourne's. Dazed, Bourne went to his knees, and the Babylonian hauled him bodily toward the fire. The Babylonian's strength was incredible, even though he was bleeding profusely, even though the kidney blows would have incapacitated anyone else.

Bourne felt the intense heat of the flames on the top of his head. The Babylonian meant to feed him into the fire. He was only inches away, sliding along the floor, ever closer. He tried several different strikes, all of which the Babylonian brushed away as ineffectual. Sparks flew before his eyes, and he knew he had no time left.

Reaching over his head, he grasped one of the burning logs, and, unmindful of the pain, jabbed the burning end into the Babylonian's chest. Immediately, his clothes caught fire, the stench of charring material filling his nostrils.

Rolling away, Bourne was up and running. He saw Rebeka restraining Rowland in the kitchen. Pointing to the rear door, he ushered them through, out into the bitter nighttime cold, and into Rebeka's boat. While Bourne scooped up handfuls of snow to soothe the blistered skin of his palms, she dragged Rowland on board, then started the engine. Bourne cast off the lines, and they raced off in a spray of icy black water, vanishing into the gathering gloom.

I don't work for anyone," Peter said, lying smoothly. "At least, not permanently."

Brick stared at him. "You're freelance."

"Precisely."

They were in Brick's brand-new fire-red Audi A8. Peter was driving, taking the place of the late, unlamented Florin Popa. Brick had insisted on this arrangement so he could keep an eye on Peter, whom he still had little reason to trust. They had stopped at the pro shop so Peter could change back into his street clothes. He did this while Brick, leaning against the line of metal lockers, watched him like a pervert in a public restroom, even while he made a brief muffled call on his mobile.

Brick, in the shotgun seat, grunted now. "How do I know *you* weren't following Richards?"

"You don't." Peter was thinking as fast as he could.

"If not you, who followed Richards?" Brick asked, as Peter took back roads at his explicit direction. "Who killed my man?"

"Peter Marks. He works for the same outfit Richards does."

"He suspected Richards?"

Peter nodded, making a right, then an almost immediate left. They were heading away from Arlington, deeper into the Virginia countryside, leaving the manicured lawns and multi-million-dollar housing enclaves behind, driving into wilder terrain. Rolling hills, dense forests, damp glens stretched out before them.

"The next step," Peter said, "is to take revenge. Otherwise, this organization, having followed Richards to you, will never let you out of its sight."

"You can't be serious."

"But I am. You want to know what I was doing at Blackfriar? Okay. I was keeping an eye on you." Noting the tensing reaction throughout Brick's entire body, he said, "I was keeping an eye on you because I want to work for you. I'm tired of being on my own, with no job security, nothing to fall back on."

"Times are tough," Brick mused.

"And getting tougher."

Brick seemed to consider this seriously. Then he said abruptly, "Pull over."

Peter did as he was ordered, rolling the Audi up onto the grass that edged the two-lane blacktop and putting the transmission in neutral.

The moment the Audi came to rest, Brick snapped his fingers. "Your wallet."

Peter reached into an inner pocket.

"Careful, mate."

Peter froze with his coat half-open. "You do it then."

Brick's eyes met his in an icy glare. "Go the fuck ahead."

Using just his thumb and forefinger, Peter carefully extracted the second wallet that was in plain sight in front of the concealed pocket where his real one lay. He handed it over.

Brick allowed it to sit in the open palm of his left

hand. With his right, he peeled back the fold. Only then did his gaze drop to read the driver's license revealed. "Anthony Dzundza." The icy eyes flicked up again. "What the fuck kind of name is that, mate?"

"Ukrainian." Legends always felt it was more realistic to use a name that required an explanation. They were right.

Brick's eyes turned to slits. "You don't look Ukrainian, old son."

"My mother's a beauty from Amsterdam."

Brick grunted again. "Don't fucking flatter yourself. You're not that pretty." Reassured, he pawed through the rest of the docs in the wallet—credit cards, a bank debit card, museum membership cards, even, amusingly, an unpaid speeding ticket. Then he handed it back.

"You prefer Anthony or Tony?"

Peter shrugged. "Depends on friend or foe."

Brick laughed. "Okay, Tony, get out. I'll drop you off. You meet me at the club tomorrow at one."

"Then what?"

"Then," Brick said, his face dead serious, "we'll see what you're all about."

After Thorne apologized to the man known to the world as Maceo Encarnación, hurrying out of the *Politics As Usual* offices, Encarnación gathered up his greatcoat, and strolled to the bank of elevators.

While he waited, he allowed his practiced eye to observe the orderly pace of the workplace, the concentrated faces, the purposeful strides, the pride puffing out chests. Above all, the sense of superiority and security that, he knew full well, would shatter into ten thousand pieces in the face of the chaos that was about to hurl itself full-tilt at everyone employed here.

The sense of chaos put him in mind of Moscow—the end of the story he had begun before the interview with Charles Thorne was aborted, the end Thorne would never know. Using the algorithms he and his crew had so cleverly and painstakingly devised, he had tracked down the criminals who had hacked his online account and sucked his money into the scarifying Russian underworld. After having thoroughly prepared himself, he had spent precisely three days in Moscow. By the time he had flown out, two corpses, weighed down with their own weaponry, were lying at the bottom of the Moskva River, eyes wide and staring in disbelief. As for the money, Encarnación had repatriated his *and* retrieved theirs the same way they had robbed him.

When the gleaming chrome elevator doors opened, he stepped in, placing himself next to a blonde with long legs and impressive hips. He'd always been a sucker for impressive hips and butt.

"Good afternoon," he said, basking in the incandescent glow of her wide smile.

There was frantic movement in the fisherman's cottage in Sadelöga as the Babylonian fought to strip off his clothes and minimize the damage the flames were wreaking on him. Stumbling and grimacing, he made his way to the single bathroom, turned on the shower's cold water tap, and hurled himself beneath the spray. At once, he was engulfed in a cloud of smoke, making him choke. Better than having his skin flayed off. Soon enough the smoke turned to steam.

The flames extinguished, he stripped off the remnants of charred underwear, and stepped out of the shower. His body was as lean and long-armed as that of a long-distance swimmer, all rippling muscle, hard and compact beneath taut, sun-burnished skin.

He dared not use a towel on the burns that covered much of his chest, neck, and hands. He used the mirror over the sink to check out the glass shard in his back. It took him a moment because his eyes were watering so profusely. He thought his body would retain scars, especially his neck, but he was too well trained to dwell on that. Instead, he got down to the business at hand, scrutinizing his wound with a surgical precision and thoroughness.

Even though the end of the shard had broken off when he fell on it, there was enough still visible for him to pull it out. Bracing himself against the edge of the sink and looking over his shoulder into his image in the mirror, he grasped the shard just beneath the jagged edge. He took a deep breath and let it out slowly and completely. At that instant, he pulled hard, and the shard slid free. The wound began to drool blood, but it was clean and he knew it would soon stop.

Dripping water, still pink with his blood, he returned to the kitchen, opened the back door, and, naked, threw himself facedown into the snow. The cold, he knew, would help minimize the swelling as well as numb the pain. When he'd had enough, he turned on his back, numbing the wound there.

After a few more minutes, he picked himself up and, returning inside, rummaged in the kitchen cupboards until he found a package of baking soda. Shaking out the powder into a bowl he took down from a shelf, he mixed it with water, stirring it into the consistency of a thick paste. Then, breath hissing through clenched teeth, he began to daub this poultice on his burns until they were completely covered in a thick salve that would both protect and begin to heal his wounds.

In the bathroom, he found a full tube of antibacterial cream, plus the remnants of the powerful prescription antibiotics Rebeka had left behind. On the tube's label were typed both her name and an address in Stockholm. The pain was already fading, the baking soda drawing it out of him. In a while, he'd throw himself into the snow again.

He guzzled down two antibiotic tablets with a beer he found in the refrigerator. Pulling his knife from between the floorboards, he paced back and forth with the silent, ferocious, cruel mind-set of a tiger until he felt his full strength flooding back.

Looking again at the label on the vial of antibiotics, he could not help but smile. Her address in Stockholm. He'd be on them again, and this time, he vowed, they'd all die.

10

"DO YOU LIKE films?" Don Fernando asked over breakfast coffee and croissants at Le Fleur en Ile.

"Of course I like films," Martha Christiana replied. "Who doesn't?"

After dinner the night before they had agreed to meet again this morning. He had not invited her back to his apartment after dinner. He wondered whether she had been disappointed.

"I mean old films. Classics."

"Even better." She sipped her coffee, served in a huge, thick cup. Outside the plate-glass windows, the magnificent rounded rear of Notre Dame rose, majestic and delicate, flying buttresses spreading like multiple wings. "But many old films aren't the classics they're reported to be. Have you seen *Don't Look Now*? When it isn't being preposterous, it's incomprehensible."

"I was thinking of Luis Buñuel's *The Exterminating Angel*."

She shook her head. Her eyes were bright in the spark of morning light. "Never saw it."

When he'd told her the synopsis, she said, "So everyone in this house is trapped, just as we ourselves are by our lives. They argue, fight, make love, grow weary and bored. Some die." She snorted. "That isn't art, it's existence!"

"True enough."

"I thought Buñuel was a surrealist."

"Actually, he was a satirist."

"Frankly, I don't see anything in the least bit amusing in the film."

Don Fernando didn't either, but that was beside the point. He had thought of the film because Martha Christiana was an exterminating angel. He knew who and what she was. He had been in the company of women of her ilk. More than likely, he would be again. If he survived her.

He knew without a shadow of a doubt that she was a sinister emissary. Nicodemo had commissioned her. This fact heartened him. He was getting close. It meant he had stirred this particular level of hell sufficiently that she had been dispatched to usher him to his death.

Smiling at his exterminating angel, he said, "The first time I saw the film I was sitting next to Salvador Dalí."

"Really?" She cocked her head. She wore a Chanel rayon suit the color of breaking dawn over a butter-yellow shantung-silk blouse, open at the throat. "What was that like?"

"All I could see were his damnable mustaches."

Her laugh was as soft and buttery as her blouse. "Did he say anything at all?"

"Dalí never said anything that wasn't for shock effect. Not in public, anyway."

Her hand crossed an invisible barrier, her fingers taking his. "You've led such a fascinating life."

He shrugged. "More than some, I suppose. Less than others."

The slanted sunlight, caught in her eyes, made them glitter like hand-cut gems. "I'd like to know you better, Don Fernando. Much better."

He allowed his smile to widen. She was good, he thought. Better than most. But he would scarcely expect anything less from Nicodemo.

"I'd like that," he replied. "More than you know."

Delia was waiting for Charles Thorne at Admitting. She had been watching people come and go through the imposing front entrance of the Virginia Hospital Center for ten minutes. She was sipping very bad coffee she had unadvisedly purchased from a vending machine on the same floor where Soraya was still in surgery.

Delia had met Soraya nine years ago, when Soraya was still working for the late Martin Lindros at CI. At that time, Delia was alone, unsure of who she was, let alone what her sexual orientation might be, which was the one area of life that frightened her. For a time, she had thought she was asexual. Soraya had changed all that.

Delia had been sent into the field to disarm a

bomb that had been found in the vicinity of the Supreme Court building. Soraya was there along with several FBI agents in an attempt to determine who had set the device and whether he was a foreign or homegrown terrorist. Either possibility was frightening.

The bomb's mechanism proved to be difficult to neutralize, which pointed to a professional terrorist. Everyone, save Soraya, had backed away to a safe distance while Delia worked on defusing it.

"You ought to get clear of here," Delia remembered saying.

"No one ought to be alone," Soraya answered her.

"If I fail, if this thing goes off—"

Soraya had engaged her eyes for the briefest moment. "Especially at the end." Then she had produced the most disarming grin. "But you won't fail."

Thorne, striding into Admitting, rudely shattered her reverie. Recognizing the anxious expression on his face as he came up to her, she said, "She had the procedure and passed a quiet night. That's all I know."

As he followed her down a linoleum-floored corridor to the bank of oversized elevators, he said, "What you told me over the phone."

"All true," she said, intuiting his meaning.

"There can be no doubt?"

His eyes were clouded, with what emotions she could not yet say.

"How many men d'you think she was sleeping with, Charles?" She shot him an angry look. "But, really, your attention should be focused on her."

"Yes, of course. I know that," he said distractedly.

The elevator doors opened, allowing people to exit. They stepped in, and Delia pressed the button for the third floor. They rode up in silence. The elevator car smelled of disinfectant, sickly-sweet disease, and the slow secretions of the aged.

As they stepped out onto the third floor, Delia said, "I have to warn you that Secretary Hendricks is here."

"Shit. How am I going to explain my presence?"

"I've thought of that," Delia said. "Leave it to me."

She led him down the hushed corridor, at the end of which was the metal door that opened onto the operating wing.

Thorne inclined his head. "That's where it happened?"

Delia nodded.

Thorne licked his lips, his anxiety living on his face. "And she's not awake yet? That can't be good."

"Don't be negative," Delia said, clearly annoyed. "The procedure's delicate. She's being carefully monitored."

"But what if she—?"

"Keep quiet!" she said, as they passed the secretary's bodyguard and entered the recovery waiting room.

Hendricks was in the corner farthest from the flat-screen TV, on which CNN was streaming soundlessly. He was on his mobile, scribbling notes on a small pad perched on one knee. He scarcely looked up when they came in. Delia stared at the oily film that had developed on her coffee and, disgusted, threw it into the trash can.

Before either of them could sit down, Hendricks finished his call and, looking up, recognized Thorne and did a classic double take.

As he rose and came over to them, Delia said, "Anything?"

He shook his head. Then he turned his attention to the man beside her.

"Charles Thorne?"

"Guilty," Thorne acknowledged, before realizing what, in the coming days and weeks, that could mean.

The two men pumped hands briefly.

"I must admit," Hendricks said, "to a certain amount of confusion regarding your presence here."

Delia kept a smile on her face. "The three of us are friends. I ran into him this morning and he insisted on coming with me."

"That's good of you," Hendricks said distractedly. "She can use the support."

"I don't want Soraya to be alone when she wakes up," Delia said.

And right on cue, one of her surgical team appeared in the waiting room. Looking from one to the other, he said, "I have news."

Tom Brick, with Peter beside him, drove the red Audi south, deeper into the Virginia countryside. The sky was filled with troubling clouds; yesterday's sun was only a memory. At length, Brick turned onto Ridgeway Drive, a bent finger that passed through dense copses of trees through which, now and again, could be seen the rooflines of large houses. Around one last bend to the left, Ridgeway came to an end at a circle off which were four houses separated by deep woods.

Brick took the right-hand driveway, graveled and well-kept. Stands of evergreens rose up on either side, so that at the dogleg left, the road vanished as if it had never existed. They were in a world of their own, cut off from everyone and everything.

Rolling the Audi to a stop, Brick got out and stretched. Peter followed him, surveying the house, which was large, stately, built as sturdily as a castle of brick and quarried stone. Architecturally, it fell neatly into the post-modern style: two stories with deep eaves, oversized windows, and a sun-splashed cantilevered deck.

Brick trotted up the front steps and, from the deep shadows of the eaves, said, "Coming, Tony?"

Peter, conscious that he was now Anthony Dzundza, nodded and went up the steps. Inside, the ground floor was light-filled and spacious. The furniture was low, sleek, modern—pale as bones stripped of flesh.

"Would you like a drink, Tony?"

Peter reminded himself why he was here. Tom Brick was the person to whom Dick Richards had run when Soraya had told him that she had it on good authority that Nicodemo was connected with Core Energy.

"*Where did you hear that?*" Richards had said. "*Tom Brick is CEO of Core Energy.*"

And here Peter—or, rather, Anthony Dzundza—was with Brick. Both Peter and Soraya had been certain that Richards would bolt to the president, to whom they assumed he reported. But no, it was to Tom Brick he had run. What in hell was going on? Was Richards a triple agent, working for the president *and* Brick?

The living room was L-shaped. Peter followed Brick around to the left as he headed toward the wet bar, but then he pulled up short. There at the short end of the L was a man standing with his legs slightly spread. His jacket was off, so Peter had a clear view of the Glock snug in its holster beneath his left armpit.

"Tony, say cheers to Bogdan."

Peter said nothing. His tongue seemed to have cleaved to the roof of his mouth. The scowling Bogdan was standing beside a plain wooden slat-back chair, incongruous in this maximally designed house. A man, his back to Peter, sat strapped and bound to it.

Brick, at the bar, said without turning around, "As they say in the movies, choose your poison."

Peter did not have to see his face to know that the imprisoned man was Dick Richards.

Not hearing an answer, Brick turned, an old-fashioned glass in one hand. "I'm having an Irish whiskey. I'll make two."

Peter, desperately trying to make sense of the scene, stood his ground while Brick poured the drinks, brought them over, and handed him one.

He clicked his glass against Peter's, then drank. "*Cent' anni*, as they say in the Mafia." He laughed. Then, seeing the direction in which Peter was looking, he gestured with his drink. "Come. I want to show you something."

Reluctantly, Peter followed him over to where Richards and Bogdan, his forbidding guard, were situated out of the line of sight of any of the windows. As if anyone would be poking around way out here. Anyone apart from Peter himself, that is.

"You said you want to work for me." Brick's voice assumed a warm, collegial tone, two men chatting at their club or on the golf links. "That's a tall order. I'm quite careful whom I hire, and never off the street. And, you see, that's my dilemma, Tony. Much as I'm grateful for the information you've provided, you're off the street."

Brick took another small swallow of the whiskey, rolling it around his mouth before he swallowed. Then he smiled amiably. "But I like you. I admire your style, so I'll tell you what I'm going to do." Slipping the Glock from Bogdan's holster, he held it out butt first to Peter. "You advocated doing away with Peter Marks, Dick's boss. While I admire your initiative, I don't think it would be wise to go after a man like that. We don't want to bring down a shitstorm, do we?" He waggled the Glock invitingly, and reluctantly Peter took it. "No, I believe a far better choice is to nip matters in the bud, take them to the cleaners—isn't that how you Americans say it?—the man who knows too much. That's the brill move. So here he is, mate, waiting for the proverbial axe to fall." Grinning, he nudged Peter forward. "We don't want to disappoint him, now do we?"

A line of pink was taking its time showing itself above the eastern horizon as they approached Stockholm.

They had made the crossing to the mainland in a minimum of light, but Bourne, having navigated the bay with Christien, guided them unfailingly to the car he had brought Rowland down in. They had bundled Rowland into the backseat, Rebeka sliding in beside him, while Bourne climbed behind the wheel.

Now, hours later, as they approached the city, Bourne exited the highway, turning left at the end of the off-ramp, and rolling through sleeping streets, eventually pulling up beside an empty lot, due for new construction. It was enclosed by a drunken chain-link fence that had seen better days.

Turning in his seat, Bourne said, "Get him out of here."

Rebeka appeared about to query him, then thought better of it. Instead, she opened the curbside door and hauled Rowland out into the pre-dawn light. Bourne shut off the engine, got out, and, coming around the front of the car, took Rowland by the collar and frog-marched him to a waist-high gap in the fence.

"Bourne," Rebeka said, "what are you going to do?"

Pressing his hand to the top of Rowland's head, Bourne guided him through the gap, then stepped through himself. As he did so, Rowland made a break for it. Bourne went after him. Owing to his two frozen toes, Rowland ran at a spastic, lurching pace, so Bourne caught up to him without difficulty. He slammed him on the back of his head, and Rowland collapsed to his knees, where he remained, his upper torso rocking back and forth as if he had lost all sense of equilibrium.

Rebeka came up to them. "Bourne, don't hurt him. Now that he's regained his memory, we need what's in his head."

"He's not going to tell us a damn thing." He slammed the back of Rowland's head a second time. "Are you, Rowland?" Rowland shook his head, and Bourne struck him a massive blow between the shoulder blades. With an animal grunt, he fell into the snow-covered dirt. Bourne reached down and hauled him back to his penitent kneeling position.

Alarmed, Rebeka said, "Bourne, what are you going to do?"

"Shut up." Bourne was filled with a murderous rage, not only because this man had tried to kill him, had, judging by his actions in the fisherman's cottage, been sent to kill him, but because he had regained his memory. Bourne had not. In all the years since being pitched into the Mediterranean, he still knew next to nothing about his previous life. It was true enough that he had managed to slot himself into the Bourne identity— he *was* Jason Bourne now—but he was still a man without a past, without a home, without any place to call his own. He floated in the air, unmoored, ungrounded, forever searching for—he didn't even know what he was searching for. But this man—who, if Rebeka was to be believed, had been sent by *Jihad bis saif* to kill him— had regained everything he had lost when Rebeka's shot had grazed his head, pitching him into Hemviken Bay. He struck Rowland again. Justice! And again. He wanted justice!

"Bourne . . . Bourne, for God's sake!"

Rebeka, both her hands wrapped around his right forearm, stopped him from a third blow.

He kicked Rowland in the kidney, and felt a measure of satisfaction as he crumpled over onto his side.

Then the acute rage subsided, and he allowed Rebeka to interpose herself. With a glare, she crouched down and began to help Rowland to his feet. This Bourne could not tolerate, and he struck the back of Rowland's knee so that he once more fell to his knees. Leaving him there, she rose to her feet and confronted Bourne.

"He was sent to kill me," Bourne said before she had a chance to speak.

"One of many, yes?" She sought to hold his eyes with her own, then she shook her head again. "Don't for a moment think I don't know what's really going on."

"I don't know what you're talking about," he said dully. He felt spent and, worse, empty.

"Let's pretend you do." She took a step toward him, lowering her voice. "What use will beating him to a pulp do? It's counterproductive," she added, answering her own question. Then, as if uncertain whether she had gotten through to him, she repeated: "It's counterproductive."

His eyes cleared, and he nodded. She smiled tentatively. "Now, let's go at him. Together, maybe we can achieve what each of us alone has failed to do."

They went around, crouching down in front of Harry Rowland, who looked at them blearily out of red-rimmed eyes.

"I know you work for *Jihad bis saif*," Rebeka

said, not yet trusting Bourne to begin this stage of the interrogation on the proper note. "Now, by your own actions, we know you were sent to kill Bourne."

"What we don't know," Bourne said, taking his cue from her, "is why."

Rowland's head swayed a little from side to side. He licked his lips, which were coated with dried blood. "Why does anyone want to kill you, Bourne?"

"You're a threat to this network," Rebeka said to Bourne. She turned back to Rowland. "Why?"

His bloodshot eyes stared at her. "You did this to me. I was besotted with you. Those nights in Dahr El Ahmar, you made me forget my mission." He cocked his head to one side. "How did you do that? I don't understand. What magic did you work?"

"This is what we do, Harry." Rebeka put a hand gently on his thigh. "The charade worked both ways. You fooled me. I had no idea you were a member of *Jihad bis saif*. Until the end."

He licked his lips again. He could not take his eyes off her. "What happened? I was so careful. What gave me away?"

Her fingers moved on his thigh. She had seized on the pleading tone in his voice. "Tell me why Bourne is a threat to *Jihad bis saif*."

"*Jihad bis saif*," he repeated with a sneer. "You don't know the first thing about *Jihad bis saif*." Curiously, he was almost laughing.

"Then enlighten us," Bourne said in Arabic, then Pashto. When Rowland didn't respond, Bourne shook his head. "There is no *Jihad bis saif*, is there?"

"Oh, but there is."

A hinted-at smile of self-satisfaction was wiped off Rowland's face by Bourne's fist as it connected with his cheek. A squeak came from him as his head snapped back on his neck. Bourne caught him before he could fully tumble over. He slapped Rowland until his eyes came back into focus.

"I guess I don't believe you." He gripped Rowland's jaw hard. "Let's put an end to this. Tell us what you know or—"

At that moment, a helicopter appeared over the rooftops, arcing across the sky.

"Cops?" Rebeka said, squinting up into the oyster-colored dawn.

"No insignias." Bourne rose, jerked Rowland onto his feet.

The copter came swinging in toward them. Clearly, it was homing in on them.

"We'd best find cover," Bourne said. But before they could move, the copter was overhead. The chattering of machine-gun fire ripped up the dirty snow. Chips of ice and clots of freshly turned earth flew in all directions. Bourne tried to pull Rowland along with them, but the fire, meant to separate them, was too intense. The men inside the copter left them no choice. He and Rebeka ran toward a stack of piled-up brick and stone from the razed building.

Bourne made one last attempt to reach Rowland, but the withering fire drove him back. The copter was moving, but instead of rising, it shot forward. The firing began again, this time clearly directed at Bourne. He dived under the cover of some wooden boards, which immediately began to splinter apart.

He rolled, snaking away from where Rebeka had hidden, conscious of keeping the bullets away from her even while he sought to protect himself. Since it had explicitly targeted him, it was clear the copter belonged to Rowland's network, that those inside had recognized him.

The copter stopped, hovering twenty feet off the ground. A door slid open and a rope ladder extended from it. Rowland was up and was running unsteadily toward it. As Bourne wriggled under more boards, Rowland grasped a rung.

Men inside the copter winched up the ladder, grabbing hold of Rowland as soon as he was within arm's reach. The copter now closed with the area where Bourne was hiding. The firing continued in brief but ferocious bursts. The boards kept flying apart, making it necessary for him to move again and thus expose himself.

The gunfire continued to track him, moving closer and closer. That was when Bourne heard the sirens. Someone had called the cops. He saw the flashing lights as a string of police vehicles rounded a corner and raced down the street toward the lot.

The men in the copter saw them too. With a last burst of gunfire at the place where Bourne had been moments before, the copter rose, banked, and, as the sirens wailed ever louder, vanished into the rising sun.

11

"Ms. MOORE IS out of surgery and in recovery," the doctor said.

There was a collective sigh of relief in the waiting room.

"Is she okay?" Secretary Hendricks said.

"We relieved the pressure and stopped the bleeding. We'll know more in the next twenty-four hours."

"What the hell does that mean?" Thorne blurted.

Delia quickly placed herself between him and the surgeon. "How is the fetus?"

"We're monitoring it. We're hopeful." The surgeon was pale. He looked wiped out. "But, again, the next number of hours are critical for both mother and child."

Delia took a breath and let it out. "So you can't rule out . . . intervention."

"At this point," the surgeon said, "nothing should

be ruled out." He looked at them. "When she wakes up, I think it would help if she saw a friendly face."

Hendricks stepped forward. "I should—"

"With all due respect," Delia said, "if she sees you, the first thing she'll think of is Peter, and he's not here, is he?"

"No." Hendricks turned to the doctor. "I would like very much to see her, if you don't mind."

The surgeon nodded. He was clearly uncertain, but cowed by Hendricks's position. "But only for a moment, Mr. Secretary."

I'm so sorry," Hendricks said, bent over Soraya's supine form. "I fear I've asked far too much of you."

Her huge, dark eyes regarded him woozily, running in and out of focus, and she mouthed two words: *My job.*

He smiled, brushing damp hair off her forehead. There was a tube running out of the side of her head, surrounded by bandages. She was hooked up to multiple machines monitoring her heart rate, pulse, and blood pressure. She looked weak, a pallor beneath her skin, but otherwise sound enough.

"Your job is one thing," Hendricks said. "But *this*—what has come about because of it, is quite another."

Beneath the ebbing torpor of the anaesthesia, her eyes showed surprise. "You know."

He nodded. "The doctors said not to worry. The baby's fine."

A tear welled out of her eye, rolling down her cheek.

"Soraya, I forced you to cross a line with Charles Thorne that should never be crossed."

"I did," she whispered, her voice paper-thin. "*I* did."

He shook his head, his expression genuinely sorrowful. "Soraya. I—"

"No regrets," she said, just before the surgeon came in and ordered an end to the interview.

At almost the very moment Hendricks returned to the waiting room, his mobile buzzed. He glanced down. "Ah, well. The president needs me."

"How is she?" Delia's anxiety was written all over her face.

"Weak, but she seems okay." He looked around for his coat, but his bodyguard, stepping into the room, handed it to him. "Listen, you have my mobile number. Keep me posted."

"Absolutely."

"Well." He shrugged on his coat. "I'm deeply relieved."

As it had been doing all morning, Delia's mind flashed back to her first meeting with Soraya. After the bomb had been defused and it had been delivered to a joint forensics team, the two women had returned to their respective offices. But late in the day, Delia's phone had rung. Soraya asked if she would join her for a drink.

They met in a dim, smoky bar that smelled of beer and bourbon.

Soraya took her hand. "I never saw anything like that." She looked up at Delia's face. 'You've got the fingers of an artist."

Delia was dumbstruck. The instant Soraya took her hand, she felt a tingling that ran all the way up her arm. It entered her torso, and where it ended up made her realize that she wasn't asexual after all. She could barely recall what they talked about as they drank, but as they moved to the restaurant next door, and the conversation turned to their backgrounds, Delia's mind snapped back into focus. Both she and Soraya viewed themselves as outsiders: They didn't hang in groups, they weren't joiners, even though the fast track in any meaningful job in DC required joining as many clubs as possible.

"We all are," Delia said now to Secretary Hendricks, though she was acutely aware that the stab of fear she had experienced when Hendricks had called her had not fully dissipated.

Silence, though somewhere a dog barked. Stasis, though somewhere a car started up.

"Well?"

Peter felt Brick's gaze descend on him like a hammer blow.

"Act!"

Peter took Dick Richards's chin in his hand, tilting his head up so that their eyes met. "Yes, it's true—I want a position at your company." Deep in Richards's eyes he could see that the other had been listening closely to every word that had been spoken in his presence. He knew that Tom Brick knew Peter as Tony. If he had any sense at all, he'd know that Peter was undercover. But Peter was looking into the eyes of a presumed triple agent. Deep down, whose side did Dick Richards want to be on? He supposed it was time to find out.

He let go of Richards's chin and, snapping free the Glock's cartridge, found it to be empty. He checked the chamber: one bullet. Had he been expected to kill Richards with a single shot?

Looking up into Brick's interested face, he said, "You've ordered me to act." Turning the handgun around, he returned it to Bogdan, who seemed to be sunk deep into a sulk, possibly because he had been denied the prospect of physical mayhem. Like a retriever who needed daily running, this guy seemed like he required a daily dose of destruction.

Peter turned to Tom Brick, who stared at him for a moment. Suddenly, Brick broke out into a fit of laughter and, going into a deep cockney accent, said, "Crikey Moses, gov, you've got some pair a cobbler's awls, you 'ave."

Peter blinked. "What?"

"Cobbler's awls. Balls," Bogdan said unexpectedly. "Cockneys're always street-rhyming. It's in their nature."

Brick pointed to Richards. "Bogs, untie the little

bugger, yeah?" reverting to his normal refined accent. "Then have a bit of a dekko outside, make sure we're comfy, cozy, and all on our onlys, there's a good lad."

Richards sat still as a statue as Bogdan untied him, kept sitting still as a statue as the hulking bodyguard loaded his Glock's magazine and snapped it into place. It was only when Bogdan stalked out of the room and he heard the front door slam that he slowly rose. He was as unsteady as a newborn colt.

Seeing this, Brick crossed to the bar, poured him a stiff whiskey. "Ice, yeah?"

"Right, yeah." Richards looked not at him, but at Peter. There was a kind of pleading in his eyes, a silent apology.

Peter, his back to Brick, mouthed: *Trust me.* To his immense relief, Richards gave a tiny nod. Did that mean he could trust Richards? Far too early to say. But his expression was confirmation of Peter's suspicion. Richards was, in fact, a double agent, reporting both to the president and to Brick. Peter fought back an urge to wring his scrawny neck. He needed answers. Why was Richards playing this dangerous game? What did Brick hope to gain?

Brick returned, handed Richards the whiskey, and said cheerily, "Bottoms up, lad!"

Turning to Peter, he said, "You know, I never would have let you put a bullet through Dick's head." At this, Richards nearly choked on his whiskey. "Nah, the little bugger's far too valuable." He eyed Peter. "Know as what?"

Peter put an interested look on his face.

"He's a stone-cold wizard at creating and cracking ciphers. Isn't that right, Dick?"

Richards, eyes watering, nodded.

"That what he does for Core Energy?" Peter said. "Crack codes?"

"There's a shitload of corporate spying, and at our level, it's bloody serious, let me tell you." Brick took another delicate sip of the Irish, which was first-rate. "We're in need of a bugger with his skills." He slapped Richards on the back. "Rare as hen's teeth, lads like him are."

Richards managed a watery smile.

"So, Anthony Dzundza, meet Richard Richards."

The two men shook hands solemnly.

He gestured. "Righto, let's get this little chin-wag started."

As they were making their way to the low, angular sofas around the bend in the L, Bogdan returned from his dekko—his recon. He nodded to Brick, who from then on completely ignored him.

"I'd like an apology," Richards said as the other two men sat down.

"Don't be a wanker." Brick waved a hand. "It's so bloody tiresome."

Richards, however, remained standing, fists clenched at his sides, glaring at his boss, or, Peter thought, one of them, anyway.

Brick snorted finally. "Oh, for fuck's sake." He turned to Peter in a theatrical stage aside. "What I won't do to keep the staff happy."

Turning back, he smiled up at Richards. "Sorry you had to undergo the Bogs Method, old thing, but I had to put Tony's feet to the fire, as it were. All in a day's work."

"Not *my* work, dammit!"

"Now you *are* being tiresome." He sighed. "There'll be a bit extra in your monthly stipend, how's that for compo?"

Richards did not reply, simply sat down as far away from the other two men as he dared.

"You know, it's a curious thing," Brick began, "but Dick has never disappointed me. Not once. That's a serious achievement." Now he looked directly into Peter's eyes. "Something for you to ponder, Tony; something for you to strive for." He smiled. "Everyone needs a goal."

"I'm self-motivated, Tom."

Brick scowled deeply. "No one calls me Tom."

Peter said nothing. There ensued a silence, increasingly uncomfortable as it drew out.

At length, Peter said, "I don't apologize unless I've made a mistake."

"That was a mistake."

"Only after the ground rules are set."

Brick stared at him. "Shall we take them out and measure them?"

"I already know who'd win."

This comment, meant to provoke, instead made Brick laugh. He shook a forefinger in Peter's direction. "Now I know the reason I liked you from the get-go." He paused for a moment, staring up at the high ceiling as if contemplating the infinite mystery of the stars in the night sky. When he looked at them again, his expression was altogether different. The British jokester was nowhere to be seen.

"Times have changed," he began. "Well, times are always changing, but now they change to our advantage. Events have taken on an iron-fisted certainty; there is no longer the will for compromise. In other words, society is made of tigers and lambs, so to speak. This has always been true, I suppose, but the change that moves in our favor is that the tigers are all weak. In times past, these tigers were vindictive—this was always true. You merely have to take a peek at mankind's history of wars to understand that. Yet now, the tigers are both vindictive and obstinate. All of them have dug in their heels. Good for us. Their pigheadedness has made them brittle, easy to manipulate, to discredit. Which leaves all society's sheep leaderless in the meadow, ready to be sheared." He grinned. "By us."

Good Lord, Peter thought, *what have I stumbled into?* Masking his face in a bland expression, he said, "How will that work, precisely? The shearing, I mean?"

"Let's not put the shears before the barber, old thing. We need to get ourselves in position first."

Peter nodded. "All right. I understand perfectly. But who do you mean by 'we'?"

The moment the question was out of his mouth he knew it was a mistake.

"Why do you ask?" Brick came forward on the

sofa like a predator who scents his prey. He became tense and wary. Peter knew he had to do something to defuse his sudden suspicion.

"I'm accustomed to knowing who I work for."

"You work for me."

"Core Energy."

"You will have an official position in the company, yes, of course."

"But I won't work there."

"Why would you?" Brick spread his hands. "Do you know anything about energy?" He waved his hand, erasing his own words. "Never mind, that isn't what I'm hiring you for."

"I assume that's not why you hired Richards here, either."

Brick smiled. "Keep up that unbridled insolence of yours, my son, and guaranteed you'll come a cropper." All at once, his voice softened. "Let me ask you a question, Tony. If you do your job right, it's the only question I'll ever ask you: Do the ends justify the means?"

"Sometimes," Peter said. "People who see the world as black or white are wrong. Life is a continuum of grays, each shade with its own set of rules and conditions."

Brick tapped his forefinger against his lips. "I like that, old thing. No one has put it quite that way. But, no matter. Here, where we are now, you're wrong. Here there are no ends, only means. We ask for—we demand—results. If one mean doesn't produce the desired result, we move on to another. Do you understand? There are no ends here; only means."

"Philosophy is all well and good," Peter said, "but it's not helping me understand what we're doing."

"An example is required." Brick lifted a finger. "All right, then. Let's take the recent earthquake and tsunami in Japan, which led the country to shut down four reactors crucial for electricity. For months now Tokyo and other major cities have had to ration their electricity needs. Even in Tokyo's main office buildings, the headquarters of its most prestigious corporations, the air-conditioning has to be set at eighty degrees. Do you know what it's like to work in eighty-degree temperature? In a suit and tie? Dress codes have had to be relaxed, a Japanese cultural taboo, fetishistic to an extreme, obliterated. Now the country is faced with having to revert to more expensive and environmentally polluting fossil fuels for its electricity needs. The alternative is sitting immobile in the dark. Full-on economic disaster. Then here we come and provide a cheaper energy alternative. What can the Japanese government say but yes? They fairly leaped at our offer.

"As I say, this is an example, but an instructive one nonetheless. Core Energy will now provide an affordable, reliably constant energy flow."

"Okay, I get that," Peter said. "But you're taking advantage of a fluke of nature, a one-off event no one could have foreseen."

"It would seem that way, wouldn't it?" A slow

smile spread across Brick's face. "But the fact is, the natural order of things isn't what caused the core meltdowns. It was human error. The reactors were twelve years old. Their emergency core cooling systems still relied on electricity, rather than the updated versions that use gravity to inundate the cores with water to cool the rods even when electricity isn't available."

Peter shook his head. "I'm not certain I understand."

"It is to our advantage to make use of human greed, old son. Nuclear inspectors and key company officials were given, um, incentives, to look the other way."

It took a moment or two for Peter to get his head around the enormity of what Brick was telling him. When the truth did hit him, he felt dizzy, sick to his stomach. "Are you...?" For an agitated moment he couldn't form the words. "Are you telling me that Core Energy was the cause of the disaster?"

"Well, I wouldn't go that far," Brick said. "But we certainly did our part to help matters along. And while it's true that France, for instance, gets eighty percent of its electricity from its nuclear reactors, and we haven't yet discovered a way to incapacitate them as we did in Japan, the country—in fact, all of Europe—gets its essential natural gas via a pipeline that originates in Russia. Now what do you suppose would happen if that pipeline were to shut down or if sections were blown to bits? What would happen if the carefully fomented so-called Arab Spring uprisings caused the blockade of the Suez Canal or the Gulf of Aqaba? Disaster or opportunity, you see what I'm getting at? Every other company in the world seeks to control supply. We, however, strive to control demand. This is how we occupy the center of the board."

The shock must have shown on Peter's face, because Brick said, "Oh, no one at Core Energy can be linked, if that's what's worrying you. There is a—what would be the term?—a black ops division that handles such matters, creating need—the opportunities necessary for Core Energy to expand its business. This is where you fit in, old thing. Why do you think I hired you?"

From his hidey-hole beneath the pile of half-splintered wood, Bourne saw a majority of the police vehicles peel off, trying to follow the flight path of the copter. One cop car and an EMS vehicle kept straight on toward the vacant lot. He'd already scanned the perimeter and knew they had entered via the only hole in the fence.

He saw movement out of the corner of his eye. Rebeka was emerging from beneath the impromptu stone-and-brick rubble fortress in which she had taken shelter. He poked his head out and, when she saw him, gestured at the wooden boards. Understanding his silent signal, she nodded and scrambled out, checking the immediate environment. Bourne did the same, digging through the layers of debris and discarded garbage lodged under the boards. His fingers found a couple of cans, and he pulled them free.

The official vehicles were nearing; they had very little time before the cops would be crawling all over the lot. They could not afford to be caught up as material witnesses or, worse, persons of interest in a police investigation. The Swedish cops took the discharging of firearms extremely seriously. There would be no end of interrogations and incarcerations.

Rebeka scuttled toward him. "I didn't find anything flammable," she whispered.

"As it happens, I did." He held up the two dented cans of paint. They were two-thirds empty, but there was still more than enough left for ignition.

As he pried open the lids, she produced her lighter. Bourne set the cans just beneath a chimney of boards, moving them to allow the right amount of draw. She lit the paint and they scrambled back around behind the pile of boards. They were very dry underneath and caught almost immediately.

The cops and EMS team spotted the flames and smoke and ducked through the rent in the chainlink fence, making directly for the fire. By this time, Bourne and Rebeka were fifty yards away.

"Nice diversion," she said, "but we're still not out of here."

Bourne led them, crouched and hidden, along the periphery, until he found a patch of protected ground. Shoving a piece of wood into her hand, he said, "Dig."

While she went to work, he grasped the bottom of the fence and tried to curl it up. It wouldn't budge.

"Stop," he said.

He stood in front of one of the leaning fence posts, kicked it hard twice, and it canted over so that the section of fence became a kind of ramp. Grasping it with curled fingers, they climbed to the top, then jumped off onto the pavement beyond the lot.

They ran.

The problem," Dr. Steen said, "is that Soraya waited so long." He regarded Delia as if she were a functional idiot. "She waited until she had an acute episode. If she had taken my advice—"

"She didn't," Delia said curtly. She hated the way doctors spoke down to everyone else. "Let's move on."

Dr. Santiago, the head surgeon on Soraya's team, cleared his throat. "Let's move to a more private space, shall we?"

Delia and Thorne had been led by a nurse through the big metal door into the sacred space where the operating theaters and recovery rooms existed, as if on a faraway shore. Dr. Santiago led them into an unoccupied recovery cubicle. It was small, close, and claustrophobic. It smelled strongly of disinfectant.

"All right," Delia said, weary of being given yet another prognosis, which would contradict the ones that came before. "Let's hear it."

"The bottom line," Dr. Santiago said, "is she's had some bleeding as the edema leaked. We've taken care of that; we're draining the excess fluid out of her brain. We're doing everything we can. Now we have to wait for her body to do the rest."

"Is she compromised because of the fetus?"

"The brain is a highly complex organ."

"Just, for God's sake, tell me!"

"I'm afraid so, yes."

"How badly?"

"Impossible to say." Dr. Santiago shrugged. He was a pleasant-looking man with black eyes and a hawk-like nose. "It's a...complication we could do without."

"I'm quite certain Soraya doesn't feel that way." She deliberately let the awkward silence extend before she said, "I want to see her now."

"Of course." Both of the doctors appeared relieved to end the interview. Doctors hated feeling helpless, hated admitting it even more.

As they went out, Delia turned to Thorne. "I'm going in first."

He nodded. As she was about to turn away, he said, "Delia, I want you to know..." He stopped there, unable to go on.

"Whatever you have to say, Charles, say it to her, okay?"

He nodded again.

Dr. Santiago was waiting for her. He smiled thinly at her and gestured. "This way."

She followed him down a corridor that seemed

to be a separate entity, breathing on its own. He stopped at a curtained doorway and stood aside.

"Five minutes," he cautioned. "No more."

Delia found that her heart was pounding in her chest. It ached for her friend. Unable to imagine what was lying in wait for her behind the curtain, she pulled it aside, and stepped into the room.

12

Y OUR CAR."

"Is registered to my friend's company," Bourne said. "He'll take care of any questions from the police."

Rebeka glanced behind them. No one was following.

"I have a small flat here," she said. "We can hole up there until we decide what to do next."

"I have a better idea."

They were in a residential neighborhood whose streets were fast filling with traffic as people rose and went to work. Bourne took out his mobile and, despite the early hour, called Christien.

"What the hell have you and Alef been up to?" Christien's voice buzzed in his ear. "I'm already fielding calls from the police."

"He's regained his memory. His name's Harry Rowland, or so he claims. There was nothing to be done." Bourne went on to explain briefly what had taken place yesterday in Sadelöga. He mentioned Rebeka, but only as a friend of his, not wanting to complicate matters further or cause his friend any degree of suspicion.

"Damn," Christien said. "But you're unharmed?"

"Yes. What we need is to somehow track the copter that snatched Rowland."

"Are you in a safe place?"

Bourne spotted a small café, open for breakfast. "We are now. Yes."

Christien got their location in Gamla Stan, told Bourne to sit tight, that he'd come to get them himself.

They went to the café, all their senses on high alert. Inside, they reconnoitered, discovered the rear entrance through the kitchen, then chose a table in the rear with a view of everyone who came in and out.

When they had ordered, Bourne said, "Tell me how the Israeli government was able to establish a research facility in Dahr El Ahmar."

Rebeka had stiffened at the words *research facility*. "So you know."

"I thought you had brought me to a temporary Mossad forward outpost in Lebanon."

He waited while the server set down their coffee and sweet rolls.

"When I escaped in the copter I had stolen in Syria, I realized that Dahr El Ahmar isn't a military encampment. The Mossad is there to guard a research facility."

Rebeka stirred sugar into her coffee. "What did you see?"

"I saw the camouflage netting, and I swung low enough to see the bunkered building underneath. There are experiments going on in that building, and I have to ask myself why these experiments are being undertaken in Lebanon, not Israel, where they'd be far more secure."

"But would they be more secure in Israel?" Rebeka cocked her head. "Why would our enemies look for Israeli research on Lebanese soil?"

Bourne stared at her. "They wouldn't."

"No," she said slowly. "They wouldn't."

"What's in the bunker lab? What are they working on?"

Three people came in, one left. She stirred more sugar into her coffee, then took a sip. She was gazing at a space between him and the door, looking at nothing but her own thoughts, as if weighing her next action.

At last, she said, "Have you ever heard of SILEX?"

He shook his head.

"For decades now, there has been a theory knocking around the nuclear fuel industry that posited the theory of extracting U-235, the isotope used for enriched uranium fuel rods, via lasers. For a long time it was overhyped, and all designs proved either ineffective or prohibitively expensive. Then, in 1994, a pair of nuclear physicists came up with SILEX— separation of isotopes by laser excitation. The Americans control that process, and a project with SILEX at its center is even now going forward. At Dahr El Ahmar, we have come up with a parallel methodology. It's being tested in such secrecy because of fears that, if stolen, the technology could be used by terrorist cells or nations like Iran to accelerate weapons designs."

Bourne thought a moment. "Rowland was trying to steal the technology at Dahr El Ahmar."

"That's what I thought. But the fact is that Harry knew nothing about the real purpose of Dahr El Ahmar, let alone the experiments. No, he was looking for you, and, ironically, in pursuing him, I led him directly to you."

"You couldn't know that."

She made a face.

Outside in the street, they watched a long black car slide past, more slowly than the rest of the traffic. It could mean nothing, or everything. They kept their eyes on the plate-glass door. Two elderly ladies walked in and sat down. A suit with an iPad under his arm rose and went out. A young mother and child pushed in and looked around for a free table. The three servers passed to and fro. When several minutes went by and nothing untoward happened, Rebeka relaxed.

"I'm taking a chance telling you this," she said.

"Colonel Ben David is already convinced I know Dahr El Ahmar's secret. The question to be answered is why Harry Rowland was sent to kill me."

"Why? Do you think it's all connected?"

"We can't rule out the possibility until we know the network's goal."

"For that we need Harry."

He nodded. "Our only lead is the copter that snatched him."

Rebeka frowned. "How do you propose we—?"

Her question was cut short as two uniformed police came through the door and began to scrutinize the customers.

Martha Christiana, sitting next to Don Fernando Hererra in a private jet, was used to walking a tightrope—in fact, she welcomed it. But, for the first time since she had begun taking on commissions, she wasn't certain of her footing. Don Fernando was proving to be more of a challenge than she could have anticipated.

For one thing, he was something of an enigma. For another, he didn't act like any older man she had ever met. He was a dynamo of physical energy, and mentally he wasn't stuck in the reminiscences of a former age, unable to embrace an increasingly complex technological present. More than anything, he wasn't afraid of the even more challenging future. Experience had taught her that older men, having expended their reserves of creative energy, were now content to fade into the comfortable background, letting the present whiz by them in an uncomprehensible blur. Don Fernando's grasp of cutting-edge technology was both comprehensive and dazzling.

On a fundamental level, she found Don Fernando charming, erudite, and psychologically astute. He drew her in as the sun does a planet. The two of them made intimate connections that both exhilarated and alarmed her. She found herself basking in these connections the way a beachgoer toasts in sunshine. When she was with him, she was happy.

In this, she was deviating from the successful execution of her commission. She knew this, but she didn't stop. Such behavior was completely foreign to her and, as such, a mystery.

Another thing: There was in Don Fernando something of a memory for her, of a time before Marrakech, before she ran away from the lighthouse. A time of raging storms and walls of water crashing furiously against the rocky promontory into which her home was driven like a massive spike. Or had her thoughts turned in this direction because Don Fernando was flying her to Gibraltar?

"I'd like to take you to dinner," he had said earlier that day.

"What restaurant?" she had said. "How shall I dress?" She wore a black sheath skirt and matching braided bolero jacket, beneath which was an oyster-white silk shirt, pinned at the top with an onyx oval.

"It's a surprise." His eyes twinkled. "As for how to dress, I see nothing wrong with what you're wearing."

The surprise had been the jet, waiting for them on the tarmac of a private field on the outskirts of Paris. It was only after they had raced down the runway and lifted into the air that he had told her their destination.

Heart racing, she had said, "What's in Gibraltar?"

"You'll see."

Now they had landed. A car and driver were waiting for them. As soon as they climbed in, it swept away down a coast all too familiar to her. Twenty minutes later, the lighthouse came into view, rising from the rocky promontory of her youth.

"I don't understand." She turned to him. "Why have you brought me here?"

"Are you angry?"

"I don't know how you…I don't know…No, I—"

The car stopped. The lighthouse loomed high above them.

"It's automated now. It has been for years," Don Fernando said as they got out. "But it's still functioning, it still serves its original purpose."

Leading her around to the west side of the lighthouse, he walked with her several hundred yards to the grave site. She stopped, reading the headstone. It was her father's grave.

"Why have you done this, Don Fernando?"

"You *are* angry. Perhaps I was wrong." He took her elbow gently. "Come. We'll leave immediately."

But she did not move, stood her ground and shook off his hand as gently as he had gripped her. She walked several paces away until she was directly in front of the grave. Someone had left flowers in a zinc container, but that was some time ago. The flowers were dried, many of the petals missing.

Martha Christiana stared down at the stone below which her father lay buried. Then, surprising even herself, she knelt down to touch the earth. Above her, clouds raced across the azure sky. Sea birds swooped, calling to one another. Lifting her head, she saw a sea eagle's nest and thought of family and home.

Unaccountably, her fingers went to the pin she wore at her throat. She unfastened it, dug a shallow depression in the earth over her father, and placed the pin in it. Then slowly, almost reverently, she covered it over, placed her palm onto the earth, as if she could still feel it, like a beating heart.

When she rose, Don Fernando said, "Do you want to go inside?"

She shook her head. "I belong out here."

He nodded, as if he understood her completely. Instead of annoying her, that gesture of their unspoken, innate connection comforted her. She linked her arm in his, walked him away to the edge of the rocky promontory. Below them, the sea rose, foaming against the granite teeth far below.

"When I was a little girl," she said, "I used to stand here. The sea looked like brittle glass as it broke apart on the rocks. It made me think of my family. It made me sad."

"This is why you left."

She nodded. Back in the car, as they drove slowly away from the shore and the glowering lighthouse, she said, "How did you find out?"

"Everything is knowable," he said with a smile, "these days."

She said nothing more. It did not matter how he had found her history, only that he knew. One more astonishment: She was not unhappy that he knew. Somehow, even without asking, she understood that it would remain their secret.

She stared at the countryside, and like a sleeper waking from a pleasant dream into harsh reality she remembered that she had been sent here to kill this man. The idea seemed absurd to her now, and yet she knew that she had no choice. She never did once she took a commission from Maceo Encarnación.

Emerging from her difficult thoughts, she saw that they were turning off Castle Road into an area of Gibraltar unfamiliar to her. After several small streets, they came to a triangle of parkland, dotted with pencil cypress and palm trees. Martha rolled down the tinted window, heard the clatter of swaying fronds. A bright spray of gulls flickered by. Sunlight glimmered off a bisque-tile roof, which came nearer as the car rolled up a driveway and came to rest before a pillared portico.

"Where are we?" Martha said.

Without a word, Don Fernando accompanied her up the stone steps, across the portico, and into a large, airy entryway, dominated by a cut-crystal chandelier and a high mahogany banc behind which sat a young woman, efficiently fielding calls while entering data on a computer console.

A business of some sort, Martha thought. *Possibly one of his.*

Leaning forward, Don Fernando handed over a folded sheet of paper, which the young woman unfolded as if it were an official document. Her clear eyes scanned it, then they flicked up to take in Don Fernando and, briefly, Martha Christiana herself. She picked up a phone, spoke only a few words into it. Then she nodded at them, and, smiling, pointed in the direction of double swinging doors.

Inside the doors, a uniformed woman, somewhat older, with a kind face and demeanor, waited for them, her hands clasped in front of her like a nun. When she saw them, she turned, leading them down a wide, thickly carpeted hallway, interspersed with closed doors between which hung various photos of

Gibraltar down through the years. The only thing that hadn't changed was the great shrugged shoulder of rock, uncounted ages old.

At length, the woman stopped in front of a door and gestured. "Take as long as you wish," she said. She retreated down the hall in the direction they had come before Martha had a chance to ask her what this was all about.

Don Fernando looked at her without an expression she could read.

"I'll be right here if you need me."

She was about to query him, but immediately realized that it would do no good. Resigning herself, she pushed open the heavy door and stepped inside.

How can they be looking for us?" Rebeka said. "They can't know our faces."

"Nevertheless, they're here. Whether or not they know our faces, they're looking for the people at the construction site who escaped on foot."

"Anyone who looks guilty or is trying to hide."

Bourne looked at her. "Hit me."

Her eyes found his, found the answer she was seeking there. Leaning across the table, she slapped him hard across the face, back up, upending her chair, and shouted, "Bastard!"

The cops looked, but then so did everyone else in the café, even the servers, who stood frozen in place.

"Calm down," Bourne said loudly, still seated.

"Calm down? How could you do this to me! And with my own sister!"

He rose now, the second scene of the play beginning. "I told you to calm down!"

"Don't tell me what to do!" She tossed her head. "You have no right."

"I have every right," he said as he grabbed her wrist.

Rebeka jerked back even as he held on. "Let me go, you sonofabitch!"

The physical contact was enough for the police, who stood up simultaneously and approached the table. "Sir," the older of the two said, "the lady wants you to let her go."

"Stay out of this," Bourne said.

"Do it!" The younger one moved forward menacingly, and Bourne at once dropped his hold on Rebeka's wrist.

"Are you all right, ma'am?" the older cop said. "Do you want to press charges?"

Eyes flashing, Rebeka said, "I just want to get out of here." Gathering up her coat and shoulder bag, she turned and stalked out of the café, all eyes following her.

The older cop turned his attention to Bourne. "Pay your bill and clear out. And stay away from the woman, hear?"

Bourne put his head down, threw some krona on the table and swept out. As the door closed behind him, the café returned to life. The cops sat back down and finished their coffees, the incident evaporating instantly from their minds.

Bourne met Rebeka around the corner. She was laughing.

"How's your cheek?"

"I'll turn the other one."

She laughed even harder. It was a rare light-hearted moment in their time together. Across the street, he saw Christien standing beside a black late-model Volvo. He was smoking a small cigar and eying the almost steady stream of young women, wrapped in their winter coats, as if he had not a care in the world.

Evading the traffic, Bourne and Rebeka crossed the street. He grinned at them—especially Rebeka—as he let her into the backseat. Bourne sat beside him in front. Christien had left the engine running, and he nosed out as soon as he glimpsed a break in the traffic.

"I have a trace on the copter," Christien said. He was far too savvy to ask Bourne any more about Rebeka than Bourne had seen fit to tell him over the phone. "That proved to be no problem. There aren't many with those markings—in fact, only one."

"What kind of markings are they?" Rebeka asked.

Christien gave her the once-over in the rearview mirror. "This is where the abduction gets interesting."

He handed Bourne a folder filled with high-resolution photos. Rebeka leaned forward between the bucket seats to get a good look.

"We have access to a number of the city's surveillance cameras." Christien made a turn onto Prästgatan, moving more slowly with the increasing crush of traffic. "I had those blown up, and our computer enhanced the images. Page through them; you'll see why."

There were four 8x10 photos. The enlargements

and enhancements had drained them of almost all color, but both Bourne and Rebeka recognized the helicopter that had shot at them and had snatched Harry Rowland. As if they needed confirmation, the second photo showed Rowland through the window of the side door. Bourne flipped to the third photo.

"Kungliga Transport," Rebeka read. "It looks like a typical commercial aircraft."

"Yes," Christien said, "but it's not. Look at the last photo. Up past the tail rotor."

Bourne flipped again; this photo was an even closer shot. He held it up so more light fell on it.

"That's a corporate logo," he said, "but I can't make out the name."

"It's too small, even for the enhancements." They stopped at a light. Christien tapped the logo. "See the shape? It's kind of unusual, so we ran the outline through one of our bleeding-edge computer recognition programs, and what do you know, we got a hit. This copter belongs to SteelTrap."

"Internet security," Rebeka said. "Top-shelf stuff."

Christien nodded. "Talk about bleeding edge. SteelTrap software is light-years ahead of anyone else's."

"What," Bourne said, "is SteelTrap doing trying to kill me and, at the same time, rescue Harry Rowland?" He turned to Rebeka. "You said Rowland worked for a terrorist network?"

"Which one?" Christien said.

"*Jihad bis saif*," Rebecca said. "I overheard Colonel Ben David talking about it in Dahr El Ahmar. He thought I was still unconscious."

"Who was he talking with?" Bourne asked her.

She shook her head. "I don't know." She sat back, arms crossed under her breasts. "One thing seems clear, though: it looks like SteelTrap does more than produce bleeding-edge software."

"Like what?" Christien said.

Bourne grunted. "Bleeding-edge, period."

13

WHEN MARTHA CHRISTIANA saw the old woman sitting beside the large picture window, she saw herself. The room was sparsely furnished and even more sparsely decorated. There were few personal items: a comb, a hairbrush with a silver handle. A small yellowed scrimshaw of a lighthouse standing alone on a promontory, a faded photo of a beautiful but frail-looking woman, holding against her shins a small girl. That was all. But the room was filled to brimming with a loneliness so profound it took Martha's breath away.

The old woman did not turn as she crossed the room and picked up the photo of her and her mother. There was another photo, she saw now, placed behind the first. It showed a slim man in a peacoat, standing beside the cut-glass beacon of the lighthouse. Raking daylight streamed in, illuminating him, but also emphasizing his separation from anything except that fierce beacon.

Martha Christiana stared at the photo of her father, but she did not pick it up. She did not touch it at all. She felt, in her heart, that touching it would be a desecration, though she could not say why. At last, she put down the photo and walked over to the old woman. She was staring out at the view: a swath of lawn, a clutch of palms, and beyond, nondescript buildings across the street. Not much to look at, but her concentration was absolute, fearsome. Martha did not think she was looking at the grass, the trees, or the buildings, none of which would have any meaning for her. She was sitting slightly forward, tensed, peering, as if through a telescope, into the past.

"Mom," Martha said in a shaky voice, "what do you see?"

At the sound of the voice, her mother began to rock back and forth. She was thin as a rail. In places her bones shone whitely beneath her tissue-thin skin. Her pallor gleamed like the sun in winter.

Martha moved around until she was standing in front of the old woman. Though her cheeks were deeply scored, her entire face ravaged by time, pain, and loss, still something inside her remained unchanged. Martha felt a pang deep inside her chest.

"Mom, it's me, Martha. Your daughter."

The old woman did not—or could not—look up. She seemed locked in the past. Martha hesitated, then reached out, took the skeletal hand in hers. It was as cool as marble. She stared at the raised veins, blue, seeming ready to burst through the skin.

Then she looked up into her mother's eyes, gray and gossamer as passing clouds shredded by conflicting wind currents.

"Mom?"

The eyes moved imperceptibly, but there was no recognition—none at all. It was as if she did not exist. For so many years, her parents had ceased to exist for her. Now, here, with her father already gone, at the end of her mother's life, there was nothing for her. She was a stone thrown into the sea, sinking out of sight without even a ripple to mark its passing.

For some time, she stood as still as that great shoulder of rock at the edge of Gibraltar, holding her mother's cool hand. Once, her mother's lips parted, and she whispered something that Martha didn't catch. It wasn't repeated, even at Martha's insistent urging. Silence settled over them both. The years had flown by and were now like fallen leaves, brittle and dead.

At last, when she could breathe again, Martha Christiana let her mother's hand slip from hers. She crossed to the door, though she was barely aware of what she was doing. Opening the door, she found Don Fernando waiting patiently in the hallway. She opened the door wider.

"Come in," she said. "Please."

So, old thing." Brick took a bite out of a colossal olive, sucked the pimiento between his lips like a second tongue, and chomped down, grinding it to orange paste. "I have a bit of work for you. Ready to have a go?"

"Sure," Peter said, "now's as good a time as any."

"That's the lad."

His heart rate spiked. He had no idea what Brick was going to ask of him, but it wasn't going to be good. *In for a penny, in for a pound.* And continuing that thought, *There's a damn good reason clichés were born.*

The two men sat in the kitchen of Brick's Virginia safe house. Between them were several plates of food—rounds of Italian salami and mortadella, crumbles of pecorino cheese, a deep-green glass container of olive oil, handfuls of crusty bread, a dish of olives, and four oversized bottles of dark Belgian beer, two of them empty. Dick Richards had left an hour ago with Bogs, who was taking him back to within three blocks of the Treadstone headquarters.

Wiping his lips, Brick rose and crossed to a drawer, rummaged around in it until he found what he wanted, then returned and sat across from Peter.

"So," Peter said, "where d'you want me to go?"

"Nowhere."

"What?"

"You're staying right here." Brick slid a small packet across the table.

"What's this?"

"Double-edged shaving blades."

Peter picked up the packet and opened it. Sure enough, he discovered four double-edged blades. Plucking one up carefully, he said, "I can't remember when I last saw one of these."

"Yeah," Brick said, "they're from the last century."

Peter laughed.

"No joke, mate. Those there'll take off your finger if you look at them wrong. Specially honed, they are."

Peter dropped the blade back on top of the others. "I don't understand."

"Easy-peasy, old thing. You stay here. You wait. Bogs'll be bringing someone here. He'll make the intros, you chat the mark up, all nice'n'larky-like. Wait for Bogs's signal, then..." He tilted his head toward the box of blades.

"What?" Peter felt the gorge rise into his throat. "You mean you want me to kill this person with one of these blades?"

"Use all four of 'em, if that's your cuppa."

Peter swallowed. "I don't think—"

Brick's torso shot forward, his hand imprisoning Peter's right wrist in an iron grip. "I don't give a fuck what you think. Just get it done."

"Jesus." Peter fought down the panic that threatened to undo him. *Think fast*, he berated himself. "We're isolated here. Wouldn't a gun be simpler?"

"Any shite-arse off the street can pop a bloke at close range." He made a gun of his free hand, pushed the end of his finger-barrel into Peter's temple. Then, in a dizzying shift, he broke out into a grin, letting go. "I want to see what you're made of, old thing. See what lurks beneath, see if I can trust you to go on to bigger'n'better." He rose. "You wanted to work for me. This is the path you chose. Your chance to grab the gold ring." He winked, his grin evaporating. "Don't make a fucking hash of it, yeah?"

* * *

The one society Soraya did belong to was a weekly poker game at the mayor's townhouse. But that, too, was something that bound her and Delia together: both women were naturally shy, but fiercely competitive, especially when it came to poker. Being ushered into the high-stakes game was one of Delia's great joys, and the incident that cemented her friendship with Soraya. It was at these intimate sessions, sitting around a green baize table with the elite of Washington politics, that Delia came to know Soraya best, and to sort out her feelings toward her. Gradually, the sexual charge resolved itself into the warm glow of a deep and abiding friendship. She realized that she was attracted to Soraya, but not as a lover. She soon discovered an acute relief that Soraya was neither gay nor bi. No possibility of complications to get in the way of their friendship. As for her friend, Soraya accepted Delia for who she was. For the first time in her life, Delia felt no hesitation, no shame, no obstinacy in revealing herself to another human being. She never felt judged, and in return she opened her heart and her mind to Soraya.

Now, having pulled up a chair, Delia sat beside her friend's bed and took her hand. Soraya's eyes fluttered open. Her lids were blue, bruised-looking. In fact, she had the dazed look of someone who had just received a thorough thrashing.

"Hello, Raya."

"Deel—"

Tubes ran in and out of both arms. There was

still a drain poking through the bandages on the side of her head. *Hideous thing*, Delia thought, trying to avert her gaze without being conspicuous about it. She failed.

"I guess you shouldn't show me a mirror." Soraya tried for a smile and just missed. It looked lopsided, grotesque, and for a breathless moment Delia was terrified that the operation had done something to the nerves on that side of her face. Then, as Soraya started to talk more, she realized it was merely fatigue combined with the remnants of the anaesthesia.

"How d'you feel, Raya?"

"Bad as I look. Maybe worse."

Now it was Delia's turn to smile. "It's fine now. Everything's fine."

"Hendricks told me the baby's okay."

Delia nodded. "That's right. No problems."

Soraya sighed, visibly relaxing. "When can I get out of here, did the doctors say?"

Delia laughed. "Why? You itching to get back to work already?"

"I have a job to do."

Delia bent over her. "Right now your job is to get better—for yourself and for the baby." She took her friend's hand. "Listen, Raya, I did something...something you warned me not to do. But under the circumstances, I thought...I told Charles about the baby."

Soraya, overwhelmed with guilt, closed her eyes. But she knew she had to continue on down this path, step by ugly step.

"I'm sorry, Raya. Truly. But I was so afraid for you. I thought he had a right to know."

"It's your basic decency, Deel," Soraya said. "I wasn't thinking clearly. I should have known." In fact, she *had* known. She had been banking on Delia's basic decency.

"Where's Charlie now?"

"He's been here for a while," her friend said. "I'm kind of surprised he's stayed so long."

"Does his wife know he's here?"

Delia made a face. "Ann Ring is up on the Hill, engulfed day and night in her senatorial legislative package on next year's Homeland Security procurements and expenditures."

"How d'you know that?"

"I read Politico. They don't like her, either."

"Who does, except her constituents? And, of course, *The Beltway Journal*."

"Now you're going to say you can't understand why he married her."

Soraya's lips curled in the semblance of a smile. "*She* married *him*. She was like an unstoppable force. He couldn't say no."

"Any adult can say no and mean it, Raya."

"But not Charlie. He was bedazzled."

"Senator Ring has that effect on a lot of conservative Republicans. She could do a spread in *Playboy*."

"If only," Soraya said. "Then we'd all be rid of her."

"I don't know. I have a feeling she'd be able to somehow spin it to her advantage."

Soraya laughed and squeezed her friend's hand. "What would I do without you, Deel?"

Delia squeezed back. "Heaven only knows."

"Listen, Deel. I want to see Charlie."

Delia's face clouded over. "Raya, do you think that's such a good idea?"

"It's important. I—"

All at once, her eyes opened wide, and she gasped. Her hand turned into a claw and her torso arched off the bed. The monitors to which she was hooked up started to go crazy. Delia started screaming, and Thorne pushed open the door, his face white and drawn.

"What is it?" He looked from her to Soraya. "What's happened?"

Delia could hear the soft slap of running rubber-soled shoes, voices raised in alarm, and she shouted, "Help! She needs help! Now!"

Bourne and Rebeka silently entered the apartment she had rented on Sankt Eriksgatan in Kungsholmen. It was on the third floor, a block and a half from the water. Christien was waiting for them downstairs in the Volvo, along with a bodyguard-messenger from his office he had picked up on a prearranged street corner in Gamla Stan.

The pair went stealthily through all the rooms, checking the shallow closets, even under the bed, and behind the shower curtain. When they had assured themselves that the apartment was secure, Rebeka knelt down on the tile floor of the bathroom.

"How much money have you stowed away?" Bourne said.

"I always establish a private vault in a secure location. It's not safe to carry so much on my person."

Bourne, kneeling beside her, helped her carefully peel up two thin lines of grout, making certain they wouldn't crumble. This left an island tile, which she plucked up. Beneath lay a thick wad of bills—krona, euros, American dollars.

Stuffing the wad into her pocket, she stood up. "Come on," she said. "This place gives me the creeps."

They left the apartment, hurrying down the twilit stairs.

Ilan Halevy, code name the Babylonian, sat behind the wheel of the rental car he had parked in a strategic spot across the street and down the block from the entrance to the building in which Rebeka had rented her apartment. He had been waiting for hours, but for him those hours felt like minutes. It seemed as if he had been waiting for something to happen all his life. As a boy of ten, he had waited for his parents to divorce; as an adolescent of fourteen, he had waited for the bully he had put into the hospital to die; shortly afterward, he had found himself waiting for a train to take him out of the heartland of his country into the capital, the busiest, shiniest, most confusing place he could think of in which to get lost. He had killed again, but this time on his own terms. He chose well—a wealthy American businessman, with whom he had struck up a conversation in the bar of the capital's poshest hotel. Now, with money in his pocket and an alternate identity, he shaved his beard, bought himself two sets of the best Western clothes from the Brioni boutique in the selfsame hotel, charging it to one of the businessman's credit cards. Before that moment, he had never before seen a credit card in the flesh, let alone handled one.

Soon after, he had slid quite naturally into Tel Aviv's criminal underbelly, making a name for himself quickly, ruthlessly, remorselessly. He supposed that was how he had come to the attention of Colonel Ben David. In any event, when Ben David had approached him, he was properly wary. But, in time, the two men established a relationship. Despite its undisputed closeness, no one would mistake it for friendship, especially the two principals.

Halevy sighed, longing for a shwarma whose delicious muttony grease he could dribble over a pile of Israeli couscous. He hated the Nordic countries—Sweden in particular. He hated their women, blond, blue-eyed, upholding the abhorrent Aryan ideal of the superman. There wasn't a Swedish runway model he didn't feel compelled to kick in her perfect, chiseled face. Give him a dark-skinned, dark-haired Amazon with Mediterranean features any day.

He was still enmeshed in these sour thoughts when he saw the late-model Volvo draw up to the building under his surveillance. Rebeka stepped out, crossing the pavement to the front door. He was about to emerge from his car when he saw Bourne striding after her.

Why the hell are they still together? he asked himself. *She's working with him?* He ground his teeth in fury and sat back against the seat, forcing himself to wait. A familiar state for him, but sometimes, as now, it maintained its power to drive him crazy.

Along the E4 motorway, Christien turned off into a fast-food and gas lay-by. Since stopping off briefly at Rebeka's apartment, they had been heading steadily north out of Gamla Stan, where Christien had picked them up. Bourne wondered where they were going.

Sovard, the bodyguard-messenger, handed a slim packet to his boss as soon as he had parked in a spot away from other cars.

"Two tickets," Christien said, handing the packet to Bourne.

Rebeka accepted hers with a certain reluctance. "Where to?"

Fishing an iPad out of Sovard's briefcase, Christien used the touch screen to access a video. "In this instance, Sweden's fetish for surveillance has served us well," he observed.

The three of them watched a video that had obviously been quickly and roughly spliced together from several fixed CCTV cameras at various locations. In the beginning there was nothing of much interest: a swath of tarmac, overalled workers with ear-dampening headphones in small motorized carts heading back and forth. Arlanda airport.

Then, in a flurry of activity, a sudden backwash sent people scurrying. A moment later, the disguised SteelTrap copter descended into view, settling onto the ground. Almost immediately, the side door slid back and three men clambered down. One of them was clearly Harry Rowland. He hustled between the two men, moving left to right, vanishing out of camera range.

Jump-cut to another camera in another area of the airport. Three men were seen hustling across the tarmac. Though the view was from farther away, it was clear from their gait that these were the same three men from the SteelTrap copter. A long-range private jet was waiting for them. An immigration official checked their passports, stamped them, and nodded them up the mobile stairs.

Another jump-cut, this time a different angle on the same scene, closer up, probably through a telephoto lens, judging by the jittery images. One by one, the men bent down, disappearing into the belly of the jet.

A final jump-cut to the jet rolling down the runway, gathering speed. When it lifted off out of the frame, Christien stopped the video and stowed the iPad.

"The pilot was required to file a flight plan with the tower at Arlanda. The plane is headed to Mexico City via Barcelona." Christien smiled. "It so happens that Maceo Encarnación, the president of SteelTrap, has his main residence in Mexico City."

"Nice work," Bourne acknowledged.

Christien nodded. "Your AeroMexico flight will be following virtually the same route as the SteelTrap jet, but they'll have a two-hour head start. Jason, I know you have a passport. Rebeka?"

"Don't leave home without it," she said with a wry smile.

He nodded. "Good. We're set then."

·

Putting the Volvo in gear, he rolled out of the lay-by, back onto the E4, heading for the Arlanda airport.

Sovard was on his way back from security, to which he had accompanied Christien's VIP guests when a man asked him for the time. The moment he glanced at his watch, he felt an immense pain at the nape of his neck. As he pitched forward, the man caught him under the arms and half-dragged him into an airline lost-luggage office. It was currently unlighted and unmanned, beyond its hours of operation. In his current semi-paralyzed state, Sovard had no idea how he had gotten into the locked office. In any event, he was set down against a pile of suitcases, duffel bags, and backpacks. His equilibrium shot, he teetered. As he did so, he caught a glimpse of the livid scars on the man's neck. When he tried to right himself, the man delivered a massive blow to both ears that caused Sovard's eyes to roll up in their sockets. He felt sick, incapable of stringing two thoughts together, let alone trying to figure a way out of his imprisonment.

"I have little time." The man touched Sovard on a nerve bundle behind his right ear, and a firework of pain exploded in Sovard's brain. "Where are they going?"

Sovard stared up at him blankly. A sliver of drool escaped the corner of his mouth, discolored his shirt. It was pinkish with his own blood.

"I will only ask you one more time." Again, the Babylonian used only one finger, this time stopping the flow of blood through Sovard's carotid artery, then released it. "You have ten seconds to answer my question. After that, I will bring you to the point of unconsciousness, over and over until you beg me to kill you. Frankly, I'd like that, but I'm thinking altruistically, I'm thinking of you."

He repeated the procedure twice more before Sovard lifted a trembling hand. He'd had enough. The Babylonian leaned forward. Sovard opened his mouth and spoke two words.

Eighty minutes later, Bourne and Rebeka were settling into their first-class seats, accepting hot towels and flutes of champagne from the flight attendant.

"Feel nostalgic?" Bourne said, his gaze following the attendant back down the aisle.

Rebeka laughed. "Not at all. My life as a flight attendant seems like a lifetime ago."

Bourne stared out the window as the crew made its last-minute preparations, then they strapped themselves in. The massive engines revved as the jet taxied toward the head of the runway. Over the intercom the captain announced that the plane was number two for takeoff.

"Jason," she said softly, "what are you thinking?"

It was the first time she had called him anything but Bourne. That made him turn toward her. There was a softness—almost a vulnerability—in her eyes he hadn't seen before.

"Nothing."

She watched him for a moment. "Do you ever ask yourself whether it's time to get out?"

"Get out of what?"

"Don't do that. You know. The great game."

"And do what?"

"Find an island in the sun, kick back, drink a beer, eat fresh-caught fish, make love, sleep."

The plane slowed, turning onto the runway, strings of yellow lights running away in front of it.

"And then?"

"Then," she said, "do it all over again the next day."

"You're joking."

There was a silence, broken by the soft push forward as the brakes came off, and the jet hurtled down the runway. They lifted off, the wheels retracted, they rose higher.

Rebeka put her head back against the seat and closed her eyes. "Of course I'm joking."

During the meal service, she pushed away her tray, unsnapped her seat belt, rose, and went forward, standing out of the flight attendants' way. When she made no move to use the restroom after the OCCUPIED light flicked off and a middle-aged woman emerged, Bourne followed her. A sense of melancholy, sharp as the scent of burning leaves, seemed to have enveloped her.

They stood side by side, shoulders pressed together in the cramped space. Neither of them spoke until Rebeka said, "Have you been to Mexico City?"

"Once that I can remember."

She had wrapped herself in the protection of her own arms. "It's a fucking snake pit. A gorgeous snake pit, admittedly, but a snake pit nonetheless."

"It's gotten worse in the last five years."

"The cartels are no longer underground since they've integrated with the Colombians. There's so much money that all the right officials, even the police, are in on the action. The drug trade is out of control. It's threatening to inundate the entire country, and the government doesn't have either the will or the inclination to stem the rising tide. Anyway, anytime someone in authority pops up trying to take charge, he gets his head lopped off."

"Not much incentive to swim against the tide."

"Unless you're swinging the hammer of God."

Another silence descended, as if from the high, clear sky through which they were flying. Bourne listened to her soft, even breathing, as if he were lying in bed next to her. Despite this, he was acutely aware of how separate from her—from everyone—he felt. And, abruptly, he understood what she was trying to get out of him. Was he incapable of feeling any deep emotion about anyone? It seemed to him now that each death, each parting he had memory of, had inoculated him over and over, until he was now fully anaesthetized, incapable of doing anything more meaningful than putting one foot in front of the other in the darkness. There was no escape for him, and Rebeka knew it. That was why she had brought up the notion of an island in the sun. Leaving the darkness behind was not an option for him. He had spent so many years negotiating its mysterious byways that he would only be blinded in the sunlight. This realization, he understood, was what had saddened her, wrapping her in melancholy. Whether it was because she had seen herself in him or because she actually desired the exile for herself remained to be seen.

"We should go back to our seats," he said.

She nodded distractedly. They left the bathroom and went back down the aisle. That was when he saw Ilan Halevy, the narrow brim of a hat pulled low, sitting in the last row of first class, reading a copy of the *Financial Times*. The Babylonian looked up over the rim of the newspaper, delivering a wicked grin.

14

WHAT D'YOU MEAN I can't see her?"

"She's crashing, Charles." Delia put her hands against his chest, pushing Thorne back from the recovery room.

He stood against the wall as doctors and nurses pushing stainless-steel carts hurried past.

He followed them with his eyes. His mouth was half open and he seemed to have trouble breathing. "What's happening, Delia?"

"I don't know."

"You were in there." His restless gaze lit on her. "You must know *something*."

"We were talking and she just collapsed. That's all I know."

"The baby." He licked his lips. "What about the baby?"

Delia reared back. "Ah, now I get it."

"What d'you mean?"

"Why you're here. I get it. It's the baby."

Thorne appeared confused—or was that alarm on his face? "What are you talking—"

"If the baby dies, all your troubles die with it."

He came off the wall, his eyes blazing. "Where the hell do you come off—?"

"The baby dies and you don't have problems with Ann, do you? No explanations needed, it's as if the baby never existed, your affair with Soraya a distant memory, far away from the press and the bloggers, looking for dirt twenty-four–seven."

"You're nuts, you know that? I care about Soraya. Deeply. Why can't you accept that?"

"Because you're a cynical, self-centered sonofabitch."

Thorne took a breath, gathering himself. His eyes narrowed. "You know, I thought we could be friends."

"You mean you thought you could recruit me." She produced a steely laugh. "Fuck off."

Turning her back on him, Delia went to talk to Dr. Santiago as he emerged from Soraya's room.

"How is she?"

"Stable," Dr. Santiago said. "She's being moved to the ICU."

Delia was aware that Thorne had come up behind her. She could almost hear him listening. "What happened?"

"A slight blockage developed at the surgical site. Rare, but it happens sometimes. We've cleared it and we're giving her a low dose of blood thinner. We'll try to get her off it as soon as we deem it safe."

"Safe for her," Delia said. "What about what's safe for the baby?"

"Ms. Moore is our primary patient, her life takes precedence. Besides, the fetus—"

"Her baby," Delia said.

Dr. Santiago regarded her enigmatically for a moment. "Right. Excuse me."

Delia, melancholy and forlorn, watched him disappear down the hallway.

Thorne sighed. "Now I see how it is between you and me, I'll lay my cards on the table."

"When will you learn I don't give a shit about your cards?"

"I'm wondering whether Amy will feel the same way."

Delia spun on him. "What did you say?"

"You heard me." The challenge in his voice was unmistakable. "I have transcripts of your voicemails with Amy Brandt."

"What?"

"Surprised? It's a simple hack. We use a software program that imitates caller ID. It's how we can gain access to your mobile phone—anyone's, really—and bypass the password protection."

"So you have—"

"Every message you and Amy have left for each other." He could not hide a smirk. "Some of it's pretty hot."

She slapped him across the face so hard he rocked back on his heels.

"You hit like a guy, you know that?"

"How the hell d'you live with yourself?"

He laughed thinly. "It's a dirty job, but someone's got to do it."

She eyed him warily. "If you have a point, make it."

"We each have something on the other." He shrugged. "Just something to remember."

"I don't care—"

"But Amy does, doesn't she? In her line of work she has to be careful. A shitload of parents don't like their kids being taught by a lesbian."

Delia thought of several choice things to say, but at that moment a pair of grim-faced nurses wheeled Soraya out of recovery, past them, down the hall to the ICU. There was silence for a time after that.

"So there's our truce," Thorne said, "laid out for you."

Delia turned back to him. "Did you ever care about Soraya, even for a moment?"

"She's a hellcat in bed."

"What's the matter? Ann's not enough for you?"

"Ann has sex with her job. Otherwise she's a cold fish."

"My heart goes out to you," she said acidly.

He gave her a lupine grin. "And mine to you." He grabbed his crotch. "You don't know what you're missing."

Maceo Encarnación, staring out the Perspex window as his jet circled Mexico City prior to landing, saw the familiar fug of brown effluvia that hovered over the sprawling metropolis like a filthy carpet. A combination of the happenstance of geography and the unbridled emissions of modern progress formed this almost permanent atmospheric layer. Mexico City, built upon the ruins of the great Aztec megalopolis Tenochtitlán, seemed to be drowning in its own future.

The first thing his lungs inhaled when he stepped onto the rolling stairs was the stink of human shit, used to fertilize many of the crops. In the street markets where fruits and vegetables were laid out on the ground, dogs and toddlers alike pissed and shat on the wares without consequence.

Encarnación ducked into a black armored SUV, its motor running so that it sped off the moment he had settled into the backseat. His elaborate colonial California-style house, with its pseudo-baroque quarry windows, front garden, and elaborate wood-clad interior hallways, was on Castelar Street, in Colonia Polanco. Situated less than a mile from Chapultepec Park and the Museum of National History, it was constructed of pale yellow stone and *tezontle*, the indigenous reddish volcanic stone that marked so many of the city's great structures.

The ground on which his urban estancia sat was the most valuable in all of Mexico City, but because it was protected from development by the powerful National Fine Arts Institute, of which Encarnación was, not coincidentally, an influential member, no high-rises could be built there, as they had been in Lomas de Chapultepec or Colonia Santa Fe.

"Welcome home, Don Maceo. You have been missed."

The man sitting beside Encarnación was short, squat as a frog, with dark skin, a belligerent hooked Aztec nose, and pomaded black hair swept back from his wide forehead, thick and lustrous as a horse's mane.

His name was Tulio Vistoso; he was one of the three most powerful drug lords in Mexico, but almost everyone except Encarnación called him the Aztec.

"There is tequila to share, Don Tulio," Encarnación said amiably, "and news to digest."

At once the Aztec was on guard. "Problems?"

"There are always problems." Encarnación fluttered a hand back and forth. "What matters is the level of difficulty these problems present in the solving."

The Aztec grunted. He was wearing a black linen suit over an elaborate guayabera shirt. His feet were clad in caiman-skin huaraches dyed the color of polished mahogany. The driver was Encarnación's bodyguard, the stolid armed man beside him belonged to the Aztec.

Nothing more was said on the drive to Encarnación's mansion. Both men knew the value of silence and of presenting business at the proper time and place. Neither man was possessed of an impetuous nature. They were not prone to make a move before its time.

The familiar streets, avenues, and squares slid by in a blur of color and cacophonous noise. Bursts of bougainvillea crawled up the stucco sides of restaurants and tavernas, lumbering buses belched carbonized particulates. They passed by the square of Santo Domingo, inhabited by *evangelistas* with their old bulky typewriters, banging out for the city's illiterates letters of love or condolences, simple contracts to be explained and signed, eviction notices to be delivered orally, occasionally short, stark missives of bile and hate. The sleek armored SUV maneuvered nimbly in the rattling sea of taxis painted in violent colors and trucks and buses packed with stinking men, women, children, and animals. While church and cathedral bells clanged incessantly, it passed through the thick, grainy, wallowing morass of the city on its way to the cleanly exalted Colonia Polanco, and nestled within its heart, the villa, screened by high walls and pines, secured by electrified fences.

Beautiful as it was, with finely wrought designs and magnificent scrollwork, Encarnación's mansion was built like a fortress, an absolute necessity, even for him, in the city's crime-ridden environs. Yet it wasn't the increasingly powerful drug lords the premises were fortified against, but the shifting political landscape, unstable as quicksand. Over the years, Encarnación had witnessed too many of his supposedly invulnerable friends plowed under by regime changes. He had vowed that would never happen to him.

It was the time of *la comida*, the grand theatrical lunch of the City of the Aztecs, a meal taken as seriously as a saint's festival and with an almost religious fervor. It started at 2:30, often lasting until 6 PM. Grilled meat with assertive *pasilla* chilies; baby eels, white as sugar, in a thick, vinegary stew; grilled fish; flour tortillas, hot and steaming from the griddle; chicken *mole*; and, of course, bottles of aged tequila set the long plank table in Encarnación's paneled, light-filled dining room to groaning.

The two men sat opposite each other, drank a toast with tequila the color of sherry, then set about sating their immense appetites, at least for the time being. They were served by Anunciata, the nubile daughter of Maria-Elena, Encarnación's longtime cook. Seeing something special in her, he had relieved her of learning the finer points of cooking with the thousand varieties of fried peppers and exquisite *moles*, and was instead teaching her the finer points of disruptive technology in cyberspace. Her mind was as active and nubile as her body.

When their bellies were full, the dishes cleared, and the espressos and cigars served, Anunciata brought in enormous mugs of hot chocolate laced with chilies, which she proceeded to whip into a froth with a traditional wooden *molinillo*. This was the most important part of the ritual. Mexicans believe that the powerful spirit of the drink lives in the foam. Placing a mug in front of each man, she vanished as silently as she had appeared, leaving the two men alone to discuss their Machiavellian plans.

The Aztec was in a jovial mood. "Little by little, like hair falling from an aging scalp, the president is ceding power to us."

"We run this city."

"We have control, yes." Don Tulio cocked his head. "This does not please you, Don Maceo?"

"On the contrary." Encarnación sipped his hot chocolate meditatively. It wasn't until he tasted this magnificent drink that he truly knew he was home. "But gaining control and maintaining it are two very different animals. Succeeding at the one does not guarantee the other. The country abides, Don Tulio. Long after you and I are dust, Mexico remains." Like a professor in a classroom, he lifted a finger.

"Do not make the mistake of taking on the country, Don Tulio. Governments can be toppled, regimes can be replaced. To defy Mexico itself, to take it on, to think you can overthrow it, is hubris, a fatal mistake that will bury you, no matter the length and breadth of your power."

The Aztec, not quite seeing where the conversation was going, opened his spatulate hands. Besides, he wasn't altogether certain what *hubris* meant. "Is this the problem?"

"It is *a* problem, a discussion for another day. It is not *the* problem." Encarnación savored a draft of the chilied chocolate foam, sweet and spicy. "Yes," he said, licking his lips. "*The* problem."

Extracting a pen and pad from his breast pocket, he scribbled something on the top sheet, tore it off, folded it in half, and passed it across the table. The Aztec looked at him for a moment, then lowered his gaze as his fingers took hold of the folded sheet and opened it to read what Encarnación had written.

"Thirty million dollars?" he said.

Encarnación bared his teeth.

"How could this happen?"

Encarnación, rolling the hot chocolate around his mouth, looked up at the ceiling. "This is why I asked you to meet me at the airport. Somewhere between Comitán de Dominguez and Washington, DC, the thirty million disappeared."

The Aztec put down his cup. He looked distressed. "I don't understand."

"Our partner claims the thirty million is counterfeit. I know, I couldn't believe it myself, so much so that I sent two experts, not one. Our partner is right. The real thirty million that started its journey in Comitán de Dominguez ended up counterfeit."

The Aztec grunted. "How did the partner find out?"

"These people are different, Don Tulio. Among other things, they have a great deal of experience counterfeiting money."

Don Tulio wet his lips, his brow furrowed in concentration. "The thirty million changed hands a number of times over many thousands of miles." Comitán de Dominguez, in the south of Mexico, was the first distribution point for the drug shipments originating in Colombia, transshipped through Guatemala, crossing the border into Mexico. "It means there is a thief inside."

At that, Encarnación's fist slammed down on the table, upsetting his cup, spilling hot chocolate over the embroidered lace tablecloth, a present his paternal grandmother had received on her wedding day. The Aztec's eyes opened wide even as his body froze.

"A thief inside," Encarnación echoed. "Yes, Don Tulio, you have caught the essence of the problem in its entirety. A very clever thief, indeed. A traitor!" His eyes blazed, his hand trembled with barely suppressed rage. "You know who that thirty million belongs to, Don Tulio. It's taken me five years of the most delicate, frustrating, and nerve-racking negotiations to get to this point. Our buyers must take possession of that money within forty-eight hours or the deal, everything I've worked toward, will be flushed. Have you any idea what it took to make those people trust me? *Dios de diablos*, Don Tulio!

There is no reasoning with those people. Their word is ironclad. There is no wiggle room, no elasticity whatsoever. We are bound to them, and them to us. Till death do us part, *comprende, hombre*?"

His fist came down again, rattling cups and saucers. "This does not happen in my house, this cannot happen. Do I make myself clear?"

"Absolutely, Don Maceo." The Aztec knew when he was being dismissed. He rose. "Rest assured this problem will be solved."

Encarnación's eyes followed the Aztec as a predator will its prey. "Within the next twenty-four hours you will bring me both the thirty million and the head of this traitor. This is the solution I demand, Don Tulio. The only solution possible."

The Aztec, eyes as opaque as those of a dead fish, inclined his head. "Your will, Don Maceo, my hand."

When Bogs reached the area surrounding the Treadstone headquarters, he pulled the car up to the curb but restrained Dick Richards as he was about to get out.

"Where d'you think you're going?" Bogs said.

"Back to work," Richards answered. "I've already been away from my desk for too long." He glanced down at Bogs's meat-hook hand on his arm. "Let me go."

"You'll go when you're told to go, not before." Bogs looked at Richards intently. "It's time for you to go to work."

"Go to work? I *have* been working."

"No," Bogs said. "You've been sleeping. Now you will *create*. I will give you specific instructions. You're to carry them out to the letter. You do what I tell you, in the way I tell you, no more, no less, got it?"

Richards, his insides suddenly turned liquid, nodded uncertainly. "Naturally."

"What we have in mind isn't easy." He leaned toward Richards. "But what in life ever is?"

Richards nodded again, even more uncertainly. He had not expected this. Up until now his life as a triple agent had gone relatively smoothly, settling into a pattern that was easy to follow. Now he knew that he had been lulled into a false sense of calm and security. Bogs was right, he had been sleeping. Now came the deep; now came the unknown, where monsters that could swallow him whole lurked.

"What..." His words stuck in his throat. He licked his lips, as if to grease the way. "What do you want me to do?"

"We want you to set a Trojan inside the Treadstone intranet."

"Treadstone has electronic safeguards. The Trojan will be found almost immediately."

Bogs nodded. "Yes, it will." His eyes glittered ferally. "And, if you're clever enough not to get caught, your bosses will assign you to neutralize the Trojan."

Richards didn't like this; he didn't like it at all. "And?"

"And you'll do your job, Richards, in your usual quick and efficient manner. You'll impress them. You'll quarantine the Trojan, neutralize it, shred it."

He leaned in so close that Richards could smell the onions on his stale breath. "As you're shredding it, you'll implant a virus that will corrupt all the files on Treadstone's servers."

Richards frowned, shaking his head. "What good will that do? I'll never get to the remote archives off-site. They're isolated from the servers. The on-site server system will be cleansed. It will re-establish the files from archives. The system will be up and running within twelve hours."

"You must extend the downtime to twenty-four."

"I…" Richards swallowed. He felt both frozen and as if he had a high fever. "I can do that."

"Sure you can." Bogs's grin looked a mile wide. *The better to eat you with, my dear.* "That's the amount of time we'll need."

15

PETER HAD EXPECTED Tom Brick to stay in the safe house with him, but following his murderous instructions, he left. Alone in the vast house, Peter wandered for some moments, then sat down in a chair and took out the key he had found in Florin Popa's shoe as he dragged him into the boxwood maze at Blackfriar Country Club.

Holding it up to the light, he turned it over and over, studying every square inch of it. It was small, with a round plug at the end, covered in a blue rubberized material similar to what had been used on public locker keys, back in the days before 9/11 when there were such things as public storage lockers. This key had no markings whatsoever, but he figured there must be something to distinguish its use.

Utilizing one of the super-sharp razor blades Brick had given him to kill whoever Bogs brought through the door, he slit open the covering and peeled it back. He was immediately disappointed. The plug was blank on both sides. Turning it on end, however, he saw etched into the end: *RECURSIVE.*

He looked at the key in a new light and considered that it might not be for a lock, after all.

Now that he had a substantial clue to follow, he was unwilling to stay in the house, trying to figure out how he would get around killing someone he most certainly did not want to kill. He rose and went to the front door, only to find it locked. The same was true for the back door. All the windows were locked. He could see the tiny wires that would raise an instant alarm if any of the panes were broken.

The same was true for the windows on the second floor, but up here in the bedrooms the panes were smaller. Back down in the kitchen, he rooted around in the drawers without finding what he needed, but a closet revealed a tool chest. Inside, he found a glass cutter. Racing back upstairs, he chose a window that looked out on a spreading oak and scored a line between the glass and the sash. The super-sharp blade dug deeply into the glass. He made the same scores on two other sides. Setting down the glass cutter, he crossed to the bed, removed a case from a pillow, then, wrapping it around his left hand, returned to the pane of glass he'd been working on. Slowly and carefully, he scored down the fourth side.

With the fingertips of his right hand on the glass, he struck it with his protected left hand, and it moved a little. He hit it again, harder this time, dislodging the pane from the sash. He grabbed it between the fingers of his right hand before it could

fall and shatter. Then he turned it, laying it flat, careful not to disconnect the alarm wire. With infinite
care, he climbed through the open space, turned his
body and leaped to the crotch between two thick
branches of the oak. He teetered vertiginously until
he threw his arms around one of the branches.
Steadying and orienting himself, he climbed down
to the lowest branch, and, from there, dropped the
last two and a half feet to the ground.

Retrieving his mobile from its hiding place in his
crotch, he phoned Treadstone for a car to pick him
up, giving his approximate location. Then he began
to walk out of the cul de sac, toward a road whose
name he could recognize and relay to the driver.

It took him three calls to determine that there was, in
fact, a boat named *Recursive* tied up at slip 31 at the
Dockside Marina at 600 Water Street SW. By that
time, his driver had dropped him where he had left
his car outside the Blackfriar Country Club. Forty
minutes later, he was pulling up to Dockside, rolling
into a parking space.

He sat for a moment, turning the key over and
over between his fingers, as the car engine cooled,
ticking like a clock. Then he got out and walked
down to the boardwalk where the boats were tied up.
Most of the boats were battened down for the winter, covered against the weather. Some of the slips
were empty, their occupants dry-docked and shrink-
wrapped. On a few boats, people were working,
stowing fishing gear, hosing down decks, coiling
ropes, cleaning seats and brass railings. He nod-

ded to them, smiling, as he ambled past. He had to remind himself that everything slowed down at a marina, that a careful and unhurried manner held sway.

It seemed odd to him that Florin Popa, a bodyguard, would own a boat. But then, considering how carefully the key had been hidden, maybe Popa didn't actually own the *Recursive*. Maybe he was just using it.

Peter followed the slip numbers until he came to 31. The *Recursive* was a 36-foot Cobalt inboard. Judging by the open deck and the seating arrangement, it was a pleasure craft, not a fishing boat. Taking hold of one of the dock's wooden uprights, he swung aboard. The first thing he did was check to make certain no one was aboard. This was an easy enough task, considering that the Cobalt had no closed cabin or, apart from a minuscule head, belowdeck area.

Taking the key, he slid it into the ignition slot. He could only get it in halfway, however. It would not start the boat. Removing it, he began a thorough search, removing cushions that covered storage areas, opening the small dash box facing the passenger's seat, pulling on the metal ring that opened another, larger storage area, all to no avail. There was no slot anywhere on the *Recursive* in which to insert the key.

By this time, twilight was falling on DC, and a chill wind whipped across the water. Peter sat on the rear cushions, staring out at nothing, trying to figure out what he had missed. The key was etched with the name *Recursive*. He was aboard the *Recursive*.

Why couldn't he find what the key was meant to open?

He pondered this vexing question for another fifteen minutes or so. By then, darkness had fallen, the lights had been switched on, and he was forced to admit defeat, at least for the moment. He called Soraya at home, then disconnected, remembering that she had told him that line was out of order. Instead, he punched in her mobile number. It went right to voicemail. He left a brief, necessarily enigmatic message asking her to call him, and disconnected.

At home, he fixed himself a meal cobbled together from leftovers, but he scarcely tasted a thing. Afterward, he wandered around, touching things absently, while his mind whirred away a mile a minute. Finally, recognizing that he was as exhausted as he was wired, he slipped a DVD into his system and watched several episodes of *Mad Men*, which calmed him somewhat. He fell into a reverie where he was Don Draper, only his name was Anthony Dzundza. Roger Sterling was Tom Brick, Peggy was Soraya, and Joan was the strength-training guy at the gym Peter had been trying to approach for months.

Martha Christiana, watching the terrible inertia of what was left of her mother, said, "Is this how it ends?"

"For some." Don Fernando stood close beside her. "For the broken."

"She wasn't always broken."

"Yes," he said, "she was." When she turned to

look at him, he smiled encouragingly. "She was born with a defect in her brain, something that wasn't working correctly. In those days, it wasn't something that could be diagnosed, but even today, there's not much that can be done."

"Drugs."

"Drugs would have turned the young woman she used to be into a zombie. Would that have been better?"

Martha's mother moved uncomfortably, made a mewing sound, and Martha went to her, helped her over to the bathroom. She was inside with her for several minutes. Don Fernando crossed to the dresser, picked up the two photos, and one by one, studied them. Or rather he studied the young girl Martha Christiana had been. He had the unusual ability of being able to glean people's psychological quirks from "reading" old photos of them.

The door opened behind him, and, putting down the pictures, he helped Martha bring her mother over to the bed, where they sat her down. The old woman seemed exhausted or, perhaps, not there at all, as if she were already asleep.

The nurse came in then, but Martha waved her away. By silent mutual consent, she and Don Fernando got the old woman into bed. As she laid her head on the pillow and Martha arranged her hair around her emaciated face, a tiny spark appeared in her eyes as she looked up at her daughter, and it was possible to believe for just that instant that she recognized Martha. But the ghost of a smile evaporated so quickly that it might never have existed.

Martha sat on the edge of the bed while her

mother closed her eyes, drifted deeper into the impenetrable jungle of her mind. "We'll all end up here, in the end."

"Or we'll die young." Don Fernando's mouth twisted. "Except me, of course." He nodded. "'No one here gets out alive.'"

"'Five to One.'" Martha recognized the line written by Jim Morrison.

He smiled. "It isn't only Bach and Jacques Brel I'm partial to."

Martha turned back. "How can I leave her here?"

"You left her before." She turned on him, but before she could say anything, he said, "That's not a criticism, Martha, simply a statement of fact." He approached her. "And the fact is, she's best off here. She needs care, and these people are caring."

She turned, looked down at her mother's sleeping face. Something had happened. She no longer saw herself there.

At length, Peter slept, dreaming of the Cobalt running at full throttle, while he desperately swam to keep from being chopped to kelp by the whirring prop. The next morning, as he disinterestedly poured cold cereal into a gaily striped bowl, he got a brainstorm.

Firing up his laptop, he Googled *recursive*, which referred him back to the noun *recursion*, whose main definition in the postmodern world was "the process of defining a function or calculating a number by the repeated application of an algorithm." That told him nothing, but when he looked up the origin, he discovered that the Latin *recursio* meant "running back, or repeating a step in a procedure," as in, say, shampooing: lather, rinse, repeat.

That led him to consider that there might be a recursive *within* the *Recursive*. The trouble there was that he had checked everything within the boat and had found nothing. But what about the area *around* *Recursive*?

He showered and dressed in record time, drove back to the marina, where he arrived at slip 31 and jumped onto the Cobalt. It looked just the same as it had yesterday. He moved methodically around the boat, peering over the side. There was nothing on the port side, bow, or stern, and it seemed the same for the starboard side, until he reached down under the second bumper and found a rope tied to the underside.

With mounting excitement, he hauled up the rope, hand over hand, until he had retrieved what was on the end of it: an immense rubberized watertight satchel. With some difficulty, owing to the weight, he set it on one of the aft cushions. Sure enough, the satchel was locked. When he inserted the key and turned it to the right, the lock popped open.

Removing it, the satchel's top opened like an animal's jaws. Inside, he found stacks of five-hundred- and thousand-dollar bills. All the breath went out of him. Instinctively, he looked around, peering through the bright morning sunlight to see if anyone was watching him. No one was. The few people he had passed earlier had taken their boats out. The marina was deserted.

He spent the next half hour counting the bills, adding up the sums of the stacks, which, he quickly discovered, each held the same number of bills. When he was finished, he couldn't believe the figure he had come up with.

Good God, he thought. *Thirty million dollars!*

Bourne and Rebeka deplaned in Mexico City with the Babylonian on their backs.

"There's no way out," Rebeka said. "He has us trapped in here."

"There's still customs and immigration to consider." Bourne was aware of the Babylonian, ambling five or six people behind them. He needed to stay there in order to keep them in sight.

"We should split up," Rebeka said, passport out and open as they joined the first-class line to be processed into Mexico.

"That's what he'll expect us to do," Bourne said. "I imagine he'll welcome that, a man like him. Divide and conquer."

They inched forward toward the white line painted on the concrete floor that marked the last staging area before handing over their passports.

"Do you have a better idea?" Rebeka asked.

"I will," Bourne said, "in a minute."

He looked around at all the faces—the men and women, the children of all ages, the families traveling with strollers and the paraphernalia endemic to babies and toddlers alike. Three teenage girls with teddy bear backpacks giggled and did a little dance, a woman drew up in an airline wheelchair, a three-year-old broke away from her mother and began wandering through a thicket of people who laughed and patted her on the head.

"What we have to do," Bourne said, moving, "is make something happen."

"What?" But she followed him as he stepped over to the longer line of economy-class passengers that snaked through the hall.

He came up beside the woman in the wheelchair. She was dressed in a chic pinkish Chanel suit, her thick black hair pulled severely back from her face in a complex bun. Bending over, he said, "You shouldn't be waiting on a long line. Let me give you a hand."

"You're very kind," she said.

"Tim Moore," he said, giving the name on the passport he was using.

"Constanza." She had a face in which the DNA of the Olmec and their Spanish conquerors mingled as it had in their centuries-old bloody battles. Her skin was the color of honey, her features hard, almost brutal in the unquestionable beauty that seemed timeless. "Honestly, I don't know why they deposited me here. The attendant said to wait just a moment, but she hasn't come back."

"Don't worry," Bourne said. "My wife and I will have you through here in no time."

With Rebeka following, he pushed the wheelchair off the long line and headed straight through to the head of the first-class line.

"Halevy is watching," Rebeka whispered to Bourne.

"Let him," he said. "There's nothing he can do."

Constanza cocked her head, her clever eyes questioning. "What's that, Mr. Moore?"

"I'll need your passport."

"Of course." She handed it over as they came up to the immigration cubicle.

He handed over the three passports. The official opened them, stared into their faces. "This woman is a Mexican citizen. You two should be in that line over there."

"Señor and Señora Moore are with me," Constanza said. "As you can see, I can't get around without them."

The official grunted. "Business or pleasure?" he said to Bourne in a bored voice.

"We're on vacation," Bourne said, matching the official's tone.

Their passports were duly stamped and Bourne pushed the wheelchair through into the baggage claim area, Rebeka just behind him. They stayed with Constanza, helping her with her baggage, while, some yards away, the Babylonian fumed, pacing, helpless to come nearer.

Outside security, she was met by her chauffeur, a burly Mexican with tiny piggy eyes, a pockmarked moon face, and the demeanor of a doting uncle. He unfolded a beautiful aluminum wheelchair, transferring his charge into it without seeming effort.

"Manny," Constanza said as they all headed for the exit doors, "this is Señor Moore and his wife, Rebeka. They were kind enough to help me through immigration. They're nice people, Manny, and one so infrequently meets nice people nowadays, isn't that so?"

"Absolutely, Señora," Manny said dutifully.

She turned her head. "Mr. Moore, you and Rebeka must be my guests. There's plenty of room in the auto and, since it's lunchtime, I insist you take the meal with me." She waved a hand. "I'll not hear a word to the contrary. Come along now."

She wasn't kidding about having room. Her "auto" was a Hummer limo with a custom interior that made it as comfortable as a living room.

"Tell me, Mr. Moore, what is your line of work?" Constanza said when they had settled themselves and Manny, behind the wheel, had pulled out into the circular traffic flow leaving the airport. She had the sort of body most women of twenty would kill for: big-breasted, slim-waisted, long-legged.

"Import-export," Bourne said without hesitation.

"I see." Constanza, watching Rebeka as she stared back at the pick-up area, continued, "I so love people with secrets."

Rebeka turned. "I beg your pardon?"

"My late husband, Acevedo Camargo, was a man composed almost entirely of secrets." She smiled slyly. "Sometimes I think that's why I fell in love with him."

"Acevedo Camargo," Bourne said. "I've heard that name."

"I expect you have." There was a distinct twinkle in Constanza's eyes as she addressed Rebeka. "My late husband made his money, like so many clever men in Mexico, in the drug trade." She shrugged. "I'm not ashamed of it, facts are facts, and, besides, it's better than kowtowing to Gringos with your face in the dust." She waved a hand. "No offense, but we're in my country now. I can say what I want, when I want."

She smiled benignly. "You mustn't misunderstand me. Acevedo was a good man, but, you see, in Mexico, more often than not, good men die. Acevedo turned his back on the drug trade. He became a politician, a crusader against the people who had made him a multimillionaire. Brave or stupid? Possibly both. They killed him for it, gunned him down in the street between his office and his armored car, a hail of bullets; no one could have saved him, not even if he had had a dozen bodyguards instead of three. They all died that evening. I remember the sun was red as a bullfighter's cape. That was Acevedo—a bullfighter."

She sat back, apparently exhausted by her memories. Manny drove along the Circuito Interior Highway, heading into the dusky west.

"I'm so terribly sorry," Rebeka said, after exchanging a quick look with Bourne.

"Thank you," Constanza said, "but there's really no need. I knew the life I was drawing when I fell in love with him." She shrugged. "What can you do when desire and destiny become entwined? This is life in Mexico, which is made up of equal parts poverty, hopelessness, and shit. An endless series of defeats. Excuse my bluntness, but I've lived long enough to know how tedious it is to beat around the bush."

Her hand, slender, elegant, and burnished with nail polish and jeweled rings, made circles in the air. "Because this is what life is here, we learn to take any path that will lift our faces from the mud. I chose Acevedo. I knew who and what he was. He would not, *could* not, hide those things from me. Over the years, I advised him. No one knew, of course. Such things are frowned upon for a woman." She smiled, almost wistfully. "I gave him more money instead of children. Being tied to the kitchen and the nursery was not for me. I told him that at the very beginning. Still he loved me and wanted me." Her smile broadened. "Such a good man. He understood so much. Except how to survive." She sighed. "Smart as he was, what he never figured out was that it made no difference whether the law was raped and pillaged by the government or by the criminals."

She lifted her head, a brave smile on her face. "Thinking back on it, I'm certain now that he knew he would be killed. He didn't care. He wanted to do what he wanted to do." That enigmatic smile again. "Brave and stupid, as I said."

The limo, exiting the highway, turned left onto Avenue Rio Consulado and then the Paseo de la Reforma. As they entered the city proper, the navel of the Distrito Federal, home to twenty-two million souls, Constanza's eyes snapped back to focus on Bourne and Rebeka.

"*Dios mio*," she said, as they drove through the choked streets of the Historic District, "listen to me rambling on about my life when I so want to know about yours."

So," Don Fernando said, "who do you belong to?"

Martha Christiana, plucking off a bit of buttery

croissant, concentrated on her breakfast. "Why should I belong to anyone?"

"All women yearn to belong to someone."

She took a sip of her café au lait, served in a thick white porcelain cup the size of a small bowl. "What about the independent women?"

"*Especially* the independent women!" he said with enthusiasm. "Independence needs to be attached to something, otherwise it is meaningless. It has nothing to contrast with. It withers and turns bitter."

The two of them were sitting at a round table with a glass top and heavily filigreed wrought-iron legs, one of perhaps a dozen scattered across the rooftop restaurant that overlooked the busy harbor at Gibraltar and, further out, the deep-turquoise Mediterranean. The high blue sky was dotted with benign-looking meandering clouds. A freshening breeze stirred her hair. It had been late when they had finished in the room where her mother sat, locked inside her own mind. Martha had needed to talk, though it shamed her at first. Later on, after he had helped her put her mother to bed, much to her astonishment, the shame had evaporated like mist in sunlight.

She looked up now into his strong, lined, sunbronzed face. He saw her expression, and his hands opened wide. "What? I'm the man who loves women."

"At the moment you don't sound like it."

"Then you've misunderstood me." He shook his head. "No one chooses to be alone, no one wants it."

"I do."

"No," he said evenly, "you don't."

"Please don't tell me what I want."

"My apologies," he said without really meaning it.

The eggs came then, along with *papas bravas* and *salsa verde*. They ate silently for a time. A tension was building between them. At the moment Martha Christiana realized that it was deliberate, he said, "So now who do you belong to?"

A tiny smile broke across her lips, which she hid by mopping a runny yolk with several potato bits and popping them into her mouth. Now she understood what this conversation was about, and why he had taken her back to Gibraltar. She chewed thoughtfully and swallowed.

"Why do you want to know, Don Fernando?"

"Because," he said calmly and evenly, "you came to me as the angel of death." He caught the flash of her eyes, their ever so slight widening. "Now I'm wondering whether we have gone beyond that."

"And if we haven't?"

He smiled. "Then you must kill me."

She sat back and wiped her lips. "So you know."

"It would seem so."

"When?"

He shrugged. "From the very beginning."

"And you let me go about it?"

"You intrigue me, Martha."

Her serious eyes studied him for a moment, then she laughed raucously. "I must be losing my touch."

"No," he said. "You no longer wish to be alone. You want to belong."

"I belong to Maceo Encarnación."

There, she had said the dreaded name. It was out.

He shook his head. "That, my dear, is an illusion."

"Now, I suppose, you'll tell me it's an illusion created by Maceo Encarnación."

"In fact, it's an illusion you yourself created." Don Fernando, knowing she loved fresh-squeezed blood-orange juice, refilled her tall, narrow glass. "Maceo Encarnación does not possess that power." He paused for a moment, as if in deep contemplation. "Unless, of course, you have given it to him."

He shrugged again, his gaze tangling with hers. "You're stronger than that. This I know without question."

"How?" she said. "How do you know?"

He answered her with his eyes.

"I have been with Maceo Encarnación for a number of years, after a long line of—" She was about to say *after a long line of men who used me and who I used, after I escaped Marrakech*, but she bit her tongue instead. She could not recount those months of humiliation, even with this man, whom, she realized now, she had come to trust, an utterly astonishing revelation, considering she had been quite certain she could never trust a man. That included Maceo Encarnación, who paid so generously for her services, just as he had paid for her training. *"You're a natural at killing,"* he had told her once. *"All your skills need are more options to choose from, a bit of refining."* The concept of trust had never been raised between them. Theirs was a strictly transactional relationship, nothing more, but nothing less, either. The fact remained, however, that she had never once contemplated betraying him. Until now.

Don Fernando Hererra, the man sitting across from her, staring, it seemed, into her very soul, had changed everything, upending her life, causing her to transgress every rule she had imposed on herself. But, on second thought, maybe not. Perhaps he was an emissary, perhaps he had just handed her the key. The rest had been her choice, as he had intimated. It was she who had opened the door, stepping through into an entirely new world. He hadn't told her how to act or feel—he had been trying to tell her that she had already made her decisions.

She knew without having to ask that this was how Don Fernando saw it, and she was immensely grateful for that. He was the sort of man she had dreamed of, but had convinced herself she would never meet, that he could not possibly exist.

And yet...

Breaking her gaze away, she stared out over the rocking boats, the furled sails, the drying nets on the decks of the just-returned fishing fleet. The granite boulders rising like a giant's shoulders from the sea.

"When I was a child," she said, "I used to think I lived at the end of the world." She waited, afraid, almost, to go on. Then she took the next step into the brightly lit room. "I was wrong. It was the beginning."

16

CONSTANZA CAMARGO LIVED at the corner of Alejandro Dumas and Luis G Urbina, in Colonia Polanco. From her jalousied front windows Bourne looked out at the modernist, angular man-made pond in the center of Lincoln Park, beyond which, to the north, past the thick, geometric stands of trees, was Castelar Street. The interior of the colonial mansion was warm and comfortably furnished, made welcoming and even intimate by the profusion of personal items, photos, memorabilia, and souvenirs from half a lifetime of world travel.

"Someone in this family loves Indonesia," Bourne said, as he and Rebeka followed Constanza into the dark wood-beamed dining room. It was wallpapered in a dark-green semi-abstract forest pattern and had French doors that led out to an inner courtyard dominated by a lime tree and a concrete fountain sculpted into the shape of twin dolphins, caught in mid-leap. Purple and pink bougainvillea clung to the pale stone walls.

"That would be me," Constanza said. "In Java, I stood atop the Buddhist sanctuary, Borobudur, at sunrise. In the late afternoon, I heard the Muslim voices of the muezzin calling and echoing all across the dusky, sun-bronzed valley. Astonishing. I fell instantly in love."

As they sat at the thick trestle table, they were surrounded by servants, each carrying a tureen of stew or a platter of food or bottles of tequila, wine, and spring water.

As lunch was methodically, almost ritualistically, served, Constanza said with that same twinkle in her eyes, "Now I've told you my history, you must tell me yours."

"We've come to Mexico City looking for someone," Bourne said before Rebeka could answer.

"Ah." Constanza smiled. "Not on a vacation."

"Sadly, no."

She waited while a servant spooned a dark, rich pork *mole* onto her plate. "And may I assume that your search is urgent?"

"Why would you say that?" Rebeka asked.

Constanza turned to her. "Did you think I didn't see that evil-looking man lurking in the arrivals hall? I may be getting on in years, but I'm not senile!"

"I want to be as sharp as you are," Rebeka said, "when I'm your age."

"Flattery will get you everywhere," Constanza said with a wink. "Why do you think I offered you a lift?" She leaned toward them, lowering her voice conspiratorially. "I want in on the action."

"Action?"

"Whatever you two are up to. Whatever that evil-looking man wants to stop you from doing."

"Since we're speaking bluntly," Bourne said, "that evil-looking man wants to kill us."

Constanza frowned. "Now that I won't put up with!"

Rebeka shook her head. "You're not shocked?"

"After you've lived my life," Constanza said, "nothing is shocking." She turned to stare at Bourne. "Especially for people who say they're in import-export. For many years, that was my husband's line of work!"

She put her hands together, no longer interested in eating, if she ever had been. "So, tell me what you can and I will help you find whoever you're looking for."

"His name is Harry Rowland," Bourne said.

"Or Manfred Weaving," Rebeka added.

"Legends," Constanza said, a sprightly gleam in her eye. "Oh, yes, I know about legends. Acevedo used them in the early days when we traveled abroad."

"There's something that may make this man easier to locate," Bourne said. "We think he works for SteelTrap."

Something new overcame Constanza's expression, something powerful and dark and thoroughly unpleasant. She looked from one to the other. "This will undoubtedly sound overheated, even melodramatic. I wish it were either of those things." Her eyes had turned dark and unfathomable with secrets best left untouched. "My best advice is to forget this man Rowland or Weaving. Whatever your business is with him, forget it. Leave Mexico City on the next flight."

After enduring a restless night during which Charles Thorne was pursuing her through a labyrinth of dank corridors that smelled of anaesthetic and death, Delia awoke in her own bed with a pounding headache even three ibuprofen couldn't quite eradicate. She checked her phone to see if there had been any calls from Soraya's ICU nurse, even though she knew there hadn't been. One voicemail and two texts from Amy, wondering how she was. Amy and Soraya did not get along, which was a great sadness to her. She hadn't wanted to believe it, but Amy was jealous of the intimacy she shared with Soraya. Even though she had assured Amy there was no physical component to their friendship, that Soraya was strictly hetero, she had come to the realization that Amy didn't believe her. *"I've read all the articles about how rampant homosexuality is in the Arab world,"* Amy said in one of her less than finest moments. *"It's all been pushed underground, it's all sub rosa, which makes the urge all the stronger."* Nothing Delia could say would dissuade Amy from her point of view, so she had stopped trying, and gradually the subject of Soraya dropped from their conversations.

Showered and dressed, she grabbed a bite at a McD drive-through. She might as well have been eating the cardboard packaging for all she could taste the food.

Arriving at the office, she occupied herself with figuring out a fiendishly clever double-blind detonation mechanism. When, at length, she looked at her watch, over two hours had passed. She stood up, stretched, and took a walk around the lab in an attempt to clear her head.

It was no use. No matter what she did, she remained alone with her thoughts and her seething anger at Charles Thorne. Her first concern, of course, remained Soraya, but now she was at a total loss to understand what had drawn her friend to that monster. *Maybe it's a heterosexual thing*, she thought, with both amusement and bitterness. He had humiliated her. Far worse, she had allowed him to humiliate her.

She returned to her workstation, but now she was unable to concentrate, so, grabbing her overcoat, she returned to the hospital. It seemed important, somehow, to be near Soraya, especially because she was unconscious and vulnerable.

Already exhausted and terribly hungry, she went down the hall to the ICU, but once she was assured by Soraya's nurse that there was no news, she took herself down to the basement commissary, filled up her tray with a mishmash of dishes, added a soda and, after paying, sat down at a Formica table. She ate staring at the huge analog clock on the wall, her thoughts with her friend, hoping that with every breath she took now she'd be closer to healing.

Dear God, she thought, *stay close to Raya, protect her from harm, let her and the baby be okay.*

Her eyes burned and her skin felt parched, products of spending time in the hospital's canned air.

She knew she should leave, take a break, walk around the block even, but somehow she could not get herself to do it. She waited for her mobile to ring, willing there to be good news.

And, at last, there was. Her mobile vibrated, she jumped up, and listened to the nurse even as she was on her way upstairs, her heart pounding in her chest. Too long a wait for the elevators, so she turned to the stairwell, taking the treads two at a time, thinking, *Come on, Raya. Come on!*

Pushing the large square button on the wall to open the automatic doors, she went into the ICU. On either side of a wide central aisle were screened-off bays from which issued the mechanical beeps, whistles, and sighs of the various machines keeping the critical care patients alive, in some cases, breathing.

She hurried past the burn and cardiac units. Soraya's bay was the last one on the right. Her nurse, a young woman with her hair pinned back, looked at Delia with caring eyes.

"She's awake," the nurse said, reacting to the acute anxiety on Delia's face. "Her vitals have stabilized. Dr. Santiago and one of his colleagues have been in. They seemed pleased with their patient's progress."

Delia felt as if she were walking on burning needles. "So the prognosis?"

"The doctors are cautiously optimistic."

Delia felt a bubble in her chest deflate. "Then she's out of the woods?"

"I would say so, yes." The nurse offered one of those nursely smiles that could mean nothing at all. "Though there's still a ways to go, she's made remarkable progress."

Delia said, "I want to see her."

The nurse nodded. "Please don't overtax her. She's still very weak and is working for two."

As the nurse was about to turn away, Delia said, "Has anyone else been in to see her?"

"I called you the moment the doctors were finished with their examinations."

"Thank you," Delia said fervently.

The nurse ducked her head. "Call me if you need me." She pointed. "I'll be at my monitoring station."

Delia nodded, then, pushing aside the fabric curtain, went in to see her friend. Soraya, hooked up to a bewildering array of machines, was propped up on the high hospital bed. Her expression brightened considerably when she saw Delia.

"Deel," she said, lifting her hand for her friend to take. She closed her eyes for a moment when she felt the warmth of Delia's hand. "I've come from the back of beyond."

"So the doctors tell me." Delia's smile was genuine. Raya looked far better than she had in recovery. The dusky-rose color had returned to her cheeks, happily replacing yesterday's deathly pallor. "It's been a rough ride, but now the worst is over, I know it."

Soraya smiled and Delia burst into tears.

"What is it? Deel, what is it?"

"That's your old smile, Raya. The smile I know and love so much." She leaned over and kissed her friend tenderly on each cheek in the European manner. "Now I know I have my best friend back. Everything's going to be all right."

"Come here," Soraya said. "Sit by me."

Delia perched herself on the edge of the bed, keeping hold of her friend's hand.

"I've been dreaming non-stop, Deel. I dreamt I was in Paris with Amun, that he hadn't been killed. I dreamt I was with Aaron. And I dreamt that Charlie was here." Her eyes, clearer now, gazed into Delia's. "Is Charlie still here, Deel?"

"No, he left." Delia's eyes cut away, then returned to her friend. "He said the baby changed everything, that he wants to keep you in his life."

"In other words, you misread him."

"I guess so." She had no intention of telling Soraya that Thorne had threatened her.

"Good. That's so good." Soraya squeezed her hand. "You did precisely what I wanted you to do."

"What?" Delia's head came up.

Soraya's smile was tinged with regret. "I used you, Deel. Before the attack, I went to see him, but what I wanted so disgusted me, I couldn't tell him. I needed you to do that for me." She squeezed her friend's hand. "Don't be angry."

"How could I be angry with you?" Delia shook her head. "But I don't understand."

Soraya gestured. "Could I have some ice water?"

Delia rose and poured water from a plastic pitcher into a plastic cup and handed it to Soraya, who drank deeply.

When she handed the empty cup back, she said, "I need a way to keep Charlie tied to me."

"Once again, not understanding."

Soraya laughed softly and put a hand on her belly. "Come here, Deel. I can feel the baby moving."

Leaning over, Delia put her hand next to Soraya's, and when she felt the baby kicking, she laughed as well. Then she sat back. "Okay, Raya, time to tell me how we're all linked, you, me, and Thorne."

Soraya studied her for a moment. At length, she said, "My relationship with Charlie is not what I've made it appear to you."

Delia shook her head mutely.

"It's business."

"Having an affair with him was business?" The shock reverberated straight through Delia. "Are you fucking kidding me?"

"I wish I were." Soraya sighed. "It's the reason I hooked up with him in the first place." She smiled. "That's all I can tell you. I feel so guilty using you like that."

"Jesus, no, Raya. I ..." Now things that had made no sense to Delia slid into focus. "Frankly, I could never understand what you saw in him."

"Secrets, Deel. Secrets. They rule my life. You know that."

"But this. Hopping into his bed because—"

"A centuries-old tradition. Ask Cleopatra, Lucretia Borgia, Mata Hari."

Delia looked at her friend as if in an entirely new light. "And the baby?"

Soraya's eyes glittered. "It's not his."

"Wait, what? But you told me—"

"I know what I told you, Deel. But I need Charlie to believe it's his." She rubbed her belly. "It's Amun's."

Delia felt dizzy, as if she had lost her moorings in this new world Soraya was revealing layer by mysterious layer. "What if he asks for a paternity test?"

"What if I tell his wife about us?"

Delia stared at Soraya with a new understanding, a kind of astonishment, and something else entirely. "Raya, you're scaring the hell out of me right now."

"Oh, Deel, I don't mean to. You're my friend. We're closer than sisters. Even Peter doesn't know what I've told you. Please try to understand."

"I want to, Raya. Honestly, I do. But this just goes to show that you never really know anyone no matter how close you think you are."

"But we *are* close, Deel." She reached out. "Listen to me, ever since I came back from Paris I've come to realize that there's more to life than secrets. That's all I have, really." She laughed. "Except you, of course." She sobered immediately. "But now I have the baby and—I've been thinking—using the baby as a weapon against Charlie—it's heinous. For the first time in my life I feel dirty, as if I've crossed a line that sickens me. I can't use my child in this way. I don't want that for him. I don't want this life for him. He deserves more than shadows, Deel. He deserves the sunshine and kids his age. He deserves a mother who isn't always looking over her shoulder."

Delia leaned over and kissed her friend on the cheek. "This is good, Raya. Ever since you told me about the baby, I've been waiting for you to come to that conclusion."

Soraya smiled. "Now I have."

"You'll have to tell Peter."

"I already have, more or less."

"Really? How did he take it?"

"Like Peter. He's so rational. He understands."

Delia nodded. "He's a good guy." She frowned. "What will you tell Thorne?"

"Not a fucking thing. I don't have to tell you what Charlie's like."

With a shudder of disgust, Delia conjured up the horrible, humiliating conversation, culminating in the moment when he had grabbed his crotch and said, *"You don't know what you're missing."*

She felt the urge to tell her friend what Thorne had done, how he had hacked into her mobile, had tapes of the amorous voicemails Amy had left for her, but she bit her tongue. She didn't want to upset Soraya, not in the state she was in now, not when Soraya was ready to embark on the next phase of her life, ready to leave all the dark shit behind.

Instead, she smiled, bit back her bitterness against Thorne, and said, "No, I've gotten to know him much better these days." She leaned forward to kiss Soraya on the cheek. "Don't worry. Your secrets are safe with me."

Because I know you won't take my advice," Constanza Camargo said to Bourne, "I have no choice but to help you."

"Of course you have a choice," Rebeka said.

Constanza shook her head slowly. "You still have no conception of life here. There is destiny, only destiny. This cannot be explained or understood, except, possibly, in history. A story, then."

La comida was finally at an end, and they had retired to her exquisite, jewel-like living room, paneled in ebony, evoking an earlier, gilded age. She sat back in her wheelchair, her hands laced in her lap, and, as she spoke, the years seemed to melt away, revealing the magnificent, vibrant beauty she had been in her twenties and thirties.

"Maceo Encarnación not only took my husband's life, he took my legs as well. This is how it happened." She took out a flat silver case, snapped it open, and, after offering each of them a cigarillo, plucked one out. Manny, always at her side, lit it for her. "I hope you don't mind if I smoke," she said in a tone that said she had no intention of stopping.

She sat, smoking reflectively for several moments, before she began. "As I said, life in Mexico is bound to the wheel of destiny. Desire is also important—we are Latin, after all!—but, at the end of the day, desire hinders destiny. Acevedo found this out when he changed horses. He was destined to be a drug lord—this was his calling. He left it and he died.

"I should have learned from his mistake, but the truth is my desire for revenge blinded me, cut me off from my destiny, and, at the end of the day, cut me off from my legs. What happened was this: after Acevedo was shot dead, I summoned a cadre of men, Colombians who owed their livelihood, even their very lives, to Acevedo. They came here, and, at my direction, set out to end the life of the miserable Maceo Encarnación."

She took another long drag from her cigarillo, which emitted smoke like a just-fired pistol. Then she continued: "I was foolish. I miscalculated, or, rather, I underestimated Maceo Encarnación's power. He is protected by an almost mystical power, as if by gods. Acevedo's loyalists were beheaded, and then he came after me himself."

Her fist pounded against her useless legs. "Here is the result. He didn't kill me. Why? To this day, I don't know. Possibly, to him my living as a cripple was a more fitting punishment than death. More likely, it was raw cruelty."

She lifted a hand, fluttering it back and forth, as if the reason for her continued life was unimportant. "This is a cautionary tale, Mr. Moore, not an attempt to elicit sympathy." She turned to Rebeka. "But now you see, my dear, how the great wheel of destiny works. It has brought you to me or me to you, and there is a reason for that. Destiny has now combined with my desire for revenge. It has brought me the weapons I need because, Rebeka, I do not for a moment believe that you are Mr. Moore's wife—" she smiled "—any more than I believe his name is Moore." Her gaze shifted back to Bourne. "Mr. Moore, you would no more bring your wife to Mexico on such a mission than you would allow her to walk into a tiger's den."

She lifted a forefinger. "And make no mistake, going after Maceo Encarnación is walking into tiger territory. There will be no mercy, no second chances, only, if you are lucky, death." She stubbed out her cigarillo. "*But* if you are *very* lucky and extremely clever, you may yet walk out of the tiger's den with what you and I desire."

17

TULIO VISTOSO ARRIVED in Washington, DC, with anxiety in his mind and murder in his heart. How difficult was it, he thought, for Florin Popa to keep safe what he, Don Tulio, had so cleverly stolen on the steep, treacherous trail along the Cañon del Sumidero, outside Tuxtla Guttiérez, replacing the real thirty million with what he had been certain were undetectable counterfeit bills? And yet, Popa had failed, and his life was forfeit if he could not placate Don Maceo and his holy, all-powerful buyers within thirty-six hours.

He was still fulminating about the monumental fuck-up when he arrived at the Dockside Marina and saw the Cobalt in slip 31 crawling with cops. And not just cops, he realized with a jolt. *Federales.* He could smell them a mile away. They moved with a certain measured gait, like dray horses in their traces. He stared, horrified. The boat was well guarded, cordoned off with yellow CRIME SCENE tape.

Christ on the cross, what in the name of all that's holy has happened? Instinctively, he looked around, as if Popa might be lurking somewhere in the vicinity. Where the hell was Popa? Don Tulio wondered with a sinking heart. Had Popa absconded with the thirty million? Don Tulio's thirty million. This prospect terrified him. Or, worse, did the *federales* have it? Was Popa in their custody? With a trembling hand, he began to fire off a series of text messages to his lieutenants in a frenzied endeavor to recoup the thirty million as quickly as possible.

The Aztec felt like pulling his hair out. His crazed brain kept churning out dire possibilities, but a sliver of civilized veneer stopped him cold. Instead, he turned on his heel and stalked away. He swiped a hand across his forehead. Despite the chill, he was sweating like a pig.

Up ahead, a car pulled into a parking space in the lot and, a moment later, a young man leaped out. He pushed by Don Tulio as he hurried down the gangplank, onto the dock, and out to slip 31. Sensing something unusual, the Aztec turned. Sure enough, the *federale* ants crawling all over the *Recursive* began kowtowing to the new arrival: *el jefe*. This interested Don Tulio so, instead of hightailing it, he decided to hang around as unobtrusively as possible. This meant going down the gangplank himself and onto the dock. Choosing a deserted boat as far away as practical from the activity on the *Recursive*, he climbed aboard and busied himself doing nothing at all while he spied on the new arrival.

Happily for him, the marina's quiet atmosphere, combined with how the water carried the voices, allowed him to overhear snatches of conversation. In this way, he determined that *el jefe's* name was Marks. Turning for a moment, he noted that the vehicle Marks had arrived in was a white Chevy Cruze. He jumped off the boat, then went at an unhurried pace back up the ramp and into the lot, where he jotted down the Cruze's license plate number. Back on the boat, he returned his attention to Marks himself, his mind already plotting his next several moves.

It had been his experience that meeting with the chief of your enemies was preferable to working your way up the plantain tree. But meeting with *federales*, especially on their own turf, was a tricky business, one, Don Tulio knew, that needed to be thought out in considerable detail. He also knew that he would get one shot at confronting *jefe* Marks, so he was obliged to make the best of it. The danger of such a maneuver did not disturb him; he lived with danger every day of his life, had done so from the time he was ten years old and already raging through the streets of Acapulco. He had loved the sea, even before he became a cliff diver, showing off for Gringo money. He jumped from the highest cliff, dove the deepest, stayed down the longest. The churning water was his father and his mother, rocking him into a form of peace he could find nowhere else.

He became king of the divers, taking a cut from all their winnings. That might have continued indefinitely, until the moment a Gringo tourist accused him of fucking his teenage daughter. That the Gringa had initiated the liaison meant nothing in the face of her father's colossal wealth and the authorities' desperation to keep Acapulco a world-class tourist destination.

He got out just ahead of the cops, fleeing north, losing himself in the immense urban sprawl of Mexico City. But he never forgot how the Gringo had ruined his life, for he loved the ocean waters, desperately missed his old life. Years passed and a new life began to weave around him. Anarchism first. When he was older, he took out his rage at the institutional corruption with bouts of extreme violence against anyone who held a steady job. Eventually, he got smart and joined a drug cartel, working his way up the power grid by any and all means, which impressed his superiors up until the moment he directed his followers to cut their heads off with machetes.

From that bloody moment on he had been *jefe*, consolidating his power with the other cartel heads. He was uncomfortable in society. He had no expertise navigating the capital's deep and treacherous political waters, so he had forged an alliance with Maceo Encarnación, which had served them both well.

The Aztec made himself busy all over again while he leaned his ear to the prevailing wind and discovered that Popa was dead. *Jefe* Marks had killed him, after which he had inadvertently found the key. *The fucking key*, Don Tulio thought with a savagery that shook him to his core. *He has the fucking key*. But then, his mind cooling a single degree, he dredged up this hopeful thought: *He has the fucking key, but that doesn't mean he has the thirty million.* Which was followed by a second hopeful thought: *If the* federales *have the money, why are they searching the boat so frantically?*

Fuming, the Aztec finished coiling a rope for the seventeenth time. Noting that the *federales* were breaking up, he went down into the cabin, waiting there patiently while he counted the number of rivets in the deck, perched uncomfortably on a narrow seat. Shadows passed as the *federales* left the *Recursive* and went back up the dock to the parking lot. He listened for the car engines starting up. When, like popping corn, they ceased, he knew it was time.

Emerging from the cabin, he looked at the *Recursive*. It appeared deserted, but he resisted the urge to board it. Even though the clock that now measured his life was ticking mercilessly away, he knew it would be foolish to risk everything by going over there in daylight. Better by far to show patience, to wait for night to fall. He returned to the boat, lay down on the deck, and fell instantly into a deep and untroubled sleep.

Midnight," Constanza said. "Manny will come and collect you."

After she bade them goodnight, Bourne and Rebeka retired to the two adjoining bedrooms in the guest wing. But almost immediately she appeared on the threshold of his room.

"Are you tired?" Rebeka asked.

Bourne shook his head.

She walked in, went past him, and stood by the window, arms wrapped around herself, staring out at the inner courtyard. Bourne came and stood beside her. They could hear the wind clatter through the palms. By a sliver of moonlight, they watched the rustling of the leaves on the lime tree.

"Jason, do you ever think about death?" When he said nothing, she went on. "I think about it all the time." She shivered. "Or maybe it's just this place. Mexico City seems steeped in death. It gives me the creeps."

She turned to him. "What if we don't survive tomorrow?"

"We will."

"But what if we don't?"

He shrugged.

"Then we die in darkness," she said, answering her own question.

She stirred, then said, "Put your arms around me." When he did, holding her tight, she said, "Why don't we feel the way other people feel, deep down, not just on the surface, like water glancing off water? What is the matter with us?"

"We can do what we do," Bourne said softly, "only because we are what we are." He looked down at her. "There's no turning back for us. There's only one exit from the life we live, and none of us who are good at what we do want to take it."

"Do we love what we do so much?"

He was silent. The answer was evident.

He held her that way until, with a discreet knock on the partially open door, Manny announced himself.

* * *

His name is unimportant," Manny said as he drove them through Mexico City's bright-night streets. "He is known as *el Enterrador*." The Undertaker.

"Isn't that a little over the top?" Rebeka said from the plush backseat of the armored Hummer.

Manny looked at her in the rearview mirror and smiled with his teeth. "Wait till you meet him."

Flashing lights up ahead revealed a semicircle of cop cars, blazing headlights illuminating six cops using truncheons to beat down on a dozen teenagers armed with switchblades and broken beer bottles.

"Just another night in Mexico City," Manny said with no apparent irony.

They traveled on, through the Zona Rosa, the Historic Center, seemingly across the entire broad expanse of a city that sprawled, octopus-like, across the mile-high plain toward the great looming volcano, Popocatépetl, brooding like an ancient Aztec god.

They witnessed fires, street gangs stalking one another, they heard raucous Gringo techno and native *ranchera* music spilling out of nightclubs, vengeful brawls, the occasional gunshot. They were passed by roaring, souped-up cars driven by drunken kids, with *cumbia* or rap blasting from custom speakers, on and on, a nightmare scenario without end.

But at last they reached Villa Gustavo a Madero, and Manny slowed the Hummer, rolling it through darkened, sleeping streets, into the heart of the city within the city. Up ahead, the bonnets of trees, black against the twinkling, indistinct skyline, rose up like a prehistoric world until, through tree-shadowed by-ways, they reached the very center of the heart: the Cementerio del Tepeyac.

"Of course," Rebeka said to relieve the almost unbearable tension, "where else would *el Enterrador* hang out but in a cemetery."

However, it wasn't to one of the crypts that Manny took them, but to the Basilica de Guadelupe. He had no difficulty unlocking the door to the basilica and ushering them inside.

The incredibly intricate and exquisitely painted interior was ablaze, the gilt chandeliers illuminating the host of cherubs that spilled across the domed ceiling. Manny remained just inside the doorway while gesturing them down the central aisle. Long before they reached the draped altar, however, a figure appeared: a man with a pointed beard and mustache. His black eyes seemed to penetrate their clothes, their very skin, as if peering into the heart of them.

He possessed the pallor and demeanor of a ghost, speaking so softly Bourne and Rebeka were obliged to lean forward to hear him.

"You come from Constanza Camargo." It was not a question. "Follow me."

As he turned to go, he pushed up the wide sleeves of his ecclesiastical robe, revealing forearms knotted with muscle and ropy veins, crawling with tattoos of coffins and tombstones, beautiful and horrific.

It was almost 4 AM by the time the Aztec awoke,

according to his unerring internal clock. He was hungry. No matter. There were thirty million reasons to ignore the gnawing in his stomach. Finding a rubberized waterproof flashlight, he took it topside.

Outside, Washington glittered, seeming far away across the water. Don Tulio looked across to where the *Recursive* lay tied up at slip 31. No one was visible. In fact, the entire marina appeared deserted. Still, the Aztec stood on the boat, aurally cataloguing the night noises—the slap of the wavelets against hulls, the creaking of masts, the pinging of rigging against those masts—these were all the normal sounds of a marina. Don Tulio listened beyond those for any anomalous sounds—the soft tread of feet, the low sound of voices, anything that would indicate the presence of human beings.

Finding none, he was at last satisfied. He climbed onto the dock, first looking to the darkened harbormaster's hut, then swiftly and silently made his way to slip 31, stepping, at last, aboard the *Recursive*.

He went immediately to the second bumper on the starboard side and felt under it with his fingers. The nylon rope was still there! Heart pounding, he pulled in the rope, hand over hand. The weight felt just as it should; with every foot he reeled in, he became more and more certain that his thirty million was safe and secure at the nether end of the rope.

But when he had pulled it all in and switched on the flashlight, what he saw tied to the end was a lead weight.

"Looking for this?"

Don Tulio whirled, saw *jefe* Marks holding up the watertight satchel, deflated, empty, the thirty million and his life gone. Engulfed by the final wave of his murderous rage, he leaped at his tormentor, heard the explosion rocket through his ear, felt the bullet enter, then exit his left biceps. He kept going, a full-on bull-rush that took both Marks and him over the railing, both plunging down, the chill black water robbing them both of breath.

Chinatown? Really?" Charles Thorne sat down at the Formica table opposite the tall, slender man, dressed in one of those shiny Chinese suits that imitated the American style, but none too well.

"Try the moo goo gai pan," Li Wan said, gesturing with his chopsticks. "It's really rather good."

"Christ, it's four in the morning," Thorne said with a sour face. There was no point in asking Li how he managed to get a restaurant to stay open for him in the waning hours of the night when nothing, not even the cats, was roaming Chinatown's streets. "Besides, it's not really a Chinese dish."

Li Wan shrugged his coat-hanger shoulders. "When in America."

Thorne shook his head as he unwrapped his chopsticks and dug in.

"I suppose you were expecting beef sinew and fish maw," Li said with a visible shudder.

"My friend, you've spent too much time in America."

"I was *born* in America, Charles."

Thorne lapped a slick of MSG off his chopsticks. "Exactly my point. You need a vacation. Back to the homeland."

"Not *my* homeland. I was born and raised right here in DC."

Li, a prominent intellectual rights lawyer, had graduated from Georgetown University, which made him wholly homegrown. Still, Thorne couldn't help needling him; it was part of their relationship.

Thorne frowned. Despite what Li had said, he didn't like the moo goo gai pan at all. "As an outsider, you're privy to an awful lot of their secrets."

"Who said I'm an outsider?"

Thorne regarded him thoughtfully before hailing a passing waiter, who stopped and stood before him with the air of someone who, despite the hour, had many things better to do. Picking up the grease-stained plastic menu, Thorne ordered General Tso's chicken. "Extra crispy," he said, though it's doubtful the waiter heard him or, if he did, cared, until Li spoke to him in the withering Cantonese only a Mandarin could manage. Off the waiter went, as if Li had lit his tail on fire.

After pouring them both chrysanthemum tea, Li said, "Really, Charles, after all these years it would behoove you to learn Cantonese as well as Mandarin."

"What? So I can intimidate waiters in Chinatown? That's all it's good for these days."

Li regarded him again with his patented inscrutable look.

"You do that deliberately," Thorne complained. "You know that, don't you? I'm on to you."

The waiter set down a platter of General Tso's chicken, and, after giving Li a questioning look and receiving an answering nod, beat a hasty retreat.

"Is it extra crispy?" Li said.

"You know it is," Thorne replied, piling some into his bowl of rice.

The two men ate in companionable silence amid the sizzle and steam of the open kitchen behind them. The usual bustle, shouting, and shoving, however, were missing. The unaccustomed hush lent the place a forlorn air.

At last, when the first frenzy of shoving the food into his mouth had abated, Charles said, "I've known you a long time, Li, but I still can't figure how an outsider like you is trusted with—"

"Hush, Charles."

Their waiter, wiping his hands on his filthy apron, walked past them to the men's room.

Li pointed at Thorne's dish. "There really was a General Tso, you know. Zuo Zongtang. Qing Dynasty. Died in 1885. From Hunan. Odd since the dish is mainly sweet, not spicy like most Hunan dishes. It's not indigenous to Changsha, the capital of Hunan, nor Xiangyin, the general's home town. So what is its origin? There's speculation that the name of the dish was originally *zongtang* chicken."

"Meaning 'ancestral meeting hall.'"

Li nodded. "In that event, nothing to do with the good general." He swirled some tea around his mouth and swallowed. "Of course, the Taiwanese have claimed they created the dish." Li put down his chopsticks. "The point being, Charles, that no one knows these things—no one can."

"Are you saying that it's impossible to know how you became such a trusted guardian of—"

"Listen to me," Li said, abruptly and finally. "I'm

saying that in Chinese culture there are many reasons for many things, most of them too complicated to comprehend fully."

"Try me," Thorne said with a mouthful of food.

"I can't go into my lineage. It would make your eyes pop and your head spin. Suffice it to say, I am among the elite residing outside of Beijing. As to your suggestion of returning to the motherland, I'm far too valuable to the powers that be precisely where I am."

"'The powers that be.'" Thorne flashed a lopsided grin. "One of those opaque, distinctly Chinese phrases."

"As they say," Li said, returning the lopsided grin like a forehand over the net, "Beijing is composed of equal parts quicksand and cement."

"What do 'the powers that be' think of your bedding Natasha Illion?" Li and Illion, a supermodel of Israeli background, had been a breathless item for over a year, something of a record for that rareified, hothouse species.

Li, silent on the subject of his inamorata, watched Thorne return to his eating, waiting a decent amount of time before he said, "I understand you have a bit of an issue."

At that, Thorne's chopsticks froze halfway to his mouth. He covered his consternation by making a show of putting them down slowly and carefully. "Exactly what have you heard, Li?"

"Exactly what you have. You and the rest of the senior staff at *Politics As Usual* are about to be investigated for illegal voicemail hacking." He cocked his head. "Tell me, does the illustrious Senator Ann Ring know?"

"If she did," Thorne said acidly, "she'd be jumping out of her skin." He shook his head. "The investigation has not yet begun."

"For the time being."

"She must, on no account, find out. It will be the end."

"Yes, the end of your gravy train. How many millions is your wife worth?"

Thorne regarded him bleakly.

"But the senator will find out the moment the investigation begins, if she hasn't already."

"She hasn't, believe me."

"Tick-tock, Charles."

Thorne winced inwardly. "I need help."

"Yes, Charles," Li Wan said, "you most certainly do."

El Enterrador led them to the back of the apse, down a short, dimly lit corridor, into the rectory, which smelled of incense, polished wood, and man-sweat. Beneath an enormous figure of Christ on the Cross were laid out the architectural plans for Maceo Encarnación's villa on Castelar Street.

"Are you sure this is where our man is going to be?" Bourne had asked Constanza Camargo earlier in the evening.

"If, as you say, he was flown here to Mexico City," she had replied, "this is the reason why."

El Enterrador took them floor by floor, room by room, through the house. "Two floors," came his papery whisper, "plus, most importantly, a basement." He told them why.

"The roof is made of traditional unglazed Mexican tiles. Very sturdy. There are two exit doors on the ground floor—front and back. None on the second floor, save the windows. And as for the basement—" his long, stiletto-like forefinger showed them on the plan.

Then he lifted the top sheet, exposing another. "Those were the original plans. Here are the modifications Maceo Encarnación made when he moved in." His forefinger stabbed out again. "You see, here—and here—and again here." His black-ice eyes cut to them for an instant. "Good for you, possibly. Possibly not. That is not my business. I told Constanza Camargo that I would get you in. The rest is up to you."

He stood up, his cowl throwing an oblique shadow across the modified plan. "Afterward, if you are successful, if you manage to escape, you will not come here, nor will you go to Constanza Camargo's home."

"We discussed with her what would happen," Rebeka said, "after."

"Did you?" Clearly, *el Enterrador*'s interest was piqued. "Well, well."

"She must like us."

El Enterrador nodded. "I believe she does."

"How do you know Señora Camargo?" Rebeka asked.

El Enterrador flashed them an evil smile. "We met in heaven," he whispered, "or in hell."

"That's hardly helpful," Rebeka said.

"We are in Mexico, Señorita. Here there are volcanos, serpents, madness, gods, sacred places. Mexico City is one such. It is built upon the navel of the Aztec world. Here, heaven and hell meet."

"Let's get on with it," Bourne said, "shall we?"

The evil smile returned to the false priest's lips. "An unbeliever."

"I'm a believer in doing," Bourne said, "not talking."

El Enterrador nodded. "Fair enough, but..." He handed a small object to Bourne. It was a tiny replica of a human skull, studded with crystals. "Keep this safe," he said. "It is protection."

"Against what?" Bourne asked.

"Maceo Encarnación."

At that moment, Bourne recalled what Constanza Camargo had said: "*I underestimated Maceo Encarnación's power. He is protected by an almost mystical power, as if by gods.*"

"Thank you," he said.

El Enterrador inclined his head, obviously pleased.

Rebeka said, "Are we to stay here?"

"No. You will be transported to the mortuary, where you will stay until the call comes."

"The call will come to this particular mortuary?" Bourne said.

"This one and no other."

Bourne nodded, accepting *el Enterrador*'s word.

They were led out of the rectory, through a small, unobtrusive door, out into the churchyard beyond which stretched the vast cemetery, a city unto itself. There was a hearse awaiting them, its engine purring richly.

El Enterrador opened the wide rear door, and they climbed in.

"*Vaya con Dios, mis hijos,*" he said in a pious

voice, and made the sign of the cross. Then he slammed the door shut, and the hearse rolled out of the churchyard, away from the basilica, making its funereal way through the blackened byways of Cementerio del Tepeyac, heading deeper and deeper into the mystical heart of the city.

18

P ETER, DOWN IN the depths, felt the chill of
death. Hands were at his throat. He kicked out, but
the water, seeming thick as sludge, defeated his attack. Bringing his hands up under those at his throat,
he exploded them outward the moment they made
contact. The pressure came off, but the two of them
were still sinking down.

He scissored his legs, arrowing upward, but
hands caught at him, dragging him back. Didn't this
man need to breathe as badly as he did, weren't his
lungs aching, his head pounding, his heart thumping
painfully in his chest?

Peter could not see his antagonist, had never seen
him, in fact. The moment his flashlight picked him
out on the boat, he was blinded by the man's own
flashlight. Then came the attack, and both of them
went into the water.

Down and down.

Peter felt the cold sucking the strength out of him. His limbs felt like lead weights. Then there was an arm around his throat, a choke hold, which he could not tolerate. Feeling for the man's face, he jammed a thumb into one eye, pushing and pushing with all the strength left in him, and though the water impeded him, he had enough leverage that the choke hold vanished.

Peter spun to confront his attacker face-to-face. No light in the darkness. He had no idea how deep they had drifted, only that there was less than a minute before his lungs ran out of oxygen.

He rose, feathering his lower legs, then, instead of an ineffective kick, shoved the heel of his shoe into his attacker's face. Instantly, then, he scissored his legs again, reaching upward with his arms, his first priority now to get to the surface.

With that goal fixed firmly in mind, he kicked harder than ever. It seemed an eternity, during which he might have blacked out for seconds at a time, reality drooling by in discrete segments, connected by nothingness, as if his mind had completely fled his body. But, at last, he saw wavering above him the shadow of illumination—the opposite of a shadow, casting itself on what, as he neared, he realized was the skin of the water.

As he broke the surface, strong arms reached down, powerful hands gripped him—his men, alerted by the shot he had fired, must have been searching for him from the moment they boarded the *Recursive*.

He heard grunts above him, lifted his head to see two or three faces, among them Sam Anderson, his deputy, picked out in the glare of the spotlights. He squinted, half-blinded by the spots, like a creature from the depths. He heard Anderson turn and call for the spots to be angled slightly away, and was grateful when his men promptly complied.

That was when he felt something pinion his legs, then an immense weight pulling him inexorably back down into the water. Dimly, as he shouted, he wondered how his assailant could manage to stay underwater so long and still have the strength to try to pull him under.

Above his head, he heard shouts of consternation, above all, Anderson's firm voice, calmly calling out orders. As the men redoubled their grip on him, Anderson rose, and, drawing his sidearm, fired it into the water near Peter.

When the fourth bullet streaked into the water, Peter felt the weight come off, and his men drew him up, back over the railing and onto the deck of the *Recursive*. Immediately, they wrapped him in blankets. Red lights spattered the deck and cowling in rhythmic bursts. Peter saw that one of the revolving lights belonged to an ambulance. A pair of burly EMT paramedics lifted him onto a gurney.

"Anderson," he said in a voice that sounded unsteady even to his ears, "get these people off me. I'm not going anywhere."

"Sorry, boss, but we've got to get you checked out."

The gurney was lifted off the boat onto the dock. Peter discovered he was strapped down and helpless. Anderson trotted at his side. They rolled him up the dock to the parking lot where the ambulance waited.

"That fucker's still down there. We have to ID him. Call out the divers."

"Already done, boss." Anderson grinned. "In the meantime, we have spotlights on three Coast Guard boats scanning the harbor."

Just before the paramedics loaded him into the back of the ambulance, Anderson placed his mobile onto his chest, and said, "While you were getting wet, you got a priority call from SecDef." *Hendricks.*

The paramedics were already taking his vitals.

"The moment I get out of restraints," Peter said with no little sarcasm. Then: "Anderson, find this fucker."

"You got it, boss."

The door slammed shut and the ambulance took off. Anderson retraced his step to slip 31 and got back to work. The boss said to find the fucker, and that's precisely what he was going to do.

Early that morning, Maria-Elena had driven out of the heavily protected compound on Castelar Street, heading, as she always did, to her favorite markets to shop for that night's dinner. She was a creature of habit. She had worked for only one person in her life. Maceo Encarnación had taken her off the streets of Puebla when she was fourteen, a terribly thin, undernourished girl, and introduced her to his household. As it happened, she had a natural gift for preparing food—all that was needed was a bit of polishing from the then cook. From the moment Maria-Elena cooked her first dinner in his house, she had become an immediate favorite of Maceo Encarnación. He elevated her above others on his staff who had been with him longer, which, of course, caused friction.

Later, looking back on it from her lofty perch, Maria-Elena realized that the temporary chaos her rise had caused among the staff had been deliberate. It was a form of harrowing, Maceo Encarnación seeking to root out the malcontents and trouble-makers before anything untoward happened. With their firing, the household returned to a peacefulness deeper than it had experienced before. Maria-Elena was certain Maceo Encarnación was a genius at handling people, not only his staff. Her keen eye observed how he dealt with his guests—how he engaged some, flattered others, humiliated still others, and proposed ultimatums, either by guile or directly, depending on the guest's personality—to get what he wanted out of them.

In the end, it was the same with me, she had thought as she shopped for fresh fruit, vegetables, chilies, meat, chocolate, and fish. She knew all the vendors, and they, in turn, knew her, mindful of who she worked for. Needless to say, she received the best of everything, all at prices significantly under those they proposed to their other customers. From time to time, they gave Maria-Elena little treats for herself and for her daughter, Anunciata. After all, she was important in their world, and, besides, in her early forties, she was still a beautiful and desirable woman, though she didn't consider herself beautiful, not like Anunciata. Anyway, she desired no man at all.

After shopping, she always walked a bit down Avenida Presidente Masaryk, where Maceo Encarnación shopped at all the chic, high-end designer boutiques. Seventeen years ago, just after Anunciata had been born, while she still lay in the hospital, Maceo Encarnación had arrived with a jeweled Bulgari bracelet for her. For weeks afterward, she was terrified to try it on, though she fondled it every day and slept with it on her pillow every night.

That morning, after peering in some heavily fortified windows, she had abandoned Avenida Presidente Masaryk for her real destination, the Piel Canela boutique, at Oscar Wilde 20. She stopped in front of the window, staring at the butter-soft handbags, gloves, clutches, and belts that reminded her of the beautiful serpents she used to dream about in her youth. Her eyes slowly filled with tears as desire burned in her heart and lungs like the fire from which the phoenix once rose. There, in the center of the window, was the handbag she coveted and, half wrapped around its double strap, the elegant gloves. Both were the color of *dulce de leche*. Maria-Elena wanted them so badly her throat itched. But she knew she would never buy them. Tears leaked from her eyes, making rivulets down her cheeks. She wept and wept. It was not that she didn't have enough money. She had been in Maceo Encarnación's employ long enough, and he had been generous enough with her, that she could afford both items. But she was a girl of the streets; she could no more buy these high-priced items for herself than she would ever leave Maceo Encarnación's employ, even after what had happened.

The final stop on her early morning excursion had been La Baila, on the Paseo de la Reforma, just four blocks south of Lincoln Park. The beautiful restaurant, lined in colorful Mexican tiles, turned out delicious and authentic food. In fact, over the years, Maria-Elena had been able to inveigle the recipe for the amazing thirty-ingredient *mole de Xico* from the owner-chef.

As the morning was mild, she had sat at an outside table, ignoring the fumes from the hellacious traffic on the Reforma. When Furcal, her favorite waiter, arrived at her table, she ordered her usual, *atole*, a boiled maize drink, flavored today with nopal, *empanadas de plátano rellenos de frijol*, and a double *espresso cortado*.

She had time now all to herself when, for the moment, she was free of obligations to Maceo Encarnación, when her mind could be itself, much as it was each night in the moments between the time she got into bed and the time she fell asleep. Except even then, within Maceo Encarnación's compound, where his will could stretch out its hand and reach her any time of the day or night, she wasn't truly free. Not like now, anyway, sitting by herself in a familiar restaurant, the sooty air of the city rushing by her on mysterious errands from the great volcano, Popocatépetl.

A female waiter she didn't know had smiled warmly at her as she set down Maria-Elena's *atole*.

"I hope the drink is to your liking," she had said.

Maria-Elena, always polite, thanked her, took a sip, then another, deeper one, and nodded, allowing the waitress, whose name was Beatrice, to depart.

She wrapped her hands around the hand-thrown mug. She had time now to consider the implications of what she had read in Anunciata's diary. Last week she had come across it by accident when she was cleaning her daughter's room. It had been kicked, no doubt inadvertently, under the bed. Maria-Elena recalled with perfect clarity the moment, holding the book in her palms, when she had become aware that it was a diary. She recalled in vivid detail the fateful moment before she opened the diary, when everything was as it had always been. She almost didn't open it. In fact, she had bent down to return it, unread, to its place beneath Anunciata's bed. What would have happened then? Reality would not have been ripped and reshaped.

But curiosity had crawled through her like an evil serpent. Even then she had extended her arms, about to drop the diary under the bed. But something—the serpent of desired knowledge?—had stopped her, and she saw herself withdrawing her arms until the diary came back into view.

She did not stand up, and she wondered at that now. On her knees, as if in prayer, she opened the forbidden book, and read what she should never have read. Because in there, near the end, were lines of fire that seared her brain. She would have cried out then if she hadn't immediately jammed her fist into her mouth.

Anunciata—her daughter, her only child—had been taking herself regularly to Maceo Encarnación's bed. In horrific detail, the words of fire recounted the first time and every time thereafter. Maria-Elena slammed the diary shut. Her mind was aflame, but her heart, mortally wounded, had already fallen to ash.

She took a sheet of paper out of her handbag, unfolded it, and with a careful, cramped hand, began to write. As she did so, tears slid down her cheeks, staining the paper. She did not care. Her heart overflowed with shame and sorrow, but that did not stop her. Grimly, she kept writing until she came to the dreadful end. Then she folded the sheet away without looking at what she had written. Why bother? It was seared into her heart.

Once again, possessed by the evil serpent and having drained her *atole*, leaving the rest untouched, she threw some bills on the table and rushed down the sidewalk. Returning to the Piel Canela boutique, at Oscar Wilde 20, she pushed through the door, and, egged on by the serpent inside her, pulled out the credit card with which she purchased the food for Maceo Encarnación and bought her longed-for purse and gloves. She ran her hands over them as the saleswoman rang up the charge, then she asked for them to be gift wrapped, watching as they were buried in layers of pastel-colored crepe paper, carefully interred in a thick box with the name of the boutique embossed in gold ink on either side. The lid was placed on and all was wrapped with a pink-and-green bow.

On the card the saleswoman handed her, she wrote the name of her beloved daughter. And below it, she wrote, "This is for you."

Accepting her altered desire, she exited the shop into sudden blinding sunshine. She stood on the sidewalk, unable to take another step. Her legs refused to work, and now a sharp pain pierced the left side of her chest. *Dios*, what was happening to her? A terrible taste in her mouth. What had been in her drink?

Vertigo overcame her, and she fell. Shouts and the sounds of running feet came to her as far-away echoes, unattached to her or what was happening to her.

As she lay, staring up into the dusky sky, tears came again, along with a sob torn from the depths, where the evil serpent coiled and uncoiled, flicking its forked tongue. Her mind, encased in amber, flickering on the edge of a lethal unconsciousness, retreated to the only thing that mattered: the moment of the revelation a week ago.

The catastrophe was her fault. If only she had told Anunciata, but she had wanted to spare her daughter the sordid details of her origin. Now the mother had read those same sordid details in her daughter's diary, knowing, God help her, that both mother and daughter had shared the same colossal bed, the same monstrous, all-powerful man, the same defilement. Maceo Encarnación was Anunciata's father. Now he was her lover as well.

That was her last thought before the poison she had ingested at the café stopped her heart completely.

Martha Christiana sat brooding on the flight back to Paris from Gibraltar. Beside her, Don Fernando leafed through the latest *Robb Report*. She stared out the Perspex window at the infinite blue sky. Below her, the clouds looked so billowy that she imagined she could lie down and rest on them.

Rest is what she desired most now. Rest and the deep, untroubled sleep of the righteous, neither of which, she knew, were available to her. Don Fernando had astonished her at every turn. Now, after visiting her father's grave, after seeing what her mother had become, how could she continue on the same path she had been traveling for years? *How can I not?* she asked herself.

She turned to Don Fernando. "I'm thirsty. Where's the flight attendant?"

"I sent the cabin crew back to Paris last night," he said, not looking up.

She returned to her brooding. She realized that she had become unmoored in a world in which she had been certain she knew all the angles. She was confronted now with one she could not have anticipated and did not know how to play. She felt like a little girl again, lost and alone, wanting only to run from where she was into the void of the unknown. She was dizzied, as if falling from a great height. It was only now that she realized how completely Maceo Encarnación had fashioned a world around her, an environment in which she could function— but as what? His iron fist or his puppet, dancing to the tune of each new assignment. Death, death, and more death. She saw now how he had mesmerized her into thinking that killing was all she was good for, that without him, without the assignments he brought her, without the money she received from him, she was nothing.

"*You live for the moment of death,*" Maceo Encarnación had told her. "*This makes you special. Unique. This makes you precious to me.*"

She saw now the load of goods he had sold her, how he had flattered her, stroked her ego, caressing her with his words. She had a mental image of herself as a puppet, dancing to his tune. An icy wind knifed through her, and she shuddered inwardly.

"What do you think of this new Falcon 2000S?" Don Fernando said, plopping a two-page spread featuring the private jet onto her lap. "This plane is due for a major overhaul. Instead, I'm thinking of upgrading."

"Are you serious?" She looked at him, not the photos of the Falcon. "This is what's on your mind?"

He shrugged and took the magazine back. "Maybe you don't have a feel for jets."

"Maybe you don't have a feel for what's going on," she said, a good deal more hotly than she had intended.

He put aside the magazine. "I'm listening."

"What are we going to do now?"

"That's entirely up to you."

She shook her head, exasperated. "Do you not understand? If I don't kill you, Maceo Encarnación will kill me."

"I understand."

"I don't think you do. I won't be able to escape him."

"Again, I understand."

"Then what am I—?"

"Are you still planning to kill me?"

She snorted. "Don't be absurd."

He turned toward her fully. "Martha, this sort of change of heart is not so easily accomplished."

"No one knows that better than me. I've seen the mess it can make. At the last minute—"

"The person can't go through with it."

"Even though they want to."

"Sometimes," he said, "sensing no exit, they kill themselves instead."

She looked at him levelly. "That won't happen to me."

He took her hand in his. "How can you be certain, Martha?"

"In Gibraltar, you took my heart and dissected it, picked out all the black bits, then put it back together."

"No," he said. "You did that."

A smile formed slowly on her face. "Who handed me the scalpel?"

The plane was descending, touching the top of the clouds, and then, all at once, it was in them, the sky going gray and featureless, as if they were alone in the air, lost to the world. The drone had become a kind of silence, a shroud.

"We'll be landing soon," Martha said. "I'll have to call him."

"By all means do."

"What will I tell him?"

"Tell him what he wants to hear," he said. "Tell him you have completed your assignment. Tell him I'm dead."

"He always demands proof."

"Then we'll give him some."

"It will have to be convincing."

"It will be," Don Fernando assured her.

Her brows knit together. "I don't understand."

Unbuckling his seat belt, he stood up. "The plane isn't going to land."

The waters of Acapulco were turquoise, clear down to the rocky bottom. Diving into them from great heights took both skill and lungs of steel. To survive the depths to which a cliff diver plunged, to hold your breath for the time it took to descend and then fight the currents, eddies, and undertow on your way up to the frothy surface took long practice and, again, lungs of steel.

By the time he was eleven, Tulio Vistoso, the best cliff diver in the sun-bleached resort city, could hold his breath for just under nine minutes. By the time he was fifteen, it was at least a minute longer.

The water around Dockside Marina was black as oil, but the lack of light was no deterrent for the Aztec. He had let go of *jefe* Marks's legs when the bullets hit the water; there was no sense in being stupid. If he didn't pull Marks under then, he knew it was just a matter of time. Not that Maceo Encarnación had given him much time. In fact, half of it was gone. He had to return to Mexico City with someone's head and at least the promise of the return of the thirty million.

The moment the bullets stopped and *jefe* Marks was pulled out of the water, Don Tulio made his move. He knew it would be only a small matter of time before Marks's people dropped divers into the water. He had to be either securely hidden or out of the water entirely before that happened. With the boats in the water, he could hardly swim out of the marina. Besides, he had to assume the Gringo *federales* would already have established a secure perimeter.

Rising near one of the slimy piers near the *Recursive*, he felt the vibrations of other boats. Then powerful floodlights were switched on, probing the darkness of the water, pushing back the shadows in which he had thought to secret himself. Clearly, now, that would not do. Neither would the network of pilings and crossbeams beneath the pier, his next choice. As he popped his head experimentally out of the water, he heard the panting and sniffing of dogs. They'd find him for sure under the pier.

That left only one alternative, one he was reluctant to use. Ducking back down to avoid a moving spotlight, he moved slowly and deliberately, causing no ripple at all, moving stealthily into the narrow crevasse between the dock and the starboard side of the *Recursive*. He edged his way along until he was directly beneath the second, and larger, bumper.

Feeling only with his fingertips, he found the metal ring, painted the same color as the hull. If you didn't know it was there, you would never have seen it. But the *Recursive* was, first and foremost, a smuggler's boat; it contained all manner of tricks and traps. This particular one ran along the starboard side just above the waterline. It was meant for plastic bags of china white or heroin, but it could, in an emergency, accommodate a man. The trouble was that it wasn't entirely watertight, not, at least, with the Aztec's weight in it. This was why he had been reluctant to consider it. Being able to hold your breath for over nine minutes was one thing, but being trapped in a coffin-sized space while it slowly filled with seawater was quite another.

Still, entombment was the only chance Don Tulio had now, and he took it. Twisting the ring, he opened the hatch from the top and swung himself into the space. Water splashed in with him, filling the bottom. Quickly now, he closed the door and turned the ring into the locked position from the inside so it could not be seen.

Then, his heart beating fast, he began to pray to a god he had long since abandoned, except in name.

Forty minutes after he reached the ER, Peter was allowed to sit up while he was hydrated with fluids via an IV. He called Hendricks, waking him up.

"Where the hell have you been?" the secretary said grumpily.

When Peter told him that he had infiltrated Core Energy, that its CEO had verbally implicated himself, that Dick Richards was secretly working for Tom Brick, and that he had followed leads to the thirty million aboard the *Recursive*, Hendricks sounded mollified. But only for a moment.

"I hate it when both my directors are out of circulation."

Instantly, Peter was on the alert. "What are you talking about?"

"Soraya's in the hospital," the secretary said. "She collapsed and had to have an emergency procedure."

In his extreme agitation, Peter nearly tore out his IV. "How is she?"

"Stable, from the last update I got. Delia's with her. She's barely left Soraya's side."

"Where is she?"

"Same hospital you're in, but you don't sound as if you're in any shape—"

"I'm fine," Peter snapped, a bit too aggressively. Even he realized that, albeit belatedly. "Sorry, sir, this whole business at the marina has got me on edge."

"Right. Keep me wired into that. The moment you ID the man who attacked you, I want to know, got it?"

"Yessir."

There was another pause. "As for Richards, do you want to pick him up or let him run?"

Peter considered this question, among thoughts of Soraya. "Give me a day or two to see what he's up to. Now that I've flown Brick's coop, I want to see what's going to happen."

"I wish we knew who he was bringing back for you to kill."

"Me, too, boss. But it might have been no one. Brick is into playing games with your head. I had had enough of that, and there was this key lead to run down."

"I hear you. But as of this moment we have to treat Richards as a threat."

"Absolutely, boss. But if we can use him to gain solid evidence of what Brick is really up to, I don't want to miss the chance."

"Fine." Hendricks sounded reluctant. "But any backup you need—"

"I'll call ASAP."

"Do that. And, for the time being, I'm ordering you up protection."

"That's precisely what you won't do, sir. With all due respect, I can't do my job with a shadow. I'm not a desk jockey. I can handle myself."

Silence on the other end of the line.

"Sir?"

"Peter, for God's sake, take better care of yourself," Hendricks said before he disconnected.

You have two choices," the mortician said, "sleep on the floor or in one of these coffins."

"Nice silk," Rebeka said, sliding her hand along the rim of a coffin.

The mortician grinned. "Soft as a cloud, too." He was a pale, thin man with a sunken chest, a pencil mustache, and the bee-stung, ruddy lips of a woman. His hands looked as delicate as porcelain. He had lacquered nails. He told them his name was Diego de la Rivera.

"Your choice," he said. "Either way, I'll notify you when it's time."

"You're sure Maceo Encarnación's people will call you," Bourne said.

"More than that," de la Rivera said, "I'm sure Maceo Encarnación himself will call me."

"How's that?"

De la Rivera's lips twitched. "I'm married to his sister."

This made Bourne uneasy. "Isn't blood thicker than water here?"

De la Rivera's lips curled fully into a sneer. "Maceo Encarnación is not my blood. The man is made of money, but still he treats his sister like shit." He spat onto the floor. "And me? He likes giving me business; he thinks it demeans me. 'All you're interested in is my money,' he tells me, when what I want is for him to treat us like people. But, what? He doesn't even invite us to his home. So there's no blood here, not for me, not for my wife. He can go fuck himself for all I care." He waved his hand. "So whatever chaos you cause when you're inside, I'll fucking applaud."

He went out then without another word, cutting the overhead lights as he left. The lamp on his desk was left burning as, it seemed, it always was, even when he wasn't there. All that remained was the deep, steady humming of the massive refrigeration units in the basement, rising through the concrete floor in spectral sound.

"Do you want to lie down?" Rebeka looked from Bourne, whose expression made her laugh, to the open coffin. "Neither do I."

Bourne opened the detailed map of the city *el Enterrador* had given him, and, by the dim lamplight, began to study it. "Are we clear on what we need to do," he said, "once we get in?"

"Rowland first, then Maceo Encarnación."

Bourne shook his head. "Rowland first, then we get out."

"What about Encarnación?"

Bourne glanced up. He could see the lamp reflected in her eyes, a corona of light surrounding her pupils. "Listen, I've been thinking," he said softly. "I'm beginning to suspect that *Jihad bis saif*—"

"It's hiding in plain sight."

"Really?"

She nodded. "It's part of Encarnación's empire. It must be."

He returned to studying the map of the labyrinthine city. "Why do you say that?"

"We arrived here, drove through...I listened to what Constanza Camargo said, and I knew."

"You're wrong," Bourne said. "*Jihad bis saif* is a ghost. It doesn't exist."

"But what about what I overheard in Dahr El Ahmar?"

"Dahr El Ahmar. That's the key, isn't it?" Bourne looked up again. "It was Colonel Ben David you overheard. You say he thought you were still unconscious, right?"

She nodded.

"What if he knew you were listening?"

She stared at him.

"Think this through, Rebeka. Ben David knew you brought me into Dahr El Ahmar, a top secret Mossad camp in a foreign country, harboring even more top secret research on a procedure parallel to SILEX, the separation of isotopes by laser excitation, in order to quickly and efficiently enrich nuclear material to weapons grade.

"Now, all of a sudden, he doesn't know whether to trust you. So he sets a trap. He discusses *Jihad bis saif* within your hearing. Come on, why would he do that when you're within earshot? Would he really take the chance that you were unconscious? The hell he would. No, he talked about *Jihad bis saif* to see what you would do. And what did you do?

You cut and ran. No wonder he sent the Babylonian after you."

Rebeka shook her head. "No. It can't be."

"But you know it is," Bourne pressed her. "We know Ben David better than most people. I think we've both seen him at his worst."

"Then what about Rowland?"

"He was sent by Maceo Encarnación," Bourne said. "Encarnación is the one who wants me dead. You saw how his copter came after me in Stockholm."

He could see her taking deep breaths, gathering herself. When she turned back to him, her eyes were glistening and a tiny tremor went through her like an arrow. "I thought I was so smart."

"Forget it. We all make mistakes."

"There was no one inside Mossad I could trust, and in the end Ben David betrayed me."

"I imagine he sees the betrayal from a different perspective."

She took another slow breath. "What really happened between you and him? Before, I mean."

Bourne regarded her for a long time. She became acutely aware of the open coffins, pale silk linings spectral islets in the semi-darkness. They didn't look soft and comforting at all.

"In the twilight of Mubarak's reign in Egypt, his government lost control over the Sinai," Bourne said. "But I'm sure you already know this."

She nodded.

"That's where Ben David and I first met. A contingent of IDF was in there policing the local bedouin caravans, which were smuggling drugs, arms, and human slaves from Eritrea into Israel. Ben

David was there with five of his Mossad agents, investigating a rumor that Mubarak or someone highly placed inside his government was behind the shipments, greasing the wheels with the bedouin chieftains. I was in the midst of my own investigation that peripherally involved the IDF. Suffice it to say that our goals clashed."

"He wouldn't have liked that."

"He didn't," Bourne said. "In typical Ben David fashion, he concocted a story about me and sold it to the IDF commander. As a result, the IDF went after me."

"Which accomplished the dual goal of getting you and the IDF off his back, giving him a free field to pursue his own objective without interference. Clever."

"Not clever enough," Bourne said. "I evaded the IDF by impersonating an arms dealer and joining one of the bedouin caravans. When Ben David and his unit attacked them, there I was."

Rebeka indicated that they should sit on the floor. "What happened?" she said, when they were settled.

"Ben David got the surprise of his life. According to the caravan leader, the shipments originated in Pakistan, Syria, and Russia, not with the Egyptian government."

"You believed him?"

Bourne nodded. "He had no reason to lie. As far as he was concerned, I was there to supervise one of my own shipments. He received his payments from Russian arms dealers, like the one I was impersonating, and from terrorist cells with connections to the Colombian and Mexican cartels."

His eyes glittered. "Ben David's intel was either incorrect or deliberate disinformation. Either way, he was wasting his and the Mossad's time in the Sinai. Trouble was, Ben David refused to believe me. He ordered me executed, and I almost was."

"But you escaped."

"With the help of my newfound bedouin friends. Ben David was infuriated, vowing to hunt me down and kill me."

"That's the end of the story?"

"Until it picked up again when we flew into Dahr El Ahmar."

"Shit, I wish I had known."

"What would you have done differently?" Bourne said. "You needed immediate medical assistance. The Mossad camp was the closest safe haven."

"I would have warned you."

Bourne grunted. "Seeing Ben David again was warning enough."

"He took off half a mountaintop trying to bring you down," she said. "But then again, you scarred him for life."

"He got what he deserved."

Her eyes studied the shadowed contours of his face. "He'll never forgive you."

"I don't want his forgiveness."

"He'll never stop hunting you."

Bourne gave the hint of a smile. "He isn't the first. He won't be the last."

"It must be..." She seemed to lose her voice, or her nerve.

"It must be what?"

"A difficult life you've chosen."

"I think," he said softly, "it chose me. I'm an accidental passenger."

She shook her head. "You're an agent of change."

"Maybe just the center of a balancing act."

"That's enough...more than enough, maybe, for one man."

They sat silently then, their eyes locked, thinking their own thoughts, until they heard a sharp scrape. The overhead lights flickered on, revealing Diego de la Rivera.

"The call's come in," he said. "It's time."

19

"YOU'RE INSANE." Martha Christiana stared up at Don Fernando. "You're telling me we're alone on the plane?"

"Yes."

"The pilot and navigator have parachuted out."

"Three minutes ago. It's on autopilot."

"And you plan to crash the plane—"

"Crash it, yes." He slipped off a thick engraved gold ring with a pigeon-blood cabochon ruby in its center. "The recovery team will find this. It is unique. It will be identified as mine."

Martha, breathless, still had trouble believing this crazy plan. "But they'll find no body remains."

"Oh yes, they will."

She followed him to the rear of the plane, where, when she saw stacked up three body bags, she recoiled. She stared at him. "This is a joke, right?"

"Unzip the bags."

He said this with such utter calmness that she felt a chill run down her spine. This was a side of him he had not revealed until now. Brushing past him, she leaned over the top body bag and, with a convulsive gesture, unzipped it. She found herself staring into the blank white face of a corpse.

"Three men," Don Fernando said. "The pilot, the navigator, and me. That is the way it will be reported."

She whirled on him. "And you'll just what? Disappear from running Aguardiente Bancorp?"

"It's a leap of faith," he said, turning away. "Come now. Our time has run out." He broke out a pair of parachutes and handed one to her. "Or do you want to die in the crash?"

"I can't believe this is happening."

"But it is." He shrugged into his harness, tightening the bands across his chest. As if noticing her hesitation for the first time, he frowned. "Are you having second thoughts?"

"I don't understand..."

"Then kill me now and have done with it. You're running out of time. Fulfill Maceo Encarnación's commission. I doubt I can stop you."

Her frown deepened. "He said you wanted to take everything away from him."

"How much do you know about his empire?"

She shook her head.

"Well then, there is no reason for his comment to affect you."

She thought about her meeting with Maceo Encarnación at the Place de la Concorde, encircled by constant traffic, the shouts and laughter of unknowing tourists. In the shadow of the guillotine and the Reign of Terror. "But it did."

"And so..." He spread his hands wide. When she didn't answer, he stepped toward her, taking the parachute out of her hands and manipulating the straps over her shoulders. But when he began to cinch the wide strap across her waist, she gripped him.

"Wait."

Their eyes met.

"Last chance, Martha," he said. "You must decide now. Stay with Maceo Encarnación or take the first step into that new beginning you spoke about in Gibraltar."

He removed her hands and cinched the waist strap tight. "It seems to me that your past has been defined by following a series of men." He led her to the door, put his hand on the huge metal bar that would unlock it. "Continue or change, Martha. Your choice is as simple as that."

"You call this a simple choice?"

"Call it what you will, it's yours to make." His voice softened. "No one can help you with this decision, Martha. I wouldn't even try."

She took a breath. She thought about the lighthouse, her father's grave, her mother lost in a world where Martha was still a child, still a part of her life. She stared into Don Fernando's eyes, wanting to read something there, but he was true to his word: he wasn't going to try to influence her. And all at once, she realized that he was the first man in her life who hadn't sought to manipulate her.

She nodded then and replaced his hand on the door's locking bar. "Let me," she said.

He laughed and kissed her on both cheeks with great affection. "Best I show you something first."

"You said we were out of time."

He guided her back up the aisle to the front of the plane, opened the door to the cockpit, and showed her the pilot and navigator alive and well in their seats.

"Better strap in, boss," the pilot said. "We'll be landing in five minutes."

Charles Thorne turned, restless in bed. The truth of the matter was he hated and feared Li Wan, yet the two men were bound together by the stream of secrets they passed back and forth as if through a delicate membrane. They were conduits; they needed each other. Thorne turned again, trying and failing to get comfortable.

Worse, by far, was that he envied Li Wan. He had been in love with Natasha Illion, the Israeli supermodel, Li's inamorata. And he could swear that Li knew. Each time they were together, Li presented Natasha as if she were bathed in a follow spot, or so it seemed to him. And Natasha, perhaps being in on Li's little running joke, always wore the most provocative designer outfits—necklines down to her navel or mesh tops through which Thorne stole clandestine peeks at her small but perfect breasts, the nipples like cherry buds. Thorne moaned, imagining his mouth enclosing them.

He was certain that Li, and possibly Natasha as

well, were laughing at him on their nights out, as if he were an animal they constantly taunted through the bars of his cage.

The light of the bedside clock penetrated his eyelids. Barely an hour since he had returned from his 4 AM rendezvous with Li at the restaurant in Chinatown. The General Tso's chicken lay in his stomach like a ball of wax, unmoving and indigestible.

He turned once more, then rolled to the side of the bed and sat up. Today there was to be no respite in sleep, no way out of the noose tightening inexorably around him. Of course, he could ask Soraya for immunity from the coming phone hacking tsunami, but that would mean crawling back to her on his knees, groveling like the basest supplicant. He would be in her power forever, and he knew from bitter experience that she could be merciless when she felt she had been wronged. But what if she was his only recourse? Li had made noises about helping him, but he'd rather be tied to a third rail than be in that bastard's debt.

No, he thought now, as he swung his legs over the side of the bed, Soraya was his last best hope of getting out of the water before the Justice Department investigation sank all boats.

Then he remembered that she was in the hospital, that she was carrying his baby, and all at once, the General Tso's chicken moved inside him in an altogether unpleasant manner.

He jumped up, and, sprinting, just made it across his bedroom, over the bathroom tiles, to the toilet before vomiting with such force that he felt as if his intestines had turned inside out.

* * *

Li Wan, luxuriating between the impossibly long legs of Natasha Illion, picked up his enciphered mobile and pressed one button. The sounds on the line went immediately hollow as the call was shunted through a series of encrypted substations that hopscotched across the country, across the Pacific, at last ping-ponging dizzily through a cluster of top secret listening posts within Beijing. The offices of the State Administration of Grain were housed in the massive Guohong Building in the Central Government District. Though the top three floors bore the same SAG logo, none of its workers on the floors below were allowed access. There was a separate elevator that rose from the colossal lobby to those top three floors without stopping at the intervening levels. As far as the workers below were concerned, those floors above them housed the offices of the ministers who directed the State Administration of Grain, connected directly to the Politburo itself. No one harbored a desire to go up there; in fact, for them it did not exist.

But for Li Wan, and people like him, those floors were all that existed in the Guohong Building. Their interests did not include grain production, quotas, or yearly allocations. The final destination of the call he initiated that morning in Washington, between Natasha Illion's silky legs, was a vast office on the very top floor of the Guohong Building.

It was 6 PM in Beijing, but the hour of night or day was of no import, as that office, those three floors, in fact, were fully manned 24/7.

The High Minister stood at the edge of an immense open-plan room whose fifteen hundred computers, linked through a proprietary intranet, were manned by youngsters ranging in age from ten to nineteen. These youngsters were hackers all, handpicked by the Chinese military, and their sole job was to hack through the firewalls and intranets of foreign governments and multinationals supplying foreign governments and militaries with cutting-edge weaponry and technologies. To do this, they were broken up into cadres, each one working on the next generation of Trojans, worms, and viruses, be they Stuxnet, Ginjerjar, or Stikyfingers. Anyone trying to backtrace the origins of these attacks would, after a long, arduous search, find that the ISP number belonged to Fi Xu Lang, a disgraced economics professor in a backwater village in Guangdong Province.

The Minister felt an unalloyed sense of pride at the operation that he himself had argued for and set up. The intelligence stolen from a variety of sources had already proved highly valuable to his friend General Hwang Liqun and the rest of the Chinese military.

The Minister felt the vibration of his mobile phone and went out of the cyber sweatshop, down to the far end of the hall, and into his office. He sat behind an ebony-wood desk, inlaid with elephant ivory, that was entirely clear of clutter. There was a rank of six corded phones on one side, a paperweight made of a thick chunk of rhino horn adorning the other side. In front of him was an open dossier marked TOP SECRET. The Minister, perhaps fifty, was possessed of the long, elegant face of a conductor or a choreographer. His black hair was slicked back from his wide, intelligent forehead. His hands, long and spidery-thin, were as carefully groomed as his hair and face. As he answered his mobile, he stared at a photo stapled to the inside cover of the dossier. He waited patiently as Li Wan's call was routed to one of his phones. He held the phone to his ear without letting his gaze leave the photo, which was a black-and-white surveillance snapshot made with a long lens.

As soon as the encrypted connection opened, he said, "Speak." His voice was high and keening, like that of a child being punished.

"Minister Ouyang, there has been a significant development."

Ouyang's eyelids dropped halfway. He was imagining the room his agent was calling from. It was five in the morning along America's East Coast. He wondered whether Li Wan was alone or with his long-legged girlfriend.

"This could have a positive or negative impact on my evening, Li. What is it?"

"Through the auspices of stupidity, we have been given an extraordinary opportunity."

"With Mr. Thorne?"

"Yes."

"He and his coven of executives at *Politics As Usual* have been caught in a phone-hacking scandal that netted them some extraordinary exclusives over the past nineteen months, boosting their bottom line, but leaving them open to investigation by the American Justice Department."

"This is not unknown to me." In fact, Ouyang had a contact inside Justice. "Please continue, Citizen Li."

"From day one, my mission in establishing a mutual conduit with Charles Thorne has been to get to his wife."

"As chair of the newly formed Homeland Strategic Appropriations Committee, Senator Ann Ring is of extraordinary importance to us." Ouyang kept staring at the photo, as if trying to unlock the secrets inside the brain of the man caught by one of his surveillance teams. Then he said pointedly, "So far, however, you have failed to engage her on any level apart from the superficial."

"That time is at an end," Li said. "Thorne's back is against the wall. He needs my—our—help. I believe now is the time to extend our hand to support him in his hour of need."

Ouyang grunted softly, delicately. "In return for what?"

"In return for Senator Ann Ring."

"I was under the impression—an impression you gave me, I might remind you—that Thorne's marital relationship is not all it might be, all it *should* be."

The insane implication, via the stressed word, was that the couple's personal troubles were somehow Li's fault. This was Minister Ouyang through and through. Li set his mind to navigating the increasingly choppy waters.

"That slight estrangement will now work in our favor," Li said.

Ouyang, running his fingertips ever so lightly over the face of the man in the photo, said, "Please explain."

"If Thorne and Ann Ring were closer, I feel certain he would have confided in her about the impending investigation. He has told me nothing could be further from the truth. But if I— we—can provide him with a way out, a method of inoculating and indemnifying himself against implication, he would be grateful—and so would she.

"Senator Ring has an exemplary congressional record. Any hint of scandal—even from her husband—could be devastating to her position as chair of the Homeland Strategic Appropriations Committee. If she is disgraced and steps down, we will be back to square one. We will have lost valuable time. We cannot afford to start all over."

No, Minister Ouyang thought, *we most certainly cannot*.

"I despise stupidity," he said.

Li wisely held his tongue.

"There is danger in exposing ourselves to the extent required to extricate Thorne from his predicament." At the moment, Ouyang appeared to be talking to himself, trying to work out the pros and cons of Li's suggestion. "As you know, Li, there is a very thin line between an asset and a liability."

His eyes never left the face he now knew so well, a face he saw in long, drawn-out nightmares to which he returned again and again, an endless repetition that infuriated him.

"I understand, Minister. But I have trained Thorne. He is our unwitting conduit."

"The best kind," Ouyang acknowledged.

"Precisely."

The face had a name, of course, and he knew it as well as he knew his own—a name that was hideous, a name he was determined to eradicate as if it had never existed.

"I have worked long and hard cultivating this conduit. He can be saved from the oncoming storm," Li said with the full force of his conviction.

"As long as you aren't exposed, as long as our plan isn't jeopardized, you have my permission." He cocked his head to one side, concentrating on both his important conversation with Li and the equally important photo. He grunted. "Do not disappoint me, Li."

While Li Wan rambled his gratitude, Ouyang tapped the eyes of the man in the photo, first one, then the other, in his mind's eye blinding him before he was killed, and his name echoed and reechoed in his mind.

Jason Bourne, Jason Bourne, Jason Bourne.

Hey."

"Hey yourself." Soraya smiled when she saw Peter enter her room, heard his familiar voice. But seeing him in his bedraggled clothes, her expression immediately changed. "What the hell happened to you?"

"Thirty million dollars." He pulled up a chair and began to relate the story of the increasingly visible web that included Richards, Core Energy, Tom Brick, Florin Popa, all leading to the thirty million sunk in a watertight satchel off the *Recursive* at Dockside Marina.

"What does it all mean?" Soraya asked when she had absorbed the various strands.

Peter shook his head. "I don't know, but I'm going to find out."

"What about Richards?"

The same question Hendricks had asked him. "I've decided to give him his lead. Whatever Brick is up to, it runs through Richards."

"Won't Brick be suspicious that you didn't wait around to kill whoever it was he was bringing back to the house in Virginia?"

Peter hitched his chair forward. "I don't think so. Anyone with half a brain wouldn't stay around. I think that was just a test."

"An intelligence test."

"Brick doesn't trust me fully." Peter shrugged. "Why should he? As far as he's concerned, I crawled out of a hole and saved him a lot of grief. But so what? In his business, he's got to run me through a maze before he can accept me completely."

"So you'll contact him again?"

Peter winked at her. "You bet." He stood up. "Now relax. I want to see you on your feet before long."

Don Tulio sat in his rental car watching as Sam Anderson, his team having scoured and dredged the marina basin for any sign of the man who had attacked his boss, berated the crew and sent them back down to try again. Anderson stood giving orders to a man Don Tulio knew from conversations overheard as Sanseverino. Sanseverino nodded and went back up to the parking lot. Don Tulio followed Sanseverino as he drove Peter's car to the hospital. Don Tulio was an expert driver; he knew how to tail someone without being discovered.

Now he sat in his car, watching as Sanseverino trotted into the ER entrance and disappeared into the bowels of the hospital complex. He had no intention of following Sanseverino inside, where there was sure to be security and every chance he would be made. Why bother, when all he had to do was wait here for *jefe* Marks to emerge, get in his car, and drive off? Don Tulio, time running out, would follow him and take his pound of flesh. The plane he had chartered back to Mexico City was ready and waiting for him.

As to the thirty million, he knew for certain it was gone. The *federales* had it, which meant it had evaporated like smoke. His lieutenants, having decapitated the sacrificial lamb Don Tulio had chosen from within his ranks, were hard at work replacing the thirty million. Rehabilitating his image with Don Maceo weighed just as heavily on his mind. Don Maceo would have already been placated, at least temporarily, by the head the Aztec's lieutenant had delivered. But he would not be impressed until the money was returned and Don Tulio delivered the second head and informed him to whom it belonged.

The Aztec checked the 911 handgun, its hollow-point ammo, one more time. Then, setting the gun on the seat next to his gravity knife, he leaned his head back, closing his eyes halfway. He had developed the ability of sleeping with his eyes half-open, like a reptile. Nothing got by him when he was in this state. His mind relaxed and rested while his senses remained on alert. It was this peculiar ability that alerted him to *jefe* Marks emerging from the hospital, accompanied by Sanseverino. The two men went directly to Marks's car. A brief altercation broke out as Sanseverino insisted on driving. Marks acquiesced, and his deputy got behind the wheel while Marks himself climbed in beside him.

Don Tulio turned on his ignition a moment before Sanseverino did. He followed the car out of the hospital parking lot at a discreet distance, varying the number of vehicles between them. As he drove, he hummed a *cumbia* tune that reminded him of sleek arms and powerful legs, sweat-slicked bodies, minds lubricated with mezcal, all moving to the insistent beat.

Sorry we haven't found him yet, boss," Sanseverino said as he negotiated a turn. "Maybe the currents took him, 'cause if he was down there the divers would've found him by now. The current was sucking out, they told me, so Anderson sent them down to search a wider circle."

"Dammit," Peter said, "I needed to ID him in order to follow the money trail back to its source. Without him, we're at a dead end."

"Dead is dead," Sanseverino said.

"It ain't over till it's over," Peter grumbled. He was in a foul mood. *Everything is going wrong to-*

day, he thought, refusing to admit how worried he was about Soraya. Plus, he didn't like that she had shut him out; it wasn't like her.

"Anderson said to leave it and go home," Sanseverino said. "Take the day and night to recuperate."

Peter shook his head. "With Soraya down, Treadstone is undermanned as it is."

"We're kind of circling, you realize that?" Sanseverino said. "I have no idea where we're going."

"Take a deep breath." Peter pulled out his mobile. "In a moment you will." He looked up Delia's mobile in his address book and clicked on the highlighted number. A moment later, Delia answered.

"It's Peter," he said, brusquely. "We need to talk."

"I'm—"

"Now."

"Uh-oh."

He grinned fiercely. "That's right. 'Uh-the-fuck-oh.' Where are you?"

"Out of the office. On a case."

"I'll come to you." He snapped his fingers. "Address."

Don Tulio followed *jefe* Marks's car out into the countryside, moving farther and farther away from the more populated areas of the section of Virginia closest to DC. Quite soon, he was lost. The rental car wasn't equipped with a GPS, but his mobile was. He fumbled it out with one hand and turned it on.

Not that it mattered exactly where they were, not at this moment, anyway. All he had to do was to keep his eye on the car in front of him and, as the traffic began to thin out, figure out ways to keep his own car from being spotted by either Marks or Sanseverino. This included some fancy maneuvering, but luckily, even when the traffic was at its sparsest, there were always trucks to hide behind for a time.

Don Tulio narrowed his cruel Aztec eyes against the glare and kept pumping his foot on the accelerator. It wouldn't do to maintain a constant speed, which would mirror that of Marks's car, and, therefore, bring attention to himself. By moving in and out of the sight line of their mirrors, he made himself all but invisible.

They had been traveling for close to forty minutes when Don Tulio saw the large red-brick building off to their right: Silversun High School. A group of official-looking vehicles were parked helter-skelter near its front entrance. Peering more closely, he spotted figures in loose-fitting jackets with ATF printed on their backs in oversized bright yellow letters.

A moment later, Marks's car slowed, preparing to take the next right onto the approach road to the school.

This is it, the Aztec thought. *I'll never get a better chance.*

Accelerating, he came up right behind Marks's car as if from nowhere. The touch of a button slid his window all the way down. The Chevy sped up. He grabbed his 911 off the seat. Then he swerved to the right, overtaking the Chevy within seconds.

As he came abreast of the car, he glimpsed *jefe* Marks's pale face turn inquiringly toward him. He saw the muzzle of Marks's police Glock. Aiming the 911 directly at Marks's face, he squeezed off one, two, three shots, then he stamped on the brakes, negating any chance of return fire.

Ahead of him, the Chevy slewed wildly, then swerved, tires squealing as the driver put on the brakes and began a sweeping U-turn. That was the Aztec's cue. Accelerating again, he broadsided the Chevy, staving in both doors on the driver's side. His own front end crumpled, jarring him so hard his teeth clacked together.

His head snapped back against the seat and the airbag deployed, but he was ready, puncturing it with the point of his knife, slashing it away from him with the blade. The seat belt was jammed, and he used the knife like a machete to hack through it as if it were a fibrous jungle vine.

He kicked out, impatient now to view his handi-work, and the door swung open, screaming a bit as metal abraded metal. The hinges were askew. He got out, a little dazed by the sudden brute force of grav-ity rushing back in.

Staggering over to the Chevy, he could see that Sanseverino had been caught in the broadside. His entire left side, trapped by the airbag, was crushed by the metal hammer of the collapsed door. His head was canted at an unnatural angle, as if he were inspecting the footwell. He wasn't inspecting any-thing, the Aztec observed. He was dead.

Bending over, he peered more deeply into the Chevy's interior. Where was *jefe* Marks? The door on his side was open, the window down, but there was no sign of a body, alive or dead. How could that be? The Aztec had put three bullets through the Chevy's window, as close to point-blank as it was possible to get in a moving vehicle.

The most infinitesimal movement alerted him, and, hurrying around the front of the wreck, he saw Marks, who looked as if he were pinned under his own car. The *jefe* was conscious.

"How?" the Aztec said in English. "I shot you three times. How did you survive without a scratch?"

Marks looked up at Don Tulio and said in a voice like the rustle of dry leaves, "Bulletproof glass."

"Fuck!"

"Who are you?"

"The one who brings your death." The Aztec stalked toward where Peter lay. "You stole my thirty million, fucker."

"And who did *you* steal that thirty million from?"

Don Tulio held the 911 in one hand, his opened knife in the other. Now he pointed the handgun at Marks. "Since you'll be separated from your head thirty seconds from now, I'll tell you. Don Maceo Encarnación."

"I spit on Don Maceo Encarnación," the *jefe* said. "And I spit on you."

Within the blink of an eye, Peter brought the Glock he had been clutching into view, and, squeezing the trigger, shot the man standing over him in the left side of his chest. But Peter heard two shots, not one. As the man staggered back, Peter felt a blinding pain engulf him. He tried to breathe, coughed, felt a hot gout of blood rushing into his throat, choking him. He could not breathe. His heart labored as he lost strength.

So this is how it ends, he thought. And, strangely, he didn't seem to mind.

20

REBEKA LAY UNMOVING on top of Bourne as the hearse drove through the burnt, bitter pre-dawn of Mexico City. They were enclosed within the polished elm coffin Maceo Encarnación had ordered for Maria-Elena, his deceased cook. Diego de la Rivera himself sat beside the driver. The coffin, locked into its stainless-steel rails, was the only thing in the capacious rear. Black curtains covered the windows.

"The coffin is how Maceo Encarnación has the deceased travel back to the mortuary," Diego de la Rivera had told them just before they had departed. "The coffin material and style are already picked out. His security guards know me; they'll look into the interior, but they won't bother searching it. Trust me."

Events transpired just as Diego de la Rivera had said. The hearse was stopped outside the gates. From inside the coffin, Rebeka and Bourne could hear muffled voices. A moment later, the wide rear door opened, more voices were heard, closer this time. Then the door slammed shut. Some rude laughter, then the hearse was granted entry to Maceo Encarnación's estate. Gravel crunched beneath the hearse's tires as the vehicle traveled at a funereal pace along the semicircular driveway, then around to the rear of the villa.

More voices, less querulous. Again, the rear door was opened, but this time the coffin was unlocked from its position, and Diego de la Rivera and his driver carried it into the house, presumably to where Maria-Elena was laid out.

At some point, the coffin was set down. A triple knock followed by a double informed them that their journey was at an end. The coffin's lid was lifted up, and, like vampires in the night, they climbed out into the dimness of a room that smelled of perfume and death.

Apart from the corpse of the unfortunate Maria-Elena, Diego de la Rivera and his driver were the only other people visible. They were in the woman's bedroom. It was filled with trinkets, entire shelves covered with miniature skulls and skeletons, gaily painted in Day-Glo colors, obviously collected over the years from Day of the Dead festivals. The body lay on the white cotton coverlet, which was edged in decorative eyelets. Maria-Elena had been a handsome woman: wide Olmec face, large in bosom and hips, but with a narrow waist. Her hands were folded on her stomach. She wore a yellow dress printed with red poppies, making her seem as festive as the papier-mâché skulls and skeletons that surrounded her.

"There's an armed man outside the door. He's the one who greeted us at the back door," Diego de la Rivera whispered to them. "*Vaya con Dios*. You're on your own from now on."

Bourne grabbed him by the elbow. "Not quite yet."

Maceo Encarnación's man turned as Diego de la Rivera exited Maria-Elena's bedroom.

"I left something in the hearse," he said sheepishly.

The man nodded. "I'll come with you."

As the guard moved off after de la Rivera, Bourne stepped out and slammed him in the back of the neck. Dazed, the man half-turned into Bourne's smash to the side of his head. He went down, unconscious.

Bourne dragged him into the bedroom and disarmed him, sticking a Sig Sauer into his waistband. He found a gravity knife and pocketed that as well. Selecting a piece of clothing from Maria-Elena's dresser drawer, he stuffed it into the security man's mouth. Then he tied his hands behind his back with a scarf and shoved him under the bed, settling the end of the coverlet over him so that he was completely out of sight.

"Now," Bourne said as de la Rivera reentered the bedroom, "it's *vaya con Dios*."

Just outside Maria-Elena's closed bedroom door, Bourne and Rebeka stood silent and still, listening to the sounds of the house, alert for any footfalls, voices, anything at all that might indicate there were security guards inside the house as well as outside, but, apart from a radio, dimly playing Tino Rossi's 1945 version of "Besame Mucho," there was no sign of life.

It was very early, barely sunrise. It was a good bet that the principals of the house were still sleeping. But someone must be up, listening to the sinuous music. And now they heard soft footfalls down the hallway, so they ducked into a bathroom, leaving the door ajar just a sliver.

Bourne saw a beautiful young woman, wrapped in a long, silken robe intricately embroidered with flowers and vines, come down the wide, curving polished-wood staircase and hurry along the hallway past them. She was clearly naked beneath the robe. Judging by her features and her grief-stricken expression, he guessed she must be Maria-Elena's daughter. Peering out carefully, he saw her disappear into her mother's room. A moment later, as they emerged from their hiding place, they heard a low wail of despair from behind the bedroom door.

"Poor thing," Rebeka whispered in Bourne's ear.

Bourne mentally surveyed the layout of the two-floor villa that *el Enterrador* had showed them. The non-help bedrooms were upstairs. Bourne noted with curiosity that Maria-Elena's daughter had come from there, not the main floor, where by all rights she ought to have her sleeping quarters. Plus, the dressing gown she had wrapped around her must have cost as much as her mother's yearly salary. These small oddities were pushed aside as they began to ascend the staircase, their senses on high alert.

Once they had assured themselves that no one else was on the stairs, they raced the rest of the way up, reaching the second floor landing without incident. This upper floor was divided in two. The west wing—to their left—was Maceo Encarnación's immense master bedroom suite, which included a sybaritic bathroom and a massive wood-paneled study. The east wing—to their right—contained four en suite guest bedrooms. It was toward the east wing they crept, keeping their heads below the railing until they reached the wall where the bedrooms started, two on each side.

Bourne signed that he'd check the bedrooms on the left while Rebeka should take the ones on the right. Nodding in affirmation, she stepped down the hallway. He watched her for a moment before he went to the first door.

Placing one ear against the door, he listened, but, apart from the low hum of the HVAC system, he heard nothing. Hand on the knob, he turned it, opened the door, and silently stepped into the bedroom. Heavy curtains hung across the window. In the dimness, he made out the basic furniture: bed, dresser, desk, and chair. No one was in the bed, whose coverlet was undisturbed. The air in the room smelled stale; no point checking the bathroom.

Returning to the hall, he saw Rebeka emerging from the first bedroom on her side. She shook her head: no one there, either. They moved farther down the hall until they were standing in front of the third and fourth bedrooms.

Hearing soft footfalls on the staircase, they turned, crouching down, pressed back against the

walls. Maria-Elena's beautiful daughter came float-
ing up the stairs as if on a cloud, trailing her ex-
travagant robe behind her. Reaching the landing, she
turned to her left, moving into the west wing and
vanishing behind the heavily carved mahogany door
to the master suite.

Bourne and Rebeka exchanged glances before
they went back to work. As before, Bourne put his
ear to the bedroom door, but this time he heard, very
faintly, the sound of running water. Signaling for
Rebeka to join him, he slowly turned the doorknob,
opening the door just enough to peek inside. This
bedroom was as dim as the previous one, but here
the bedcovers were rucked back, the pillow clearly
showing the indentation of a head.

Bourne slipped inside the room, Rebeka following him soundlessly. The shower was on, the door
to the bathroom slightly ajar. Signing that he would
go in while she checked the closets, Bourne stole
across the bedroom and, turning his body sideways,
tapped the door slightly and slipped through the
wider opening into the steam-bound bathroom.
Bright lights were on, blindingly reflected off the
shiny white tiles.

In one motion, Bourne was across the space, his
arm extended, hand pulling back the opaque shower
curtain. Water streamed from the showerhead, cas-
cading down on empty space. There was no one in
the shower.

Understanding bloomed. With an inarticulate
growl, Bourne whirled, retracing his steps, out of the
bathroom and into the bedroom. Rebeka, half inside
the closet, turned as he came in. As she did so, Harry

Rowland, emerging from the depths of the closet, slammed his fist into her side, where she had been knifed in Damascus six weeks ago. Before Bourne could move, he had a knife across her throat. From behind her, he grinned like a death's-head.

Bourne was certain Rebeka knew at least a dozen ways to free herself. She wasn't able to; Rowland saw to that. He bent her torso cruelly, causing her to gasp like a fish out of water. A red stain slowly spread across the side of her shirt where she had been struck.

"One of the useful bits of intel I picked up when I was nosing around the Dahr El Ahmar camp," Rowland said, eyes darkening, "was where she was wounded and how bad it was."

He moved infinitesimally, shifting something Bourne couldn't see because Rebeka was in the way. Then he punched her in the side, and she hissed her pain through clamped teeth. The bloodstain widened. She stared at Bourne with bloodshot eyes.

"Let her go, Rowland," Bourne said.

"Is that a request or a threat? Either way." Rowland shook his head. "This fucker has been following me halfway around the world, and now you have joined the hunt." He smiled with his teeth. "See, this is what it's like to regain your memory." Nodding, he continued: "Oh, yeah, I know who you are, you poor amnesiac freak. I actually feel sorry for you, living half a life, carrying that shadow around with you, day and night, awake or asleep. A nightmare of unimaginable proportions." Rebeka moved and he struck her again in the same place. Blood welled up out of the fabric, dripped onto the floor. "Only I know what it's like to have no past, to be adrift in the present."

"What do you want?" Bourne was seeking a way to forestall more damage being done to Rebeka.

"I want an end to the hunt. I want your deaths."

Bourne could see Rebeka gathering her reserves of strength, and he knew for what. He signaled with his eyes for her to stand down, to do nothing. *I have a plan*, his eyes said. *Let me handle Rowland.* But she ignored him, drew on her training, fierce and indomitable.

"There's another way out for all of us," Bourne said, doing whatever he could to distract Rowland an instant before Rebeka made her move.

Afterward, Bourne could not determine what went wrong—was Rebeka too depleted by the pain? Rowland too fast? She moved in a blur, he countermoved into her, the blade of his knife penetrating her side even as she whirled, delivering a blow to the point of his chin.

He staggered back, letting go of her, but she reeled back, the knife buried to the hilt in her side, and, as Bourne moved forward, collapsed into his arms. Lifting her off her feet, Bourne ran out of the bedroom, down the hallway to the door to the basement.

The plan of the house was clear in his mind, everything *el Enterrador* had told them about the basement echoing the only promise of escape. With Rebeka lying bleeding in his arms, he could think only of escaping from Maceo Encarnación's estate and getting her to a hospital as quickly as possible.

He took her down the concrete stairs. With a

flick of a switch the basement blazed with light, illuminating the space and its contents. He found a flashlight in a tool chest and switched it on. Crossing to the electric panel, he cut the power to all the breakers. The lights went out, not only down in the basement, but all through the house, along with the alarm system.

"*In the center of the basement is a storm drain,*" *el Enterrador* had told them. "*The water table beneath the house dictates a large one.*" Large enough to accommodate a human being.

Using the flashlight's beam, Bourne found the drain. Rebeka moaned as he set her down. The hilt of the knife still stuck out of her side. He could not pull it out without a resultant gush of blood. Even if he bound the wound, it would bleed far more than it was now. Curling his fingers around the grate that covered the drain, he hauled upward. It wouldn't budge.

All of a sudden, he heard the sound of running boot soles on the floorboards above his head. He looked over at Rebeka, the blood staining the bare concrete near her. Upstairs, there would be a clear trail to the basement door.

Charles Thorne, in his enormous king-size bed, drifted restlessly in and out of sleep. He heard the front door click closed, and he sat up. Or had he dreamed it? He heard soft footfalls coming toward the bedroom. He knew the gait as well as he knew his own.

His wife was home.

"Did I wake you?" Ann Ring said from her position in the open doorway.

"Would it matter?" He was trying to shake the sleep out of his head.

"Not really."

That exchange, as much as anything, defined their relationship. A marriage fueled by hot sex had been transformed into a marriage of convenience as the chemicals cooled and dissolved into the routine of daily life.

He watched his wife as she strode into the bedroom, crossing to her dresser, where she began to take off her jewelry.

"It's almost seven in the morning. Where were you?"

"The same place as you. Out."

Staring at Ann's back, pale and shimmery in the city light, as she unzipped and shrugged off her dress, Thorne could recall a time when the heat between them was so unbearable all they could think of was melding together, no matter where they were. Now he seemed to be watching a photograph. Now it was unbearable to look at her and admit to himself what he had lost.

What has become of me? he wondered. *How did I wander so far off course?* There was no answer, of course, apart from the obvious one: Life happened, one decision at a time, a tiny incision in a rock face becoming a landslide under which he was now in imminent danger of being buried.

Naked, Ann went into the bathroom and flicked on the lights. A moment later, as he heard the shower come on, he got out of bed and padded over to where her clothes were puddled on the floor. By the wedge of light thrown from the bathroom, he went through the hip pockets of her dress, then rooted in her small clutch.

A shadow passed across him and he froze.

"Can I help you with something?" Ann stood in the doorway, watching him with the coldly luminous eyes of a reptile.

She hadn't stepped into the shower after all. He closed his eyes, raging at himself for falling into so obvious a trap. Obvious in retrospect. His hate for her was so powerful he could taste it.

Then she moved. "Get away from my things, you pathetic sonofabitch."

He stepped back hurriedly as she snatched her purse from his hand.

"You want to know where I was?" Ann's nostrils flared as she shook her head, contempt altering her expression. "I had a little visit with Mr. Li." As his eyes widened, a smile curled her lips. "That's right, *your* Mr. Li." She opened a drawer of her dresser, put the clutch inside, then leaned on the open drawer as if to show him how much he wearied her. "Only, he never was your Mr. Li. Not exclusively, anyway."

"How...?" Thorne felt paralyzed. His brain seemed to have lost the ability to string two thoughts together. "How did you...?"

She laughed silently. "Who do you think introduced him to his Israeli girlfriend?"

Back at the toolbox, Bourne grabbed a crowbar and used it to pry up the grate. Setting it aside, he trained the beam of light down to see the trajectory of the drain. It was a sheer vertical drop for only about seven or eight feet, after which there was a bend as it sloped slightly farther down. He gripped the flashlight between his teeth and gathered Rebeka into his arms. Holding her against him, he slid down the storm drain, the soles of his shoes thudding hard against the bottom of the vertical drop.

Shifting her slightly in his arms brought no response from her. Tilting his head so the beam of light lit up her face, he saw that her eyes were closed. The wound in her side was deep, and he wondered if the knife blade had nicked, or even penetrated, a vital organ. There was no way to tell. He tried again to stanch the flow of blood but was only partially successful.

"Rebeka," he said softly. Then forcefully. But her eyes opened only after he had slapped her cheek. "Don't pass out on me," he said. "I'm getting you out of here." Her eyes gazed up at him, slightly out of focus. "Just hold on a little longer."

The urgency of escape weighed on him, and he negotiated her through the bend, then scuttled along the slope, which became less and less severe. Their escape route smelled of concrete, dead leaves, and rot. The bottom of it was wet and dank. Echoes of their progress followed them like ghosts fleeing into the darkness.

He tilted his head upward, playing the beam of light across the top of the drainpipe, looking for the service junction *el Enterrador* had told them was three hundred yards beyond the wall of the estate and emerged onto a heavily treed area of Lincoln Park.

The pipe was slowly narrowing, something *el En-terrador* had failed to mention. Bourne's progress was slowed by the constant maneuvering of Rebeka's body to fit the changing dimensions. He kept going, murmuring a soft litany to keep her conscious. There was still no sign of the service junction. Just then, the beam of light began to stutter. Darkness replaced light. It returned, but with a dimmer wattage. The batteries were failing.

Bourne redoubled his efforts to move forward quickly, but the drainpipe continued to narrow, obliging him to inch along, headfirst, Rebeka's body on top of him. He could feel the beat of her heart, the shudder of her breathing, which was becoming ragged as she fought for air. He had to get her out of the ground and into the air immediately.

He kept going forward, inch by bloody inch, every second crucial now. The flashlight failed again, took longer to come on, the beam faded, worn-out and flickering. But in its inconstant illumination, Bourne at last saw the outline of the service junction, a vertical shaft up to the park.

Trying to pick up speed, he dragged Rebeka along with him, his back raw and wet through his clothes from scraping along the bottom of the pipe. A semicircular rim, shimmering like a sliver of moon in a nighttime sky, beckoned to him and then winked out as the flashlight's batteries finally failed. He was plunged into the pitch black.

Natasha Illion?" Thorne felt the world slipping from beneath his feet. "I don't—"

"Understand?" Ann held her icy smile. "Poor Charles. Let's just say Tasha and I are friends and leave it at that."

"You bitch!" he cried and leaped at her.

Ann took her hand out of the dresser drawer. She gripped a small Walther PPK/S. Thorne either didn't see it or didn't care. Enraged, he came on, his hands raised, seeking to strangle her.

Ann pulled the trigger once, twice, holding her hand rock-steady, squeezing the trigger. The powerful .32 ACP bullets tore through him, knocking Thorne against the wall with such force he ricocheted off.

His eyes opened in shock and disbelief. Then came the blinding pain, and he pitched into her. For a moment he gripped her as he once had when they were lovers, desperate in their feverish lust.

His mouth opened and closed, a speared fish gasping for air. "Why...? You..."

Ann watched him dying with a cold, almost clinical eye. "You're a traitor, Charles. To me, to our marriage, but most of all to our country." He slipped to his knees. "Do you know what you were up to with the estimable Mr. Li? Estimable as a spy, that is."

Thorne felt as if there were no more shocks left for him to endure. The landslide had come and it was covering him completely.

"Good-bye, Charles." Ann pushed him away, found his blood on her. Stepping over him, she returned to the bathroom, where she stepped into the shower and began to scrub her body clean.

* * *

Bourne kept moving forward, judging the distance from the last after-image of the shaft's rim still shining in his mind's eye. The pipe was now so narrow that he could feel the top by lifting his arm in his prone position. This is how he traversed the last few feet to the rim. Feeling it with his fingertips, his heart lifted.

Setting Rebeka down, he stood up into the shaft. Reaching above his head, he felt the bottom of the hatch. There was a metal ring distended from the bottom. He turned this to the left, then pushed, and was rewarded by a rush of light and fresh air.

Freedom!

Ducking back down, he once more gathered Rebeka up and, lifting her into the shaft, pushed her up to the surface. A moment later, he followed her up. Daylight glowed around them. They were in the center of a copse of trees, planted in a perfectly symmetrical square, four trees deep on each side.

Keeping Rebeka down and out of sight, he lifted his head, listening for sounds of pursuit. He heard the distant rumble of traffic from the perimeters. It was too early for any strollers to be visiting the park. They were alone.

Checking Rebeka again, he saw that the wound was already suppurating. He tried using one of the bits of cloth he'd taken from the toolbox to stanch the flow, but almost immediately the cloth was saturated. The difficult travel through the drainpipe had exacerbated the wound. He listened to her heart, then her lungs, and didn't like what he heard. He tried to calculate how much blood she had lost—more than she had on their flight from Damascus to Dahr El Ahmar. Her face was ashen, all color drained from her eyes. She tried to speak but couldn't manage it. If he didn't get her to a hospital soon, she'd surely bleed out.

She opened her mouth, said something unintelligible.

"Save your strength," he whispered. "Only a little way to go now until the hospital."

He picked his head up again. What they needed now was transportation.

"Rebeka," he said, "I'm going to get a car for us." Rising, he wove his way out of the square of trees, went across the park, and down a bit, where he saw a car park. Traffic drove by. A taxi passed. He thought about hailing it, but cruising cabs were all too often driven by gang members out to mug and rob unsuspecting tourists. Instead, he stood by the side of the parked car. He was about to break in when a police cruiser drifted past. The cops marked him and the cruiser slowed. Bourne turned away. The cruiser stayed put, and he cursed under his breath.

Another taxi turned the corner and came his way. It was free, and he flagged it down. From the corner of his eye, he saw the cruiser pull away and drive on. When the cab pulled to a halt, Bourne told the driver to wait. Retracing his steps, he returned to the grove. As he brought Rebeka across the park to the waiting vehicle, she murmured something again. This time, he put his ear close to her mouth. Her eyes opened, focusing on him with an obvious effort, and forced herself to repeat it. A name.

They reached the waiting taxi. The driver turned, watching Bourne deposit Rebeka in the backseat and climb in after her.

"*¿Qué pasa con ella?*" the driver said.

"*Ponernos al* Hospital General de Mexico," Bourne ordered.

"Hey, she's bleeding all over my seat!"

"She's been stabbed," Bourne said, leaning forward. "*¡Vamos!*"

The driver grimaced, put the taxi in gear, and pulled out into traffic. Within three blocks, Bourne knew they were going the wrong way. Hospital General de Mexico was south of here; they were heading north. He was about to say something when the driver began to pull over to where two squat Mayan-looking men were loitering on a corner, smoking furiously.

Lunging forward, Bourne wrapped one arm around the driver's throat and pulled hard. At the same time, his free hand groped beneath his jacket, found the pistol, and jerked it out of its shoulder holster.

"The hospital," Bourne said, pressing the muzzle against the side of his head, "or I pull the trigger."

"And risk the car going out of control?" The driver, still heading for his partners in crime, shook his head. "You won't."

Bourne pulled the trigger and the driver's head exploded in a welter of blood, brains, and bone. The taxi lurched forward, heading directly toward the two men. They recognized the oncoming vehicle, threw down their butts, and got ready to go to work. Then the taxi jumped the curb and, yelling, they scattered.

By this time, Bourne had clambered over the front seat. Shoving the driver out the door, he slid behind the wheel, veered away to just miss a street-light and several pedestrians before he was able to muscle the car's trajectory back out onto the street.

He made a spectacular U-turn, running up and over the divider. Brakes screeched, horns blared, and angry shouts were raised. But, moments later, they were all behind him as he raced in and out of lanes, heading pell-mell south toward the hospital.

He glanced at Rebeka in the rearview mirror, saw her extreme pallor, could not detect even a shallow breath coming from her. She was bathed in blood.

"Rebeka," he said. And then, more forcefully, "Rebeka!"

She did not respond. Her eyes stared upward blankly. He sped on through the increasingly chaotic streets, past modern buildings and squares embed-ded in the ruins of the ancient past, into the smoky, raw-flesh–colored Mexico City dawn.

Book Three

21

TREADSTONE'S INTERNAL ALARM sounded at precisely 7:43 AM. Anderson, the ranking Treadstone officer, called Dick Richards at 8:13 AM, after his staff had been unable to identify the Trojan that had jumped the firewall to attack the on-site servers, much less quarantine and exterminate it.

"Get down to HQ," Anderson said, "ASAP."

Richards, who had been sitting on the edge of his bed, literally biting his nails to the quick while he waited for the call, jumped up, splashed water on his face, and, grabbing his raincoat, headed out the door. On the way to work, he allowed himself a self-satisfied smile.

When he arrived fourteen minutes later, the office was in something of a quiet uproar. No one had yet figured out how a Trojan could have invaded the on-site servers, and it was this question, just as much as how much damage it had done, that occupied the discussion around the IT department.

After checking in with the hastily convened team, Richards set himself up at the server terminal and began his "tracking" of the Trojan he had created and set like a time bomb inside the Treadstone intranet. Creating the Trojan had been the fun part, but inserting it had proved far more difficult than even he had imagined, and he cursed himself for not paying more attention to the intricacies of the firewall during the short time he had been at Treadstone.

He had made the mistake of assuming that the Treadstone firewall was built on the same cyber architecture as those at the DoD and the Pentagon, with which he was familiar. Much to his consternation, he had quickly discovered that it was a completely different animal, one whose algorithms were alien to him.

He had spent hours racking his brain, trying to understand the architecture. He couldn't find a way in until he discovered how the base algorithm functioned. Close to 4 AM, he had cracked it. In celebration he rose, took a long-delayed pee, then selected a beer and some sliced ham from the refrigerator. He rolled the slices into cigars, dipping them into hot mustard, ate them one by one, washing them down with the beer. He chewed and swallowed while considering the possible routes he could take to insert the Trojan through the firewall. It had to be done that way, as if an outside agency were responsible.

He washed his hands and returned to his desktop, starting the tricky and delicate process of breaching the Treadstone firewall. The program he had devised was tiny but supremely powerful. Once inside, it mimicked the server, rerouting Treadstone requests for information to a dead end that would quickly bring all intranet traffic to a screeching halt.

Now, as Richards sat typing away at the server terminal, his job was to insert the virus he had prepared while at the same time quarantining the Trojan before eliminating it. This was just as tricky as the original insertion. He had to make it appear as if the virus was triggered out of the Trojan as it was being isolated. Hair-raising enough, but then Sam Anderson pulled up a chair and sat down next to him.

"How's it going?"

Richards grunted, hoping Peter's deputy would get bored and leave. Still he sat, staring at the computer language racing across the screen. Stuxnet was so last year compared to the mutated program he had devised: an advanced viral form that incorporated the best parts of the Stuxnet algorithm and grafted it onto an entirely new architecture, known in his circles as Duqu, which, among other neat devices, used both faked and stolen digital certificates to insinuate itself into the boot program, the core of every operating system. From there, it twisted every command.

"Making progress?"

Richards ground his teeth together in frustration and anxiety. He hadn't counted on being observed. "I've identified the Trojan."

"Now what?"

On the other hand, he thought, Anderson doesn't know dick about software programs, so what could make him suspicious? "Now I need to quarantine it."

"Move it, you mean?"

"In a way." The constant stream of idiotic questions was making it difficult for Richards to concentrate. "Although 'moving' in the cyber world is a relative term."

Anderson leaned forward. "Can you explain that to me?"

It was all Richards could do not to let out a howl. Working for three masters was nerve-racking enough without this interference. "Some other time maybe."

Anderson was just about to ask another question when his mobile buzzed. Answering it, he listened to the voice on the other end of the line. "Fuck." The more the voice spoke, the more he scowled.

Richards risked a glance over at him. "What is it?"

But Anderson was already striding across the room. Snatching up his coat, he raced out the door.

Shrugging, Richards returned to his intricate sabotage.

I need a body." Secretary Hendricks spoke to Roger Davies, his first adjutant, on his mobile. "Male, no family ties. A B&E rap sheet would be ideal. Also, I need you to send over a hand-picked clean-up crew. An apartment needs to be sterilized." He listened briefly to the buzz of Davies's voice on the other end of the call before he interrupted. "I understand. Just make it happen now."

Hendricks disconnected and looked down with distaste at the body of Charles Thorne. "That's damn good shooting, Ann," he said. "But I wish to God you'd found another way."

"So do I." Ann stood beside him in her bedroom, a thick bathrobe tied around her. After she had called her handler, she had considered getting dressed, but Hendricks had trained her too well. She didn't want to disturb the scene until he arrived with further orders. "But he gave me no choice. I guess he just snapped."

Hendricks, hands in the slash pockets of his overcoat, wiped his brow with the back of his hand. He'd had Ann pick up her dress off the floor while he checked it for blood spatters. Then he directed her to hang it in her closet. Her shoes were another story. He discovered several blood spatters and placed them in a plastic garbage bag he had brought with him. He had donned disposable gloves and booties before crossing the threshold into the apartment.

He picked up her Walther PPK/S and began to methodically wipe it clean of her prints. "You think you can handle Li by yourself?"

"I've worked for you in secret for, what? Sixteen years?" Ann nodded. "I sure as hell can handle him." She eyed Hendricks. "But it isn't really Li you're concerned about."

"No." Hendricks sighed. "It's whoever he reports to." He turned away, not wanting to look at the corpse again until Roger arrived with his burden. He could have given this dirty job to any one of a number of subordinates, but he knew that was the way leaks developed, even in the most secure of clandestine organizations. The dirtier the job, he had learned, the more imperative it was that you handled it yourself. And this was an exceptionally dirty business. He sighed. "The structure of the Chinese

Secret Service is more than a bit opaque. It would be immensely helpful to know who we're really up against."

He turned back to her. "That's what I'm going to need from you now, Ann. We couldn't ask it of poor Charles." Of course they couldn't. Thorne had been a dumb conduit—he was passing on disinformation to Li without knowing the intel was false. His overweening urgency for power had blinded him. Bad for him, but good for Hendricks. As Hendricks had anticipated, such urgency led to mistakes in judgment, which was just what Charles Thorne had made when he climbed into bed with Li in order to gain scoops for *Politics As Usual*. Now, sadly, that phase of the operation was prematurely terminated.

It was possible, the secretary mused, that Ann had mismanaged her private life with him. He shrugged mentally. That was the chance you took when manipulating human beings; their behavior wasn't always predictable.

"Don't worry," Ann said.

One thing you could say about Ann Ring, Hendricks thought, she had ice in her veins.

"Nevertheless, you do look worried."

"It's Soraya."

"Ah, yes. I heard." Ann tilted her head. "How is she?"

"She almost died," Hendricks said with more emotion than he had intended.

Ann regarded him coolly, her arms crossed over her chest. "But she hasn't died, has she?"

"No."

"Then let's thank our lucky stars."

"I should have chosen—"

"You chose her because she was the right person for the job."

"Once you told me that your husband was infatuated with her."

"Really, Christopher, that wasn't the reason at all. Charles's infatuation with her just made the assignment you gave her that much easier. She would have found another way; she's an exceptionally clever girl. And from what you've told me, she enjoyed passing on the bits of disinformation to Charles."

Hendricks nodded. "It gave her a great deal of pleasure to have a direct hand in taking down Li and his cohorts."

"There," Ann said. "You see? You're just feeling remorseful because her concussion landed her in the hospital."

That wasn't it at all, Hendricks thought sadly. Or, at least, not all of it. What worried him most of all was Soraya's pregnancy. It seemed clear to him that she was carrying Charles Thorne's child. If that was the case, how was Ann going to react? She was his most closely held, and therefore his most precious, asset-in-place. He could not afford to lose her, especially now that they had made such definitive contact with Li.

The question that vexed Hendricks most was the identity of Li's handler. Not one of the DoD's vaunted sources could tell him who might be running Li Wan.

Hendricks turned his mind to more practical matters. "Ann, I want you dressed and out of here before the team arrives. You have a place?"

She nodded. "A room at the Liaison. I use it when I have late nights on the Hill."

"Go there now. Tomorrow you will assume your role as a grieving widow."

"What about Li?"

"He'll want to convey his condolences," Hendricks said. "Encourage him to do so in person."

"It won't be easy. As we've seen, he is a very wary man. If he becomes suspicious now, we'll never find out who's running him and what they want."

"You're right." Hendricks thought for a moment. "You're going to have to give him something that will allay any suspicions he might harbor."

"It'll have to be something big—something important."

Hendricks nodded. "Agreed. Give up his girl."

"What?" Ann, plainly shaken, stared at him, stupefied. "We can't. You know we can't."

"Do you have a better idea?"

Silence.

"Good God," Ann Ring said, "I didn't sign up for this."

"But you did, Ann. You know you did."

She licked her lips. Her face was pale. "It's people's lives we're manipulating."

"Not civilians," Hendricks said. "We all signed the same document."

"In blood."

He did not contradict her.

She glanced over one last time at the corpse of her husband. "At what point," she said, "are you completely drained of all human emotion?"

"You'd better get going," Hendricks said. He had no clear answer for her.

Four minutes after Ann Ring departed, the clean-up crew arrived. Shortly thereafter, Davies delivered the man who had shot Charles Thorne to death in the midst of a break-in robbery. Hendricks settled the Walther into the corpse's right hand, curling the fore-finger over the trigger. When he and Davies had set it in place and made certain everything was correct, he called Eric Brey, director of the FBI, and emotion-lessly filled him in on the murder.

Fuck," Peter Marks said, "I'm alive."

"You sound disappointed," Anderson said.

There was a jouncing, along with the steady vi-bration of a vehicle engine. His eyes roved.

"Ambulance," Anderson said. "It was Delia who got to you first. She was inside the school when the shooting took place. She called me first thing."

Peter licked his lips. "How am I?"

"You're fine," Anderson said.

"Where was I shot?"

"You..." Anderson's eyes cut to the paramedic on his right.

Peter felt a sudden lurch in the pit of his stomach. "I can't feel anything."

Anderson's expression betrayed nothing. "Trau-ma. Doesn't mean a thing."

"But I can't feel..." Peter braced himself. "Is my spine involved?"

Anderson shook his head.

Better off dead, Peter thought, *than a cripple*.

Anderson put a hand on his shoulder. "Boss, I know what's going through your mind, but right now nothing's set in stone. Just relax. Keep still. A surgical team is standing by. Let them do their thing. Everything will be okay."

Peter closed his eyes, willing his screaming brain to shut up. He needed to concentrate on this moment. *Que sera sera.* The future would take care of itself. "The man who shot me. I need to know his identity."

"He had no ID on him, boss."

"Fingerprints, dental records, DNA."

"All being taken care of."

Peter nodded. He licked his lips. "There's something else. Richards."

"I'm on it, boss. There was a breach of the intranet this morning. A Trojan. I called Richards in."

Peter thought about Richards working for Tom Brick and Core Energy. "Richards may be the one who planted it. The fucker's clever enough to get through the firewall."

"I thought of that," Anderson said. "I placed an electronic keylogger on the server terminal he's using to ID and quarantine the Trojan."

"Nicely done, Sam." Peter winced, feeling some pain now. "I don't yet know why Brick wants to get inside Treadstone."

"We'll find out. Take it easy now, boss."

He saw Anderson nod to the paramedic beside him, who slipped a needle into a vein on the inside of his elbow from which a delicious warmth drifted, washing through him.

"It's important. It's all important," he said, his words already slurry.

"I'll see to it, boss." And, good as his word, as Peter slipped into unconsciousness, Anderson punched in a number on his mobile, making the first of many calls.

Bourne, heading through the relentlessly beating heart of Mexico City, the smell of blood in his nostrils, hadn't forgotten about the Babylonian. He was somewhere within the brightly colored whirlpool of the city, standing in a plaza, watching, driving the same chaotic streets as Bourne, using what contacts and conduits he might have in Mexico to reestablish contact with his quarry.

Thinking about Ilan Halevy was preferable to thinking about Rebeka, who he had failed to protect adequately, who died before she could finish the mission she had assigned herself, a mission that was important enough for her to abandon Mossad and strike out on her own.

Her mission was now his own.

Bourne, heading through the city streets, the stench of fire and fear in his nostrils, looked for Halevy, wanting to find the Babylonian as badly as Halevy wanted to find him.

He drove east, toward the airport, and when he saw the radiant sign for Superama, he turned off. At Revolution 1151, Merced Gómez, Benito Juárez, he pulled into the colossal parking lot, slid the taxi into an empty slot, and got out.

Opening the trunk, he discovered a pile of rags. He used one to wipe down all the interior surfaces. He paused when he was finished and looked at Rebeka. Her shirt had been ripped open. Inside, he saw an aluminum-mesh wallet. Lifting it out with his fingertips, he wiped off the blood. Inside was her legend passport, the money she had taken from beneath the floorboards of her rental apartment in Stockholm, and a delicate silver necklace with a star of David. She had never shown the talisman to him. Leaving the wallet and its contents behind seemed like leaving a part of her to be picked over, so he took them. He knew there was nothing more he could do for her. Saying his silent goodbye, he slammed the door, using the rag, and picked his way through the lot to the store.

In the bathroom, he threw away the rag and washed her blood off his hands. Then he dumped his blood-stained coat and shirt, and went in search of a new outfit. He bought black jeans, a white shirt, and a charcoal-colored jacket.

Returning to the parking lot, he moved through the rows, looking for an older car. Behind him, he heard the throaty gurgle of a motorcycle engine. It was a large one—an Indian Chief Dark Horse. He saw it approaching out of the corner of his eye. It was traveling so slowly that he gave it scant attention, but the instant it put on a burst of speed, he turned. The driver was male, but a mirrored faceplate on his helmet obscured his face. Sunlight spun crazily off the crown of the black impact-resistant plastic.

The Indian went down a parallel row, and Bourne turned back to the car he had chosen. Unbending a wire hanger he had taken from the store where he bought his clothes, he stuck the hooked end down between the door frame and the window. The lock popped up. He was about to open the door when the Indian reappeared, coming at him very fast from the opposite side.

Bourne stood by the door, watching the motorcycle coming closer. It was almost upon him when he swung the door out. The Indian's front wheel struck the metal with a dull clang, and the motorcycle bucked like a stallion. Its back reared up, flinging the driver out of his seat. He somersaulted up and over the car's crumpled door, and landed on the roof.

As he slid down, Bourne grabbed him, slammed him back against the car's side. He ripped off the helmet and saw up close the damage the flames had done to Halevy's neck.

As the Babylonian leaped at him, Bourne drove a knee into Halevy's crotch, then smashed a fist into the side of his head. Bourne grabbed him as he fell sideways. Halevy kicked him in the side of the knee, then, twisting free, drove his fist into the pit of Bourne's stomach. As Bourne's body turned, he struck the Babylonian in the kidney.

Bourne went down, Halevy on top of him. Halevy flicked out a knife, slicing a shallow arc toward Bourne's throat. Bourne reached up, scraped his nails down the Babylonian's fire-wounded throat. Halevy reared back, his eyes tearing with the fiery pain, and Bourne smashed his wrist against the bottom of the car. The knife clattered to the tarmac, and Bourne pressed his forearm against Halevy's throat.

"Tell me about Ouyang." Ouyang was the name Rebeka had spoken just before she died.

Halevy stared up at him balefully. "Who or what is an Ouyang?"

Bourne dug into the nerve bundle at the side of his neck. Halevy bared his teeth and his eyes popped. Sweat broke out on his face. The left side was scorched red, rippled and rent by the inroads the flames had made as they ate away and blackened the layers of his skin. He began to breathe hard.

"Ouyang," Bourne prompted.

"How d'you know about Ouyang?"

Bourne did that thing again, and this time Halevy's body arched up, his straining muscles trembling involuntarily. Little grunting noises emanated from his open mouth, like an animal caught in a trap, about to gnaw his leg off.

"Ben David deals with Ouyang."

"Not the Director or Dani Amit?"

Halevy, blowing air through his mouth as if to cool himself off, shook his head. "This is private. It isn't Mossad."

"Then how do you know about it?"

"I won't—" The Babylonian gave a silent howl as Bourne worked on him for a third time. His face was blue-white. Even his fire wound was now a pale pink, livid against the starkness of his stubble. Sweat flew off him like rain. "Okay, all right. Ouyang's a high minister in the CSP. Ben David has something going with him, but I swear I don't know what. Ben David recruited me to run interference with Tel Aviv, to make sure neither the Director nor Amit find out what he's up to." His gaze turned briefly canny. "But Rebeka found out, didn't she? She's the one who told you about Ouyang."

"It doesn't matter," Bourne said.

"Oh, but it does." The Babylonian gave Bourne a smile tainted with pain. "Ben David has a thing for her. He always did."

"And yet he sent you to kill her."

"That's the kind of man he is." Halevy took several shuddering breaths. "Divided, always divided, just like our country, just like every country in the Middle East. He loves Rebeka. I don't know what it took out of him to order her termination." Those oddly porcine breaths again. "There's no reason for you to believe this, but I'm glad she's still alive."

At that, Bourne rose, and, hauling the Babylonian up by his shirtfront, walked him back to the taxi. He shoved his face against the window.

"See her there? She's dead, Halevy," Bourne said. "I hold you and Ben David to account."

"I didn't do it. You know I didn't." Even as he was saying this, he whirled, a needle-like weapon in the palm of his hand. Its point glinted wetly with what must be some kind of fast-acting poison. Bourne, lifting an arm, felt the needle snag in the fabric of his jacket. The needle point scraped against his skin but did not break it. Bourne smashed the heel of his hand into Halevy's nose. He delivered a second strike to the Babylonian's throat, fracturing the cricoid cartilage.

Jerking his arm away from the needle, he struck Halevy flush on his ear. The Babylonian, gasping for air that would not come, staggered to his knees, still trying desperately to swipe at Bourne with the needle. Bourne grabbed him, and drove his knee into his groin, then struck him over and

over again until he felt the bones in Halevy's
chest give way.

With the Babylonian dead, Bourne slipped into the
old car he had chosen, hot-wired it, and drove out
of the lot. At Benito Juárez International Airport,
he bought a first-class ticket, then went in search of
something to eat.

While he waited for his food, he took out the tiny
skull studded with crystals that *el Enterrador* had
given him as protection against Maceo Encarnación.
"He is protected by an almost mystical power,"
Constanza Camargo had told him, *"as if by gods."*

His food came, but he found that he was no
longer hungry. As he turned the skull around and
around between his fingers, he thought about everything that had happened to him and Rebeka
since coming to Mexico City, all of which had
been dictated, in one way or another, by Constanza Camargo. And then he began to wonder
about something else. Why would Henry Rowland secrete himself in the closet of his bedroom
unless he had known they were coming? But how
had he known with such precision where they
were?

Bourne stared at the crystal-studded skull and
into his mind came thoughts of other gods—the
gods of technology. Placing the skull on the table,
he smashed the bottom of his fist down onto it.
Carefully, he picked through the shattered bits and
pieces, extracting the minuscule tracking device that
had been embedded in its center. He left it amid the

debris without destroying it. He wanted the signal to continue broadcasting, just as if he had never discovered the device.

He rose, paying for the meal he hadn't touched, then exited the departure lounge, heading for the long-term parking lot, to find a suitable vehicle to drive back into the city.

There are any number of ways to remain alive after you're dead." Don Fernando Hererra laughed, seeing the expression on Martha Christiana's face. "This is only one of them."

The pilot had landed the private jet in a vast field south of Paris. There was no runway, no windsock, no customs shed. The plane had deviated from its flight plan and, after a frantic Mayday call, was now off the grid as far as the towers at Charles de Gaulle and Orly airports were concerned.

"There are no magicians in the world, Martha. Only illusionists," Hererra said. "The idea is to create the illusion of death. For this, we require an authentic disaster, which is why the plane has landed here, where no one will be hurt."

"Those bodies I saw on the plane," Martha said, "are real."

Hererra nodded as he handed her a folder.

"What's this?"

"Look inside."

Opening the file, she saw forensic reports on three bodies retrieved from the wreckage of the plane that had not yet crashed. The three bodies were burned beyond recognition, of course, but were identified by dental records. Hererra was named, as well as the pilot and the navigator.

Martha picked her head up. "What about their families? What will you tell them?"

Hererra nodded to the two men who were exiting the jet, whose engines were still running. "These men have no families, one of the reasons they were hired in the first place."

"But how—?"

"I have friends inside the Élysée Palace who will control the accident scene."

The pilot approached Hererra. "The three corpses have been placed correctly," he said. "We can proceed anytime."

Hererra checked his wristwatch. "We've been off the radar for seven minutes. Do it now."

The pilot nodded, then turned to his navigator, who was standing apart from them. The navigator held a small black box in his hand. When he pressed a button on the box, the jet's engines rose in pitch until they became a scream. Another button remotely released the brakes, and the jet bucked forward, quickly gaining speed until it slammed into the line of trees at the far end of the field. A ferocious noise flared, momentarily deafening them. The ground shook, and an oily black-and-red fireball puffed out in the sky.

"We go," Hererra said, herding them all toward a large four-wheel-drive SUV crouched at the edge of the field. "Now."

The Cementerio del Tepeyac and, especially, the

Basilica de Guadelupe looked completely different in daylight. All the sinister qualities, burned into the Mexican night, had been washed away, leaving a thin veneer of religiosity that no doubt hid a multitude of sins, both venial and mortal.

Parking his stolen car a hundred yards away, Bourne spent several minutes circumnavigating the immediate area around the basilica. There was no sign of the hearse that had conveyed him and Rebeka to the establishment of Diego de la Rivera, Maceo Encarnación's brother-in-law. There was also no sign of the mysterious pseudo-priest, *el Enterrador*. Bourne recalled in vivid detail the tattoos of coffins and tombstones adorning his forearms.

He went around to the entrance and slipped through. The interior was filled with echoes and incense. A choir of angelic voices lifted heavenward. Mass had commenced. Bourne made his way to the back of the apse, returning to the dimly lit corridor that led to the rectory.

Before he arrived, however, he paused, hearing voices from within the small office. One was a female alto. Moving stealthily forward, Bourne caught a sliver of the rectory, the enormous crucified Christ dominating as usual. Then into his restricted line of vision came the source of the alto. With a start, he recognized the beautiful young woman who had drifted down the staircase in Maceo Encarnación's villa, who had cried out when she had seen what Bourne understood must have been her mother, laid out, ready for the mortician's art. The anomaly of her coming from an upstairs bedroom where no servant ought to be, naked beneath her expensive robe, now returned to the forefront of Bourne's mind. Upon returning upstairs, she had gone into the master suite, where Maceo Encarnación presumably lay beneath the bedcovers.

What was she doing here? Bourne moved slightly, his gaze following Maria-Elena's daughter as she moved anxiously around the rectory. He'd heard de la Rivera, the mortician, use the dead cook's name. A moment later, she stopped in front of a robed and hooded man. His spade beard announced him as *el Enterrador*.

"Give me absolution for my sins," she said softly. "I harbor murderous thoughts."

"Have you acted on these thoughts?" he replied in his raspy whisper.

"No, but—"

"Then all will be well, Anunciata."

"You can't know that."

"Why?"

"Because you don't know what I know," she said bitterly.

"By all means tell me," *el Enterrador* said with quiet menace.

She quailed for a moment, then expelled a deep breath.

"I trusted Maceo. I thought he loved me," she said, her voice abruptly changed, deeper in register and somehow darker.

"You can trust him. He does love you."

"My mother's legacy." She unfolded a sheet of paper, shoved it at him. "Maceo slept with my mother before he slept with me. He's my father."

El Enterrador touched the crown of her head.

"My child," he said, just as if he were a real priest, continuing in that ecclesiastical vein: "Fallen from the Garden of Eden, we all come from a dark place. This is our heritage, our collective legacy. We are all sinners, navigating a sinful world. However wrongful their liaison, your parents gave you life."

"And if the worst happens, if he makes me pregnant?"

"Of course we must see to it that never happens."

"I could cut off his *cojones*," Anunciata said with no little vitriol. "That would make me happy."

El Enterrador said, "I knew your mother ever since she came to Mexico City. I gave her confession. I have hope that I helped her through difficult times because she needed help and did not know where else to turn. Now it's you who comes to me for help and advice. Go to your father. Talk to him."

"What we have done!" Anunciata shuddered. "It's a hideous sin. You of all people should know that."

"Where is Maceo now?"

"You mean you don't know? He's gone. He left with Rowland for the airport."

"Where are they going?" Bourne said as he stepped into the rectory.

Both Anunciata and *el Enterrador* turned to stare at him. The priest was clearly more surprised to see him. The young woman registered only curiosity.

"Who are you, señor?" Anunciata said.

"Rebeka and I were at the villa early this morning."

"Then you—?"

But Bourne was already turning away from her.

"I should still be at the airport. That's what you're thinking, isn't it?"

"How would I—?"

"The crystal-encrusted skull you gave me. I found the transmitter inside it."

El Enterrador withdrew a long-bladed stiletto from beneath his robes, but Bourne shook his head, leveling the handgun he had taken from Maceo Encarnación's guard. "Put it down, Undertaker."

Anunciata's eyes opened wide. She seemed even more beautiful now than she had earlier. "He is a priest. Why do you call him *el Enterrador*?"

"That's his nickname." Bourne gestured with his head. "Show her the tattoos on your forearms, priest."

"Tattoos?" Anunciata echoed. She stared at her companion, clearly stunned.

He said nothing, didn't even look at her.

She reached out, pushed up the sleeves of his robe, and gasped at the intricate handiwork displayed.

"What is this?" It seemed unclear who she was addressing.

"Tell her, Undertaker," Bourne said. "I'd like to hear it, as well."

El Enterrador glared at him. "You were not supposed to come back here."

"You weren't supposed to track me, either." Bourne nodded. "Now let's get to the truth."

"About what?" *el Enterrador* whispered. "Maceo Encarnación asked for my help. I gave it to him."

"Rebeka—the woman—my friend—is dead. Put the knife on the desk."

After a hesitation, *el Enterrador* complied.

"The truth," Bourne said. "That's what I'm here for. How about you, Anunciata?"

She shook her head. "I don't understand."

"Ask the Undertaker. He's the one who is in real need of forgiveness."

She shook her head again.

Bourne said, "Rebeka and I got into Maceo Encarnación's villa via a mortician's hearse. In order for that to happen, someone inside the villa had to die."

"My mother."

Bourne nodded. "Your mother. But how would anyone know beforehand that she was going to die?" He stared directly at the priest. "People had to know your mother was going to die. Which means she was murdered."

Tears were standing out in Anunciata's eyes. "The doctor said she died of a heart attack. There wasn't a mark on her. I know. I dressed her for the . . . the mortician."

"Poison doesn't leave an external mark," Bourne said. "And if you're clever you can find a poison that won't leave an internal trace, either." He nodded. "I think that might have been your part in the murder, Undertaker." He turned to Anunciata. "Hence his nickname."

She whirled on *el Enterrador*. "Is that true?"

"Of course not," he scoffed. "The very idea that I would harm your mother is absurd."

"Not if Encarnación asked it of you."

"Did you do it?" Anunciata's cheeks were flaming. Her entire frame was shaking.

"I already told you—"

"The truth!" she cried. "This is a church. I'll have the truth!"

He went to reach for the stiletto, but she was quicker. Or perhaps she had already prepared herself. Snatching up the knife, she strode forward, and, in one powerful swing, thrust the knife into *el Enterrador*'s throat.

His eyes opened wide in shock and disbelief. He grabbed on to the edge of the desk as he was falling, but his already numb fingers slipped off, and he crashed to the floor in a rapidly spreading pool of his own blood.

22

THE BEIJING CENTRAL Committee Earth and Sky Country Club lay only five miles northwest of the capital. But it could have been a hundred. Here, beyond the massive layer of industrial smog that hung above the city like an intimation of a permanent twilight, the skies were clear. Within the twelve-foot-high spiked fence, electrified for added security, could be seen endless rows in meticulous parallels of cabbage, cucumbers, peppers and beans of all varieties, onions, scallions, *gai lan*, bok choy, and chilies, among many others. What made these vegetables special, necessitating the heavy security, was that they were all organic, grown pesticide-free in pristine conditions. In the northern section of Earth and Sky was the dairy farm, where cows were fed an all-organic diet, the milk processed in sterile conditions.

It was to Earth and Sky that Minister Ouyang

was being driven in his state-provided limousine for his twice-monthly visit. The produce of Earth and Sky was the sole property of the state, for consumption only by the Central Committee and those high-level ministers who, like Ouyang, were privy to its largesse. There were twenty-five levels of power within the many ministries of Beijing's central government. Each level was entitled to a specific amount of organic food. The higher up the minister, the larger the monthly allotment. This feudal system was a holdover from Mao's regime, made necessary by the severe pollution of China's earth and sky, which was nearing crisis level.

However, today Minister Ouyang had an altogether different reason for visiting the country club. As the cantilevered front gate opened to his driver's electronic code, he saw another car waiting just inside. The man in army fatigues stood beside the car, eating a cucumber he had apparently just pulled off the vine.

When Ouyang stepped out of his limousine and approached, he saw the livid scar down the side of the man's face.

"Colonel Ben David," he said, donning dark glasses against the sun's glare. "It has been some time."

"You know," Ben David said, lounging against the car, "I still prefer Israeli cucumbers." He chomped on the Earth and Sky vegetable, chewing slowly. "Something about the desert sun."

Minister Ouyang produced a curdled smile. "Bring your own food next time."

"I didn't say it wasn't good."

"What happened to your face?" Ouyang said in a gross breach of Chinese etiquette.

Ben David eyed him for some time. "You know, Minister, you're looking a little peaked. You haven't been drinking any of your infamous watered-down milk spiked with melamine so it can pass the protein-content tests?"

"I only drink milk from the Earth and Sky Dairy," Ouyang said coldly.

Ben David threw the stump of the cucumber onto the ground and came away from the car. "You know what occurs to me? We hate each other so much it's a wonder we can work together."

Ouyang bared his teeth. "Necessity creates strange bedfellows."

"Whatever." Ben David shrugged his shoulders. "What necessitated this face-to-face so close to our mutual journey's end?"

Minister Ouyang took out a slender file and handed it over.

Ben David opened it. His scar seemed to flare with heat as he stared at the surveillance photo of Jason Bourne. He looked up, rageful. "What the fuck is this, Ouyang?"

"You know this man," Ouyang said with maddening calm. "Intimately."

Ben David slapped the file. "This is why you insisted I travel over nine hours?"

Ouyang was imperturbable. "Please confirm my statement, Colonel."

"We have met on two occasions," Ben David said neutrally.

"Then you are the man for the job."

Ben David blinked. "What job? You're giving me a fucking *job*?"

A jet, winking silver in the bright sunshine, passed by overhead, a roar so distant it might have come from the other side of the world. Off to their left, a tractor ground slowly through the furrowed earth. The smell of loam was abruptly strong as the wind shifted. To the southwest the brown mass stained the sky, obscuring even the highest of Beijing's massive buildings.

"Tell me, Colonel, how long have we been working on our joint project?"

"You know as well as I do—"

Ouyang wiggled the first two fingers of his left hand. "Indulge me."

Ben David sighed. "Six years."

"A long time, by Western standards. Not so long as we measure time here in the Middle Kingdom."

Ben David looked disgusted. "Don't give me that 'Middle Kingdom' crap. This is business. It's always been business. This is not about politics, ideology, or cant. There's nothing mystical or even mysterious about it. You and I know that money makes the world turn. This is our ride, Ouyang, what brought us together. It's first and last on our list." He tossed his head. "This has been our program for six long, painstaking, dangerous years. Now you want to deviate. I don't like deviations."

"On all you say we agree," Minister Ouyang said. "But the world is a dynamic place, always changing. If our program cannot accommodate change, it cannot succeed."

"But we've already succeeded. In two days' time—"

"An eternity for something to go wrong." Ouyang pointed to the photo in the file. "This man Bourne has now bent his considerable talents to stopping us."

Ben David reared back as if struck. "How do you know this?"

"I am in contact with our other partners. You are not."

"Fuck!" Ben David slapped the file against his thigh. "You're not asking me to go after him."

"No need," Minister Ouyang said. "He'll quite happily come to you."

The voices of the angelic choir swelled until the massed chorale filled the Basilica de Guadelupe. In the rectory, Bourne stared down at the bloody corpse of *el Enterrador*, and said to Anunciata, "Now we must go."

Her eyes flashed along with the ruby-red blade of the stiletto she still wielded. "I'm not going anywhere with you. You were part of the plan."

"We knew nothing of the mechanisms of how we were being smuggled into Maceo Encarnación's villa," Bourne said. "My friend was killed because of that tracking device the Undertaker planted."

They looked at each other as if across a great chasm. They had both experienced loss because of Maceo Encarnación. He became a lodestone that in a peculiar way now drew them together.

She lowered the stiletto and nodded.

Bourne took her out through the small rectory entrance, through a section of the cemetery skirting the basilica itself, to where he had parked his car. They drove off slowly. A mile away, he pulled over to the curb and put the car in park, turning to her.

"If you know where Maceo Encarnación and Harry Rowland have gone, you must tell me."

Her large coffee-colored eyes stared at him without guile. "Will you kill them?"

"If I have to."

"You have to," Anunciata said. "There is no other way, with either of them."

"You know Rowland?"

She dipped her head. "He is Maceo's favorite, the protected one. Maceo looks on him as a son. He raised him from a very early age."

"Who are his parents?"

"That I do not know. I think Rowland is an orphan, though we do not speak. Maceo has forbidden it."

"Is Harry Rowland his real name?"

"He has many names," Anunciata said. "This is part of the myth."

Something icy sliced through Bourne. "The myth?"

"Maceo is obsessed with myths. 'Myths protect men.' This is what he always says. 'Myths make them safe because they separate them from other men, myths make them more than human, myths make other men fearful.'"

"How did he weave the myths around Rowland?"

Anunciata closed her eyes for a moment. "The central myth of the Aztecs is that man was created to feed the gods, otherwise the gods would rain down fire and destroy them and everything they had built. The gods ate a sacred substance in human blood."

"You're talking about the Aztecs' practice of human sacrifice."

She nodded. "The Aztec priests carved the beating hearts out of those sacrificed, offering them to the gods." She stared out the window for a moment at people passing by—a woman with a basket of fruit on her head, a boy on a dented blue bicycle. "That was a long time ago, of course." She turned back to him. "Nowadays, it's beheadings." She shrugged. "The blood is the same, and the gods are appeased."

"These are the same gods who allowed the Spaniards to defeat their people."

An enigmatic smile curled at the corners of Anunciata's lips. "Who can fathom the purposes of the gods? Mexico survived the Spaniards." Her gaze turned prescient. "The important thing is this: The Aztec struggle to control destiny is the same as our own. The coming of Jesus to Mexico has changed nothing. Blood is still spilled, sacrifices are still performed, destiny and desire are still the only things that matter."

"How does this fit in with Harry Rowland?"

"He is the advance guard, the outrider."

"The Djinn Who Lights The Way," Bourne said.

Anunciata's eyes opened wide. "You know. Yes, Rowland is the man who performs the sacrifices that increase the myth, that separate him from others, that make men fear him.

"He is Nicodemo."

* * *

The eagle sitting on a nopal cactus devouring a serpent is the modern-day coat of arms of Mexico," Maceo Encarnación said, sitting opposite Nicodemo in the wide leather seat of his Bombardier Global 5000. They had been in the air for some time. "These two creatures are at the heart of Mexican and Aztec culture. The god of sun and war told his people that they should found their greatest city in the place where they see an eagle on a nopal cactus, where the heart of his brother was buried, devouring a snake. This was where Tenochtitlán was built, and on its back Mexico City rose centuries later."

Maceo Encarnación watched Nicodemo, who hated lessons of any kind, to see his reactions. He stared at Maceo with his usual stoicism. "I tell you this tale, Nicodemo, because you are an outsider, a Colombian." He waited, should a reply be forthcoming. When only silence presented itself, he continued. "We learn to devour in order not to be devoured. Is this not the truth of the world?"

"It is," Nicodemo agreed with some animation. Speaking of death always brought him out of his brooding state. "I only wish I had been the one to kill the Aztec."

"Tulio Vistosa was the traitor I had been looking for. It was he who stole the thirty million." Maceo Encarnación chuckled. "The bundles of money were switched at the last minute. Very amusing, but not for him. He stole the counterfeit dollars and left me the real ones." Maceo Encarnación shook his head. "You have to have lived among these thieving bandits to get into their heads. You have to have been one of them."

"Like Acevedo Camargo," Nicodemo said.

Maceo Encarnación felt gratified that he was paying attention. "Constanza Camargo was a first-class singer when I met her. She was an even better actress, but she did not want to go into films."

"She wanted to spend more time with her husband, Don Acevedo."

Maceo Encarnación shook his head. "In a way. She was young and impressionable when she met Don Acevedo. He was rich and charismatic. He swept her off her feet. Within a month, they were married. At that time, Don Acevedo Camargo was the drug lord of the south. She was drawn to that life as strongly as she was drawn to other men, lovers she met with secretly. She loved the scheming. The plots she devised for him and behind his back! *Dios Mio,* that woman was bloodthirsty."

"She was ambitious."

Maceo Encarnación nodded. "Like Lady Macbeth. She enjoyed the role I gave her to play with Bourne and Rebeka."

Something dark flashed in the recesses of Nicodemo's eyes at the mention of Rebeka's name. "It wasn't supposed to work like that," he said softly. "Rebeka wasn't supposed to die. Bourne was."

"There is no way to account for the human factor. You should not have stabbed her."

"I had no choice!"

"It seems to me," Maceo Encarnación said, "there is always a choice."

"The heat of the moment precludes choice," Nicodemo said. "It's pure instinct."

At that moment, the flight attendant came down the aisle on long, lithe legs and, stopping in front of Maceo Encarnación, bent over. He studied her ample cleavage while she whispered in his ear. He nodded, and she went back up the aisle. Both men watched the ball-bearing movement of her shapely buttocks.

Maceo Encarnación sighed as he took out his mobile, punched in a number, and clapped it to his ear. "Someone will be coming for you," he said into his phone. "He'll be in Paris within the hour."

Nicodemo, grateful to get off the subject of Rebeka's knifing, said, "Don Fernando Hererra is dead. Blown up when his private jet crashed outside Paris. Why are we stopping off there when we should be heading on?"

Maceo Encarnación reversed the phone to show him the news stories. "Martha Christiana will be forwarding the coroner's report to verify that Hererra was actually on the plane. She always manages to get hold of these reports, the devil knows how. This is a beautiful thing, no? It's part of her skill set." He slid the mobile away. "You will go to her the moment we land."

"What do you want me to do?" Nicodemo said. "Kill her?"

"*Dios*, no!" Maceo Encarnación looked appalled. "Martha Christiana is special to me, do you understand?"

"I didn't think anyone was special to you, but what does it matter?"

Maceo Encarnación regarded him for a moment, as if he were a lower form of life. It seemed clear that the female Mossad agent had somehow gotten under his skin, an inexplicable feat he had thought near to impossible. He wondered what effect her death would have on him. To kill someone you cared about took an enormous amount of emotional fortitude, he knew from experience. Nicodemo had killed many people, of course, most of them in cold blood, some face-to-face, when you tried to catch that ineffable moment when life was transformed into death, when the soul fled into the shadows, when desire became destiny. He banished this disagreeable thought. "Martha Christiana is in Paris. Just bring her to me. And, Nicodemo, treat her like the lady she is."

"A lady," Nicodemo echoed. He turned to the window, his gaze far away.

"Nicodemo," Maceo Encarnación said, "what is on your mind?" When Nicodemo didn't answer, he said, "My daughter is on the other side of the world, married, and, one hopes, happy."

"I don't care about Maricruz."

You despise her, Maceo Encarnación thought. "What *do* you care about?" No response. Rebeka again. "I see."

"I'm thinking about Jason Bourne," Nicodemo said after the silence had become unendurable.

"What about him?"

"Jason Bourne represents more than just a problem. He could be the end of us."

"Calm yourself." This wasn't about Jason Bourne, and Maceo Encarnación knew it.

Nicodemo, restless in his seat, continued to stare out the Perspex window. Despite the jet's speed, the clouds seemed to drift past, as if in a dream. "We don't even know whether Rebeka is dead."

Now we get to it, Maceo Encarnación thought. "From what you tell me, it seems unlikely she has survived, even if Bourne somehow managed to get her to a hospital, which he hasn't. I have people looking; they would know if she had been admitted."

"Bourne has resources. A private doctor, maybe."

"From how you described the wound, no doctor could have saved her. She would have needed a full-fledged trauma team, and even then..." He allowed the thought to run its own course. "Forget her. That chapter is closed."

Nicodemo was brooding. "But not on Bourne."

"Of course not."

"I don't understand why you didn't leave me in Mexico City to deal with him."

"Deal with him?" Maceo Encarnación echoed. "I listened to you; we tried that once. You see how that turned out. Rebeka is dead and Bourne is still at large. Now one must create a real plan, execute it, at the conclusion of which Bourne dies. This is precisely what has been put in place. Anunciata is seeing to it."

In many ways Dick Richards's skills mimicked the finest watchmaker's. The difference was that he worked in the world of cyberspace, a place of infinite area, but without dimension. He had managed to quarantine his own Trojan and was now accessing the Core Energy network, where he had stored the preliminary codes that would activate the potent virus he had inserted like a drop of ink into its cyber heart of ones and zeros. Those codes were too complex even for his memory, and there was no way he would risk being caught with a rogue thumb drive or SD card. Besides, the attack had to seem to come from outside Treadstone, traced back to the Chinese. He could only seed the false ISP trail with a code that originated outside the Treadstone intranet.

Despite the canned air emanating from the vents in the ceiling, sweat rolled down his sides from under his arms, slid down the rills of his bent back as he sat, tensed, filled with a tremulous excitement, but also a terrible dread.

This was his big test, his ticket to the major leagues of hacking. When he pulled this off, he would prove indispensable to Tom Brick and Core Energy. This, more than anything, was what he wanted. Working for the government was soul-destroying. Other people took credit for his break-throughs, he received a puny salary, and the president treated him like a pet dog, occasionally stroked but never allowed up on the furniture where his human masters sat in daily judgment. His transfer to Treadstone had unexpectedly improved his lot. Though Soraya and, to some extent, Peter treated him with suspicion and contempt, he could not blame them. He had been sent to spy on them. He deserved their suspicion and contempt. But he also saw their willingness to give him the credit due him, if he could prove himself loyal.

True, Brick often treated him like a dog, but sometimes not. And he paid a shitload more than the government ever did—or could. Up until now, Richards had been trying to be faithful to three masters, but the tension was tearing him apart. He could no longer live this way. He needed to choose sides.

But what about Peter? How had he managed to infiltrate Core Energy? How did he know about Tom Brick? If Richards was to choose a side, then he had to decide what to do about Peter. Should he tell Peter everything he knew about Brick, Core Energy, and the secret entity that did its bidding? Should he, on the other hand, reveal Peter's real identity to Brick? Prior to working at Treadstone, the choice would have been a no-brainer. But now Treadstone had stymied him. He had to admit he liked it here. Unaccountably, the atmosphere was more like the private sector. There was little or no red tape, the co-directors saw to that.

On the horns of this dilemma, he continued his work, but his mind was elsewhere, so much so that he almost missed it. Some instinct, lodged in the most primitive part of his brain, the part humans counted on for survival, sent out a silent alarm that jerked him back to full concentration. Something was wrong. Immediately, he took his hands off the computer keyboard. Staring at the code he had been typing in, he felt an icy chill crawling down his spine. For a long time then, he did nothing but stare at the screen. Slowly, he drew his hands back from their position over the keyboard to rest them in his lap, as if he were a penitent, praying.

The normal sounds of the Treadstone office—

hushed voices, the hum of machines, the careful tread of shoes—came to him as if from a great distance. His mobile phone ringing made him start. He picked it up.

"Richards, it's Anderson."

His guilty heart leaped into his throat, closing it down for a terrifying moment. "Yessir," he eventually managed to croak.

"Made any progress?"

"The, uh, the Trojan is quarantined, sir."

"Good deal."

"It just... it's proving more difficult than I imagined to get rid of. There's... There seems to be some kind of mechanism embedded inside it." The moment he said this, he knew it was a mistake.

"What the hell does that mean?" Anderson thundered.

He had been trying to absolve himself of any culpability when the virus struck, but it seemed he had only inflamed Anderson.

"Goddammit, Richards. Answer me!"

"I'm dealing with the problem, sir. It's just going to take more time than I had expected."

"Now that the Trojan's quarantined, don't mess with it further. I don't want something else to be triggered."

Oh, you fool, Richards berated himself.

"Your number one priority is to find out how that fucking thing jumped our firewall, got me?"

"Yessir."

"I'll be back at HQ in an hour. I want an answer by then."

Richards's hand was trembling as he cut the connection. He tried to calm himself, but his mind was racing so fast that gathering his thoughts was like trying to herd cats. Pushing back his chair, he got up and, on anxiety-stiffened legs, stalked to the closest window. He stood with his forehead pressed against the cool glass. He felt as if he were burning up with fever. It seemed to him now that he had leaped into the abyss without thinking anything through, without any understanding of his capacity to bear up under a life dominated by mendacity and duplicity.

With a barely audible moan, he lurched away from the window and stumbled back to his desk. He now had what seemed an impossible deadline. Anderson would be back in less than an hour. By that time, he needed to understand his situation and find a way out.

Back at his desk, he ran his hands through his hair while he stared at the screen. What was wrong? There was the most minute lag between his pressing the keys and seeing the code on the screen. Changing screens, he checked the hardware through the Control Panel, but no recent additions had been made. Device Manager produced the same results. But when he checked the computer's CPU usage, he saw an unusual spike upward that dated back to the time he had started working. He felt a sudden rush of blood to his head. API-based keyloggers added to the CPU usage as they polled and recorded each keystroke.

That bastard Anderson, Richards thought fiercely. He had an API-based keylogger inserted into the software, which picked up every keystroke Richards made. The whole thing was premeditated, a set-up.

But how? There was only one answer: Peter Marks. Marks had betrayed him, had had no faith that he might give Tom Brick up to Treadstone.

A great rage filled Richards. He shook with the force of it. He looked one last time at the screen of incomplete virus code and thought: *Fuck it. Fuck him. Fuck them all.*

Without another thought, he disabled the keylogger software and continued with his code, working without even seeming to breathe. In the back of his mind, he prayed Anderson would show up early.

Almost fifty minutes later, six minutes before Anderson was due to arrive, Richards set the last section of the code in place. All he needed to do now was press the ENTER key and the virus would flood the on-site Treadstone servers, bringing down the entire network, freezing the communication channels, fouling the operating system itself.

He stood up, grabbed his coat, and, with one stab downward, hit ENTER. Then he crossed the room, went out the door, took the elevator to the lobby, and walked out, on his way back to his life with Tom Brick.

In the smoky distance, sirens wailed. By the sound of them, vehicles were racing toward the Basilica de Guadelupe. The Mass was finished. Someone had found the body of *el Enterrador*.

"I don't know where Maceo Encarnación and Nicodemo were going," Anunciata said. "But I know someone who might."

"Tell me," Bourne said. He kept a sharp eye on the street, on the lookout for police cars.

"I'll take you there."

"No." Bourne looked at her. "Your involvement is at an end." He produced the wallet he had taken from Rebeka's body. "It's time for you to leave." The last of Rebeka would go toward helping someone escape into a new life. He knew she would have liked that.

He opened the wallet, showing Anunciata the contents. "There's money here, more than enough to set you up somewhere far away from Mexico. And a passport." He paged through it. "You see my friend's photo. You can pass for her. You're more or less the same height and weight. Find a good salon, get your hair cut and dyed to match hers. A little makeup from a professional. That's all you need."

"Mexico is my home."

"It will also be your death. Leave. Now. After today, it will be too late."

Anunciata, holding the keys to her new life in the palms of her hands, looked up at him. Her eyes were swollen with tears. "Why are you doing this?"

"You deserve a chance at a new life," he said.

"I don't know whether I have the strength—"

"It's what your mother wanted for you."

The tears welled, falling. The sirens kept up a wail that could have come from her.

"There's something..."

Bourne waited, then he engaged her eyes. "Anunciata?"

"Nothing." She looked up. "It's nothing." She smiled. "Thank you."

"Now," Bourne said, folding her fingers over the wallet, "tell me who I need to see."

* * *

Salazar Flores was an aviation mechanic. He worked mainly on private planes, most notably Maceo Encarnación's Bombardier Global 5000. Bourne found him on the job in the maintenance hangar at the private airfield Encarnación used to house the Bombardier, exactly where Anunciata said he'd be at this time of the morning.

Flores was a short, sharp-eyed man in his middle years. His jowly cheeks were smeared with grease and his spatulate hands were permanently dyed by the fluids he used every day. He looked up sideways when Bourne approached him, then he stood and, wiping his hands on a greasy rag he pulled out of a back pocket of his overalls, faced the newcomer.

"How can I help you?" he said.

"I'm buying a Gulfstream SPX," Bourne said, "and I'm thinking of housing it here."

"You got the wrong guy." Flores indicated the office building across the runway from the hangar where they stood. "You need to talk to Castillo. He's the boss."

"I'm more interested in talking with you," Bourne said. "You'll be taking care of my plane."

Flores eyed Bourne appraisingly. "How'd you hear about me?"

"Anunciata."

"Really?"

Bourne nodded.

"How's her mom?"

"Maria-Elena died yesterday."

Bourne seemed to have passed some kind of test. Flores nodded. "An inexplicable tragedy."

Bourne had no intention of telling Flores just how explicable Maria-Elena's death was. "Did you know her well?"

Flores regarded him for a moment. "I need a smoke."

He led Bourne out of the clanging hangar where three other mechanics were at work, out onto the airfield. Keeping to the side of the runway, he shook out a cigarette, offered it to Bourne, then stuck it into his mouth and lit up.

He stared up at the high clouds as if looking for a sign. "You're a Gringo, so I suppose you know Anunciata better." He let smoke drift out between his lips. "Maria-Elena had a difficult life. Anunciata didn't like to talk about it." He shrugged bull shoulders. "Maybe she didn't know. Maria-Elena was very protective of her daughter."

"She wasn't the only one," Bourne said, thinking of the conversation he had overheard in the rectory of the Basilica de Guadelupe between Anunciata and *el Enterrador*. "Maceo Encarnación kept her like a hothouse flower."

"I wouldn't know anything about that." Flores looked around as if at any moment one of Maceo Encarnación's men was going to pop out of the shadows like a ghoul.

Bourne shrugged. "I assumed you knew the two of them well."

Flores took a last suck on his cigarette, dropped it, shredding it beneath the heel of his boot. "I have to get back to work."

"Are we getting into dangerous territory?"

Flores shot him a look. "Whatever it is you want, I can't help you."

"This can help you, though." Bourne spread the five-hundred-dollar bills between them.

"¡*Madre de Dios!*" Flores puffed out his cheeks, exhaled heartily through pursed lips. He looked up at Bourne. "What is it you want?"

"Only one thing," Bourne said. "Maceo Encarnación took off this morning. Where was he headed?"

"I can't tell you that."

Bourne stuffed the bills into the pocket of his overalls. "I'm sure your wife and kids could use some new clothes."

Flores looked around again, still jumpy, though no one was in earshot and those who could be seen weren't paying them the slightest attention. "I could lose my job...or my head. Then where would my wife and kids be?"

Bourne added another five hundred. "A couple of iPads will make you a hero."

Flores, visibly sweating, ran a hand through his hair. Bourne could see the tug-of-war between greed and fear being played out on his face. Still Flores hesitated. It was time to play his last card.

"It was Anunciata who suggested I talk to you about Encarnación's destination."

At this, Flores's eyes opened wide. "She was—"

"She wants you to tell me." A jet turned onto the head of the runway, its engines building to a roar. Bourne took a step closer. "It's important, Señor Flores. It involves Maria-Elena's death."

Flores's face registered shock. "What d'you mean?"

"I can't tell you," Bourne said, "and you don't want to know."

Flores licked his lips, took one last glance around the airfield, and nodded. As the jet shot down the runway and, in a veil of noise and fumes, lifted off, he leaned forward and whispered a word in Bourne's ear.

Martha Christiana took the call from Maceo Encarnación with an icy serenity. In an hour his plane would be landing, he would send one of his people to fetch her, and that would be the end. She would be in the center of the vortex, unable to extricate herself. The moment she stepped onto his plane, she would be in jail—she could feel it. She possessed too much incriminating information on him. One way or the other, he would never allow her to leave him.

From Don Fernando's living room windows, Martha Christiana stared longingly at the ethereal spiderwork of Notre Dame, its floodlit stone cool as marble. In the depths of night, she was wide awake. Don Fernando wasn't. He slept on one side of the large bed in the master bedroom, the curtains closed against the lights and noise of the city.

Below her, on the western tip of the Île Saint-Louis, rose the sounds of young laughter, a guitar being strummed, drunken voices raised briefly in a raucous chorus of some beer-hall sing-along. Then more laughter, a shout. A fistfight broke out, a beer bottle smashed.

Martha did not look down. She wanted no part of the ugliness below; she had enough ugliness in her own life. Instead, she allowed her eyes to trace the ancient grace of the cathedral's flying buttresses, curved like angels' harps. She was tired, but she wasn't sleepy, a semi-permanent state in her profession.

As she often did when her eyes lit on beauty, she thought of her home in Marrakech, of the beauty with which her benefactor, her captor, her teacher, surrounded himself. He had been an aesthete. He taught her how to appreciate all forms of art that brought beauty and joy to his life. *"For me, there is nothing else,"* he told her once. *"Without art, without beauty, the world is an ugly place, and life the ugliest of all states."* She had thought about this when she escaped his airless, obsessive museum-villa. She had thought about it many times afterward, after every kill, after sitting through a concert or visiting an art gallery, or flying high above the earth from assignment to assignment. As she did tonight, with Don Fernando asleep in the next room, faced once again with both the beauty and the ugliness of the world, of life.

She closed her eyes and ears to everything but the rushing of her blood. She heard her heartbeat as it might sound to a doctor. Her torso swayed a little as she drifted into a deep meditative state. She was back in Marrakech, amid the incense, chased silver services, the intricate filigreed wood screens, the colorful tiled floors and walls made up of geometric shapes. She was her young self again, imprisoned.

She opened her eyes and found that she held her

handbag in her lap, cradling it as one would a toy poodle. Without looking, she opened it, feeling around for what appeared to be a book of matches. She took it out. It said MOULIN ROUGE on one side. Where the striker ought to be was a thin metal rod. When she dug a nail beneath it and pulled, a nylon filament unspooled to a length of eighteen inches. She had constructed this murder weapon herself, using principles handed down by the *hashashin*, the ancient Persian sect whose objective was to assassinate Christian knight infidels.

She stood so abruptly that her handbag slid off her lap to the carpet. Landing, it made no sound. On bare feet, she picked her way across the living room, to the doorway beyond which Don Fernando lay asleep in his bed.

He had told her that he was different from all the other men in her life, men who had sought to manipulate her in one way or another, bend her to their own ends, use her like a gun or a knife, to work out their need for power and revenge.

From the moment she stepped aboard his plane, Don Fernando's plan to turn her from her assignment had been set in motion. He had played on her long-buried emotions, bringing her face-to-face with her past, her dead father, her demented mother. He had brought her home, seeking to soften her to his will, which was to live. And in the plane on the return flight, he had turned the screws on her even tighter by lying to her over and over until she had made the decision he had wanted her to make all along: abandon her mission.

But she was not so easily duped. She was in far

more control of her emotions than he could know. There was a job to do, she could see it so clearly now, see through all the bullshit men threw at her as smokescreens. At last, she had seen the path through the bullshit to, once and for all, make her way to the other side.

Always imprisoned.

She stepped over the threshold and entered Don Fernando's bedroom. He lay on his back on the side of the bed nearest her, veiled in deep shadow. Moving to the window, she pulled back the drapes. His patrician face was illuminated by Paris's mellow glow. Returning to him, she reached out, touched him on the shoulder, and he gave a snort and rolled over on his side, facing away from her. Perfect.

She lifted the strangler's filament, concentrating solely on her purpose. When her vision narrowed to a pinpoint, when all she could hear was the rhythmic beating of her heart, purpose became action.

She moved with perfect, deadly intent.

23

THE MOMENT DR. SANTIAGO removed the drain from the side of her head and bandaged the wound, Soraya felt as if she had returned from the gray land of near-death to a world full of color and promise. Everything looked sharp-edged. Her acuity of vision and hearing was like that of a hawk. Every surface she ran her hand over felt new, different, and exciting.

When she remarked on this to Dr. Santiago, he broke out into a wide smile. "Welcome back," he said.

For the first time since she had been admitted, she was free, untethered by lifelines to fluids and monitors. She moved around her room on legs made unfamiliar and shaky by her ordeal.

"Look at you," Delia said. "Look at you!"

Soraya embraced her friend, held her tight, aware of the baby between them. She did not want to let go. Brushing tears away, she kissed Delia on both cheeks. Her heart was full.

Only one thought clouded her return from the back of beyond. "Deel, I need to go see Peter. Will you help me?"

Without another word, Delia went and got a wheelchair into which Soraya lowered herself. Hours before, on his last visit, Hendricks had told her that Peter had been shot. *"We don't know how badly yet,"* he had said, *"but I want you to be prepared. The bullet lodged near his spine." "Does he know?"* she had asked. Hendricks had nodded. *"Right now he has no feeling in his legs."*

Before he left, Hendricks had signaled to Delia, and they had walked out of Soraya's room together. Now, as Delia pushed her along the hospital's hushed corridors, Soraya asked, "What did you and Hendricks talk about outside my hearing?"

There was a telling hesitation. "Raya, concentrate on Peter. I don't think this is the time—"

Soraya put her hands on the wheels, stopping them. "Deel, come around where I can see you." When her friend had complied, she said, "Tell me the truth, Deel. Does it have something to do with my baby?"

"Oh, no!" Delia cried. She knelt in front of Soraya and took her hands in hers. "No, no, no, the baby's fine. It's…" Again the telling hesitation. "Raya, Charles is dead."

Soraya felt the shock of disappointment, nothing more. "What?"

"Ann shot him."

Soraya shook her head. "I don't...I don't understand."

"There was an altercation. Charles came at her and she defended herself. That's not the official story. He was shot during a B and E, that's what the news outlets are being fed."

Soraya said nothing for some time. Nurses squeaked by on rubber-soled shoes, phones rang softly, doctors' names were called, some urgently. Everything else was still.

"I don't believe it," Soraya breathed.

Delia searched her friend's face. "Raya, are you okay? The secretary left it up to me to tell you, but I don't know whether this was the right time."

"There is no right time," Soraya said. "There's only the present."

Searching through the corridors of her mind, she could find no feeling for Charles Thorne other than disappointment that their business relationship was at an end. Conduits weren't easy to find, especially one so perfectly placed at the center of the information superhighway. But, on the other hand, if Charles was right about the impending investigation, his usefulness would have been at an end anyway. What she felt most was relief. It had been distasteful to her to lie to him about the baby. She could absolve herself, at least, of that sin.

"Raya, what are you thinking?"

Soraya nodded to Delia. "Let's go see Peter."

He had been out of surgery for over an hour and he was awake. He seemed happy to see them.

"Hey, Peter," Soraya said in an overbright voice. He looked ghostly, arms pale, pierced by needles whose tubes ran up and out of him. His face was contorted by pain though he tried his best to hide it. His lopsided smile broke her heart.

"You look good," he said.

"You, too." She was standing, clutching the railing of his bed for support.

"I have to get going," Delia said. She and Soraya embraced.

"Later," Soraya whispered into her ear.

"You're full of shit," Peter said when Delia was gone. "As always."

Soraya laughed, touched his knee beneath the overstarched bedclothes just to reestablish the link between them that she found so important. "I'm glad you're still here."

He nodded. "I wish I could say I'll be as good as new when I get out of here."

Her heart turned to ice. "What do you mean? What have the doctors told you?"

"The bullet didn't hit my spine."

"That's good news!"

"I wish it had."

"What d'you mean?"

"The impact shattered it. Pieces lodged everywhere, including my spinal column."

Soraya felt a sudden dryness in her throat, and she swallowed convulsively. She met his gaze head-on.

"I have no feeling in my legs," Peter said. "They're paralyzed."

"Oh, Peter." Soraya felt her heart beating faster, a certain churning began in the pit of her stomach.

"Are they sure? It's early yet. Who knows what will happen next week, or even tomorrow?"

"They're sure."

"Peter, you can't give up."

"I don't know. The president going after our asses, you talking about leaving, then this happens." His laugh sounded weak and hollow. "That's three, isn't it? It's the end."

"Who said I'm leaving?" It was out of her mouth before she had a chance to think about it.

"You did, Soraya. Remember our walk in the park, you said—"

"Forget what I said, Peter. I was just shooting my mouth off to a friend. I'm not going anywhere." Much to her astonishment, she realized she meant it. While moving to Paris sounded great, it was a pipe dream. Her life was here with Treadstone, with Peter. Looking into his face, she knew she couldn't leave him in this state, perhaps she never would have, even if this hadn't happened to him.

"Soraya." He smiled.

He seemed more relaxed now. She could see how heavily the thought of her leaving had weighed on him, and she was sorry she had ever mentioned it.

"Take a pew." Blood had come back to his face; he seemed more himself again. "I have a lot to catch you up on."

In his dream, Don Fernando walked at the edge of the sea and the shoreline. The odd thing was that he was walking on the water, not on the sand, which seemed to steam and bubble, as if it were being stirred in a vast cauldron. His feet were bare, his trousers rolled up to his calves. His feet looked pale and indistinct, as they would if viewed underwater. He walked and walked, but the curve of the landscape never changed, he never seemed to get anywhere.

In the next heartbeat, he was awake, a shadow like a giant bird passing over him, so close he could smell it. It had Martha Christiana's scent. For the instant she was above him, and he felt paralyzed, as if stuck between two dreamworlds, one where he walked on water, the other where Martha spread her wings, flying above him.

Then the shadow was gone, Martha was gone with it, and he heard, like the cathedral bells of Notre Dame, the sound of shattering wood and glass. In the space of the next heartbeat, a chill breeze off the river invaded the room.

He turned over, still half-asleep, and saw the curtains billowing crazily, the window's panes and sash demolished as if by a great force. It wasn't until he heard the screaming from outside that he rose, curious, and, then, as he approached the ruined window, his curiosity turned to a mounting horror.

"Martha," he called over his shoulder. And then more loudly, "Martha!"

No answer. Of course there was no answer. He stuck his head out the window, unmindful of the glass shards that penetrated his palms. He looked down, and saw her, spread-eagled on the cobbles of the narrow street. Around her, like a princess's bed of diamonds, glass shards glittered wetly. Blood leaked from beneath her, running in rivulets, as a crowd gathered. The screaming continued, even after the unmistakable sounds of police and ambulance sirens made their way along the quay, coming ever closer.

My dear Senator Ring," Li Wan said, "let me be one of the first to express my sincere condolences for your loss."

Ann Ring smiled wanly. Inside she was pleased that Li had made an appearance. "Thank you," she murmured. *How stupid words are*, she thought. *How inadequate, how mendacious.* She was disgusted by the dog-and-pony show inherent in funerals, eulogies, mourning periods. The dead were gone, let them go in peace.

Li Wan wore a black suit, as if he, rather than she, were in mourning. Belatedly, she recalled that white was the Chinese color of death and mourning. Well, she thought wryly, he *is* wearing a white shirt, so crisply starched it appeared as if the collar points might at any moment do him harm.

Ann, in an ox-blood St. John nubbly wool suit, sat in the cloistered family room at Vineyard Funeral Home on Fourteenth Street NW. Even in mourning, she was the kind of woman who radiated sex and allure. She was surrounded by her usual entourage, along with a smattering of friends. The official viewing, which would attract hundreds of her colleagues, allies, and enemies from inside the Beltway, was mercifully a day away. Now it was quiet. The air was perfumed with the huge wreaths and bouquets of flowers that lined the walls and exploded from vases set on tables and even on some unused chairs.

"There was a history," Li Wan was saying now in a low monotone, "and history means everything."

"That's something we have in common, Mr. Li," she said in an even tone.

He bowed his head slightly and risked a slight smile as he handed over a wrapped parcel. "Please accept this inadequate token of my sorrow."

"You're too kind." She took the package, laid it squarely on her lap, and watched Li's face. She was waiting, and she thought he knew she was waiting.

At last he said, "May I sit with you a moment?"

She gestured. "Please."

He sat primly, almost as if he were a turtle, trying to pull its arms and legs into its shell. It was an almost womanly attitude she found repellent.

"Is there anything I can do, Senator?"

"Thank you, no." *Curious*, she thought. *He's acting like a mainland Chinese, not like a Chinese American.* Because of the special nature of this man and the relationship with him laid out for her by Chris Hendricks, she felt the need to explore that notion. "And please call me Ann."

"You are far too kind," Li said, ducking his head again.

What is his behavior telling me? she asked herself.

Li looked across the room to the flowers bedecking the console table against the opposite wall. "I have many memories of your husband, Senator." He paused a moment, as if debating whether or not to continue. "Memories that might, in time, be shared."

Now comes the light, she thought. But it was altogether unclear whether he was on an official mission. Her heart leaped at the thought that it might be a personal one, that something had happened between Li and Charles that might have changed their dynamic or, if not that, Li's own goals as opposed to his government's.

"You know, Mr. Li, I have my own memories of my husband. It might be pleasant to hear some others."

Li's thin shoulders twitched infinitesimally. "In that event, I would welcome the opportunity to invite you to tea, Senator, when you feel up to it, of course."

"How kind of you, Mr. Li." She had to be careful here, very careful. "I have a full slate of subcommittee and budgetary meetings that have been thrown into disarray. You understand."

"I do, Senator. Of course I do."

She turned on a wistful expression. "On the other hand, it would certainly be refreshing to speak of matters unrelated to Capitol Hill." She fingered Li's present. "Perhaps this evening, after my vigil. I have allotted time for a meal."

Li Wan looked hopeful. "Possibly dinner then."

"Yes," she said, ratcheting up her wistful expression. "That would be lovely."

"I'll pick you up here if you like." Mr. Li's smile was like a sliver of moon. "You have only to decide when."

Sam Anderson spent fifteen fruitless minutes sending Treadstone personnel to scour the building for

Richards. Not having found him, he recalled his people and sent out a BOLO via FBI and the Metro Police with a priority tag.

Then he joined the assembled IT team, which was feverishly working to ID the virus that was overrunning the Treadstone servers, rendering them useless. He had peeled off one man, Timothy Nevers, who he assigned to check the software keylogger and its hardware companion that he had placed on the terminal Richards was working from, to parse the results.

Peter had chosen the perfect person to be his right-hand man. Anderson was neither ambitious nor complacent. He was wholly focused on the job he had been given to do, and he did it better than anyone else at Treadstone. Unlike many of his colleagues in the clandestine services, he was a people person, an exemplary manager. Those who followed his orders did so without question. They believed in him, believed he could work them out of any trouble they ran into.

This virus was trouble of an exponential order. Every minute the IT team delayed in identifying its basic algorithm, the virus broke through and annihilated another barrier. The on-site Treadstone servers were beginning to look like Swiss cheese; there was almost nothing to pull off them, even if the IT team could find a way around or through the virus, which, as of now, they couldn't.

"Keep on it," Anderson said, and, turning to Tim Nevers, said, "Speak to me of the unspeakable."

"You got that right," Nevers said. "This guy Richards is a freakin' genius at software programming. I'm still getting a good look at the Trojan, which, by the way, he definitely coded and entered into the system."

"What about the virus?"

Nevers scratched his scalp. He was just over thirty and already shaved his head because he was going bald. "Yeah, well, it's the freakin' velociraptor of viruses, that much I can tell you."

"Not helpful," Anderson said. "You have to give me something I can export to the other IT guys."

"I'm doing my best," Nevers said, fingers blurred over the keyboard.

"Do better."

That was what Anderson's father had always said to him, not unkindly, but in a way that made Anderson *want* to do better, not simply to please his father, though, of course, that loomed large. Doing better made him succeed, as well as learn something important about himself. Anderson's father was a military man—intelligence—who ended up at Central Intelligence. He had revamped many of their clandestine intel gathering methods and was rewarded by being kicked out because of a bad heart. He hated idling at home and died sixteen months after he had been let go. His bosses all said, "We told you so," but Anderson knew what his father had known: At home he couldn't "do better." Useless he went to sleep one night and never woke up. Anderson was quite certain his father knew that, too, as he drifted off.

"Got something!" Nevers said. "I've coded out the virus algorithm from the Trojan's. It's endlessly regenerative. Amazing, really."

"What I want to know, Nevers, is whether it can be stopped."

"Intervention," Nevers said, nodding. "Not the way you'd ever think to nullify a virus, which is what makes it so clever. You have to flip a switch, so to speak, from *inside* the algorithm."

Anderson hitched his chair forward in order to get a better view. "So do it."

"Not so fast," Nevers said. "The virus is encoded with traps, fail-safe mechanisms, and dead ends."

Anderson groaned. "One step forward, two steps back."

"Better than being in the dark." Nevers hit the ENTER key. "I've just transmitted everything I've discovered to the rest of the IT team." He turned, grinned at his boss. "Let's see if they can do better."

Anderson grunted.

"Richards destroyed the software keylogger just before he activated the virus. That's the kernel of the problem. The software recorded only the partial code, not all of it. We can't stop it until we have the code in its entirety."

"Don't you have enough information to make an informed assumption, intervene, and flip the algo-rithmic switch?"

"I could," Nevers said, "but I won't." He turned to Anderson. "Look, this virus is so full of thorns—triggers, in other words—that if I don't know pre-cisely what I'm doing, I could inadvertently set off one of these triggers and make things infinitely worse."

"Worse?" Anderson said, incredulous. "What could be worse than all our data being obliterated?"

"The motherboards overloading, the servers becoming nothing more than a pile of silicon, rare earths, and fused wire circuits. Vital enciphered communications would be down for God knows how long."

Then he grinned. "But on the bright side..." He pulled a tiny oblong from beneath the desk and held it up. "Richards didn't find the Bluetooth transmitter. If he downloaded anything from outside, it'll be recorded right here. Even better, we'll be able to back-trace it to the source."

When Nicodemo saw Don Fernando Hererra, he froze, still as a statue. Hererra was dead—at least, according to Martha Christiana. But she had lied, and now she herself was dead, lying on the cobbled street on the Île Saint-Louis. Whether she had jumped from the fifth-floor window or had been pushed was impossible to say. But what was irrefutable was the presence of Hererra talking to the cops while the photos were being taken and fingerprints lifted from the crime scene.

Craning his neck up, Nicodemo could see through the windows detectives treading through what must be Hererra's apartment. More flashbulbs lit up the night, more fingerprints were being taken up there in every room. What they expected to find, Nicodemo had no idea, nor was he interested. His focus, which had been on Martha Christiana, the woman Maceo Encarnación had told him to pick up and bring back to the waiting jet, now shifted to Hererra. There was nothing Nicodemo could do for Martha Christiana anymore, but there was certainly something he must do about Hererra.

Retreating to the shadows around the corner, he pulled out his mobile and called Maceo Encarnación.

"I'm standing around the corner from Don Fernando Hererra's apartment," he said when he heard the other man on the end of the line. "I don't know how to break this to you, but Martha Christiana is dead."

He pulled the mobile away from his ear at the tirade of curses that emanated from it.

"Fell or pushed, I don't know which," he continued when Maceo Encarnación had expended the depths of his shock and rage. "I'm sorry, truly. But we have other matters to occupy us. Martha Christiana lied about Hererra being dead....I know, I am too....But he's standing big as life....Of course I'm sure it's him."

Nicodemo spent the next few moments absorbing every word Maceo Encarnación spoke, at the end of which he said, "You're sure that's what you want me to do."

More withering talk, during which Nicodemo began his preparation for the assignment Maceo Encarnación had given him.

"Get it done," Maceo Encarnación concluded. "You have twenty-four hours. After that, if you haven't appeared, I take off without you. Clear?"

"Perfectly," Nicodemo said. "I'll be back before the deadline. Count on it."

Disconnecting, he pocketed his mobile and walked back to the crime scene. Martha Christiana had been loaded into the ambulance. Hererra was still talking with the detectives. He spoke, they nodded. One of them scribbled notes as fast as he could.

Nicodemo flipped out a cigarette, lit up, and smoked languidly as he continued to assess the scene. When, at length, the detectives were finished with Hererra, they gave him their cards, and he turned away, returning to his building. Nicodemo watched as he pressed a four-digit code into the panel on the right side of the huge wooden doorway to the street.

He waited until the detectives left and, amid the slowly dispersing crowd of onlookers, stood confronting the panel, which consisted of ten raised brass buttons, numbered one through zero. Taking out a small vial, he blew a white powder, finer than talcum, over the buttons. The powder adhered to the residue of oil left by Hererra's fingerprints, revealing four whitened buttons. On the third combination, the door's lock clicked open, and he stepped inside.

He stood for a moment in the cobbled inner courtyard where, centuries before, horse-drawn carriages full of passengers would pull up and liveried footmen would fall over themselves to help the patricians down and into their residence. Now, of course, many people lived in the building, but the history remained, rising off the cobbles like steam from the horses' glistening flanks.

Two women, one young, one older, were lounging against a wall beside the front door, discussing the tragedy. The older one smoked. Nicodemo took out a cigarette and, approaching them, asked for a light.

"Terrible thing." The young woman shuddered. "Who can sleep after something like that?"

"Now the street will be clogged with the morbidly curious," the older woman said, shaking her head.

Nicodemo nodded sympathetically. "Why would someone throw themselves out a window?" he wondered out loud.

"Who can say?" The older woman shrugged her meaty shoulders. "People are mad, that's my position." She sucked down more smoke. "Did you know the poor girl?"

"A long time ago," Nicodemo said. "We were childhood friends."

The older woman looked sorrowful. "She must have been so unhappy."

Nicodemo nodded. "I thought I could help her, but I arrived too late."

"Do you want to go upstairs?" the younger woman said, as if struck by a sudden idea.

"I don't want to disturb Señor Hererra."

"Oh, I'm sure he could use the sympathy. Here." She crossed to the door, slipped her keys out of her pocket. She pressed the attached disc against a metal pad beside the door and it buzzed open.

Nicodemo thanked her and went into the vertical vestibule. A large iron staircase curved upward, and he ascended. The building was eerily still, as if everyone in it were holding their breath in horror. No one was on the stairs, all the apartment doors were firmly closed, as if against a rapidly spreading disease.

Don Fernando's floor was likewise deserted. He

went soundlessly down the landing to stand in front of the apartment. He listened but heard nothing.

Then he put his ear to the door.

Inside the apartment, Don Fernando could still smell the stale clothes of the cops and detectives. He felt as if his home had been broken into. He didn't want to smell anything but Martha Christiana's distinctive scent, and he resented deeply the official invasion. He stood stiffly, his back ramrod-straight, and tried to separate his thoughts from his emotions.

He was responsible for Martha Christiana's death, he had no doubts on that score. He had manipulated her, put her in what turned out to be an untenable position, pitting himself against Maceo Encarnación. He had twisted the screws on her, slowly to be sure, but in the end that hadn't mattered. In the end, she hadn't been able to follow either him or her employer. She had taken the only way out that would give her surcease. Perhaps this had been her destiny from the moment she was born into a loveless home and ran away, she thought, to save herself. Instead, she had run pell-mell toward her destiny, toward this apartment on the Île Saint-Louis, toward her death on the cobbles of the Quai de Bourbon.

Perhaps it had nothing to do with him, but he did not believe that. In Martha Christiana desire had warped her destiny. Now she was dead. Turning in a slow circle, he felt the lack of her, as if there were more shadows in these rooms he had come to know so well, as if there were suddenly another room he had never noticed and hadn't explored, a room whose contents frightened him.

He checked once more to be certain he was alone even though the rational part of his brain told him that he was. Padding silently into the bathroom, he knelt down on creaky joints and extracted Martha Christiana's handbag from the narrow space between the claw-foot tub and the marble-tiled floor, where he had shoved it before the cops had asked for entrance.

Putting down the toilet seat cover, he sat, placing the handbag on his thighs. He stayed like that for long minutes, his fingers exploring the soft leather, his nostrils dilated to take in her scent, which rose from the handbag's interior and caused tears to form in his eyes.

Though he had been acting out of self-preservation, he had genuinely liked Martha. He had also felt sorry for her, trapped as she was. But what good had his empathy done, except to drive her the last few yards to her destiny?

He sighed, and his head came up abruptly. He had heard a sound, and he listened, as if for her soft bare footfalls, as if she might still be alive, as if the last several hours had been a nightmare from which he had just this second awakened, her handbag in his lap. Then he looked down and knew with absolute clarity that what he held between his hands was all that was left of her.

Slowly, he opened the bag and, with a curious trepidation, peered inside. He encountered the usual tools of the female trade: lipstick, compact, eyeliner, a small pack of tissues, her wallet, astonishingly thin, as if what little was inside might evaporate as quickly as her life. He opened it briefly, then fished out her mobile phone.

It was locked, but he knew many of the things she liked, and he tried several of them on the keypad until he stumbled upon the right one, and the mobile opened to him as it had so many times to her. This door opening, as it were, moved him deeply. It was as if she were inviting him into the guarded part of herself.

"*Mea culpa*, Martha," he said. "I wish you were here."

Just outside the front door, Nicodemo heard these words as they wafted through the apartment, and he pressed his ear harder against the door. In doing so, he caused the old wooden panels to creak.

He froze, scarcely allowing himself to breathe.

Don Fernando's head came up, and, like a dog on point, his body began to quiver. The creak from the front door had arrowed through the apartment, piercing his heart like a presentiment of death.

Placing Martha's handbag aside, he rose and, leaving the bathroom, went through the bedroom to the living area. There he stood for a moment, immobile, scenting the air for a new spoor. He stared hard at the front door, which he had been careful to lock the moment the last of the detectives had vacated the premises. He watched the wooden boards, as if they might tell him what or who was on the other side of the door.

At length, he crept to the door and, with his back arched, bent to put his ear to the old wood. He heard breathing, but whether it was the building or some- one standing on the other side of the door, he could not tell. He felt, if not frightened, then profoundly uneasy. He did not keep a handgun in the apart- ment, which was lucky for him. The cops would have confiscated it, and it might have aroused their suspicions that Martha Christiana's death was mur- der rather than suicide. Now, though, he regretted not having stashed one somewhere. He did not feel safe.

After taking another fruitless listen through the door, he backed away, returning to the bathroom, where he took up Martha's handbag and resumed his melancholy journey through its contents.

He checked her mobile's call log first. The last incoming call had been made perhaps fifty minutes before she went out the window. Considering the hour it had been made, he thought that significant, especially because it was from a number in Martha's phonebook. The name attached had been reduced to initials, but there was no doubt to whom "ME" be- longed: Maceo Encarnación.

What had Maceo Encarnación said to her that had made her snap, caused her to decide to kill herself? There was no doubt in his mind that she had felt trapped between himself and Encarnación with no way out.

He checked her voicemails, texts, all the usual stuff that almost invariably clogged up people's mo- biles, but there was nothing. Martha Christiana had been too careful. As he was scrolling through her phonebook, his own mobile buzzed. He picked it up. Christien was calling.

"Are you still dead?" Christien said with a chuckle.

"Sadly, no." Don Fernando took a breath. "But Martha Christiana is."

"What happened?"

Don Fernando told him.

"Well, at least she won't be a threat to you anymore. I'll take care of the press release correcting the news of your death." There was a slight pause. "Do you know where Bourne is?"

"I thought you were keeping track of him?"

"No one can keep track of him, Don Fernando. You know that better than anyone."

Don Fernando grunted. Without thinking, he slid Martha's mobile back into her handbag. His fingers found the compact, smooth and warm, as from contact with Martha's skin. He found that circling his thumb over its lacquered surface gave him a measure of solace.

"Our enemies are on the move," Christien said. "Maceo Encarnación and Harry Rowland have left Mexico City. They landed in Paris over an hour ago. I thought I'd better warn you."

"Something's happening."

"Yes, but I hope it's not what we have been afraid of."

Don Fernando ran a hand across his face. "There's only one way to find out."

"With Maceo Encarnación in Paris, I'm concerned about you."

"Maceo Encarnación knows better than to show

his face in Paris. I have too many eyes and ears on the ground. Rowland is, however, another matter."

"Jason and that Mossad woman, Rebeka, were following Rowland."

Don Fernando stared at his bare feet on the bathroom tiles. Martha had liked his feet. She said they were sexy. "If that's the case, then they've failed."

"I don't want to think about Jason failing."

"Neither do I." Don Fernando's heart grew even heavier as he stared at the lapis face of Martha's compact. "Listen, Christien, there must be something we can do for Jason."

"It's progressed too rapidly, gone too far. It's out of our hands," Christien said. "All we can do now is have faith that Bourne will come through."

"If anyone can…" *Vaya con Dios, hombre,* Don Fernando thought as he disconnected.

He was tired—beyond tired. He rose and, still holding the compact, padded back to the bedroom. It was early morning, when the city, still wrapped in sleep, began to shudder with the rumble of the first of the day's traffic, when people queued up at bakeries to buy breakfast baguettes and croissants, when bicyclists crossed the bridges, taking their owners to work.

He lay down on his bed, the covers rucked beneath him, but that only brought into view the window Martha Christiana had ruined on her way out of his life. Rolling over, he sat up, his gaze once again fixated on the compact. It was odd, he thought, that Martha carried a compact when he had never seen powder on her cheeks or forehead. She used lipstick and lash color; her natural beauty required nothing more. And yet…

He turned the compact over and over in his hand. Then, on a sudden impulse, he snapped it open. The thin puff was there, but, when he lifted it out, there was no powder underneath, just a tiny gold flange set into the base. Using a fingernail, he lifted the flange, and the base came up, revealing an eight-gigabyte micro-SD card.

Just then he stiffened, his head cocked to one side, trying to capture the tiny noise again. There was no doubt about it, someone was outside his front door. Rising silently, he crossed to the kitchen and slid out a large-bladed carving knife.

Back in the living room, he paused in front of the door, listening. He heard the sound again, as of the scrape of shoe soles against the hallway floor. Stepping closer, he grasped the lock and turned it over slowly and quietly.

Keeping the point of the knife at the ready for an instantaneous thrust, he grasped the doorknob, and, with a quick, efficient turn, pulled open the door.

24

DICK RICHARDS, WAITING TO be shown into Tom Brick's palatial offices at the Core Energy headquarters on Sixteenth Street NW, felt like a fugitive not only from Treadstone, but from life itself. He had been waiting for what seemed like hours while a veritable parade of people were ushered in and out of the executive office suites.

For what seemed like the eighth or ninth time, he hauled himself up and reintroduced himself to the young woman behind the slab banc. She had the young person's knack of wearing her wireless earpiece like jewelry, somehow making her look more human rather than like an alien. She smiled up at him with her bee-stung lips.

"Mr. Richards—" he was astonished that she remembered "—Mr. Lang would like a word with you."

Stephen Lang was senior operations VP.

Richards wondered why he wanted to see him. "I'm here to see Tom Brick."

The receptionist smiled and touched the carapace of her earpiece. "He's not in the office at the moment."

"D'you know where he is?"

The smile stayed in place, another piece of postmodern jewelry. "I believe that's what Mr. Lang wants to talk with you about." She held out a shapely bare arm. "D'you know the way?"

Richards nodded. "I do."

Passing through the pebbled translucent doors, he turned right to the end, then right again. Ahead of him lay Lang's spacious corner office. He had been in there a handful of times when Brick had brought him in on the logistics of one project or another.

Stephen Lang was an ex-athlete running to fat. He still had the basic frame and musculature of a Michigan linebacker, but his face had broadened and his gut had deepened. The moment Richards entered his office, he came around from behind his desk, bouncing on the balls of his feet. He grinned, extended his hand in a brief, bone-crushing grip, and nodded at one of the upholstered chairs in front of his smoked-glass–topped postmodern desk.

"So I hear that the Treadstone computers are hopelessly snarled." Perched on a corner of his desk, he nodded. "Good work, Richards."

"Thanks. But I'm now fucked. I can't go back there."

"Not to worry. You've helped us achieve our goal at Treadstone. Time to move on." Lang clapped his hands together. "Listen, Tom wants to congratulate you himself. He was called away at the last minute, so he's arranged for a car and driver to take you to him."

"Is he at the safe house?"

"Yeah, about that, the safe house is no longer safe." Lang clapped his hands again. "As I said, time to move on." He stood, indicating that the interview was at an end. Extending his hand again, he said, "Safe travels, Richards. You've become invaluable to us, so a significant bump in pay is waiting for you, not to mention a bonus." He waved his hand. "Tom will explain it all."

Richards, cheeks flushed, went out of the office suite. He barely felt his feet on the carpeting. Finally, he was getting the recognition he deserved. A chubby blonde greeted him with a smile on the elevator ride down to the lobby. He was so astonished when she said something to him that he scarcely heard a word she said. She looked vaguely familiar, but all he could muster was a stupid grin by way of reply. Watching her walk across the lobby, he thought, *Other women will smile at me—beautiful women*, because they existed—especially here inside the Beltway—to respond galvanically to money and power.

Outside, as Lang had said, a black Lincoln Navigator was waiting for him. It was a raw, gloomy late afternoon, with drizzle slanted by the wind. Richards hurried over. There was no need to introduce himself. Bogs, recognizing him, smiled and swung open the passenger door for him. Then he climbed in behind the wheel and peeled out, driving very fast through the congested streets of the city.

•

Richards sat back, luxuriating in the beginning moments of his new life. He had made the right choice. Government service was for fools who were content to work unconscionably long hours, take home their meager pay packets each week, and eventually retire into obscurity, worn out, beaten down by the endless bureaucracy.

They went over the Woodrow Wilson Memorial Bridge into Virginia, then turned north. Ten minutes later, the Navigator turned in to a side entrance to Founders Park in Alexandria, which fronted the water. The driver got out, opened the door for Richards, and guided him down a long wharf that jutted out into the Potomac. At the far end was a large weathered-wood gazebo under which he saw Tom Brick talking to a figure in shadow.

He turned when Richards and the driver entered the gazebo's overhang. "Ah, you made it, Richards. Good deal." He gestured toward the other figure with him, the chubby blonde who had accompanied Richards down in the elevator.

Richards had just a moment to register his surprise when he felt a ghastly pain in his side. He opened his mouth to shout, but the driver's thick hand clamped hard over the lower half of his face. Blood ran out of him, and his knees sagged. The driver was half holding him up.

He looked at Tom Brick who, along with the blonde, was watching him without any apparent emotion.

"What?" he stammered. "Why?"

Tom Brick sighed. "The very fact that you're asking these questions confirms that your usefulness to me is at an end." He stepped toward Richards, grabbed his chin, and lifted his face to stare into his eyes. "You idiot, what did you think you were doing announcing yourself as the saboteur?"

"I…I…" Richards's slowly freezing brain, already shutting down at its periphery, was desperately trying to grasp what was happening to him. And then, out of the corner of his eye, he saw the blonde grinning at him and he realized that she was a Treadstone employee—an assistant, someone in the unique position of watching everyone in the organization. *Jesus*, he thought. *Jesus Christ.*

"This is the price you pay for having multiple masters, Richards." Tom Brick's voice was gentle, rueful, understanding. "There was no other ending possible."

Richards's brain, robbed of blood, was turning more sluggish by the second. But still, he got it. Finally. "You recognized Peter Marks right away."

Brick nodded. "Thanks to Tricia here, I did."

"Then why did you let him—?"

"Once I knew he had followed me, that he knew more than I had dreamed, it was imperative to find out what his game was." Brick pinched Richards's chin between the pincers of his thumb and forefinger. "You didn't tell me who he was, Richards. Why didn't you tell me?"

"I…" Richards closed his eyes, swallowed hard. He was dying, so what the hell. "I thought if he and Soraya Moore liked me, took me in, I could—"

"What? What could you have, Richards? Friends? Colleagues?" He shook his head. "No one cares about you, Richards. No one wants to work with you. You're an insect I'm about to squash. You have a gift, but your human flaws outweigh your usefulness to us. You can't be trusted."

"I made my choice. I chose you." Richards's voice sounded pathetic, even to him. Tears leaked out of his eyes and he began to weep. "It's not fair. It's not fair."

Clearly disgusted, Tom Brick let him go, lifted his gaze, and nodded to his driver, holding Richards up. The knife slid in farther, was twisted so violently Richards's eyes nearly popped out of his head. The sound that emerged through the hand clamped over his mouth was not unlike that a pig makes when the slaughtering blade comes down.

The moment the door to the apartment swung open and the carving knife slashed out, Bourne caught Don Fernando's fist.

"Easy, Don Fernando."

Don Fernando stared at him, obviously shaken. "It was you, Jason? You were outside my door earlier?"

Bourne shook his head as he stepped into the apartment and closed the door behind him. "I only just got here." He cocked his head. "Someone was trying to get into the apartment?"

"That or he was keeping watch on me."

"There was no surveillance on the building," Bourne said, taking the carving knife from the older man's hand. "I checked."

"Maceo Encarnación and Harry Rowland are here in Paris. I think it was Rowland at my door earlier."

"Don Fernando," Bourne said, "Rowland is Nicodemo."

"What? Are you certain?"

Bourne nodded. "He's with Maceo Encarnación. I followed them here from Mexico City."

"The woman?"

"Rebeka was a Mossad agent." Bourne sat on a sofa. "She's dead."

"Ah, well, then we both lost someone." Don Fernando sat heavily next to Bourne. "I'm sorry."

"What happened?"

Don Fernando told him briefly about how Maceo Encarnación had sent Martha Christiana to kill him, and what had happened after he and Martha met. "She went out the bedroom window, leaped across me while I was sleeping. She could have killed me, but she didn't."

"You were lucky."

Don Fernando shook his head. "No, Jason. Today I don't feel in the least bit lucky." He laced his fingers together. "Hers was a soul in torment. Perhaps she needed a priest. I am no priest. In this case, I might have played the role of the devil."

"We're all pursued by shadows, Don Fernando. There are times when they catch up to us. There's nothing more to be done; we have to move on."

Don Fernando nodded. He picked up Martha Christiana's compact, popped it open, and showed Bourne the micro-SD card hidden beneath the false bottom. "I can't help but think she left this for me to find." He shrugged. "But perhaps that's just wishful thinking."

"Have you looked at what's on the card?"

Don Fernando shook his head. "Not yet."

"Well," Bourne said, plucking up the card, "it's time we did."

Maceo Encarnación went up to the cockpit of his private jet. The door was open, the Chinese pilot going through a pre-flight checklist.

"Do you think he'll make it back in time?" the pilot asked without looking up.

Maceo Encarnación grunted as he slipped into the navigator's seat. "Impossible to say."

"Your attachment to him is well known."

Maceo Encarnación contemplated the pilot for some time. "What you mean," he said slowly and finally, "is that Minister Ouyang disapproves of my attachment to Nicodemo."

The pilot, who was also Minister Ouyang's agent, said nothing. He sat very still, as if attempting to divine the air currents.

"Nicodemo is my son. I raised him, taught him."

"You took him from her."

The pilot spoke without judgment, his voice perfectly neutral. Nevertheless, Maceo Encarnación took offense. He could not do otherwise; it was in his nature.

"His mother was married to someone else," Maceo Encarnación said, more to himself than to the pilot. "I loved her, but her husband was a powerful man, and I needed his power. She could not keep the child, could not even be with the husband while it was growing inside her. She took herself to Mérida, to her aunt's estancia for the five months she was showing. I took the boy from her, raised him."

"You said that already."

Maceo Encarnación hated these people, but he was forced to deal with them. No one else had their power, their expertise, their deep pockets, their vision. Nevertheless, he often, as now, had to exert an iron will to keep himself from beating them to a bloody pulp. The fact that he could not treat them as he treated his own people was like a knife in his gut. He often dreamed of this Chinese agent on the edge of the Pacific, his severed head rolling fish-eyed in the surf, while his trunk twitched, spewing blood like the fountain in Chapultepec Park.

"I repeated it because it's important in the understanding of my attachment, and I can never be certain of your grasp of Spanish." Maceo Encarnación did not bother to wait for a response from the agent, knowing none would be forthcoming. Was there ever a poorer match in allies, he thought, than extrovert Mexican and introvert Chinese?

This agent had a name, but Maceo Encarnación never used it, assuming that it was false. Instead, he thought of him as Hey-Boy, a despicable term that amused him no end. He would tell him the story—part of it that he would take for the whole—because it amused him to do so. What he would not tell him was the private part. The identity of Nicodemo's and his sister Maricruz's mother remained locked inside him. Constanza Camargo had given birth to Nicodemo early in their years-long affair. Maricruz was born three years later. Constanza was the one woman he had ever loved, the one woman he could never have, first, because of Constanza's husband, and then because of Constanza herself, who loved him, loved her two children with him, but had vowed never to see them, never to interrupt the flow of their lives with the truth, to complicate and warp their destinies in the name of her desire.

"So," Maceo Encarnación said now, "Nicodemo, parted from his mother, became mine, body and soul. As soon as he was old enough, I sent him to a special school in Colombia. I felt it imperative that he learn the trade."

"The drug trade," the agent said, with unnecessary venom. The Middle Kingdom had been done irreparable harm by the opium trade in the 1800s. The Chinese had memories centuries long.

"That and the arms trade." Maceo Encarnación pursed his lips. "As Minister Ouyang well knows, my prime interest is in arming those who need it most." When speaking with the agent, he always assumed he was speaking with Ouyang, the spider in the center of his Beijing web.

"You are most altruistic."

Maceo Encarnación's left hand twitched. Not for the first time, Hey-Boy had crossed the line that would, in any other circumstance, have cost him, quite literally, his head. Once more it was necessary for Maceo Encarnación to remind himself of the extreme importance of Minister Ouyang and his minions. Without Ouyang's assistance, the deal with Colonel Ben David would never have been possible.

"My altruism is matched only by Minister Ouyang's," he said, enunciating slowly and carefully. "You would do well to remember that."

The agent stared out the cockpit window. "When do we leave?"

"When I tell you to start the engines." Maceo Encarnación looked around. "Where is it?"

The pilot looked at him with his long Mandarin eyes. His spidery fingers drew out from beneath his seat an olive-drab metal box with a fingerprint lock. Maceo Encarnación pressed the end of his right forefinger onto the pressure-pad, and the lock opened.

He opened the top and looked down at the close-bonded stacks of thousand-dollar bills. "Thirty million. Amazing to look at," he said, "even for me."

"Colonel Ben David will be pleased," the agent said, deadpan.

Maceo Encarnación gave a silent laugh. "We all will."

Soraya was about to leave Peter's hospital room when Secretary Hendricks bustled in.

"Good to see you out of bed, Soraya," he said. Then he looked past her to where Peter lay. "How are you feeling?"

"Numb," Peter said, "in every way imaginable."

Hendricks dredged up a bark of a laugh. "Look, Peter, I don't have a lot of time. We have a bit of a situation up at headquarters."

"The computer network is down."

"That's right," Hendricks said, at the same time Soraya said, "What?"

"Dick Richards." Peter looked at Hendricks, who nodded. "I told Sam to pick him up."

"Anderson made a command decision to try and definitively link Richards with Core Energy." Hendricks gestured. "Brick has been ultra-cautious. Despite what he allegedly said to you—"

"He did say it to me, dammit!" Peter said heatedly.

Hendricks let Peter expend himself. "A court of law will rule against you," he said, after a time. "We've tried to follow a money trail, but if Richards is being paid by Core Energy or any of its subsidiaries, we have yet to find any evidence of it. Anderson knew this, which was why he put a keylogger onto the terminal he set Richards up at."

"Don't tell me," Peter said sourly. "It didn't work."

"What makes you say that?"

"I assume you have Richards in custody."

For the first time, Hendricks appeared chagrined. "He's gone, disappeared."

"Find Brick," Peter said. "That's where Richards went, guaranteed."

Hendricks spoke softly into his mobile. When the conversation concluded, he said, "For some reason Brick wants the Treadstone system down. Why?"

"Assuming you're right," Soraya said, "it's likely our overseas monitoring he wants to go silent."

Peter snapped his fingers. "You're right! But what is he afraid of us finding out?" He gnawed on his thumb for a moment.

Hendricks shifted from one foot to the other. "Peter..." He looked suddenly uncomfortable. When Peter looked up, he continued. "Considering everything that's happened to you—the serious nature of your current injury, I think it's best if you're relieved of duties as co-director of Treadstone."

"What?" Peter said.

Soraya took a step forward. "You can't."

"I can," Hendricks said. "And I am."

"It's my legs that are paralyzed," Peter said, "not my brain."

"I'm very sorry, Peter, but my mind's made up."

As he turned to go, Soraya said, "If Peter goes, so do I."

Hendricks swiveled back, leveling his heavy gaze at her. "Don't be foolish, Soraya. Don't throw away your career for—"

"For what? My loyalty to my friend?" she countered. "Peter and I have served together from the beginning. We're a team, end of story."

Hendricks shook his head. "You're confusing dedication with loyalty. That's a terrible mistake, one you're not likely to recover from."

"It's Treadstone that won't recover from losing its co-directors," she said with all the force she could muster.

The secretary appeared shocked. "You talk about Treadstone as if it's a family. It's not, Soraya. It's a business."

"With all due respect, Mr. Secretary, Treadstone *is* a family," she said. "Every one of its contacts overseas belongs to me. If I leave, they'll leave with me—"

"They won't."

"—just as they did when I was let go from CI during the regime change." She stood toe to toe with Hendricks, unafraid because, really, she had nothing to lose. She had no desire to remain at Treadstone without Peter. "I told you at the time that regime change was a mistake and that's turned out to be true. CI is a shell of its former self. It's dysfunctional, and morale is far worse than it was in the weeks following nine-eleven."

"I don't react well to being threatened," Hendricks said.

"I don't think I'm the one doing the threatening here."

"Look, Anderson's in the field, even as we speak. Peter put him in charge and—"

"I like Sam as much as the next guy," Peter said, "but he's not seasoned enough to run field ops for Treadstone for any length of time."

"Are either of you going to do it?" Hendricks gestured. "Look at you. Neither of you could walk out of here under your own power."

"There's nothing to stop us setting up a temporary HQ right here in Peter's room," Soraya said. "In fact, given that the Treadstone servers have been rendered useless, a substitute network seems like the best possible course of action right now."

Peter, who had been watching the dispute like a spectator at a tennis match, now said, "Wait a minute! Soraya, that thirty million I found. I assumed it was drug money, but what if it's not?"

She turned, frowning. "What d'you mean?"

"What if it was being used to pay for something else?"

"The money's proved to be counterfeit," Hendricks said dismissively.

"What?" Peter's head turned. "Really?"

Hendricks nodded. "Uh-huh."

"But that doesn't make sense. The guy who almost killed me—"

"Tulio Vistoso," Hendricks said. "Aka the Aztec. A top-line Mexican drug lord."

"I don't understand," Soraya said.

"We think it was a feint," the Secretary said. "Classic misdirection on Maceo Encarnación's part. When he's in Mexico City, the two are practically joined at the hip."

Peter shook his head. "I'm not so sure. The Aztec went to extreme lengths to protect that money."

Another short silence ensued.

"Is it possible," Soraya mused, "that Vistoso didn't know the money was counterfeit?"

Peter was intrigued. "That would mean he'd been scammed."

"That doesn't track," Hendricks said. "Vistoso was one of the Mexican Big Three. Who would dare to scam him?"

"Someone with more juice." Peter looked from one to the other. "Someone like Maceo Encarnación."

Soraya turned to Hendricks. "Have you been tracking him?"

"Encarnación was in Washington several days ago, giving an interview for *Politics As Usual*."

"I'm still back on the counterfeit thirty mil," Peter said. "Something about it is totally off." He snapped his fingers. "There must be an expert we can get hold of who might be able tell us who the counterfeiter is."

"It's already being worked on," Hendricks said. "But why should we be interested?"

"Thirty million is an enormous amount," Peter mused. "It had to be very, very good work. A master forger was involved. Maybe we can use him to implicate Maceo Encarnación."

Soraya crossed her arms over her swollen breasts, noticing how tender they had become. "Speaking of Maceo Encarnación, do we know where he went after his interview?"

"He flew back to his headquarters in Mexico City," Hendricks said.

"Is he there now?" Peter said.

Hendricks was already on his mobile, barking orders. He waited, staring at Peter. A moment later, he got his reply. "He's in Paris now, but has yet to disembark, which is odd because his plane has been on the ground for a good six hours."

"So okay," Peter said, "because Vistoso was Maceo Encarnación's prime lieutenant and because thirty million, even in counterfeit money, is a helluva sum, we've speculated that Encarnación must be involved."

"I'm thinking of Brick wanting the Treadstone system down," Soraya said. "Could there be a connection between him and Maceo Encarnación?"

"That system," Peter said, "is our best listening post in the Middle East."

"And Paris," Soraya said, "is a helluva lot closer to the Middle East than Mexico City."

Hendricks gave a quick nod. "Maceo Encarnación's pilot will have to file a flight plan out of Paris."

"We get that." Peter nodded. "We know precisely where he's going. If it's to the Middle East we have our proof of Encarnación's involvement."

Hendricks, the mobile to his ear, started giving them orders.

"Hold on," Soraya said. "You forget we don't work for you anymore."

"Who the fuck said that?" Hendricks gave them a hint of a smile just before he stepped through the door.

25

THINK OF IT AS a troika," Bourne said as he scanned the information on Martha Christiana's micro-SD chip. "Maceo Encarnación, Tom Brick, the Chinese."

Don Fernando shook his head. "What I don't understand is why Martha had this material in the first place."

"It was her fuck-you stash," Bourne said. "She amassed this information to use as leverage."

Don Fernando was silent for some time. He stared at the screen of his laptop with a melancholy sorrow. At last he heaved a great sigh. "But, in the end, she didn't use it." He turned to look at Bourne. "Why?"

"This was a way out, but only one of several. It would still leave her a life of constantly looking over her shoulder."

"She wouldn't have wanted that," Don Fernando said.

"From what you've told me about her, no. But, on the other hand, I doubt that she wanted out at all. That was her essential dilemma. She could no longer go forward, and, for her, there was no way back. There was no other way, no other life that she could conceive of."

"I told her about it," Don Fernando lamented. "I laid it all out for her."

"She couldn't hear it, or she couldn't believe it."

Don Fernando sighed and nodded with a kind of finality. "You're a good friend, Jason. There aren't many like you."

Traffic rolled endlessly by outside. The amplified voice of the guide aboard a passing Bateau Mouche rolled up the stone walls to them, then drifted away as if on a watery tide. The bare trees whipped in the wind off the Seine. Downstairs, on the Quai de Bourbon, there were still gawkers, murmuring among themselves about last night's suicide. The circus hadn't died down.

Bourne pointed to the screen. "According to Martha's information, the Chinese have been laundering money through Maceo Encarnación."

"They're going to use the thirty million to buy something from an unknown entity in the Middle East—something very important," Don Fernando said. "But Martha didn't know what it was or from whom it was to be bought."

Bourne did know, however, because Rebeka had whispered the name to him just before she bled out in the backseat of the taxi in Mexico City.

Don Fernando sat back. "What I don't understand is what Maceo Encarnación gets out of this deal. A ten percent laundering fee? That's hardly worth the risk he's taking."

Bourne scrolled through Martha's information again. Something he had seen before had stuck in his mind. Then his forefinger stabbed out as he pointed. "There! Tom Brick's involvement." He turned to Don Fernando. "What does Core Energy stand to gain in a deal with Maceo Encarnación and the Chinese?"

Don Fernando thought a moment. "That depends on what the Chinese are buying."

"It's energy-related," Bourne said. "Don't you see? Energy is the element that ties all these people together."

"Yes. With their huge upsurge in economic expansion, production, infrastructure, and population, the Chinese are always after alternative forms of energy. I can see how Brick and Core Energy would want a piece of whatever technology the Chinese are after." He shook his head. "But Maceo Encarnación?"

"The troika only makes sense if Maceo Encarnación and Core Energy are somehow allied."

"What? But Christien and I would know about that, surely?"

"Would you?"

"We've had our eye on both Maceo Encarnación and Core Energy, Jason. We could find no money trail between the two."

"If Brick and Maceo Encarnación went about the alliance in the right way, there wouldn't be one. A money trail would be the first thing they'd conceal. From what I've read, Core Energy has more than enough subsidiaries worldwide to conceal a money trail."

"Not from us," Don Fernando insisted. "Christien has developed a proprietary software program that drills down through any mare's nest of shell corporations and holding companies. I'm telling you there's no money trail."

Bourne laughed. "Of course! That's where Maceo Encarnación's drug lords come in. They're the ones who reverse-launder the money flowing between Maceo Encarnación and Core Energy."

"Reverse-launder?"

Bourne nodded. "Instead of funneling dirty money through legitimate sources, Brick and Maceo Encarnación have done the reverse. They've taken the legitimate money that flows between their two companies and funneled it through the drug lords, making it dirty, and therefore, untraceable. It's all cash, back and forth. No matter how clever and sophisticated Christien's software program is, it isn't going to pick up those kinds of transactions. No one else is, either."

"It's brilliant." Don Fernando passed a hand across his forehead. "I wish to God I had thought of it."

"Don Fernando," Bourne said, "Maceo Encarnación and the thirty million are going to Lebanon to consummate a deal."

The older man brightened considerably. It was clear Martha Christiana's death had hit him hard. "Then we need to get there as quickly as possible."

Bourne regarded him warily. "We're not going anywhere until we take care of Nicodemo. You told me you went to a lot of trouble to prove to Maceo Encarnación that you died when your private jet crashed. But if Nicodemo was at your door earlier, then chances are he saw you outside the building. Encarnación knows you're alive. Nicodemo won't allow you to leave Paris alive."

So many things can go wrong."

Minister Ouyang, a tiny, translucent teacup balanced between his fingertips, stood in the large central chamber of the magnificent Chonghuagong, the private suite of Qianlong, emperor of the Qing dynasty, buried in the secret center of the Forbidden City. Few people were allowed into the chambers, which gleamed with the emperor's jaw-dropping collection of precious jade figurines and historic calligraphic scrolls, and none but Minister Ouyang and several others of the Central Committee at such a late hour. The flames from tiers of thick yellow candles threw off flickering, glimmering light that both illuminated and shadowed the array of the Middle Kingdom's treasures.

The woman to whom Ouyang had directed his concern was curled like a cat on a Mandarin divan brought in for the occasion and followed him with her coffee-colored eyes. Even in this position, the power in her long legs was apparent. Cloaked in a gleaming orange shantung silk robe, she looked like the emissary of the sun. "If you think that way, darling, you will make it so."

Ouyang turned sharply enough for the hot tea to sting one fingertip. He ignored the pain to stare at his wife. "I will never understand you, Maricruz."

She bowed her head slightly, her thick waterfall of hair covering one eye, acknowledging the compliment in the restrained manner of the high-caste Chinese with whom she had lived since coming to Beijing a decade ago. "This is as it should be."

Ouyang, in a long, traditional Mandarin's robe, took a step toward her. "But, really, you are not like a Westerner at all."

"If I had been," she said in a voice of stillness and depth, "you never would have married me."

Ouyang studied her the way a painter eyes the model for his most important work of art. Transformation was the painter's skill; it was also Ouyang's. "Do you want to know what ultimately attracted me to you?"

Maricruz opened her eyes slightly.

"Your patience." Ouyang took a sip of his tea, held it in his mouth for a moment, then swallowed. "Patience is the greatest of virtues. It is almost wholly unknown in the West. The Arabs understand the value of patience, but they are primitives compared to us."

Maricruz laughed. "I think that's what I like most about you Chinese—your incredibly high opinion of yourselves." She laughed again. "The Middle Kingdom."

Ouyang took another sip of tea, savoring it much as he savored these intellectual boxing matches with his wife. No one else had the guts to talk to him in this blunt manner. "You're living in the Middle Kingdom, Maricruz."

"And loving every minute of it."

Ouyang crossed to a narrow niche and took up a small jade box, exquisitely engraved with rampant dragons on a field of stylized clouds. He held this box in his two hands.

"The Middle Kingdom has always been a rich source of mythology. I think you know this, Maricruz. Your own civilization is steeped in myth and legend." Ouyang's obsidian eyes glittered. "However, our history is so long and twisted that we have had several setbacks, all of them egregious. The first one occurred many centuries ago, in two thirteen BC, when Emperor Shi Huangdi of the Qin dynasty ordered the burning of all books on subjects other than medicine, prophecy, and farming. Thus were lost many of the Middle Kingdom's root mythological sources.

"As often happens here, Shi Huangdi's order was reversed in one ninety-one BC, and much of the literature was reconstructed. However, it was rewritten to support ideas popular with the then current emperor. Mythological history was rewritten, as it is over and over again, by the victor. Valuable information was lost forever."

He came toward her with the box held like an object of infinite value. "Rarely, however, a piece of the precious past is somehow discovered, either by fate or by the desire to find it."

Standing in front of her, he held out the box.

Maricruz eyed the jade warily. "What is this?"

"Please," Ouyang said, bending down to her.

Maricruz took the box, which weighed far more than she had expected. It was cool to the touch, smooth as glass. With one hand, she opened the top. Her fingers trembled. Inside was a folded square of paper. She looked up at Ouyang.

"The name of your mother, Maricruz."

Her mouth opened but no sound emerged.

"Should you wish to find her."

"She's alive?" Maricruz breathed.

Ouyang watched her, eyes alight. "She is."

Very slowly, she closed the box and set it down on the settee beside her. She uncoiled with a lithe strength he found intoxicating. She reminded him of the American movie stars of the 1940s. As she rose, her robe parted. *How did she manage that magician's sleight of hand?* he wondered. The inner hemispheres of her firm breasts revealed themselves like beautiful bronze bowls. She pressed her body against him.

"Thank you, Ouyang," she said formally.

"What will you do?"

"I don't know," she whispered. "I want to know. I don't want to know."

"You have the chance to undo the revision of your own personal history."

"It means defying my father." She rubbed her forehead against his shoulder. "What if my mother doesn't want to see me? Why didn't she try—?"

"You know your father," Ouyang said softly, "better than anyone."

"There must be a reason," she said. "Do you know what it is?"

"I have reached the limits of my knowledge in this affair." But, of course, Ouyang knew the reason, just as Maricruz would the moment she saw the

name of her mother, married to a powerful drug
lord, a friend, a business partner, who Maceo Encarnación cuckolded without a scintilla of remorse. He
had desired Constanza Camargo. That was Maceo
Encarnación in a nutshell.

"I need time," Maricruz said now. "I need to concentrate on what is about to transpire."

Even as Ouyang felt his body respond to hers, his
mind returned to what she had said. "You are correct, Maricruz. I have the perfect partners. Nothing
is going to go wrong."

She smiled at him, her arms wrapped around him.

"This plan would not have been possible without
you," he said, nuzzling her ear. "Without the partic-
ipation of your father and brother."

Maricruz's laugh was a gurgle deep in her throat.
"My poor brother, Juanito, saddled with the name
Nicodemo, with the sobriquet the Djinn Who Lights
The Way, both given to him by our father in order to
bury himself even more deeply in the shadows."

"Your father moves in a circle of light in his legitimate business dealings as CEO of SteelTrap. He
moves in a circle of shadow with his illegitimate
dealings with the cream of the drug lords and arms
dealers."

His fingertips caressed her bare shoulders beneath the slithery robe.

"But I know a different Maceo Encarnación, the
one who moves in darkness, the one who makes
plans like a master chess player, the one who
brings disparate elements together, often without
their knowledge or consent, the one who is invaluable to me."

Maricruz, breathing softly and evenly, lowered her head into the crook of his neck. "There is no end to his cleverness, to his ruthlessness, to his ability to use anyone and everyone when it suits his purpose."

Ouyang smiled. "Your father and I have no illusions about our relationship. We use each other. It's symbiotic. We accomplish so much more that way."

"And Colonel Ben David?"

"A means to an end."

"You will make a lifelong enemy."

Ouyang smiled as his hand encircled her breast. "This is not an issue. He won't survive."

She drew back with a tiny indrawn breath. "Ben David is a colonel in the Mossad. Do you really think you can get an assassin close enough to him?"

"I have already done my part," Ouyang said, drawing her back to him. "Your father has arranged everything else."

He smiled. "It will be Jason Bourne who terminates Colonel Ben David with extreme prejudice."

Sam Anderson was in a foul mood when he got off the phone with Secretary Hendricks. He felt that he had let Peter down. He was angry at himself for not being able to be in two places at once, for not delegating, for not ordering one of his subordinates to keep an eye on Dick Richards.

As he climbed into his car along with an agent named James, he cursed the evil gods that raged over Treadstone. The organization had been ill-fated ever since it had first come into existence. Sometimes, as now, it seemed to him that the current

Treadstone staff was paying for the missteps and sins of its founders. There was no other interpretation of both co-directors being down at the same time.

As he raced through the Washington traffic, he nodded to James. "Do it now."

James dialed a number on his mobile, then put the call on speakerphone. When a female voice, smoothly efficient as a robot's, answered, he asked for Tom Brick.

"May I ask who is calling?" the female voice asked.

James turned to Anderson, who nodded.

"Herb Davidoff, editor in chief of *Politics As Usual*."

"Just a moment, please."

There was a pause during which Anderson slewed the car around a lumbering truck. Half on the sidewalk, he hit the horn, scattering nearby pedestrians.

Take it easy, boss, James mouthed at him.

"Mr. Davidoff?" The female voice had returned.

"Here."

"I'm afraid Mr. Brick is currently unavailable."

"Please tell him that I need a quote from him for a front-page story," James hurried over her. "Time is of the essence."

"I'm afraid I can't, Mr. Davidoff. I'll switch you to his voicemail. I assure you Mr. Brick accesses it several times a day."

"Thanks very much," James said, terminating the connection. He glanced at Anderson. "The house in Virginia?" He meant the house to which Peter had been taken by Tom Brick.

"Deploy our best COVSIC," Anderson said as he put his foot to the accelerator. He meant a covert forensic team. James nodded and got on it.

Just then a call came in to Anderson's mobile.

"Handle it yourself," he barked. He was in no mood for office decisions.

"Sir, it's Michaelson. I'm three blocks south of Founders Park in Virginia. The police just fished a body out of the Potomac. It's Dick Richards."

"Fuck, fuck, fuck," Anderson said, even as he put the car into a controlled skid, making a sharp U-turn, and accelerated away.

Tell me why Colonel Ben David is at the nexus of the troika's plan," Don Fernando said.

"It started with SILEX." Bourne shifted on the larger of the apartment's two sofas. "The methodology draws on the extraordinary purity of laser light to selectively agitate uranium's enriched form. The needed isotope is identified, culled, and extracted. If it works, the process is a game-changer. Enriched uranium for nuclear power plants could be manufactured in a fraction of the time and at a fraction of the cost it now takes.

"The problem," Bourne went on, "is that SILEX would also make weapons-grade uranium easily available. Yellow-cake to nuclear warheads in a matter of days."

"But it doesn't work," Don Fernando said.

Bourne nodded. "GE bought the rights to SILEX in 2006, but it has yet to perfect the process."

He turned, staring out the window at the slow

river traffic. He seemed always to be looking at people going about their peaceful daily lives while the world hurtled toward the precipice of war.

"SILEX was just the beginning. Three years ago, the Israelis set up an underground research facility in northwest Lebanon, just outside a small town known as Dahr El Ahmar. The facility was guarded by a small, select unit of Mossad agents under the command of Colonel Ben David."

He turned back to Don Fernando. "It was to Dahr El Ahmar that Rebeka guided me after we were both wounded in a firefight in Damascus six weeks ago. It was the closest safe haven, at least for her. She was feverish, very badly wounded. I imagine she wasn't thinking clearly. Bringing me to Dahr El Ahmar was a breach of security.

"Colonel Ben David tried to have me killed. I managed to escape in the helo we flew in on, but as I left I caught a glimpse of the bunkered facility. Rebeka told me the rest. The Israeli scientists had a breakthrough. Their version of SILEX works."

There was a deepening silence, into which, after a time, Don Fernando cleared his throat. "So let me get this straight. Colonel Ben David has agreed to sell this process to Maceo Encarnación?"

"To the Chinese," Bourne said. "My guess is Maceo Encarnación is a peripheral figure in all this—maybe he's the broker, the one who put Colonel Ben David together with the Chinese."

"That could very well be." Don Fernando tapped his teeth ruminatively with his forefinger. "After all, SteelTrap employs a good number of Israeli technicians. It sells its proprietary Internet security to the Israeli government, among many other huge clients."

He shook his head. "What I don't understand is why Colonel Ben David would betray his country."

"Thirty million. Dangle enough money in front of a man like that, a military man, a disgruntled officer who's probably never made more than fifty thousand dollars a year, and the crystal ball clears."

"How did you come by that figure? Did you pull it out of the air?"

"So to speak," Bourne said, waggling his mobile.

Don Fernando made a whistling sound. "Even for Christien and me that's a trainload of money. I can only imagine that it would be irresistible to Ben David."

He sat down heavily on the smaller sofa. "The problem is we're trapped here in my apartment. Nicodemo could take me down with a sniper rifle the minute I walk out my door."

"He won't," Bourne said. "Nicodemo comes from a tradition of hands-on killing. It's a matter of honor. Killing you at a distance won't satisfy him. He wants to take your head off."

"Cold comfort," Don Fernando grunted.

"Nevertheless, it works to our advantage." Bourne, staring out the window again, lifted his view across the river to the Right Bank. "I need to bring Nicodemo into my territory."

In the far distance, he could just make out the sugar-white dome of Sacre Coeur, atop Montmartre. "Tell me, Don Fernando, when was the last time you went to the Moulin Rouge?"

* * *

Peter and Soraya looked at each other after Secretary Hendricks left his room.

"Why did you do that?" Peter said.

Soraya smiled and came and sat on the edge of his bed. "You're welcome."

"Seriously?" he said.

She nodded. "I don't want to leave."

"Because of me."

She shrugged. "Is that so terrible a reason?"

He studied her a moment, then took a drink of water from a plastic cup. He seemed to be debating something internally. "I have to ask myself...Soraya, you've been lying to me."

"Withholding some information. That's not the same thing."

"If we can't trust each other, what's the point of either of us staying together?"

"Oh, Peter." She leaned over and kissed his cheek. "I trust you with my life. It's just that..." Her eyes cut away for a moment. "I didn't want anyone to know about my pregnancy. I figured it would jeopardize my position."

"You thought I'd betray you to Hendricks?"

"No, I...To be honest, Peter, I don't know what I thought." She touched the bandaged side of her head. "Obviously, I wasn't thinking clearly."

He took her hand in his, and they sat like that, wordless, full of emotion, for some time. Outside, in the corridor, orderlies wheeled gurneys, nurses hurried by, doctors' names were called. All of that seemed part of another world that had nothing to do with them.

"I want to help you," Soraya said at length.

"I don't need help."

But that was an instinctive, knee-jerk response, and they both knew it. That shared knowledge seemed to break the newly formed ice, to return them to the time when they were closer than siblings, when they shared everything.

Soraya leaned closer and spoke to him in low, intimate tones while he listened intently as she outlined the top-secret mission Hendricks had given her. "Listen, Peter," she concluded, "Charles is dead, it's over now, but this liaison with him was strictly Hendricks's idea. He came to me with it, said it was a matter of national security, and I felt that I...well...that I couldn't refuse him."

"He shouldn't have asked that of you."

"I've been through that with him. He knows he crossed the line."

"And yet he did it," Peter said, "and he'll do it again. You know it and I know it."

"Probably."

"What will you tell him the next time?"

She touched her belly. "I have my child to think of now. Things will be different."

"You think so?"

Her gaze drifted from him to the middle distance. "You're right. I can't know."

He squeezed her hand. "None of us can—ever—no matter the circumstances."

A small smile wreathed her lips. "True enough." Leaning over again, she hugged him. "I'm so sorry, Peter."

"Don't be. Everything happens for a reason."

She drew back, watching him. "Do you really believe that?"

He laughed without much humor. "No, but saying it helps keep my spirits up."

She looked at him steadily. "It's going to be a long haul, no matter what happens with your legs."

"I know that."

"I'll be here."

"I know that, too." He sighed. "They'll order a psych eval to determine whether I'm fit for duty."

"So what? They've already ordered one for me. We're fit for duty, Peter. End of story."

Once more, they sat in companionable silence. Once, a tear overran Peter's eye and slid down his cheek. "Damn it to hell," he said, and Soraya squeezed his hand again.

"Tell me something," he said. "Tell me something positive."

"Let's start with Jason Bourne," she said, "and how he needs our help."

26

LA GOULUE HAD BEEN the first of the Moulin Rouge's famed Cancan Queens. Each night she entered the famed theater via the well-hidden and almost unknown *entrée des artistes*, a tiny staircase that led to heaven from the grubby back alleys of Montmartre. The well-worn staircase, trod upon by generations of the Moulin's dancers and cabaret artists for over a century, had in years past been supplanted by a newer backstage entrance. Don Fernando, however, knew not only of its existence, but the fact that it was still a useful way to gain access to the halcyon environs of the Moulin Rouge, when all other methods failed, or when one of the Doriss Girls of his acquaintance wanted to sneak him in for some backstage shenanigans between shows.

He called his current Doriss Girl, Cerise, who, he assured Bourne, was absolutely reliable.

Just after 8 PM, they exited Don Fernando's building on the Quai de Bourbon. A driver and car from Don Fernando's favored service were waiting.

"Tell the driver you've changed your mind," Bourne said.

When Don Fernando dismissed the car and driver, he and Bourne crossed the nearby bridge to the Right Bank without incident.

"I don't see him," Don Fernando said.

"You won't," Bourne assured him. "But there was a better than even chance he had suborned someone inside the car company you frequent."

The thing to avoid was crowds, so they headed for the taxi *tête de station* near the Hôtel de Ville and climbed into the waiting cab. Don Fernando gave the driver the address of the Moulin Rouge, and the Mercedes nosed out into traffic.

"You seem very sure of yourself, Jason," Don Fernando said as he settled back into the seat.

"It never pays to be sure of anything," Bourne replied, "apart from putting one foot in front of the other in the dark."

Don Fernando nodded as he stared at the back of the driver's head. "I never asked you about the female Mossad agent."

"Rebeka," Bourne said. "She and I were both after the same man, Semid Abdul-Qahhar, the head of the Mosque in Munich and one of the seminal players in the Muslim Brotherhood. We joined forces, we helped each other. She was a good person—someone trying to do the right thing, even though it might very well have cost her her position at Mossad."

Don Fernando nodded absently. "There's always a price to pay for doing the right thing," he mused, "the only question is, how heavy is the price?" He rubbed his knuckles against the side of his face. "There's also a price for not being able to do the right thing." He sighed. "That's the nature of life, I suppose."

"Our life, especially."

Their discussion was interrupted when they were rear-ended by the car behind them. It was at a slow speed and didn't amount to much; nevertheless, their driver threw the Mercedes into park and got out and started an altercation with the driver of the other car.

"Get out!" Bourne said suddenly. He pushed against Don Fernando. "Get out now!"

Bourne pulled on the door handle, but the central lock had been engaged from the driver's console. The driver who had hit them handed the taxi driver a small packet.

Bourne launched himself over the front seat-backs, but at that moment a figure ducked into the Mercedes and pointed a Sig-Sauer at him, forcing him to return to the backseat.

"No escape now," Nicodemo said, as he slid behind the wheel.

He nodded, and the taxi driver returned to the car. Keeping the Sig trained on them, Nicodemo disengaged the central lock. The driver wrenched open the rear door and bound Bourne's wrists behind his back with a length of plastic zip cord, then did the same to Don Fernando.

"Take them to the trunk," Nicodemo said.

"You came into us too hard," the driver said. "The lock's bashed in and the trunk won't open."

"Okay. Get out of here," Nicodemo said.

The driver slammed the rear door shut, and went back to the car Nicodemo had been driving.

Nicodemo, behind the wheel of the Mercedes, grinned at them. "Now the real darkness comes, Jason."

Bourne said nothing. He was testing the tensile strength of the zip cord. He wouldn't be able to snap it without outside help.

Placing the Sig on the bench seat beside him, Nicodemo turned away from them to face front. "Much better to have tame animals," he said, watching them in the rearview mirror as he put the Mercedes in gear and pulled out into the nighttime street, "than wild ones to the slaughter."

A funny thing happened to me on the way to your office, Mr. Brick," Anderson said. "Funny, odd, that is."

"And what would that be, Agent Anderson?"

"I just came from looking at a body fished out of the Potomac River. Hadn't been there long, a couple of hours max."

Tom Brick, sitting at ease behind his large, masculine desk in his massive office that took up an entire corner of the top floor of Core Energy, spread his hands. "Yeah? So?"

"Knifed twice in the side."

"What's it got to do with me?"

"'What's it got to do with me?' the man says." Anderson, with James at his side, stood in the approximate center of the office. Having shown his government ID to the phalanx of secretaries, assistants, and assorted flunkies, they had been ushered into Brick's office where, it appeared, he was having a meeting with a suit seated on a sofa facing the desk. Brick did not invite the newcomers to sit. Anderson checked the expression on the professionally scrubbed face of the suit before he returned his gaze to Brick.

"I'm curious, Mr. Brick, as to why you haven't asked the victim's name."

Brick stared at him with dead-fish eyes. "His name is of no interest to me."

"You said *his*, but I said a *body*."

Brick snorted. "Don't play *NCIS* with me, Anderson."

"I'll tell you anyway, because you know him. His name is Dick Richards."

Brick sat for a moment, unmoving. Then he rose and gestured to the man with whom he had been talking when Anderson and James had entered.

"Perhaps it's time you met Bill Pelham."

"As in Pelham, Noble and Gunn?"

Brick couldn't contain a smile. "That's right."

Pelham, Noble and Gunn was in the top tier of Washington law firms. It counted among its clients many presidents, former presidents, and senators, not to mention the head of the FBI, as well as the mayor and the police commissioner of DC. Its juice was potent; it flowed directly from the hallowed Beltway source.

Anderson, trying his damnedest to ignore the broadside, said, "In any event, Mr. Brick, we need to talk. Now."

"No talk," Bill Pelham said, rising from his seat on the sofa. "No talk now, not ever."

Three things I can't abide," Ann Ring said. "Confusion, complication, and dissembling." Around them, in the postmodern spaciousness of the restaurant Li Wan had chosen, silverware clinked and glasses chimed. Voices were raised in small talk. People deep in conversations on their mobile phones ignored everyone around them. She stared deep into Li's obsidian eyes. "Unfortunately, life is full of confusion, complication, and dissembling." She smiled with crimson lips. "I like neatness—clean beginnings, at least."

Li inclined his narrow head. "As do I, Senator Ring."

"And yet, here we both are in Washington, DC." Her laugh was easy to like, meant to put the listener at ease. Li was not as easy a mark as that.

"Being at a center of power is like being in a magnetic storm." He took a sip of white wine. "At once exhilarating and disorienting."

Ann tipped her head. "Is it the same in Beijing?" The change in Li's expression caused her to curse herself.

"I wouldn't know." He put down his glass with exaggerated care. "I myself have never been to Beijing. Did you just assume—?"

"A thousand pardons, Mr. Li. I meant nothing—"

"Oh, I'm most certain." He waved away her words with the flat of his hand. "Actually, Beijing seems as foreign to me as I imagine it does to you."

She allowed a small laugh to escape her lips. "Another thing we have in common."

His depthless eyes sought hers. "Commonalities are rare, I find, especially in a magnetic storm."

"I couldn't agree more, Mr. Li." She picked up her menu, a large, stiff thing with the offerings printed in a typeface simulating handwritten script. With her face shielded from his, she said, "What shall we eat?"

"Steak, I think," he said without consulting his menu. "And a Caesar salad to start."

"Creamed spinach and onion rings?"

"Why not?"

When she set aside her menu, she saw the depth of his scrutiny of her. *"Remember,"* Hendricks had told her at the very start, *"this is a very dangerous man. He seems unassuming; however, he's anything but."*

Li called the waiter over and ordered for them. The waiter gathered up the menus and departed.

"This evening reminds me of a story," Li said when they were alone again. "There was once a businessman in Chicago. He married a woman with a good head on her shoulders. So good, in fact, that following her suggestions caused his business to grow to two, then three times its original size. As you can imagine, the businessman was very happy. A flourishing business caused his standing in the community to grow by leaps and bounds. He was sought out for company mergers as well as for advice. In each instance, he consulted his wife, and in each instance, following her advice brought him more fame and riches."

Li paused to refill their glasses. "Now, you might think the businessman's life was perfect. Everyone who knew him, as well as everyone who knew of him, envied him his position and wealth. But no. In fact, he was miserable. His wife never warmed his bed, only others'."

Li stared into his raised glass. "One day, the businessman's wife died. It was very sudden and completely unexpected. Of course, the businessman mourned her, but more for the loss of her business acumen than for the woman herself.

"Several weeks later, his brother said to him, 'What will you do now?' And the businessman, after several moments of contemplation, said, 'I will do what I've always done and hope for the best.'"

Ann Ring smiled in the most neutral way. This

was not simply a story Li had once heard. In fact, he might have made it up on the spot. Either way, it was illustrative. The question the businessman's brother had posed to him was the same one Li was asking her.

Whether by design or not, his timing was impeccable. The Caesar salads arrived, set down in front of each of them in white ceramic bowls. Ann spent some time tasting the salad, asking for fresh-ground pepper, and thanking the waiter.

"I like the first part of the businessman's answer," she said carefully, "but not the second. It's never wise to sit back and hope for the best."

"The story makes me wonder who really makes the decisions in families. It seems the answer is never what it appears to be on the surface."

Ann understood that he was asking about her and Charles, which is why she chose to ignore the implied question, preferring to stick to her own agenda. She ate more salad, crunching through the garlic croutons as if they were bones.

"What surprises me, Mr. Li, is your knowledge of my intimate life with Charles."

He laid down his fork. "There is no easy way to say this, Senator. Your husband was not a happy man."

Ann watched Li with an enigmatic expression. "You mean he wasn't content." She bared her teeth just slightly. "The two aren't synonymous."

For the first time all evening Li appeared flustered. "I beg your pardon," he said.

* * *

Looking out the window of the Mercedes, Bourne could see that Nicodemo was taking them across the river to the Left Bank. The magnificent gilded light globes spanning the Pont Alexandre III spun by like miniature suns. Doubtless, Nicodemo was taking them to the killing ground he had chosen. Bourne had no intention of letting him get there.

Edging himself down on the seat until he was directly behind Nicodemo, Bourne arched his back, pressed it hard against the rear seatback. He extended his legs over the top of the front seat on either side of Nicodemo's neck, and, bringing them together, locked his ankles at Nicodemo's throat.

Predictably, Nicodemo arched backward, his body in reflex action to get away from the choke hold. Don Fernando kicked him hard on the right ear with his heel. Nicodemo's head trembled on his neck, and Bourne squeezed tighter, muscles like iron bands.

Blindly, Nicodemo scrabbled on the seat for the Sig. Bourne, exerting all his strength, lurched him away, to the left, his shoulder impacting so hard against the unlocked door that it popped open.

The Mercedes began to swerve in wider and wider arcs, and the Sig fell to the floor well, out of his reach. Horns blared, brakes squealed, abruptly halted tires left scorch marks on the bridge bed. Wide-eyed, Nicodemo was forced to try to free himself while attempting to keep control of the car. Blind instinct took over. In trying to pry Bourne's legs away from him, he removed his hands from the wheel. But as he arched back again, his right foot inadvertently stabbed down on the accelerator. The Mercedes shot forward just as it was aimed at the side of the bridge. The combination of its speed and weight lifted it onto the pedestrian walkway, slammed it into the ancient stone, crumbling in places, of the bridge's decorative balustrade.

The impact jerked everyone forward, momentarily loosening Bourne's grip, but at that moment, a light truck, attempting to circumnavigate the traffic tie-up, sideswiped the Mercedes, smashing it through the already crumbling balustrade.

The massive impact hurled the Mercedes out over the river, the driver's door swinging wide with the momentum, and the car plummeted straight down. It hit the water, which instantly rushed in on a merciless tidal wave, swamping the interior, threatening to drown the three men inside.

Ann made a sound much like that of a cat purring. She set aside her salad. "You know, Mr. Li, it occurs to me now that I know nothing about Natasha Illion—apart, that is, from what I read in *W*, *Vogue*, and *Vanity Fair*, but that's all image, publicity spin."

Mr. Li smiled. They were back on familiar ground. "Tasha and I lead very different lives," he said with a shrug of his shoulders.

"But when you come together..." The slightest hint of a smile. "I beg your pardon."

"Tasha isn't someone easy to know," Li said as if he had not heard her. "Israelis are gruff, direct, often disconcertingly so. Like all of them, she spent time in the army. That changes them, in my opinion."

"Is that so?" Ann cupped her chin in one hand. "How do you mean?"

The salad bowls were cleared away, the oversized steak knives presented and, with a brief flourish, laid out.

"In Tasha's case, it's made her wary, distrustful. She considers her entire life a secret."

"And, of course, you find this intriguing, fascinating."

He sat back as the entrées and side dishes were set before them. Several twists of black pepper later, he took up fork and steak knife and sliced. The meat was bloody, exactly as ordered. "I'm a self-professed xenophile. I'm fascinated, as you put it, by the different, the exotic, the unknowable."

"I imagine there's nothing more exotic than an Israeli supermodel."

He chewed slowly and fastidiously. "I could think of several, but I'm quite content with what I have."

"Unlike my late husband." She dragged several onion rings onto the crusty top of her steak. She looked up suddenly, her gaze like the thrust of a knife. "Charlie confided in you about his affairs."

It wasn't a question, and Li didn't take it as such.

"It seemed that Charles had very few friends and no confidants," he said.

"Apart from you." Her eyes held steady on him. "That should have been me."

"We can't always get what we want, Senator." He took a slice of meat between his teeth, chewed in his dainty way, then swallowed. "But we can try."

"I'm wondering why Charlie felt he could confide in you."

"The answer is simple enough," Li said. "It's easier to talk of intimate matters to a stranger."

But that wasn't it at all, and they both knew it. Ann was growing weary of the conversational circumlocutions required by Chinese custom. Though Li was American born, in this he was very traditional. Maybe the Chinese insisted on these long, circular verbal paths, she thought, to wear you out, soften you up for the moment when negotiation began.

"Come on, Mr. Li. You and Charlie shared secrets."

"Yes," he said. "We did."

Ann was so surprised by this bald admission that she briefly lost her breath.

"Your husband and I had an arrangement, Senator. An arrangement that benefitted both of us in equal measure."

Ann didn't bat an eye. "I'm listening."

"It seems to me," Li said, "that you have been listening all evening."

She laughed then, dry as wood. "Then we understand each other."

He inclined his head fractionally. "However, we do not *know* one another." The emphasis was subtle, but clear.

"This shortcoming has not been lost on me." She smiled without, she hoped, a trace of guile. "Which is why I would like to present you with a gift."

Li sat perfectly still across from her, his body neither tense nor relaxed. Simply waiting.

"Something precious that will correct the deficiency between us."

From her handbag, she took out a small manila envelope, which she passed across the table. Li spent several moments engaging her eyes with his own. Only then did he allow his gaze to fall to the envelope.

His hands moved, took up the envelope, and unsealed it. He shook out its contents, which consisted of a single sheet of paper, a photocopy of an official document. As if magnetized, his eyes were drawn to the seal at the top of the page.

"This is...monstrous, insane," he murmured, almost to himself.

As he scanned the information, a bead of sweat appeared at his meticulous hairline. Then he looked up into Ann's face.

"Your beloved Tasha is not just a beauty, Mr. Li, she's also a beast," Ann said. "She's a Mossad agent."

Jackknifing his body, Bourne followed Nicodemo out the open driver's door, but immediately had to turn back to fetch Don Fernando, who was floundering over into the front. With his hands bound behind him, Bourne used his teeth to grab at Don Fernando's shirt. Grateful for the help, Don Fernando scissored his legs, propelling himself through the door.

It was dark under the water, and the two men positioned themselves back-to-back, their hands together so they would not lose each other. Breaching the surface, they heard screams emanating from pedestrians on the bridge, and, in the far distance, sirens. Bourne directed them to one of the bridge's immense piers, thick with encrusted green-black weed. Beneath the weeds were barnacles, sharp as razor blades. Shoving himself back first against the pier, Bourne scraped the plastic tie against the barnacles, sawing through his bonds.

Don Fernando was beside him, treading water calmly.

"Almost out of it," Bourne said.

Don Fernando nodded. But just as Bourne reached for him, he was pulled under the water.

Nicodemo!

Bourne swiped at the pier, then kicked out powerfully as he dove beneath the water. Like a shark, he could feel Don Fernando's thrashing, along with the kicking movement that was part of Nicodemo's attack. Finding Don Fernando in the blackness, he used one of the barnacles he had grabbed to slice through the plastic tie, then propelled Don Fernando toward the surface.

This maneuver cost him. Nicodemo swerved underwater, caught Bourne a blow to the side of his head. Bourne canted over in the water, bubbles strewn from between his lips. Nicodemo struck him again, along the nerve bundle in the side of his neck. Bourne's consciousness seemed to drift away from him. He tried to move, but nothing seemed to work. He was aware of Nicodemo maneuvering behind him, and he kicked out, but a slimy rope encircled his neck, a ferocious pressure converged at his throat. His lungs burned and his throat ached. Reaching around, Nicodemo pressed on his cricoid cartilage. If that shattered, he would drown within seconds.

He felt an increasingly tenuous connection with his consciousness, felt a sharp, circular instrument against his fingertips, but he wondered whether he possessed the strength to use it. The pressure on his throat was unbearable. Any second now Nicodemo's fingertips would break through, and the black water would cascade down his throat, into his stomach and his lungs, and he would spiral down into the silty bottom of the river.

With an immense effort, he raised his arm. Everything seemed to be moving at a glacial pace, though another part of his mind was aware that time was running out far too quickly. He drew on this part, using it to arc his arm inward, grip his organic weapon more tightly as he dragged it across first one of Nicodemo's eyes, then the other.

Gouts of blood erupted. Nicodemo spasmed, and

an inhuman strength gripped him, a long moment that almost did Bourne in. But the barnacle he gripped went to work again, slashing from left to right across Nicodemo's throat.

Veils of blood, blacker than the river water, spiraled outward. Nicodemo's mouth opened and closed, caught for a moment in the lights from the bridge. Then his grip on Bourne fell away, and he passed, arms outstretched in a terrible yearning, out of what light there was, into the filthy depths of the river.

27

WHEN THE LITHE flight attendant lifted her head to emit a soft moan, Maceo Encarnación pushed her head back down between her bare shoulders, exposing the soft nape of her long neck. Her uniform jacket lay puddled on the floor; her thin pearl-white blouse rippled at her narrow waist, giving him access to her swaying breasts. Her pencil skirt was rucked up to her hips, her thong hobbling her ankles.

As Maceo Encarnación repeatedly pushed into her from behind, his pleasure produced images of the old Aztec gods of Tenochtitlán. Chief among them, Tlazolteotl, the goddess of pleasure and sin. Tlazolteotl was both feared and beloved. Feared because she was associated with human sacrifice; beloved because, when summoned correctly, she would devour your sins, freeing you to continue your life without taint.

When Maceo Encarnación thought of Tlazolteotl, he saw not the various statues of her in stone and jade residing in the National Museum, but Constanza Camargo. Only Constanza had the ability to devour his many, many sins, to cleanse him, to make him whole again. And yet, as she had made clear many times, she would not absolve him of his. The sin he had committed against her was too monumental for even Tlazolteotl, ancient and powerful, to consume.

Maceo Encarnación, thrusting into the flight attendant one last time, fell upon her bare back, trembling and sweating. His heart thundered in his chest, and he felt keenly the pain of dissolution, of a vast emptiness advancing upon him like an army of eternal night, implacable and terrifying. The one thing that frightened Maceo Encarnación was the void—the nothingness that might very well last an eternity. Not for him the constricting Mass, the meaningless platitudes contained in weekly homilies, the treacherous pabulum of "God's plan." God had no plan; there was no God. There was only man's abject terror of the unknown and the unfathomable.

In these unbearably long, unbearably empty moments after completion, Maceo Encarnación ached for Constanza Camargo as he had ached for no one else in his life. The fact that he was exiled from her was like a pain inside him he could neither reach nor cure. That it was his punishment, that it was deserved, made it no easier to bear. On the contrary, it enraged him. Not all his wealth, his dark influence, or his corrosive power was of any use to him. When it came to Constanza Camargo, he might as well be the lowliest beggar in the shit-strewn dirt of a backwater marketplace, sickly and destitute. He could not cajole her, he could not coerce her, he could not reach her.

Stepping back, he zipped his trousers. He felt sweaty and oily. His skin reeked of the flight attendant's nether regions. She had dressed herself while facing the airplane's richly fabricked bulkhead, and now strode off on long, powerful legs to resume her regularly scheduled duties, without a backward glance.

Maceo Encarnación, staring at the fabric, saw a mark where her damp forehead had pressed into it with the force of his strokes. Smiling, he caressed the stain with his fingertips. It was a sign of surrender, the stain of sin.

Constanza Camargo possessed her own stain: the sin of her serial adultery. A week after her husband's death, she had fallen down the stairs of her house, having been roused in the middle of the night by the ghostly sound of his voice, which she had either dreamed or imagined. Her beautiful bare foot had missed the first tread and down she had tumbled.

Crawling along the ground floor runner, she had found a phone and called Maceo. By that time, their affair had burned itself out; he hadn't heard from her in months. Nevertheless, he hadn't hesitated. He had found her the finest spinal surgeon in the country, who had promptly repaired the herniated disc caused by the fall. Unfortunately, as happens in a small portion of spinal procedures, she had developed peripheral neuropathy, a painful and degenerative condition that defied treatment. Nevertheless, he had made certain she had tried them all. Now her wheelchair was a constant reminder of how she had betrayed Acevedo Camargo. As it had with her husband, desire had bisected destiny, altering its course.

And what of the surgeon who had operated on Constanza Camargo? Six months after he had announced that her condition was irreversible, he had taken a week in Punta Mita with his mistress. A young man, up early, jogging at the water's edge through the misty morning, had come across two human heads, neatly severed from their bodies. At first, the police assumed they were a drug dealer and his mistress, a member of a rival gang who had tried to work territory outside his own. When the true identities of the heads came to light, the local police were at a loss as to motive, let alone as to who the perpetrators might be, and the incident was soon buried in hurried paperwork and forgotten.

Maceo Encarnación's mind returned to the present. Moments after being left alone, having checked his watch, he went down the aisle, past the flight attendant, who was busy making his dinner, and into the cockpit where the pilot and the navigator were listening to *cumbia* on their iPads, awaiting his instructions. The pilot spotted him first and removed his earbuds.

"Time to get under way," Maceo Encarnación said.

The pilot had an unspoken query in his eyes. He knew that Nicodemo had not returned.

Maceo Encarnación nodded, answering his question. "Time," he repeated, before returning to his seat and strapping in. Up ahead, in the cockpit, he could hear the pilot and navigator talking as they went through their pre-flight checklist.

The pilot contacted the tower, spoke and listened, then spoke again, and taxied the jet into their slot for takeoff.

To be frank, I don't know why I'm here."

General Hwang Liqun looked around Yang Deming's apartment. The old man was the foremost feng shui master in Beijing and, as such, much in demand. He was somewhat taken aback that he was sitting in a spacious apartment in an ultramodern beehive of a building near the Dongzhimen subway station. Filled with shiny surfaces, polished wood, marble, lapis, and jade, it seemed filled to overflowing with reflections. Outside the floor-to-ceiling windows, through the brownish Beijing smog that resembled a sandstorm fixed in time that had blown in off the Gobi, could be made out Rem Koolhaas's immense CCTV building.

General Hwang Liqun would never admit it, but he was impressed that Maricruz had been granted an appointment, and at such short notice! To be sure, she was married to Minister Ouyang, but still, she was a foreigner, albeit one whose grasp of the delicate intricacies of Mandarin was a damn sight better than many people Hwang Liqun encountered in his daily schedule.

"I think," Maricruz said to the General, as she accepted a cup of Ironwell tea from Yang Deming's narrow, blue-veined hand, "that you must very well know why I invited you here."

At this, the old man smiled, nodded to Maricruz, and, much to the General's astonishment, kissed her on both cheeks before unfolding himself like an origami stork, and, with bare feet, padding out of the room.

Maricruz indicated the small, squat iron teapot. "Will you join me?"

The General nodded in an officious and rather stiff gesture that telegraphed how ill at ease he was.

After he accepted her offering and they had sipped in an increasingly tense silence, he said, "Now, if you please..."

The General was in his early sixties, older by two decades than Minister Ouyang. Theirs was a friendship born of necessity that had gradually formed its own very real parameters. The two men shared a pleasing and deep-rooted practicality, a vital trait in modern-day China. They also had a vision for China going forward into the twenty-first century and beyond. Their real shared bond was the importance of new and innovative sources of energy and the belief that the origin of these new energy sources would come from Africa, a continent that, through the efforts of both men, was fast becoming a Chinese stronghold. There were, of course, obstacles to the two men's ambitions, both for themselves and for China. The most potent and immediate threat was the reason Maricruz had called this meeting, and why the venue was so unorthodox as to fly under every official Party radar in Beijing.

"We are here, in relative isolation and complete security," Maricruz said, "because of Cho Xilan." Cho was the current secretary of the powerful

Chongqing Party. After the last Communist Party Central Committee, Cho began his outspoken attacks on the status quo, arguing that ideology was being eroded in the frantic clamor to expand China's presence abroad. By "abroad," of course, he meant Africa, and by taking this stance he had put himself in direct opposition to Minister Ouyang and the General. Cho had decided to cleave to a party line of "building a moderately prosperous society, steeped in the ideology of socialism," and in this way avoid the cultural unrest flaring in the nations outside the Middle Kingdom, an economic divide between the upper and under classes.

"There is a war coming, General," she said.

"This is China. There are no internal wars here."

"I can feel it in my bones."

"Can you now?" the General said with a smirk that spoke of superiority.

"I come from a country steeped in the blood of class warfare."

This comment served only to more firmly establish his smirk. "Is that what the drug trade is all about?" He produced a strident laugh. "Class warfare?"

"The drug trade here in China was begun by foreigners, foisted on the population of the coast, making it dependent on the fruit of the poppy. On the other hand, we Mexicans control our trade and have done so from the beginning. We *sell* to foreigners and use the profits to fortify ourselves against the endless corruption of regional governments and the *federales*. We are people who were born into poverty. We ate dirt with what scraps we could forage, but with every breath we took, we dreamed of a free life. Now that we have that free life, we know how to hold on to it. Can you say the same, General?"

Hwang Liqun sat back, staring at this gorgeous, monstrous creature confronting him like a dark goddess of the underworld. Where had she come from? he wondered. How had Minister Ouyang found her? He and Ouyang Jidan were friends, yes, but there were limits to friendship, areas in which one must not pry. Thus did General Hwang Liqun have only the most superficial knowledge of Maricruz, though he had met her numerous times at parties, official functions, even dinners of a more intimate nature. Nothing in his past experience of her, however, would have led him to suspect that she was capable of this conversation. How much had Ouyang told her of their plans? How did he know she could be trusted? Ouyang trusted no one except the General.

He had assumed that she had called this meeting, on behalf of Ouyang, thus believing he would lose no face by agreeing to attend. Now he understood that Maricruz, deeply and inextricably involved in Ouyang's—and, therefore, his—business, was speaking for his friend, that he had cannily sent her as his emissary because the stakes were so high, the wartime strategy too fraught to chance a breach in security. Being a foreigner, Maricruz was ignored by Ouyang's associates and, more importantly, his enemies, who held her in contempt. She was secure, and the General was now grateful for it.

"It is unfortunate, Maricruz," the General said now, "that I cannot make that claim. Please continue."

She poured them both more tea. "More than five years ago, you and Ouyang pushed for building the roads and infrastructure in Kenya. You saw the endless wealth in the ground, and you were determined to claim it for China's growing energy needs. Ouyang predicted that the Kenyans would not ask the price for this desperately needed work, and he was right. And now, as a consequence, he can get whatever he wants out of Kenya—oil, diamonds, raw uranium ore, possibly even rare earth elements."

The General nodded. "Our gamble will pay off handsomely."

"And yet," Maricruz said, "this incredible payoff remains something Cho Xilan, in his overzealous manner, has worked against. Because of him, Zimbabwe is still waiting for China to make good on its infrastructure promises, and Guinea turned over oil rights in exchange for nine billion dollars in housing, transport, and public utilities that have yet to appear. All because of Cho, who has sounded the call for China's global retreat in order to 'clean house,' as he puts it, to sweep aside the entrenched corrupt political hierarchy with a new broom." She shook her head. "You gave Cho ammunition against you. He unearthed a number of African politicos who were slicing off chunks of money and lining their own pockets."

The General, slightly nettled, said in a steely voice, "That is the way deals are done in Africa. Nothing new to it."

"Except when Cho brings evidence of it to the Central Committee. He got them to stop all payments, didn't he? He built political capital, didn't he?"

She took a sip of tea, allowed the atmosphere to cool somewhat, then put down the handleless cup. "I'm sorry to be so blunt, General, but time is short. What Cho really wants is a return to the time of Mao, of a central leader, upright, righteous, ideologically dogmatic. He wants nothing less than to rule China, to rule it with an iron fist."

The General swallowed more tea to calm his teeming mind. Thoughts and ideas chased each other like schools of fish through a coral reef. At length he said, "Let us assume, for argument's sake, that I agree with your grim assessment of the situation."

"Sign off on sending a cadre of Ouyang's men to Lebanon. Our project there is in its final stages. The enormity of the energy opportunities it will bring China is virtually incalculable. Cho doesn't want either you or Ouyang to gain such power." She raked him with her eyes. "He will do anything to stop the project from being consummated."

The General's eyes began to glaze over as he lost interest. "All this is known to me. There is enough security already in place. Minister Ouyang and I agreed on this aspect of the plan months ago."

"The situation on the ground has changed," Maricruz said.

The General cocked his head as a frown deepened into a scowl. "In what way?"

"Jason Bourne has entered the picture."

Hwang Liqun blew out a small gust of breath. "Yes. He has been traveling with a Mossad agent. But that, by itself, means nothing." His hand cut through the air in a gesture of finality. "Besides, the Mossad agent is dead."

Unfazed, Maricruz pressed on. "Bourne has been to Dahr El Ahmar and escaped."

"This also is old news, Maricruz. Minister Ouyang has made arrangements to take Bourne out should he appear again in Dahr El Ahmar when the deal is consummated."

"I assume you're speaking of Colonel Ben David," Maricruz said. "The trouble is Ouyang doesn't trust Ben David."

This came as a surprise to General Hwang Liqun. Now, in a moment of revelation, he knew why Ouyang had arranged such elaborate security, entrusting Maricruz to deliver the intel in person. He looked hard into Maricruz's eyes. She was right, there wasn't much time. The deal was due to be consummated nine hours from now. He nodded. "I will sign the order immediately. Tell Ouyang Jidan an unmarked jet will be ready and waiting for his cadre within the hour."

Are you up for a swim?"

Don Fernando looked at Bourne. "I'm old, Jason, not dead." He glanced upward at the spinning lights and crowds along the Pont Alexandre III. "The police are making quite a production up there."

"We've got to get out of the area," Bourne said, "before more come and they lower divers into the water."

Don Fernando nodded.

"We'll head downriver. You can see the Pont des Invalides. It's not far."

"Don't worry about me, Jason. I'm always ready

for a good swim." He smiled. "Anyway, quick get-aways remind me of my misspent youth."

"All right, then."

Bourne slipped off the slimy bridge pier to which they had been clinging like limpets. They had to be careful, as clusters of razor-sharp barnacles lived just beneath the waterline. There were spotlights raking the water now, illuminating the area where the car had gone in. All boat traffic had been stopped upriver. A pair of police launches were coming from that direction, loaded with divers, no doubt.

Bourne watched Don Fernando slide in noise-lessly. Together, the two men stroked powerfully through the black water, away from the spotlights, the crowds, and the rapidly increasing scrutiny.

By foot, the Pont des Invalides was not a long way off, but in the water their progress was much slower. The water was very cold, and they had been wet for some time. Their sopping clothes did nothing now apart from weighing them down. However, they could not afford to stop to shuck anything off. Besides, they needed to be clothed when they emerged from the water.

Bourne kept up his powerful stroke, and, to his surprise, Don Fernando matched him kick for kick. He might be old, but he was still as strong as a marlin. The farther they went downriver, the farther behind they left the bright spotlights.

However, almost immediately they began to en-counter another problem. Away from the bridge, the currents took hold in full force, twisting and turn-ing them, even, on occasion, forcing them under the water. Bourne began to lose feeling in his extremities. The tips of his fingers were frigid, and he could no longer feel his toes at all. Even though they were protected by socks and shoes, his feet had been in the water continuously ever since the car hit the river and the water gushed in.

Slowly, stroke by stroke, they made their way downriver to the Pont des Invalides. Bourne turned just in time to see Don Fernando start to go under. Reaching over, he pulled his head up above the surface, drawing him onto the pier nearest the Right Bank.

Don Fernando's head hung down, his chin resting on his chest, which heaved like a swimmer's after he has crossed the English Channel. Bourne huddled him close, arm thrown protectively around the old man's shoulders.

"Rest for a moment," Bourne said. "Then we need to swim the last part."

"The last part? You mean there's more?"

"You see there—" he pointed "—the river wall comes down in steps to the level of the Seine. We can easily climb up at that point."

Don Fernando's head shook back and forth. His long mane of hair hung lankly down either side of his face, which was drawn with exhaustion. "I'm done." His hands trembled. "I don't think I can go on."

"Then rest," Bourne said. "Watch the light show on the Pont Alexandre III while I make a call."

That brought Don Fernando out of himself. "Make a call? How are you going to do that? Everything is soaked."

"A waterproof satphone." Bourne pulled a small oblong encased in rubber from an inner pocket.

The sight of it brought a small laugh bubbling into the older man's throat. He shook his head, then abruptly turned away. He was silent for a long time. The water lapped at the pier. Shouts from the police launches in the river at the crash site upriver carried on the night wind.

"You know, Jason, the human race seems to have an infinite capacity for rationalization." He shook his head again. "There was a time when I had hopes that my son would turn out like you. But he disappointed me. He ended up doing everything wrong, somehow his values ended upside down or inside out. I don't know."

"Now's not the time—"

"Now's precisely the time, Jason. I don't think I'll have the courage to say this at another time." He turned to Bourne. "I haven't always treated you well. Often I haven't told you the truth; at other times I've withheld information from you."

"Listen, Don Fernando—"

He held up a hand. "No, no, let me finish." With every moment that passed now, he seemed to be gathering strength. "I wish I hadn't treated you so poorly. I wish I could turn back time. I wish..."

The telltale sound of a helicopter came to them, the noise beating down off the rippled skin of the river. A huge beam of intense light lit up the sky before lancing downward to the water.

"Don Fernando," Bourne said with no little urgency, "we need to go now. I'll keep you afloat if need be."

"I know you will, Jason. I don't have to think twice about that." As Bourne was about to slip back into the water, Don Fernando grabbed hold of him. "Wait. Wait."

In the gloom, his eyes stood out, reflecting the light off the water.

"I know something now," Don Fernando said. "I know you would never disappoint me."

Sam Anderson was not a man easily intimidated, even by one of the three principals of DC's most prestigious law firm. In any event, he had come prepared for any and all possibilities. Now he pulled a document from his inside jacket pocket and handed it to Bill Pelham. While the attorney was reading it, he said to Tom Brick, "You'll come with us now, Mr. Brick. You're implicated in a matter of national security. A battalion of lawyers can't prevent it."

Brick glanced at Pelham, who nodded at him. "We'll have you out before dinnertime."

Brick came around from behind his desk and preceded Anderson and Tim Nevers out of his office, down the corridor, and into the elevator.

On the way down, Anderson said, "Forensics found some interesting material on Richards's corpse."

Brick said nothing, staring straight ahead.

"You won't be home for dinner, Brick." Anderson smiled. "You won't be home for a good long time."

The doors opened, but Brick remained in place, even when Nevers stepped forward to keep the doors from closing.

"You two are so full of shit," Brick said.

"You can share your opinion with Secretary Hendricks." Anderson came around so he could see Brick's expression. "He's the one who wants to see you."

In the car, Nevers slid behind the wheel, while Anderson sat beside Brick in the backseat.

"You're right about one thing," Anderson said as Nevers pulled out into traffic. "It's too early for forensics to tell me anything definitive."

Brick smiled. "That's the first true thing you've said since you stomped your way into my office."

"On the other hand," Anderson said, "the electronic relay I planted that connected with the keylogger tracking Richards's dirty work on the Touchstone servers has been traced back to the Core Energy network, where the activation codes for the virus he planted were stored for safekeeping."

"I had nothing—"

"Shut it," Anderson snapped. "You had everything to do with it, Brick, and we're going to prove it."

Li," Ann Ring said, "what will you do now?"

Li Wan, whose brain had been slowly exploding ever since Ann had revealed Natasha Illion's true identity, was in the bind of his life. He could not possibly reveal this to Minister Ouyang. He'd never be trusted again, and rightly so. His desperate mind tried to calculate how much intel he had inadvertently revealed to Tasha in bed or wherever else they had fucked. The dreadful truth was he could not remember. His career was stymied and in danger of not only backsliding, but being terminated with extreme prejudice. The truth was that he needed immediate help.

He looked at Ann Ring, opened his mouth once, closed it, then said, "My current situation is intolerable."

"I couldn't agree more." Her eyes were steady on him.

There ensued a short silence that nevertheless seemed to boil with thoughts and ideas. After ending the meal in a shocked near-silence, Ann, perhaps intuiting that what he needed was a change in venue, had suggested that they repair to a late-night bar, where they sat in an old-fashioned high-backed booth, completely separate from the other patrons, who were in any event intent on drinking and watching a soccer match on ESPN.

Li waited in vain for Ann Ring to suggest something. "In this type of situation," he said at last, "there is only one way to deal with things." He paused. "You have to protect me."

Ann Ring's eyes opened wide. "I'm a United States senator. I don't *have* to do anything."

Li swallowed. "I can help you in the same way I helped your husband."

"Really?" Ann Ring swung her head around. "And what did you do for him?"

"Passed on information he was able to use as scoops at *Politics As Usual*. Those exclusives made his reputation."

"Why didn't I know about this?"

"Charles was very good at keeping secrets."

"Yes. That he was." Ann considered a moment. "And what did you get from Charlie in return?"

Li passed a hand across his eyes, said nothing.

"I'm afraid I can't help you, Li," Ann said, pushing her shot glass aside and gathering her things preparatory to leaving.

"Wait! Please." He felt suddenly drained. It was a measure of the severity of his circumstances that he was even considering disclosing what he had needed from Charles. "Tell me, Senator Ring, have you heard of SILEX?"

Ann screwed up her face in concentration. "I have, but at the moment I cannot think in what context."

"SILEX stands for the separation of isotopes by laser excitation," Li said. "It's a true game-changer when it comes to quickly creating enriched fuel for nuclear reactors."

"Now I remember," Ann said. "The process was bought by GE, who formed a partnership with Hitachi. They said they could envision a SILEX plant that could enrich enough uranium per year to service sixty reactors. That would be enough to power a third of the United States."

"Then the government got involved," Li said.

"We were worried about the proliferation of weapons-grade uranium if the SILEX formula was stolen."

Li nodded. "My sole interest was in receiving up-to-the-minute reports on how SILEX was progressing."

Ann frowned. "Why is the Chinese government interested in our progress on SILEX?"

"I can't tell you," Li said, "because I don't know." That was the truth; Minister Ouyang had not confided in him. As never before, Li could appreciate the wisdom of such compartmentalization.

Following a short silence that to Li didn't seem short at all, Ann nodded.

"Okay, how can I help you?"

I'm getting nowhere fast," Soraya said.

"Going the long way around won't work," Peter said. "We don't have the time to contact every Treadstone asset in the field by secure satphone."

"I know. I've been trying to access our remote server in Gibraltar." Soraya watched the screen of the laptop that had been sent over from Treadstone HQ. The IT team assigned to her and Peter during their stay at the hospital had hooked her up to a speedy wideband connection. They had Bluetoothed her mobile into the connection as well. "So far, no luck."

"I hope to God not," Peter said. "That server is supposed to be unhackable, even if someone outside Treadstone knew of its existence."

"Well, don't worry," she said glumly. "It is."

"What worries me ..."

"Peter." Her head came up. "What is it?"

"Nothing." He looked away.

"Don't tell me 'nothing.'" Setting her laptop aside, she crossed the small space between their beds. The hospital had moved them to a large, bright room that they could share, along with the electronic equipment the Treadstone IT team had installed.

Settling herself on the edge of his bed, she took his hand. "What is it?"

"I..." His eyes came back to hers. "My legs hurt. Phantom pain."

"How do you know it's not real?"

"The doctors—"

"Fuck the doctors, Peter. They don't know everything."

"I have no nerve response, Soraya. My legs are dead."

She squeezed his hand. "Don't say that!"

There were dark circles under his eyes that had never been there before, no matter how hard he worked or how tired he'd been. Soraya's heart broke.

Perhaps Peter, knowing her so well, intuited something of what she was feeling. "The sooner I get used to the fact," he said, "the better."

She leaned in toward him. "We're not giving up."

"No one's giving up, I promise." He produced a watery smile. "What else have you been up to on that laptop of yours?"

"Trying to Skype Jason. I thought maybe he might know why Core Energy shut down our intelligence network."

"And?

"He isn't online. I've left him messages on his mobile's voicemail."

"Why don't we concentrate on what we can control, like how in hell Brick managed to get Richards past our vetting process."

"Maybe he got to him after he came to work for us."

Peter shook his head. "No way. Remember, I was with both of them in Brick's Virginia house. Theirs was a longer-standing relationship than that."

"Which means he was providing Brick with intel from NSA, possibly from the president himself."

"We'll have to interrogate Brick," Peter said, "as soon as Sam brings him in."

"You're joking, right?" She gestured. "Look at us, Peter. We're going to have him brought here? For interrogation? In our condition?" She shook her head. "No. Sam is going to have to stand in for us. We can patch into the closed-circuit TV network at the office. We'll be in constant touch with Sam via wireless earbuds. Any questions occur to us, we can tell Sam. Okay? Peter?"

He nodded, clearly reluctant. The sunlight seemed to have gone out of him, leaving him gray and bereft. She had reminded him of his condition. She was sorry about that, but there was no alternative. To make matters worse, it was going to happen again and again in the weeks and months to come.

She watched him steadily for some time. "You know, my child is going to need a male presence, a father figure."

Peter barked a brittle laugh. "Right! I'm just the one—"

"But you *are*, Peter." Her eyes were bright as she willed him to engage with her. "Who else would I want my baby to know so well?"

When Jacques Robbinet, the French minister of culture, received the call from Jason Bourne, he was sitting in the back of his armor-plated Renault. In the front seat were his driver and his longtime bodyguard. It was precisely 9:32 PM. Robbinet was on his way to dinner with his mistress, which was why he almost didn't take the call. On the other hand, the Renault was stuck in traffic, and he had become antsy and bored in equal measure.

"Jason," he said with genuine heartiness, "where are you?"

"On the stairs of the Right Bank river wall directly opposite the Pont des Invalides."

Instantly, Robbinet, whose title of minister of culture masked his real job as head of the Quai d'Orsay, the French equivalent of Central Intelligence, clicked into gear. "Was that you involved in the incident on the Pont Alexandre III?" Robbinet had received the report twenty minutes ago and had dispatched a pair of his agents to assist the police in their investigation. It wasn't every evening that a car crashed over the side of a Paris bridge, and with the heightened security in place, he wasn't one to leave any stone unturned.

"There was an abduction and murder attempt," Bourne said to his old friend. "We swam downriver."

" 'We'?"

"I'm with a friend. Don Fernando Hererra."

"Good Lord."

"You know Don Fernando?"

Robbinet leaned forward, tapping his driver on the shoulder and telling him of the change in destination. "Indeed I do, Jason." Robbinet told his driver to switch on the siren, bypass the traffic jam, use the sidewalk, if necessary, just step on it. "Stay right where you are. I'll be with you in minutes."

"Listen, Jacques, I need a jet."

Robbinet laughed in a quick moment of disbelief. "Is that all?"

"I've got to get to Lebanon as quickly as possible."

Robbinet well knew that tone of voice. "The situation is that serious?"

"Deadly. We were abducted to keep me from getting there."

"All right. Let's get you two out of the water and into dry clothes." Robbinet's mind was working at lightning speed. "By that time, I'll have a jet ready and waiting." He knew enough to take Bourne at his word. "A military jet. I want the plane armed, just to be on the safe side."

"Thanks, Jacques."

"You can thank me," Robbinet said dryly, "by not getting yourself killed."

28

THE WHOLE THING was a scam?"

"From beginning to end." Bourne could hear the incredulity in Soraya's voice. He couldn't blame her. "Maceo Encarnación went to extraordinary lengths to ensnare me."

Bourne shifted his satphone from one ear to the other; it was significantly heavier than his mobile. He was riding up in the cockpit. The Mirage fighter jet Jacques Robbinet had procured for him wasn't comfortable, but then it wasn't meant to be. It had been built for war.

"From the moment Constanza Camargo was pushed into the baggage claim area by airline personnel, I was their target."

"But how the hell did she know you'd be there?"

"Maceo Encarnación."

"And how did she manage to get through security to be at the security area in the first place?"

"Having been to Mexico City and survived," Bourne said slowly, "I can appreciate fully the complete grip Maceo Encarnación has on the capital."

Soraya paused for a moment. "And the story Constanza told you about her husband?"

"Well, the husband was real, I checked that," Bourne said. "Also, the manner of his death."

"Huh! The best liars sprinkle in as much truth as they can."

"If I knew the real relationship between Constanza Camargo and Maceo Encarnación," Bourne said, "I feel like I'd know everything." He stared through the cockpit glass. The Mirage hurtled through the aether like a weapon of revenge. Bourne had scores to settle, not only with Maceo Encarnación, but with Colonel Ben David as well.

"Everything is related, that's what you're telling me," Soraya said. "Maceo Encarnación, Nicodemo, Core Energy, and the Mossad commander at the Israeli research station outside Dahr El Ahmar."

"There's another element involved," Bourne said, "an element only hinted at because of its extreme importance."

"Do you know who or what?"

"The Chinese. Specifically someone named Ouyang."

"Hold on," Soraya said. She was back in a flash. "According to my information, Ouyang Jidan is minister of the State Administration of Grain."

"CSP, more like it," Bourne said.

"I don't doubt it. What's he doing nosing around Dahr El Ahmar?"

When Bourne told her about the Israeli SILEX

project, she nearly exploded. "What are we going to do? With Ben David implicated, we can't trust anyone in Mossad."

"Leave it to me," Bourne said. "I'll be at Dahr within hours."

"Have you considered that Dahr El Ahmar might be a trap?"

"Yes."

Soraya waited for him to provide further explanation, but when nothing was forthcoming, she went on. "Any logistics we can provide—"

"Got it."

"What still puzzles me," she said, "is the thirty million in counterfeit dollars Peter found. I don't know, maybe it's just the Aztec trying to rip off his boss. People will do just about anything to get their hands on that much money."

"True enough."

"The thing is, the counterfeiting on the bills Peter found isn't all that good. It's nowhere near the level we've found in the bills created by the Chinese, which, sad to say, are virtual masterpieces of the counterfeiting art." She paused a moment. "To be honest, that's the reason I figured the money was unrelated. What if Maceo Encarnación suspected someone in his organization was skimming? It happens all the time. So he sets up this scenario so even if the perp manages to get away with it, he's left with nothing."

"It makes sense," Bourne said. "Why don't you follow up on that premise?"

"I already have. Seems as if the Aztec's prime lieutenant got his head handed to him, literally."

"That seals it then."

She wanted to tell him about herself and about Peter's condition, but she bit her tongue. He had more than enough on his mind. Time enough when this was over to let him know. Perhaps he'd even come back to Washington to see her. She'd like that.

She cleared her throat. "Okay, then. I guess that's it for now. Keep in touch."

She said this last with such intensity that Bourne might have queried her had she not already severed the connection. He settled back in his seat, closed his eyes, and thought about his last conversation with Don Fernando.

Robbinet had his driver take them to a small but very luxe boutique hotel in the thirteenth arrondissement, where, in a top-floor suite, an elegant woman looking no more than forty was waiting for them. This magnificent creature, whose name was Stephanie, was clad in a little black dress from Dior and was Robbinet's current mistress. She already had clothes laid out for both Bourne and Don Fernando, as if she were a genie or a magician. When Robbinet had phoned her, Bourne couldn't say, but he was immensely grateful nonetheless.

While Don Fernando showered, Bourne filled Robbinet in on the scenario that had brought him and Don Fernando to Paris from Mexico City. "The identity of the body your divers will pull out of the Seine is Nicodemo," he concluded. "His real name, however, is a matter of conjecture."

"Dead is dead. I'll take it," Robbinet said, in his usual matter-of-fact fashion. "I'm just grateful no harm has come to you or Don Fernando." He grunted. "This has been quite a day, what with the abduction attempt and Don Fernando risen from the grave twice now, it seems. I was instrumental in doctoring the report of the crash of his private jet outside Paris." He regarded Bourne attentively. "It seems the two of you are made for each other."

Bourne turned to Stephanie. "Apologies for spoiling your evening."

"With Jacques, I'm used to such interruptions." Her smile was dazzling. When she stepped across the carpet to the minibar, her hips swayed ever so slightly. "It can't be helped. Besides, Jacques and I have all night."

Bourne and Robbinet conferred about the upcoming flight. Using Google Earth, Robbinet brought up the area around Dahr El Ahmar on his iPad. "I can't see this Israeli encampment."

"It's all camouflaged," Bourne said. "Plus, as you can see, the Lebanese have blocked out parts of the area so the Google cameras can't see them in detail. Try looking at the White House and its grounds using the program—you can't see a thing."

Robbinet nodded. "For security purposes, we do that in certain parts of Paris." His forefinger tapped the screen. "There's an airstrip in Rachaiya, here." His forefinger stabbed out. "It has the advantage of being both secluded and less than two miles from Dahr. There will be a driver and vehicle waiting for you when you land."

"I don't need them," Bourne said.

"This man, Fadi, has intimate knowledge of the area," Robbinet said. "My advice is to use him."

By that time Don Fernando had exited the bathroom, resplendent in the outfit Stephanie had purchased for him.

"A perfect fit," Robbinet said, admiring Don Fernando. "It's a good thing I know you both so well."

Bourne had spent the next twenty minutes scrubbing the grit, grime, and smell of the Seine off himself. Discovering a cache of disposable razors, he shaved, and by the time he climbed into his new clothes he felt reborn.

There was room for only one passenger in the Mirage jet Robbinet had ordered up, so Bourne was saved from arguing Don Fernando out of coming. They said goodbye to Robbinet and Stephanie, took the tiny elevator down to the lobby, and out onto the street, where the minister's car was waiting for them.

They traveled through Paris, out onto the Périphérique, in silence. But in the last moments, as they crossed the tarmac at the military airfield, Don Fernando turned to Bourne.

"You know, when I was younger I firmly believed that when I grew old, looking back on my life, I'd have no regrets, none at all. How idiotic! Now that I've more or less reached that age, I find that I have many regrets, Jason. More than I care to think of all at once."

The airfield was quiet. Apart from the sleek Mirage, crouched at the head of a runway, lights blinking, jets starting up, there was no activity. Robbinet must have ordered the area cleared for security purposes.

"But the one regret that stings me more than any other concerns Maceo Encarnación," Don Fernando continued. "Now, before you board, is the time to tell you."

The wind ruffled his hair. It was an unnaturally warm night, as if spring had overtaken winter before its time, as if emotions supposed dead were rising to the surface.

Don Fernando took out a cigar and, in deliberate violation of the laws, lit up. Bourne knew from past experience that smoking cigars calmed him down.

"In my lifetime, Jason, I have been loved many times. That isn't a boast, by the way, simply a fact. Many women have come and gone." He stared at the slowly smoldering end of his cigar. "And now they seem only like wisps of smoke—here, and then before you know it, gone." He stuck the cigar back in his mouth and sucked on it, producing a faintly blue aromatic nimbus around his head. "But in all that time, there was only one woman I ever loved."

Don Fernando's eyes filled with the past. "We met in Mexico City. She was very young, very beautiful, very charismatic. There was something about her..." He ducked his head. "Well, I don't know." He stared at the glowing end of his cigar again, as if it could rekindle the past. "She had not been born in Mexico City, not in any city at all, for that matter, but the way she moved and spoke you would not have known that she was a peasant. I came to learn that she was a natural mimic—she picked up accents, vocabulary, style, body movements almost instantaneously."

Bourne had a terrible premonition. "Like any great actress," he said.

Don Fernando nodded, pulling fiercely on his

cigar. "When I asked her to marry me, she laughed, kissed me, and said her destiny lay elsewhere."

"Let me guess," Bourne said. "She went on to marry Acevedo Camargo."

Don Fernando spun on his heel to face Bourne. "How did you—?"

"I met Constanza in Mexico City. She was doing Maceo Encarnación's work. She fooled me completely."

Don Fernando produced a grim smile. "She's fooled everyone, Jason. It's a long line, beginning with Acevedo. She married him on Maceo Encarnación's orders. Maceo didn't trust Acevedo, and since Acevedo's star was rising as a drug lord, Maceo considered him a security risk—possibly worse, a rival. That he would not tolerate, so he set a fox in the henhouse, so to speak."

"Constanza."

Don Fernando nodded. "She told her new spouse that she couldn't conceive, but at the same time, she was bedding Maceo as often as possible. The age when a man considers his living legacy had come upon Maceo early; he was desperate to have a child. Within a month Constanza found that she was pregnant. Of course, Acevedo couldn't know, so she went to her aunt's in Mérida for a protracted stay until she had the boy, which, according to their agreement, she gave to Maceo to raise."

Don Fernando ground what was left of his cigar underfoot and started to move toward the waiting Mirage fighter, by which Bourne surmised their discussion was nearing its end.

"Naturally enough, I found this out after the fact.

I had left Mexico City the very same night I fucked her for the last time. Pardon the crudity, but that's what one did with Constanza: fuck. She had no room in her vocabulary for making love." He shrugged. "Perhaps that was a reason I found her so irresistible. One could never believe what came out of her mouth. She was a serial liar. Much later, I came to suspect that she believed every one of her lies."

"That belief is what makes her so effective."

"Doubtless." Don Fernando jammed his hands in his pockets. He was trembling with emotion. "Still, I wanted her more than any other woman I've ever met." He looked up into the night sky, streaked with light from the Eiffel Tower. "Martha Christiana reminded me of Constanza. There was a certain—I don't know... It was as if their cores were made of the same material."

"It was hard to lose Martha."

"I killed her, Jason. That's what I'm still struggling with. Perhaps I wanted her too badly. Perhaps I thought she would make up for Maceo Encarnación taking Constanza away from me."

Bourne thought it was just as much Constanza Camargo's fault as it was Maceo Encarnación's. On the other hand, this human drama had played out in Mexico City, where anything seemed possible.

They were near the Mirage's curving flank and could smell the rich fumes of the fuel.

"Time for me to go, Don Fernando."

"I know."

They shook hands as they parted. Bourne climbed into the cockpit, the ladder was whisked away, and Don Fernando stepped backward, making his way across the tarmac without ever taking his eyes off the Mirage as it flung itself down the runway, nose up, and lifted off into the night sky, vanishing like the moon in eclipse.

You'll take her into custody."

"That's what I said, yes."

Li, standing outside the front door to his apartment, looked hard at Ann Ring. "There's no other way?"

"What other way?"

They were close to each other, speaking in whispers.

"You know what I mean, Senator." Li licked his lips. "What happened to Charles. A break-in, a death."

Ann Ring took a step back. "I'm not going to be party to murder, Li. I can't believe you're even bringing up the possibility."

He breathed softly, snorting like a horse. "It's just that there are people with keen ears. I cannot afford to have my reputation compromised."

"Believe me, Li, I will not let that happen." Ann indicated the apartment with her head. "You're certain she's in there."

"She sleeps between photo shoots. She's been going non-stop for almost two weeks."

"All right, then."

He hesitated for a moment, then, slipping his key in the lock, opened the door, and pushed inside. The interior was dark and still. They crept through the rooms until they reached his bedroom. There they found Natasha Illion fast asleep. She was on her side, the curve of her cheek, the brushed shadow of her lowered lash softly illuminated by a bedside lamp.

"She's like a child," Li whispered in Ann's ear. "She can't sleep in absolute darkness."

Ann nodded, then gestured for them to return to the living room, where she called Hendricks to send agents to take Tasha into custody. Li padded into the kitchen to get some water. She was still updating Hendricks when Li brushed past her, heading back into the bedroom.

"Wait, where—?" Without putting Hendricks on hold, she rushed in behind Li, just in time to see him stab downward with a long-bladed carving knife he must have fetched from the kitchen.

Ann screamed as he plunged the blade between Tasha's perfect shoulder blades. The girl arched up, torn out of sleep by pain and shock. Ann ran toward Li, but he had already wrenched the blade free and was now plunging it down into the side of her neck.

Ann was shouting, pulling him roughly away; blood was pouring out of Natasha Illion at a hideous rate. Within seconds, she was awash in her own blood, and Ann knew there was nothing she could do for her. Still she tried, for four long minutes, while Li stood still as a statue, his back to what he had done.

At length, Ann got off the bed. She was covered in blood. She picked up her mobile and, walking out of Li's earshot, said, "Natasha Illion's gone. Li stabbed her to death."

"Did you get it all on tape?" Hendricks seemed to be breathing fast.

Ann touched the minirecorder at her waist. "Every last frame," she said. "Li's ours now."

Making our approach."

The pilot's voice sounded through the intercom, and Bourne opened his eyes. Peering out through the windscreen, he could see nothing, not even a single light. Lebanon, near the border with Syria. Desert. Mountains in the distance. The parched wind. The nothingness.

It felt like coming home.

29

IT SEEMED TO Maceo Encarnación, as he sat brooding in his private jet, that he had left a great many people behind. Now he could add Nicodemo to the list. Even though that was not Nicodemo's real name, he had a difficult time thinking of him as anything else. Now, with him gone, left behind in Paris, dead or alive, he did not know, he understood why that was so. It was always easier to leave someone behind when he distanced himself from them, in one way or another.

Dead or alive. He thought about this phrase, while the cauldron in the pit of his stomach informed him that Nicodemo was dead. He must be dead; death was the only thing that would have kept him from returning to the plane.

He had made Nicodemo. He was wholly Maceo Encarnación's creature in a way his sister, Maricruz, never was and never would be. Maricruz was very much her own person. Even though Nicodemo had his uses, he was never the person his sister was. Maceo Encarnación loved Maricruz in a way he could never love Nicodemo. Nicodemo was a tool, a means to an end; Maricruz was the entire workshop, the end itself. Maricruz knew he was her father; Nicodemo didn't. Neither knew who their mother was.

He dozed for a while, dreaming of Constanza Camargo in the form of the great serpent that founded Tenochtitlán. Constanza opened her mouth, her forked tongue flicked out, revealing destiny and desire, and Maceo Encarnación, himself a little boy, knew he was meant to choose one or the other. Destiny or desire. He had chosen destiny, and all desire had been excised out of him. In this way, leaving people behind was as easy and, in its way, as pleasurable as swallowing a mouthful of mellow aged tequila.

When, hours later, he awoke, the jet was descending out of the sky like a great eagle toward the small airfield on the outskirts of the mountain town of Rachaiya. The plane began to judder and dip, and he fastened his seat belt. Peering out the window, he saw that the weather had changed. There was windblown snow on the ground here, as well as in the higher elevations, and more snow was falling out of the gunmetal sky. Colonel Ben David did not disappoint: one of the two AH-64 Apache attack helicopters under his command was standing by, ready to take Maceo Encarnación to the Mossad camp outside Dahr El Ahmar.

Reaching across the aisle, Encarnación drew to

him the suitcase fitted with the thumbprint lock. As the plane hit the runway and began to slow, taxiing toward the copter, he released the lock, then opened the suitcase to stare one last time at thirty million dollars.

The call came in while Soraya and Peter, both exhausted, had fallen into a deep, drug-like sleep. Delia, having taken some of her built-up sick days, was watching over them. She crossed to the table beside Soraya's bed, picked up her mobile, and saw that the call was from Secretary Hendricks.

Leaning over Soraya, she shook her. Then, seeing that her friend was slow to rouse herself, she leaned farther and kissed her on the forehead. Soraya's eyes opened, and she saw Delia holding up her mobile so she could see Hendricks's name on the caller ID.

When Soraya took the mobile from her, Delia nodded, smiling, and went out of the room.

"Mr. Secretary," Soraya said, formally.

"Soraya, are you all right?"

"Fine, sir. I fell asleep."

"No one's more entitled to sleep than you, but I've got some pressing news regarding Tom Brick. Sam Anderson brought him into custody a couple of hours ago. Forensics found traces of Dick Richards's blood on the cuffs of his trousers."

Soraya sat up straight. "Sir?"

"Brick's rolled over. He doesn't want to go to jail."

"He's made a deal."

"Given us the person who knifed Richards," Hendricks said. "But there's more—much more. I'm certain you recall the mysterious counterfeit thirty million Peter discovered."

"I do, sir." Soraya listened to what Hendricks had to say on the subject, delivered to him in writing by Sam Anderson in Tom Brick's own hand.

"Oh, my God," she said, when Hendricks was finished.

"My thought, exactly. Get your agents in Lebanon on this ASAP."

"Will do," Soraya said. "Thank you, sir."

"Thank Anderson when you see him. The man's done a stellar piece of work."

The moment Soraya cut the connection with her boss, she punched in Bourne's number on speed dial. When she heard his voice at the other end of the ether line, she said, "I have the answer to the counterfeit thirty million."

Sir," Bourne's pilot said, "I won't be able to set you down at the airfield in Rachaiya. There's a private jet sitting on the runway."

Maceo Encarnación, Bourne thought. "Options."

"Only one," the pilot said. "There's a flat space a mile to the east."

"Can you do it?"

The pilot grinned. "I've set this down in worse."

Bourne nodded. "Let's do it." Using his satphone, he dialed the number Robbinet had given him, and, after a coded exchange, gave the driver waiting for him the new coordinates.

"You understand I won't be able to wait for you,"

the pilot said as the Mirage banked to the east. "Even with Minister Robbinet's influence, the less time this plane is in Lebanese airspace, the better." The field in view, he began a rapid descent. "These days, the Lebanese government is understandably jumpy."

"Any idea how long that plane's been on the ground?"

"No more than twenty minutes, sir. It took off from Paris an hour and thirty-five minutes before we did, but the Mirage is far faster. A commercial flight takes approximately four hours. We've covered that distance in two hours and forty-five minutes. That jet is considerably slower. I calculated the respective speeds of the two planes before we took off."

"Good man," Bourne said.

"Thank you, sir." The pilot engaged the controls. "Now hold on, this is bound to be a bit of a bone-shake."

The Mirage came down very fast, but contrary to what the pilot had said, the landing was as smooth as could be expected under the circumstances. Bourne unbuckled as soon as they began to taxi and was ready with the backpack Robbinet had provided him so that the moment the Mirage came to a halt, he popped the canopy and climbed down the curved side. He ran, half hunched over, as quickly as he could, giving the pilot a clear space in which to take off. As he reached the far edge of the field, the jet turned, paused, then was released down the flat expanse and rose quickly into the air.

Bourne turned away and made for a thin stand of ratty-looking pines, beyond which the vehicle and driver would be waiting. His shoes crunched over the several inches of snow that lay on the ground, but in among the trees the snow was patchy, as if eroded away by the bed of pine needles. A chilly wind wandered with a mournful sound through the trees; the air was dry and thin, tinged with the unmistakable scent of pine tar.

Peering through a gap in the trees, he looked out to the northwest. Sure enough, there was the vehicle, an old military Jeep with open sides and a canvas top. By its side, smoking languidly, was Fadi, Robbinet's asset, a small, dark, muscular man with rounded shoulders and a shock of black hair. He must have heard the plane land because he was looking toward the field, as if anticipating Bourne's imminent arrival.

Bourne pursed his lips, producing a bird whistle. Fadi peered into the trees, then smiled when he saw Bourne step out. Clambering into the Jeep, he started it up and swung it around in a shallow arc, stopping in front of where Bourne stood.

"Right on time," he said as Bourne climbed in beside him. He reached into the backseat and handed Bourne a sheepskin coat. "Here, put this on. This high in the mountains, it's a good deal colder than in Paris."

As Bourne pulled off his backpack and slid his arm into the jacket, Fadi put the Jeep in gear. "Next stop Dahr El Ahmar."

A sudden metallic insect buzz launched Bourne out of the Jeep. He rolled across the snow-packed ground as the Jeep, struck squarely in its midsection, was hurled end over end into the fizzing air by the shoulder-launched missile. The boom of the explosion echoed off the foothills, bent the stand of pines, the tips of the nearest ones turned black and smoking. The Jeep crashed down, and Fadi, as black and smoking as the pine-tops, was thrown from the charred wreckage to lie twisted and fried in the melting snow.

Scrambling, Bourne kept the burning vehicle between himself and the area his hearing confirmed the missile had come from. A low rise in that direction was, he was fairly certain, where the enemy was lying in wait. There were numerous implications to be divined from the bombed-out vehicle, but number one, so far as Bourne was concerned, was that he had been expected. Maybe they had heard his plane land; maybe they had followed Fadi. Either way, Soraya had been right. He had been prepared for a trap at Dahr El Ahmar, but not here, after the Mirage had been diverted. It was possible, though, that Encarnación's pilot had spotted the Mirage and contacted the encampment.

Rifle shots aimed in his direction sent him scuttling toward the shelter of the copse of pines; as one struck close to his left shoulder, he gave a shocked cry and bucked his body as if hit. Biting the inside of his mouth, he allowed the warmth to fill his mouth, then spat out several globs of blood as he dragged himself between the boles of two trees.

Once hidden, he pulled a pair of high-powered field glasses out of his backpack. Robbinet had seen to it that everything he had asked for was inside.

Bourne quartered the immediate vicinity, looking for any overt sign of more of Maceo Encarnación's people. Inevitably, his attention was drawn back to the low rise. They knew he had survived; now they would think he was wounded. They wouldn't let him leave here alive, of that he had no doubt. And yet, beyond the trees there was no cover for him, even if he circled around to either the left or the right. Hidden and impregnable: They had chosen the perfect spot from which to observe and attack. No matter. Now that they thought him wounded, they'd come to him. He required only patience now, watching and listening for them to step into his copse of trees.

While he waited, he wondered how they had arrived here. He doubted they had trekked, and the rise was too small to hide a vehicle. He put the field glasses back up to his eyes, looking for a bit of camouflage. He found it off to the left, about a thousand yards from where they were hunkered down.

He had just confirmed the outline when he picked up the soft crunch of boots through snow. Not knowing how many men Encarnación had sent against him, he began to move toward the sound, which was repeated again and again at cautious intervals.

The man was following the bloody trail he had seeded. Bourne looked around at the pines. Though they had relatively soft wood and did not have ideal branch structure, he managed to find one that was suitable. Reaching up, he launched himself through the forest of needles, climbing quickly so as not to put stress on any one branch for long.

He watched the man come into view. He was holding a QBZ-95 assault rifle at the ready. Even before Bourne glimpsed his uniform, he knew from the QBZ that the man stalking him was a member of the Chinese military. So Minister Ouyang had a presence here.

At the last instant, Bourne gathered himself, dropped down onto the soldier, drove his fist into the back of his neck, and, as he turned, stumbling, took hold of his head and slammed it into the trunk of the tree. The soldier dropped like a stone, blood streaming from nose and eyes. It seeped through his hair where the skull was cracked. Bourne considered switching clothes with the soldier, but the man was too short.

Scooping up the QBZ, Bourne set off after the others who, he surmised, had entered the copse of trees from different directions. The QBZ was the newest Chinese assault rifle, but Bourne found it an awkward weapon, mainly due to the large 30-round magazine sitting just behind the trigger guard, but its cold, hammer-forged barrel, though short, made it exceptionally accurate.

With his back against the trunk of a tree, Bourne stopped, listening intently. He heard nothing. Maceo Encarnación had a head start on him; he had no time to play an extended game of cat-and-mouse with these people.

He fired a short burst from the QBZ into the trees on his right, then sprinted to his left. Sure enough, the fire drew other soldiers. They had recognized the firing sound of the QBZ and assumed their compatriot had gotten a bead on their quarry.

Bourne took one down with his second burst of fire, but the third eluded the spray of bullets. He had lost the element of surprise, but he had gained the knowledge that there were only three soldiers in the copse with him.

He took a reading on the last place he had glimpsed the third soldier; taller and bigger than the other two, the soldier had scrambled away to Bourne's right, so he circled around to his left to come upon him from the opposite direction.

A burst of fire almost took his head off as he dived onto the bed of spent needles. More shots, nearer now, and he rolled away. The soldier had obviously considered Bourne's strategy and, once out of sight, had reversed course, heading left to intercept him. His maneuver had almost worked, but now Bourne knew exactly where he was. Aiming the barrel of the QBZ high, he fired, shredding a fistful of branches, which came showering down onto the spot where the soldier crouched. Bourne was ready when he leaped up, firing, the bullets slamming into the soldier's left shoulder, twisting him off his feet. He struck the trunk of a tree, which kept him on his feet. As Bourne fired again, he darted away. Bourne fired again, but came to the end of the cartridge. He didn't have a replacement. Throwing the weapon away, he dug into his backpack while taking off after the lone remaining soldier.

The copse was suddenly very quiet. The stench of the rifles' fire hung in the air like mist. Crouching down, Bourne pushed forward from tree to tree. Bullets flew at him, striking so close to him he could feel the brush of air they displaced. He sprinted toward the flare of the weapon, and the instant he saw the soldier, he threw the knife he had extracted from the backpack.

The soldier fired, but the bullets went upward into the sky as he crashed backward, the knife buried hilt-deep in the left side of his chest. Cautiously, Bourne went to him, kicked his weapon away, then crouched down beside him. Confirming that he was dead, he quickly stripped off the soldier's clothes, then his own. The uniform was an acceptable fit. There was blood on the shirt, but this could be easily explained after a pitched battle in the pines.

Taking up the dead soldier's rifle, he struck out for the edge of the copse closest to the rise behind which the soldiers had attacked the Jeep. Rounding the left edge of the rise, he picked up the abandoned rocket launcher and saw that it had been loaded in case the first rocket missed. Keeping it with him, he quartered the area. Finding no other soldiers, he headed for the camouflaged vehicle. Dressed as he was, it wouldn't do to return to camp on foot.

He reached the vehicle and, speculating on the curious presence of Chinese soldiers so close to a top secret Israeli base guarded by Mossad, pulled off the opaque camo material, only to come face-to-face with a plainclothesman, armed with an Israeli Tavor TAR-21, small, lethal, accurate, like everything Mossad. The agent, who had obviously driven the Chinese soldiers to the site, whipped the barrel of the Tavor toward Bourne's face.

30

OLONEL ARI BEN DAVID stood facing Maceo Encarnación, and all the resentment and diminishment he had stored up from the moment he had entered into talks with the Mexican entrepreneur bubbled poisonously into his throat like mercury. He detested dealing with intermediaries, which, in this case, Maceo Encarnación was, but he detested even more having to deal with the Chinese, in the form of Minister Ouyang. He'd had no choice, a bitter circumstance he had divulged to Maceo Encarnación along about their third meeting.

It was the Mexican who had come up with the idea. This should have softened Ben David's feelings toward Encarnación, but it did not. On the contrary, the proposed solution was so ingenious, so perfect, that Ben David felt only resentment that he hadn't thought of it. From that moment on, he had been beholden to Maceo Encarnación.

Colonel Ben David, bitter by birth, paranoid by nature, persecuted by dint of both his nationality and his religion, was incapable of any positive emotion whatsoever. He was enraged that Minister Ouyang was in possession of incriminating evidence that, should it find its way to either Dani Amit or the Director, would not only end his career in Mossad, but also see him incarcerated for the rest of his life. He and Ilan Halevy had collaborated on terminations outside the sanctioned purview of Mossad. They had made tens of thousands by Ben David's soliciting kill requests from individuals and the Babylonian's enacting the murders. They had made one mistake: They had left a paper trail regarding the first hit. How Minister Ouyang had come into possession of the information, Ben David did not know. The fact was that he had it and was using it to get what he wanted from Ben David: namely, the modified SILEX formula the scientists at Dahr El Ahmar had perfected, which would allow China accelerated access to nuclear fuel and weapons.

Now, breaking his brief reverie, Colonel Ben David looked from Maceo Encarnación to Colonel Han Cong, commander of the six-man cadre Minister Ouyang had sent as his representatives.

"Your report, Colonel?" he said.

"The enemy Jeep has been destroyed," Han said.

Maceo Encarnación addressed himself to the Chinese. "Bourne and the driver?"

"The deaths have not yet been confirmed."

"And why would that be?" Ben David asked.

Colonel Han cleared his throat. "I have not yet heard from my men."

At once Ben David lost interest in him. He turned to Maceo Encarnación. "They're dead," he said. "Bourne is coming."

"Excuse me," Colonel Han said. "How do you know that?"

A slow smile spread across Colonel Ben David's face, as if he had been waiting for that question. "I know Bourne, Colonel Han."

Colonel Han frowned. "But three soldiers, highly trained and heavily armed..."

"I know what Bourne is capable of." Ben David touched the livid scar on the side of his face. "Intimately."

The dubious expression on Han's face turned into a shrug. "Then we should complete our transaction as swiftly as possible." He nodded to Maceo Encarnación, who hefted a hard-sided suitcase onto the trestle table. The fingerprint lock was duly opened, the top swung back, and the thirty million American dollars were revealed.

"It's all there. You have Minister Ouyang's word." Colonel Han held out his hand. "Now the formula."

Ben David dug into the pocket of his fatigues and drew out a USB drive, which he placed in the Chinese's palm. "It's all there," he said dryly. "You have my word."

The Mossad agent's hesitation on first seeing the Chinese uniform gave Bourne the chance to duck away.

Dropping the launcher, he grabbed the agent by the

front of his vest and flung him out of the vehicle onto the ground in a flurry of snow. The agent rolled onto his back, firing the Tavor, almost severing Bourne's head from his neck. The sting of the bullets' heat burned Bourne's cheek as he jabbed the butt of his QBZ down onto the agent's sternum. The agent smashed the butt of his own weapon against Bourne's, deflecting it at the last instant so that it slipped off his ribs and onto the ground. Kicking upward, he struck Bourne's left hip, throwing him off balance.

Bouncing to his feet, he came at Bourne, driving the Tavor crosswise into Bourne's neck, sending him stumbling into the side of the vehicle. The agent bent him backward as he pressed the weapon so hard into Bourne's throat that all air was cut off. Grinning with the effort, he bore down, his focus narrowing to his intent as the moment of his target's death approached.

It was this intent, so fervent, that caused him to miss Bourne's right heel hooking into his. As Bourne drew back his leg, the agent lost his balance. But even as he fell, he swung the Tavor around, aiming it at Bourne's chest. He pulled the trigger as he landed, the bullets firing wide when Bourne smashed the butt of his weapon into the agent's face. The second strike shattered his sternum and rib cage, driving a rib through his chest. It must have punctured a lung because pink foam boiled between the agent's lips, followed by a gout of blood, thick and clotted.

Colonel Han, having given no indication that he had registered Ben David's barb, inserted the drive into his tablet and switched it on.

Maceo Encarnación's lips twitched. "Believe it or not, Colonel Han is an expert in physics and in laser excitation in particular."

The two men watched as Colonel Han brought up the files on the USB drive and scanned them.

At that moment, Colonel Ben David's satphone buzzed. He listened for a moment, the frown on his face deepening. "No, do nothing. Just keep him in sight." He closed the connection before saying, "Our vehicle has been sighted. Only one man is in it."

"Bourne?" Maceo Encarnación said.

"He's wearing Dov's uniform." Ben David shook his head. "But I doubt it's Dov." He turned to the Chinese. "Colonel Han, I believe it's past time for you to leave."

Han looked up from his scrutiny of the equations, nodded, and closed down his tablet. Pocketing the USB drive and sticking the tablet under his arm, he nodded curtly to the two men, then stepped smartly out of Ben David's field tent.

Bourne, wearing the agent's clothes, drove the vehicle toward the Mossad encampment outside Dahr El Ahmar. The loaded launcher lay in the footwell behind him. He had a clear idea of the layout of the camp, having seen it from the air on his previous visit with Rebeka.

He found his mind, normally so calculating and pragmatic, turning back to Rebeka. He remembered the first time he had seen her, on the commercial flight to Damascus, a flight attendant about whom swirled a mystery he wanted to unravel. It was only later that she revealed herself as a Mossad agent. During their joint assault on the terrorist Semid Abdul-Qahhar's stronghold, she had proved herself to be fierce, intelligent, and brave. He felt her loss as keenly as if Maceo Encarnación had knifed him in the ribs. Constanza Camargo had told him that Maceo Encarnación was protected by the ancient Aztec gods, but the truth as he knew it now was something both more mundane and more sinister. Maceo Encarnación was protected by all those people he had seduced, suborned, coerced, tricked, and beaten into submission. Armor enough for the modern world.

As he drove, Bourne became aware of sharp glinted sunlight reflected off coated glass lenses. He was being observed by the Mossad, by Maceo Encarnación's men, or by what was left of the Chinese military contingent.

Maceo Encarnación followed Colonel Han out of Ben David's tent, walking beside him as he headed for the aircraft that would take him and what remained of his cadre back to Beijing, where Minister Ouyang waited for the bounty for which he had delivered thirty million to Maceo Encarnación.

"You played your part well," Colonel Han said in the condescending tone of the true Celestial that set Maceo Encarnación's teeth on edge.

Encarnación, imagining himself swinging a machete in the powerful horizontal arc that would sever Colonel Han's head from his body, replied, "I'll take my fee now."

Colonel Han, looking straight ahead as if he walked alone, tugged out a thick envelope from the inside breast pocket of his tunic. He held it, apparently not ready to hand it over. "What is it you did to deserve this generous payment, Encarnación?"

Feeling the blood rushing through his head, Maceo Encarnación pressed his fingertips to his temple where he could feel a distended vein beating like a second heart. He calmed himself before answering. "I acted as the go-between. I introduced Minister Ouyang to Colonel Ben David and oversaw the negotiations. Ouyang never would have got to Ben David without me."

"He might have." Colonel Han slapped the envelope against his knuckles. "*Minister* Ouyang is both powerful and resourceful." He shrugged, as if he had his orders to fulfill even though he did not agree with them. He held out the envelope, and Maceo Encarnación, made to feel like a paid employee instead of a partner, took the envelope and, in the Colonel's presence, laboriously counted the bills.

"The five million is all there," Han said in precisely the same voice he had used inside Ben David's tent.

"But is it real?" Maceo Encarnación removed three bills at random and, using eyedroppers from tiny vials he carried, subjected them to two chemical tests.

"Satisfied?" Han said with a wry smile. "They're real. Unlike the thirty million you delivered to the Zionist Ben David. He sold his precious formula for a suitcase full of counterfeit money."

With a minimum of effort, Maceo Encarnación

produced a smile of complicity. "But the bills are so well made it will take him some time to realize that he has been swindled."

"And by then," Han said triumphantly, "it will already be too late."

His plane was dead ahead. He signaled to his three remaining soldiers and they climbed on board.

"What about your other men?" Maceo Encarnación asked. "Don't you want to know whether they're dead or alive?"

"Once Bourne was spotted, they became a liability."

"Wasn't stopping Bourne part of your mission?"

"An adjunct." Colonel Han began to mount the stairs up to the plane. "I have the formula. That's all that matters."

"Not to Minister Ouyang."

"No," Colonel Han said. "But it is to my superior, General Hwang Liqun."

So saying, Han mounted the steps, disappearing inside the fuselage of the plane. A moment later, one of his soldiers swung the door closed, locking it from inside. The engines started up, obliging Maceo Encarnación to step backward at a rapid pace. He wasn't quick enough to avoid getting a face full of jet fuel backwash. Particles flew into his eyes, making them tear. He turned then, jogging back to Ben David's tent.

Bourne heard the roar of jet engines, and he diverted the vehicle in that direction. If a plane was taking off, it was a sure bet that the deal for the

SILEX formula had been concluded. He was too late.

Stepping hard on the accelerator, he roared through the periphery of the camp, shattering a wooden barrier and causing agents to fire at him even as they scattered out of the way. Seeing the jet, he accelerated away from them. It was a civilian plane with Chinese markings.

These thoughts passed through Bourne's mind like swiftly flying birds as he dug in his backpack. He was nearing the plane, which had taxied to the head of the makeshift runway and now sat, panting like a chained animal impatient to be released. He turned the vehicle hard to his left, paralleling the plane's path. Shots were being fired off to his left, and he ducked down as bullets spanged into the side of his vehicle.

He was coming up on the tail of the jet when he heard a roar off to his left. A quick glance revealed a Jeep with a driver and an armed agent riding shotgun. The agent leveled the Tavor TAR-21 at him, and Bourne jerked the wheel hard over to his right so that the offside scraped the plane's fuselage, giving the agent no chance to fire without hitting the plane.

At that moment, the jet's brakes came off and it started to taxi down the runway. Bourne, drawing closer to the plane, had pulled out the grenade Robbinet had procured for him when the agent's Jeep slammed into him. He turned back, his arm swinging out, connecting with the agent, who was jolted backward. His Jeep continued on its course, scraping along the side of Bourne's vehicle. Bourne turned right, then made a sharp left, bringing the near-side front corner jabbing into the Jeep. Both men stiffened; as the driver was about to haul the wheel hard over, the armed agent leaped into Bourne's vehicle. The Jeep, jolted hard, ricocheted away. The agent slammed Bourne in the back of the head.

The jet began to pull away.

Colonel Ben David laughed like a loon when Maceo Encarnación re-entered his tent. His fingers were hauling up handfuls of American dollars out of the suitcase. "Look at these," he said merrily, "all crap."

"Very fine crap," Maceo Encarnación said, crossing the tent. "Exquisite craftsmanship."

"Of course." Ben David nodded. "It's the work of the Chinese. Expert counterfeiters, those shitbags." He smirked. "The SILEX formula for thirty million in bogus bills. Ouyang thought he had pulled one over on me."

"He might have, without me."

Ben David nodded. "True enough. But when that formula is implemented, it will level the laboratory it was made in. Quite the joke on Ouyang." Reluctantly, he inclined his head. "I'm in your debt."

"You hate being in anyone's debt, Colonel," Maceo Encarnación said shrewdly.

"Especially yours." Ben David's expression had turned sour.

"It's not so bad. You could be in Ouyang's debt."

The Mossad agent was so powerful that he dragged Bourne halfway out of the driver's seat. The vehicle began to swerve crazily, throwing the agent off balance. Instead of resisting, Bourne flipped backward, using the agent's clasped forearms, somersaulting over his back. The agent twisted his torso, driving his elbow into Bourne's side just as the vehicle swerved again. Bourne was thrown half out of the vehicle, one leg and hip flying just above the ground.

The agent was about to pound Bourne's head with the butt of his rifle, but another, wider swerve brought the vehicle in contact with the fuselage of the plane. The agent abandoned Bourne for the instant it took him to vault over the seatback, get behind the wheel, and regain control of the vehicle.

Bourne managed to hook one leg up over the side of the vehicle so that he was lying more or less horizontally. The plane was very close, the jet outtake just in front of him, over the agent's head. The fuel made it virtually impossible to breathe, difficult to see. Nevertheless, Bourne knew that he was as close as he was ever going to get to his target. Pulling out the safety, he swung his arm back and let go of the grenade just past the apex of the arc. It spiraled through the air like a thrown football, but the engine's outtake hurled it away, so that the plane was unharmed by the explosion.

Seeing the agent distracted by the blast, Bourne clambered back into the rear compartment. The plane was lifting off now, gaining in both speed and elevation in order to clear a stand of trees. Bourne swung the shoulder-held missile launcher up, aimed through the sight, and pulled the trigger. The missile launched, speeding directly toward the plane.

The agent, shocked, turned to see Bourne leap out. As he rolled over and over, he covered his head with both arms, curling into a protective ball just before the missile exploded, rupturing the entire side of the plane, sending flames and billowing dark, oily smoke high up into the sky as it crashed back to earth and split apart. The Jeep had wandered too close. Caught in the periphery of the blast, it was lifted off its wheels. Fiery, it turned end over end, spilling the two agents, then coming down onto them in a tangle of overheated metal and burning fabric. The gas tank ignited, sending shock waves across to where the shattered plane was burning. Then it, too, burst asunder with a massive roar, incinerating everyone and everything in the immediate vicinity.

Colonel Ben David stared at Maceo Encarnación. "And the payment?"

Maceo Encarnación smiled. "And the formula?"

Ben David held up a 32-gigabyte SD card. "The real one, this time."

Maceo Encarnación opened a second envelope, spilling its contents onto the bottom of the suitcase. The diamonds sparkled and glittered in the lamplight. "Thirty million worth of perfection."

Ben David nodded. Handing over the SD card, he said, "When you insert that directly into your mobile, everything will be revealed."

Maceo Encarnación clutched it tightly in his fist. "And Core Energy will corner the market on both nuclear fuel and weaponry."

At that moment, they both heard the roar of the first explosion. They were halfway out of the tent when the shock waves from the second and third detonations threw them backward off their feet.

A flaming tire arced downward from the conflagration, heading directly for Bourne. Scrambling away, he rolled onto a patch of snow to keep the flames from getting to his clothes. By the time he raised himself up onto one knee, three armed Mossad agents were sprinting toward him. As the first shots were fired, he leaped behind a storage shed just past the edge of the makeshift runway.

The intensity of the fire incinerating the plane and the Jeep kept the agents from coming any closer, and Bourne took the opportunity to run in a half-crouch to the next building, which housed the scientists working in the camouflaged laboratory several hundred yards to his left.

Though well armed, Bourne had no particular desire to shoot the agents except in self-defense. It was their commander and Maceo Encarnación he was after. He'd much prefer to keep hidden and out of their way while he searched for his quarry.

No sooner had he entered the building than the door slammed shut. One of the windows shattered and a thick tongue of flame set the bedding on fire. The sharp odor of chemical fire filled the interior: someone was using a flamethrower.

The blaze leaped up, engulfing the interior almost immediately. Bourne turned back, but the door through which he had slipped in was bolted shut from the outside. He tried to make his way to one of the windows, but the fire had spread so quickly and the flames were so hot that he could not get to even the nearest of them. Ripping off a pillow-case, he held it over his nose and mouth, dropping to the floor, where the air was several degrees cooler. Acrid smoke billowed like storm clouds, obscuring the low ceiling.

He heard a sound over the spark and crackle of the burning wood. A figure filled the shattered win-dow, then stepped through. It was clad in a flame-retardant suit with its own breathing apparatus. The figure held the flamethrower as it looked to his right, then his left. From his position hidden away beneath one of the beds, Bourne could make out the features of Colonel Ben David through the glass face-plate.

Bourne had already witnessed the first tongue of flame and so knew that the flamethrower was using liquid—likely napalm—ignited by propane. Now, as Ben David turned again, searching for him, Bourne saw the two tanks on his back: The napalm would be housed in the tank that lay against his back, the propane tank, hidden from anyone stand-ing in front of the Colonel, just behind it. Bourne brought his rifle to bear: All it would take was a sin-gle bullet into the propane tank to roast Ben David alive. But in this enclosed space, already afire, Bourne himself would roast along with his enemy.

Trying not to cough, he watched as Ben David quartered the space, searching under one bed after another. The moment he left his post in front of the shattered window, Bourne snaked out from un-der the bed, sprinted diagonally across the smoke-

and ash-filled interior. As he left his feet, diving through the window, Ben David turned, toggling on the flamethrower. Another tongue of flame licked out, across the wall, then shot out the window, where the very end of it licked at the back of Bourne's jacket, igniting it.

Instantly feeling the heat, Bourne threw himself into a patch of deeper snow, rolling on his back to snuff out the flames. He saw Ben David step through the window, level the snout of the flamethrower on him, even as Bourne lifted the assault rifle to shoot him.

"Stalemate," Ben David said as he pulled off the suit's hood. He appeared oblivious to the building burning behind him. "It seems you're always in my way, one way or another, Bourne. What have you done with Rebeka?"

"Rebeka and I made a good team. I tried to save her."

Ben David frowned. "What d'you mean?"

"She was killed—stabbed to death inside Maceo Encarnación's villa in Mexico City."

Ben David took a threatening step toward Bourne. "Goddamn you. You never should have taken her there."

"You think her death was my fault? She was on her own mission; it coincided with mine. Besides, you sent the Babylonian to terminate her because she was getting too close to your little operation."

"What d'you know about it?"

"Now you want me to believe you still have feelings for her?"

"I asked you—"

"I know everything, down to the counterfeit money the Chinese manufactured."

Ben David leaned forward. "You don't know his name."

"You mean Minister Ouyang?"

Ben David stared at him. "Why does he hate your guts?"

Bourne stared back.

"You're not going to screw this deal for me, Bourne."

When Ben David tightened his finger on the trigger, Bourne said, "Don't you want to know who killed Rebeka?"

"I don't care. She's dead."

"It was Nicodemo, Ben David, Maceo Encarnación's son."

The Colonel stood stock still. "What?"

"You didn't know Nicodemo was your partner's son, did you?"

Ben David said nothing, but his tongue emerged briefly to moisten his lips.

"Which means Maceo Encarnación gave the order to have her killed. I could use a partner like that." Bourne laughed grimly. "But he's all yours."

"He's playing you, Ben David."

Both men turned at Maceo Encarnación's growl.

"Why haven't you killed him?" Encarnación was carrying a pistol in one hand and in the other a massive machete with an evil-looking blade.

Ben David looked from Bourne to Encarnación. "Why did you have Rebeka killed?"

"What? I don't explain my actions to anyone."

Ben David shook his head. "You had a choice. You could have captured her—"

"Are you crazy? She was far too dangerous to try to capture. Besides, there was Bourne to deal with."

"—but you had your son kill her anyway."

Maceo Encarnación looked suddenly stricken. "I have no son."

"Nicodemo. He *is* your son."

"Who told you that?" Encarnación flared.

Ben David gestured at Bourne with his head.

"And you believe him?"

"It makes too much sense to be a lie."

Maceo Encarnación spat. "Did you even hear what I said? You've inhaled too much smoke. Rebeka is dead, so is Nicodemo. The past is buried. It's our future we have to concentrate on now. Bourne is the only one standing in—"

Ben David turned the ugly snout of the flamethrower on Encarnación and pulled the trigger. A burst of napalm spat out, just missing the Mexican. Bourne was on his feet in an instant. He kicked out, sending Ben David reeling back into the flames licking out of the shattered window.

Without a backward glance, Maceo Encarnación ran around to the rear of the building. Bourne followed him at a strong lope. At the corner, a shot caused him to quickly duck back. He heard the crunch of running feet and darted around the corner, firing as he went.

Maceo Encarnación had vanished. Bourne stalked after him, checking the snowy ground for his footprints. The three Mossad agents who had fired at him previously were frantically combating the fire, which had crept close to the netting that camouflaged the laboratory from both the ground and the sky.

At the end of the building Bourne saw prints leading off toward the laboratory. Having to cross unprotected ground, he moved cautiously. He was halfway across when he noticed one of the agents answer his satphone, and he hunkered down, making himself as inconspicuous as possible. The agent, covered in soot, his clothes seared and singed in places, nodded, then abandoned his comrades, racing off toward the far side of the compound. Bourne tracked him until he passed behind the burning building, then he rose, tracing Maceo Encarnación's footprints, which led directly to the front door of the camouflaged lab. He was about to follow them when he turned, sensing movement out of the corner of his eye.

The Mossad agent had appeared from around the far side of the furiously burning building, and he wasn't alone. Colonel Ben David was with him.

Maceo Encarnación cursed the day he had agreed to Tom Brick's plan to buy the SILEX process from the avaricious Ben David. He'd bought into Brick's argument that the process would mean that Core Energy would eventually corner the market on nuclear fuel, which, despite certain setbacks, was surely the main energy source of an emissionless future without fossil fuel.

Perhaps Brick had been right. Maceo Encarnación didn't know, and he no longer cared. It had

been his idea to rope in Minister Ouyang, knowing
through Maricruz's weekly reports how desperate
the Chinese were for more energy, especially now
with their great engine of progress slowing because
of massive pollution all over the country. The Chinese were building nuclear reactors at an astonishing
rate. Their appetite for enriched uranium to fuel
these plants was increasing exponentially. Maceo
Encarnación hated the Chinese with an unrivaled
passion. They stood for everything he despised, everything he had spent his entire adult life fighting
against: repression, regulation, dampening the free
spirit of the country's population. Seeing the opportunity to fuck them over was too great a temptation.
But now, as he made himself invisible in the shadows near the front door of the laboratory, he understood how his desire had conflicted with destiny.

He was not meant to be here, on the run from Jason Bourne. He should have been back in Mexico
City with Anunciata. Now he was faced with the
moment when dominion slips through one's grip,
when expectations of wealth, influence, and power
are overwhelmed by self-preservation and survival.

He stiffened as the door to the laboratory
opened inch by inch. The interior of the building,
designed by the five scientists at work here, was
broken up into rooms where the separate processes
of the formula could be produced and refined before being chained together with the others in the
largest area at the far end of the structure. This last
space was lead-lined, and all precautions had been
taken owing to the radioactive material being created there. As far as he could tell, all the scientists

were clustered in the far lab, finishing the last of the SILEX testing.

The door opened farther. Maceo Encarnación, checking his firearm, discovered that it was empty. Tossing it aside, he raised his machete over his head, ready to strike off Bourne's head the moment he entered the building.

A shadow fell across the widening wedge of doorway, and Maceo Encarnación felt the tremor of intent run up his arm and into the fists that grasped the machete with a professional executioner's grip.

He watched the silhouette form: the nose, lips, forehead, chin, until the entire head was in front of him like that of a condemned criminal on the block. The machete whistled down, the long, wicked blade glimmering briefly before it fell into shadow as it cleaved through the neck, severing the head from its trunk.

The head bounced along the floor while the trunk danced and spun, blood spurting with each frantic pump of the heart. For an instant, Maceo Encarnación was transported back to the shoreline of Mexico, the soft Gulf waves rolling onto the shore, both seawater and sand soaking up the blood, as the head rolled back and forth in the pink foam of the surf.

Then the present returned with the speed of a rocket, and he saw the severed head facing away from him. He turned it toward him by hooking his foot against the side of the nose. It stared up at him with the unthinking eyes of a landed shark. It was a face he knew well, but it wasn't Bourne's.

He expelled a startled yelp as Bourne grabbed hold of him and slammed him back against the wall so hard he dropped the bloody machete. He stared from Bourne to the severed head.

"I thought Ben David had been burned to death."

"One of his agents saved him, and I liberated him from his agent," Bourne said. "I wanted his death to have meaning."

Maceo Encarnación's gaze returned to Colonel Ben David's face, which stared up at him from its position on the floor. There was no seawater to wash away the blood and gore, to make the death clean and neat, to dream the dream of a perfect death.

"I thought he was you," Maceo Encarnación said.

"Of course you did."

Maceo Encarnación shuddered. "Let me go. I have the secret to SILEX. Imagine the wealth you and I will share."

Bourne stared into his eyes.

"You killed Nicodemo in Paris." It was only a semi-question.

"He knifed Rebeka," Bourne said by way of answer. "She died a slow, painful death."

"For that I'm sorry."

"I looked into her eyes. I saw the pain. I saw the end coming, and there was nothing I could do."

"For a man like you, that must be terrible indeed."

Bourne drove a fist deep into Encarnación's stomach. He doubled over, and Bourne pulled him erect by his hair.

The Mexican's red-rimmed eyes opened wide. "You killed my son."

"He killed himself."

Maceo Encarnación spat into his face. "How dare you!"

"I tried to subdue him underwater, but you trained him too well. He would have killed me and Don Fernando if I hadn't killed him."

"*¡Asesino!*" Encarnación slipped a push-dagger from a sheath hidden beneath his clothes. His fist shot out, the blade aimed at Bourne's heart.

Bourne grasped the wrist, and turned it, snapping it in two. Maceo Encarnación grimaced, slammed Bourne's throat with the heel of his other hand. Bourne, a low animal growl erupting from deep inside him, spun him around, grasped his head in both hands, and cracked the neck completely in two. As he let Maceo Encarnación go, the Mexican's head lolled at an unnatural angle, as if begging to be separated from the rest of him.

Epilogue

THE DIRECTOR WOULD like to talk with you," Dani Amit, head of Mossad Collections, said.

"Talk with me," Bourne said. "Not kill me."

Amit laughed, but his pale blue eyes remained steady and grave. The two men were sitting at a small table at Entr'acte, a seaside restaurant along Tel Aviv's sweeping scimitar beach.

"The termination order was a mistake. Obviously."

"In our business," Bourne said, matching Amit's tone, "almost everything is a mistake in hindsight."

Amit's eyes drifted to the water, the lines of empty chairs set up on the beach. "That which doesn't kill us turns us gray."

"Or insane."

Amit's gaze snapped back.

"It was insane to send someone after Rebeka," Bourne said.

"She went off the grid. She broke protocol."

"Because she couldn't trust anyone."

Amit sighed and folded his hands together, as if in prayer. "Concerning Dahr El Ahmar, we owe you a great debt of gratitude."

"Rebeka suspected Ben David was rotten." Bourne would not let the subject go. "She was right."

Amit licked his lips. "Concerning Rebeka, we have received her body from the authorities in Mexico City."

"I know. You will bury her with honors. I want to be there."

"Outsiders are not permitted—" Amit bit off the automatic response, and nodded. "Of course."

A soft breeze ruffled Bourne's hair. His body ached. He could feel every place the flames had touched him, every place Maceo Encarnación had struck him.

"Did she have family?"

"Her parents are dead," Amit said. "You'll meet her brother at the funeral."

"He's Mossad also."

"Finish your espresso," Amit said, "then we must go."

Aboard the Director's boat, Bourne was provided with a panoramic view of the city. The sun beat down from a sky studded with small clouds, scudding before a following wind. He seemed far removed from the snowy highlands of Lebanon.

"You're a fine sailor," the Director said. "What other talents have you hidden from us?"

"I don't forgive."

The Director looked at him. "That's a very Mossad trait." His Brillo hair seemed impervious to the wind. "That said, we're all human, Bourne."

"No," Bourne said. "You're Mossad."

The Director pursed his livery lips. "Well, there's truth to that, no doubt, but as you've already discovered, we're not infallible."

Bourne looked back at the glaringly white city and was suddenly aware of the ages of history buried there. He took out the thin gold chain with the star of David.

The Director saw it and came and sat beside his guest. "That was Rebeka's."

Bourne nodded.

The Director took a deep breath and slowly let it out. "I go sailing whenever one of my people has been killed."

Bourne was silent. The star of David dangled between them, spinning slowly, now and then catching sunlight and redirecting it. After a long time, he said, "Does it help?"

"Out here in the clean air and the calm of the water, without the burden of the city on my back, I can finally feel how lost I am." The Director looked down at his strong, capable hands. "Is that a help?" He shrugged, as if to himself. "I don't know. Do you?"

Bourne, thinking how helpless he was when Rebeka's life slipped away, felt, like a little earthquake, echoes of identical sorrows, and understood with a terrible finality that he was as lost as the man who sat beside him.

About the Authors

ROBERT LUDLUM was the author of twenty-seven novels, each one a *New York Times* bestseller. There are more than 225 million copies of his books in print, and they have been translated into thirty-two languages. He is the author of *The Scarlatti Inheritance*, *The Chancellor Manuscript*, and the Jason Bourne series—*The Bourne Identity*, *The Bourne Supremacy*, and *The Bourne Ultimatum*—among others. Mr. Ludlum passed away in March 2001. To learn more, visit www.Robert-Ludlum.com and Facebook.com/RobertLudlumBooks.

ERIC VAN LUSTBADER is the author of numerous bestselling novels including *First Daughter*, *Blood Trust*, *The Ninja*, and the international bestsellers featuring Jason Bourne: *The Bourne Legacy*, *The Bourne Betrayal*, *The Bourne Sanction*, *The Bourne Deception*, *The Bourne Objective*, and *The Bourne Dominion*. For more information, you can visit www.EricVanLustbader.com. You can also follow him on Facebook and Twitter.

1

Lieutenant Colonel Jon Smith opened his eyes to see a shadowy figure standing at the foot of his hotel room bed pointing a gun at him. The red pinpoint dot of the weapon's laser sight skittered up the comforter cover toward his chest, making a wild pattern of loops on the way, as if the shooter were drunk and unable to aim his weapon. Smith rolled to the right, propelling himself off the mattress and onto the floor, hitting the carpet with a thudding sound and landing facedown, using his hands to break the fall. A silenced bullet tore into the pillow.

Smith reached up to the nightstand to get his gun but snatched his hand back when the laser pinpoint sight began its chaotic dance over the area near his knuckles. The killer fired again, the bullet narrowly missing Smith's fingers and piercing the alarm clock. It exploded into pieces, and bits of the drywall behind it sprayed into the air.

Smith scrambled farther to the right, and the assassin stayed with him, firing over and over, but continuing to aim in a haphazard, erratic fashion. The bullets cracked into the wall, and he took cover by sliding into the small space between an armoire and a collapsible metal stand that held his suitcase. This position had the advantage of getting him out of the shooter's direct line of sight, but put him farther from his gun and still farther from the hotel room door. The attacker dropped behind the bed, using it for cover, as if he thought Smith had access to another weapon.

Smith crouched in the dark with his back pressed against the wall while he tried to pull together his jangled nerves and think about what to do next. He was in a suburb of The Hague attending a World Health Organization meeting on infectious diseases in Third World countries, an area of expertise of the United States Army Medical Research Institute for Infectious Diseases where Smith, an MD, worked. He was due to deliver a speech the next day on the hazards of cholera in disaster areas. The routine meeting had just turned deadly, and he didn't know why.

Smith's suitcase lay open, containing his still neatly folded clothes; below it were his shoes. He inhaled, grabbed a shoe, and threw it across the room, aiming in the general direction of a lamp that he remembered sat on the desk. He heard the shoe land and then the crash of the lamp falling over and glass breaking. The pinpoint laser sight danced on the desktop. The assassin had taken the bait.

Smith didn't hesitate. He catapulted himself toward the door, moving as fast as he could, fear and adrenaline making the blood pound in his ears. The killer fired again, but Smith was now a moving target and difficult to hit. More bits of drywall exploded to Smith's right. He reached the door, twisted it open, and stumbled into the hallway, blinking in the sudden glare from the overhead lights. He turned, preparing to run to the elevator bank.

Two men carrying assault rifles, their faces covered with hoods, stood about thirty feet away at the end of the hall, facing one of the doors. One turned his head to glance at Smith, but kept his weapon aimed at the room. He returned his focus to the door, muttered something, and both men shot into the panel. The corridor rang with the staccato reports of the automatic fire. The first man kicked open the door, and both disappeared from Smith's sight as they plunged through the shattered entrance.

Smith's mind raced while he tried to understand just what was happening. The shooter in his room obviously valued silence, with his dampened weapon and what must have been a careful entrance into Smith's chamber, but the two in the hall kicked in doors and seemed unconcerned about revealing their positions.

Smith spun left but stopped when he saw the emergency exit door at the far end begin to open. It swung outward, and Smith found himself staring into the eye holes of yet another masked attacker. His own bedroom door remained ajar and he slammed back through it, dropping at once into a crouch. He crabbed to the left, hitting his temple on the corner of the desk and stepping on some broken glass from the fallen lamp. He clenched his teeth as he felt the shard bite deep, followed by a flow of warm blood.

No sound came from the shooter in the room.

The hallway erupted once again in gunfire punctuated by the screams of the other hotel guests. Smith heard an explosion and the floor shook. When the noise died down, he strained to focus his senses in the shooter's direction. No sound. He hovered in the darkness and did his best to slow his breathing, a difficult task because he was panting with a mixture of adrenaline and stress.

His cell phone lit up and began to ring. Smith froze. The phone sat on the nightstand and its display illuminated the area with a yellow color. In the weak glow he saw the shooter slumped at the foot of the bed. The phone's ring increased, getting louder each time. Smith made his way around the desk, past the motionless person and over to the nightstand. He grabbed his gun, pointed it in the direction of the bed, and flicked on the bedside lamp.

The killer remained still. Smith glanced at the phone's screen. The display read "Anacostia Yacht Club" followed by a number that Smith knew was a decoy. His other employer, Fred Klein, head of Covert-One, an organization of clandestine experts in various fields dedicated to fighting terrorism, was calling. Klein didn't call often and never without a grave reason. Another explosion rocked the hotel, punctuated with screams and the sound of sirens from emergency vehicles, still in the distance, but getting louder.

Smith picked up the phone and hit the answer key, keeping his weapon pointed at the motionless shooter.

"It's Smith. What's happening?"

"Get out of the hotel. The CIA just reported that it's targeted for an attack," Klein said. More automatic fire came from the hallway, the noise louder and closer than before and coming from both sides. The attackers were systematically entering each room.

"Is that gunfire I hear?" Smith edged around the bed past the fallen man and moved to the door. He threw the deadbolt and turned the locking bar inward before returning to the body. This attacker wore no mask, and Smith stared into the face of a man perhaps twenty-five years old, with dark hair and the broad, flat, slightly Asian features of someone of Mongolian descent. Smith crouched down and pressed his fingers on the carotid artery, checking for a pulse. There was none. He put pressure on either side of the man's jaw, forcing it open, checking for cyanide suicide pills.

Nothing. Smith could discern no reason why the man was dead.

"The CIA is a little late. They're already here. Why are they after me?" Smith transferred his phone to his left hand while he started to search the body.

"They're not after you personally, they're after American and diplomatic targets. This one is just bad luck. Coincidence. The CIA's been warning of an attack in Europe for months, but I just got the report that pinpointed the WHO conference and I knew you were there. Get the hell out of that hotel. Now."

Klein was right. The media had been reporting that certain fringe groups were planning an attack, but Smith hadn't thought much about it. He knew that US intelligence sources received hundreds of bits of information each day and that many led to nothing. Such reports were usually so vague as to be useless, and his business required that he travel to Europe.

"Tell me how many," Smith said.

"They think at least thirty. Two to four on each floor."

Smith heard more screams from the hall. A woman started wailing, the noise cut short by the report of a gun.

"They taking hostages?"

"No hostages. Body count. Get the hell out of there."

The hotel shook from another explosion and the fire alarms went off, making a high-pitched squeal so loud that Smith winced. A sprinkler set high on the wall over his bed began spraying water. Two others came to life, one over the desk and the other near the door.

He rifled the shooter's pockets, finding a spare clip for the silenced weapon and a wad of euro bills. He reached into the next pocket and withdrew a handful of photos. There were three. The first was a picture of a woman, obviously taken while she walked on the street and without her knowledge. She was dressed in a navy suit, carried a briefcase, and her long, dark hair was pinned at her neck. She looked attractive and formidable at the same time. There was no mistaking her serious demeanor.

The second picture was a candid shot of a man Smith knew and admired: Peter Howell, an agent for Britain's MI6 who had retired some years ago.

The third picture was of Smith.

2

Smith headed to the window, still talking to Klein and holding the phone, euro bills and photos in one hand, the gun in the other.

"It looks like they may be after me. Or at least someone is. There's a dead guy in my room carrying photos of me, Peter Howell, and a woman that I can't identify."

"A dead man? Did you kill him?"

"I didn't touch him. He just...died." Smith stood against the wall and used the tip of the gun to slowly pull back the curtains. Emergency vehicles filled the street, their flickering lights sending eerie red flashes that bounced off the nearby buildings. The authorities remained a safe distance from the hotel, but ringed it. "Listen, I'm going to do my best to get out of here, but if I don't, I'm going to put the photos in my pocket. Make sure one of your operatives collects my personal effects, notifies Howell, and then finds this woman and warns her." The door to his room shivered as it was kicked from the outside.

"Get out of there! I'll—"

Smith didn't hear the rest. He aimed and fired

into the hotel room door. The 9 mm bullet pierced the wood, and Smith heard the satisfying sound of a man's yell. Bull's-eye, he thought. There was a moment of silence, followed by the report of an automatic weapon firing round after round in response. Ordnance flew into the room along with bits of wood from the door, but Smith was to the right at a 45-degree angle and none of the hits came near. The bullets peppered the headboard and the wall above it with shot.

Smith shoved the phone, bills, and photos into his pocket. He'd worn loose-fitting cotton drawstring pants and a T-shirt to bed and his feet were bare. At that moment he was glad that he'd stuck to his usual, careful habit of booking rooms only on the third floor or below. Fire-truck ladders could reach the third floor, and most hotels had over- hangs at first-floor level that could break a fall if need be. Smith always thought that precautions were best when followed each and every time because you never knew when they'd become crucial. This precaution just had.

The hotel was a large, stately stone building built over one hundred years ago on a rectangular lot. The front of the hotel faced the city and the back faced the North Sea and sat directly on the beach. Smith's room was located near the end of the hall, with five rooms on one side, and ten rooms on the other. His room had a view of the city in one direction and one that was cut off by the wall that jutted out in the other. The narrow casement window swung open easily. Smith put his foot on the sill, grabbed the curtains and stepped up.

The attackers began kicking at Smith's door. He fired again, and the battering stopped. He thought the killers must be surprised that one of the hotel guests not only had a gun, but knew how to use it. Smith's military background meant he was trained in weapons and hand-to-hand combat and had learned a smattering of different martial arts moves. In his early forties, he no longer took combat duty, but that didn't mean he couldn't defend himself.

Smith was tall and slender and he had to angle his body to stand on the window's edge. He stuck his head out the window.

A six-inch decorative ledge banded the hotel at least three feet down, with a corresponding band three feet up. A quick glance to the emergency vehicles gathered in the circular front drive told Smith that he couldn't expect any help from that quarter in the time that he needed it. None had ventured closer than fifty feet from the hotel, and most stayed back even farther. The battering began again, and this time the door cracked at the leading edge. It opened, but the safety bar caught. Smith saw a hand reach around the panel. It was time to go.

He put the gun in his waistband at the small of his back and slid one leg, then the other out the window. He lowered himself, face against the brick, until his toes hit the ledge. He held on to the remains of the window and began moving to the right, toward the wall that jutted out at a right angle in the corner. He had almost thirty feet of flat hotel. Once he reached the end of the window, he'd have only the rounded decorative piece above him to grasp.

He reached the window's edge too soon and hesitated. He was sweating despite the cool spring air, and he took a deep, shaky breath. For a moment he thought he wouldn't be able to transfer his grip from the window to the small, rounded piece of stone. Every instinct in him told him not to let go of the solid window edge, and his fingers seemed locked in position. Once he managed to release his fingers, he would be committed to making it around the corner or falling to his death.

Sweat ran down his sides and he swallowed. He heard the bedroom door splinter as the terrorists finally pulled the locking bar out of the panel. With an effort he released his hand, and moved it to the rounded stone piece. His fingertips dug into the brick and mortar.

"Move." He whispered the word out loud, and the action jarred him out of his paralysis. He began inching along to the corner where the walls met. He reached it just as a masked gunman leaned out the window, an assault weapon in his hand.